THE NANNY

AND THE ICEBERG

D0182724

THE NANNY

AND THE ICEBERG

ARIEL DORFMAN

SCEPTRE

Printed and bound in Great Britain by
Clays Ltd, St Ives plc
Designed by Abby Kagan

Hodder & Stoughton
A division of Hodder Headline PLC
338 Euston Road
London NW1 3BH

For my father, who can read this.

And for my mother, who never will.

Though at times I almost believe that she can read it,

that she has been reading it all along.

This book is for both of you.

It is only for the sake of those without hope that hope is given to us.

—Walter Benjamin

•

Recently, in Zimbabwe, . . . I heard stories of rogue elephants gone berserk

after culls during which they were isolated and relocated after witnessing

the killing of the matriarch elephants, who carry the

knowledge and history of the herd and the territory. Elephants react

exactly like young men and women react to war or the disintegration of

community; they become paranoid, violent and anti-social.

—Deena Metzger

OCTOBER 12, 1992

I now believe that the light I saw earlier was a sign from God and that it was truly the first positive indication of land. When we caught up with the Pinta, which was always running ahead because she was a swift sailer, I learned that the first man to sight land was Rodrigo de Triana, a seaman from Lepe. At dawn we saw naked people and I went ashore.

—FROM THE LOG OF CRISTÓBAL COLÓN,

DATED OCTOBER 12, 1492

SEVILLA – A spokesperson for the Chilean Pavilion at the World's Fair in Sevilla categorically denied rumors that the iceberg from Antarctica that has been on display here for the last months has been threatened by a terrorist organization. Speaking on the condition that he not be identified, the official stated that the President of the Republic has ordered that when the fair closes today the iceberg is to be towed back to the eternal ice from which it was lovingly carved almost a year ago. "Everybody loves this iceberg," the official said. "Nobody would be demented enough to want to blow it up."

PART ONE

OCTOBER 9, 1992

•

It's better like this. I never should have been captured alive. . . . Tell Fidel

that he will soon see a triumphant revolution in America. . . . And tell my

wife to remarry and try to be happy. . . . I know you've come to kill me.

Shoot, coward, you're only going to kill a man.

—ERNESTO CHE GUEVARA, LAST WORDS,

OCTOBER 9, 1967

Surprise, Janice. It's me. Gabriel. Gabriel McKenzie. I'm back—though not really, not for long. I know, I know—I promised that I would write from—well, I didn't tell you what country I was going to, did I? Just those goodbye words, a year and a half ago, on July 8, 1991, promising to pop an E-mail message on your screen the next day, promising to come back and ball you, complete what we hadn't quite managed to do when we were fifteen. As if anybody keeps a promise in this world.

Sorry that I disappeared. Sorry to burden you with this bundle of pages in the real mail—the longest suicide note in history, I guess. Send it to the *Guinness Book of Records*. Send it to a dwarf I know there. Tell him he can celebrate. Tell him I killed myself in Sevilla one minute before October 12 dawned. Tell him I killed some other people, too. Yes: I've got three days left. That's how long it should take to write this and print it and send it. If I decide to send it instead of pressing the DELETE button, that is, and don't remain the only reader of my story. I could send it and still be the only reader. You could decide not to read till the end, not to reach the climax, so to speak. But I've tried to make sure you will. This is a promise I can deliver on: besides my own death at the end, there'll be violence and murder. More murder than I bargained for when I set out on this voyage back home. And sex.

Real sex. Not what I bragged to you about in my E-mail drips and drops. All that infinite experience, the ins and outs, the multiple orgasms in those many beds, what I boasted I had done to other women after I stopped seeing you, after we didn't quite make out—all that was my father, what I imagined he was doing, Cristóbal McKenzie, my dad, the greatest lover in the world. Would have been accepted as such by the *Guinness Book of Records* if I hadn't fucked up his getting recognized. So it wasn't my appendage that went into all those women and bodies, just like it never went into yours—all false, Janice. I used faraway words to seduce you. What I've always been best at. My teachers knew it. Kept on reporting to my mom that Gabriel is "too clever for his own good, mature beyond his years." Except for my face. They never mentioned my face.

There's a reason why I've refused to show you my face, to meet you when you've come to New York to visit. The first thing you asked for when we reconnected through the Internet. "Send me a photo, please send me a photo, to see how much you've changed since I left for Seattle." What I didn't want you to know is that it hasn't changed. Not at all. That it's the same face you last saw walking out the door of your parents' house nine years ago. At twenty-four, I look like I'm still fifteen. Easy to deceive you, tell you I looked thirty, thirty-five.

Not the only lie. I'm not American. Fooled you when we first met, when we almost—and kept on fooling you when we hooked up again to couple in cyberspace. Didn't want you to know I was Chilean. I came here from Chile when I was five. Me and my mother. Exiled. That's the mystery country I returned to eighteen months ago. That long dagger of a country on the Pacific Ocean. Means the end of the world in Quechua, *Chile* does. Even the Peruvian Indians thought it was too far away, too inaccessible and destitute to be conquered. Driest desert on earth, the Atacama, to the north; the Andes forbidding safe passage to the east; to the west that ocean, with no land for thousands of miles, except for the tiny isle of Juan Fernández, where poor Robinson Crusoe was shipwrecked, and Easter Island and then nothing until Polynesia. And to the south . . . I went there, to the mythical continent south of the south, first to Patagonia, then to Antarctica: I went to the white continent that for most of humanity's history did not even exist on a map. Only in dreams. I watched an iceberg being hacked from that floating mountain in Paradise Bay as the snow flurries licked my face and I tricked my father into telling me how he had fucked more women on this planet than any other man alive. As we watched that ice nobody had ever seen before in human history.

Maybe that's where I should begin the story I never told you: on a day in 1492 when snow was falling on Antarctica, it was falling and compactly forming the iceberg that my crazy *compatriotas Chilenos* have carted across the Atlantic Ocean here to Sevilla to prove how modern they are, how far they've traveled from the tropical day when Columbus sighted land. But don't get me started on snow. It was still falling on the same iceberg hundreds of years later on the night when this really begins, when I begin, when my mother and my father began what would be little lying-and-conniving me. Though my story can't really start there, my mom inserted the death of someone else into my own birth, before it. That's how she told it to me: I was alive because somebody else had died, died the day before I was conceived. Maybe it's always like that and we never know it: somebody old has to die for somebody new to live. In this case, Che Guevara. He died exactly twenty-five years ago today, come to think of it. One more coincidence, one more sign of how someone, something, is perversely playing with me.

So I'll let his death start my confession. He's sort of ubiquitous, Che is, nowadays. The man who declared that he would create two, three, many Vietnams is adorning coffee mugs and T-shirts, maybe you'll have a Guevara T-shirt on in Seattle, Janice, when you receive this confession in the mail. Che: for me, he's not something recent or merely fashionable. He's been nearby ever since I can remember, the poster with his face looming enormous on the wall of my room in Santiago as a child—and now, it's still here, the first thing I see when I wake up, the last glimmer when I go to sleep, here in this small apartment on the Calle Rodrigo de Triana in Sevilla, I put him up there of my own accord to accompany me on this last lap of my trip. Mom packed that poster in her suitcase first thing when we left Chile in 1974 after the military takeover, and seventeen years later, when we went back in July of last year for what was supposed to be a one-month visit, she brought it with her and here it still is, I brought it all the way to Spain. I hope he would approve of what I am about to do, how I'm about to avenge him and myself. If he started it all, he may as well be here for the ending.

7

"You owe that man your life," Mom answered, when one Manhattan evening I asked who that face up there on the sky of the wall belonged to, how come she was tacking it up there as soon as we arrived in the United States back in 1974, and when I asked why, what had he done? she simply added, "I'll tell you when you're ready." I looked him up, you can believe I did my research, prefiguring early on that I would be a bookish nerd—and by the age of ten, without the aid of a computer or an on-line encyclopedia, nonexistent back then, I had discovered that the Argentine-Cuban revolutionary Ernesto Guevara, known as Che, had been captured and executed on October 9, 1967, around nine months before my birth, and I got to wondering if my mother believed that the legendary guerrilla's soul had somehow magically been transferred into my body.

When I presented my transmigratory theory to her, she laughed and said that was not the link. "You were conceived the next day, *mi amor*," she said: "we were fucking you into existence, your father and me, in a hotel bed in Santiago de Chile, several thousand miles to the south of where they were lowering Che, alone and dead, into a stink-hole grave in Bolivia. I won't deny that I'd have liked Che's soul to have wandered into your tiny cells as they were developing inside me, but frankly, would the leftovers of his spirit have crossed the jungles and deserts of Latin America for thirty-six hours only to reincarnate in you, of all people? No need to resort to that sort of spiritual mumbo jumbo, because it turns out, Gabrielito, there's a more direct connection between you and Che and more than one. I'll tell you all about it in good time. Just remember: you're alive because he's dead. It's that simple. So you owe him."

I had two fathers, therefore, Janice—both of them equally mysterious and distant. Che was always there sharing my space, my time, my wall with the man who was supposed to be my father, Cristóbal McKenzie, the great McKenzie, who for—yeah, that's right—"reasons you're too young to know yet," stayed behind in Santiago when my mom escaped that military coup in our country. A mystery, my dad, even if I knew all the basic biographical facts: he was a detective of sorts, a psychologist of sorts, he brought back errant kids—that was his profession, to find runaways and persuade them to return to the family fold, and if they didn't want to, he'd put them up for a while at his own house, which he had baptized Casa Milagros in honor of my mom. And one more thing: my dad wanted me to come home.

Every week a letter postmarked Santiago would arrive at our New York apartment, and in the letter a new photo, so my eyes could accommodate the subtle changes in his appearance, so I could substitute the face in my memory with the face time and distance were molding for him far away. And in each letter, cozy, funny, humane, he was calling me back, as if all it took was to board the next plane, I felt he was rehearsing with me all the words he used to persuade those other boys to return to their parents. Full of stories, his letters, promising me—promises, Janice!—that if all else failed there was one place for me in the world and always would be. I could feel his charm oozing through the pages, I wanted to plunge my hand into the page and snatch him out of it, physically transport my father to this New York where Chile seemed ever more remote, ever more unreal, I waited for the day when he would announce a visit so I could probe his real hands and see his real face, when I could burn all his photos. But he never came. "He doesn't travel, he won't leave the country," my mother would say, hinting as usual at some enigma, "for reasons that I'll explain someday."

The reasons vaguely seemed to center on women, other women. It became clear to me that my dad was something of a ladies' man, extremely popular with "those bitches," Mom would say disdainfully, though he and my mother still loved each other and had not divorced, not because there was no divorce in Chile (there's still no divorce in Chile, Janice) but because they wanted to go on living together if he would only—and then Mom would grow quiet, and to tell you the truth, I didn't quite understand what was going on and there was nobody to ask. Even when my Abuela Claudia, Dad's mother, came to visit, if I ventured into forbidden territory, asked why Che Guevara was on my wall, why my dad couldn't travel outside the country, how my mom and dad had met, the old woman would simply lift her eyebrows, graze my cheek with her withered hand, and say, "*Querido*, I think you'd better ask Milagros about that."

And whenever I approached my mom, she'd say, "We met because of Che and we're not together because of Che, because of that damn bet your father made the night after we made you, poor thing," and before I could ask another question—What bet? Why is it so damned? What in *carajo* are you talking about, Mom?—she would cross to the rundown stereo. She always had the same cassette on hand, Mozart's *Don Giovanni*, though all she wanted to play over and over was one aria. Leporello, "that scoundrel's servant," Mom explained the first time I demanded a translation from the Italian, "he's telling Donna Elvira about his patrón's conquests, '*Madamina, il catalogo è questo,*' this is the list of all the women he's fucked, in Italy so many, in France so many, but in Spain, ah, '*in Ispagna son già mille e tre,*' in Spain he's already bamboozled a thousand and three," which left me even more puzzled: my dad was not in Spain. How was I to know he would end up here, in Spain, with me and my mom and everybody else? Outside their hotel room is the bustling Sevilla that made Don Juan famous, where he came from originally, *el burlador de Sevilla*, the trickster of Sevilla—though *trickster* cannot give you the sense of *burla* in Spanish: it is to make mockery. And he made a mockery of women and God made a mockery of him. In this very city in Andalucía, Don Juan fucked one woman too many and then killed her father when the old man came to defend his daughter's honor and then the *burlador* insulted that murdered man's statue by inviting him to dinner, not knowing that the Commendatore's statue itself would take him straight to hell. Not that my mom entertained me back then with such lurid tales. She merely pointed at the voice on the tape as if it were to blame for everything. "That bet," she said in our apartment there in New York when I was hardly even a child, that's how small I was, she would rail against that damn bet whenever something went wrong, when the clients left without paying at her restaurant, when one of the Puerto Rican waitresses had a baby in the kitchen one night—there was nothing in the world that was not directly or indirectly linked to the bet my father had made with his brother, Pancho, and their best friend, Pablo Barón, the day after he and Mom made love for the first time. Fucked me into existence: her words.

She had no problem using that sort of language around me. Very explicit about sex, my mom was. Not too typical for Chile, as you'll see—a country where everybody fucks but nobody likes to say the word, at least not in the presence of ladies, a country of hypocrites. A country where the military can put electrodes on your *pico*—but what's obscene is to say the dick word on TV. Mom was different, outspoken, straightforward, at least that's what I thought. I should have suspected, though: Mom was keeping too many things to herself. To begin with, she had never once, in her infinite depictions of labia and clitoris and glans and erections, referred to her relationship with my father, not one hint about what intimacies they had shared, how I had been born. She would only point at the huge portrait of Che on the wall. "He's responsible," she ranted, and that was as far as I could draw her out.

So it wasn't that I had no sex education—only that my father was regularly left out of those lessons. If he'd been around . . . Instead, when I was about thirteen, two years before I met you, it was my crazy mom who mentioned one evening that she'd noticed semen stains on my bedsheets. "It's called a wet dream," she announced, and then: "Did it feel good?"

"Dreamy," I answered, "but pretty good."

"Well, your father's not here so I guess I'll have to teach you how to masturbate." And then went on to explain the process to me quite graphically—as if I didn't already know! Chill out, Mom! And then escorted me to the bathroom and said that she recommended that I not use my hand. She pointed to the toilet seat. "There," she said, "use that." My whacky mom had cleaned the damn thing, scrubbed it a motherly white for my inaugural launch. "You get down on your knees"—she had put a little cushion on the floor, very considerate of her—"and just move your ass back and forth, gently. You can use some soap if you want. Remember: hands are the lazy way of doing it. Women can't help it; basically, we sort of need fingers to help us along. But men, men should find more creative ways. I'll be making dinner, *amorcito*. A great *cazuela*, to celebrate. You have a good time." And she left me there. I touched it. The glittering enamel of the toilet was glacial and the wooden seat not much better, both cold as hell, so I went ahead and did it with my hand as I usually did and then told her later, when I emerged, that I had really enjoyed the toilet seat, thanks for the suggestion.

"Wait till you do it with a woman," she crooned, doing a jerky mambo with her hips to the rhythm of Pérez Prado. "And when you do, there's something I'm going to tell you,"—it was the first time I could look forward to a concrete deadline, a moment in the future when she would reveal the secrets of my origins—"I've got a story about your dad. And about Che Guevara. But you have to be ready for it, that story."

That was the story she finally poured into my anxious ears a couple of years later when I returned home at three in the morning after having been out with you, my dear Janice Worth, and Mom was waiting up for me in the kitchen under a sad lightbulb. She was trying to imitate her Nanny. It's about time I mentioned Mom's Nana in this story, Janice, because she's the key to everything that happened: beginning with the fact that Mom was waiting for me only because her Nana had been waiting for her the night of my conception and Che's burial back in 1967. Nana realized immediately from Mom's feverish eyes that Mom was pregnant. If Mom had been that wise all those years later in New York as she worked at her interminable restaurant accounts with an eye on the door night after night, if Mom had been like Nana, known what was what, able to always guess exactly who was doing what to whom . . . But my mother jumped to conclusions, was too eager to congratulate me, and without giving me even a chance to say a word, embraced me, sat me down to tell me, now that I was a man, she said, how I had come into being.

I didn't inform her, of course, that the thing with you hadn't worked out because neither of us had considered bringing along a condom. I wasn't about to let her in on my secret: you had been adamant, hot and squirming and arching up and down under the pressure of those fingers of mine that were helping you along in accordance with my mother's advice. God, how could you move like that and still remain so stubbornly adamant? Nor did I tell Mom that you and I were going to rendezvous the next night and go for it, all the way, make 1983 the year we both lost our virginity, first because Mom had no business knowing any of this anyway, and as for me, I had been waiting forever—it seemed like forever, we had been away from Chile almost ten years by then—to find out about my dad, to unravel the mystery of the man who had made me. Get inside you so I could get inside him, inside his story.

They had conceived me the night of October 10, 1967, that much I knew, that they had met at a protest rally on the Alameda, but now I found out that it had all started seven years before, that they already had a more than passing acquaintance. They had played hide and seek, you could say. It had started one day in early 1960, at her father's house, the same gigantic house that would someday be turned into the Casa Milagros, in the vast backyard where Professor Gallardo had decided, as he did every year, to throw an *asado*, a barbecue, for his incoming students at the Universidad de Chile. A certain Cristóbal McKenzie, not yet eighteen, a freshman majoring in psychology, had come along, timid and tentative and virginal, yes, my dad hadn't made love to one lonely lady in his life. Runs in the family. But instead of using the occasion to try and bed one of the voluptuous university damsels who were flirting in that backyard under the stern gaze of none other than the Nana who did not approve of such profligate behavior but who nevertheless was dishing out her *ensalada a la chilena* in huge spoonfuls, liberally sprinkling it with enough coriander to make an army gag, instead of wriggling his way into somebody else's arms or even toadying up to the other professors munching away at the strips of steak and innards, this young McKenzie, astoundingly, spent the whole afternoon speaking to fucked-up twelve-year-old Milagros, the daughter of Professor Gallardo, the two of them talking the *asado* away in a corner.

And when he left several hours later, it was as if the world had come to an end for bobby-soxer Milagros Gallardo. His kindness toward her, the fact that he had treated her as a real human being and dispensed with the usual adult bullshit of "You're a sweet young thing, hello and goodbye, let's see if there's somebody fuckable over there," had revealed how lonely she really was and two days later she decided she could not stand another minute in that motherless home where even the Nana did not seem to understand her preteen blues. When she hightailed it out of there, the first suspect the police interrogated was, of course, none other than Professor Gallardo's psychology student. After all, this weird *tipo* Cristóbal McKenzie had spent a whole afternoon in conversation with *la niña*; he probably had something to do with her disappearance.

When the police released the suspect for lack of evidence, Cristóbal, instead of forgetting the whole unpleasant episode, grabbed the first bus back to Professor Gallardo's.

"I'm not responsible for her escape," he informed the old man, while the Nana hovered in the background, listening carefully, "but I have a good idea where she might have gone."

"Why didn't you tell the police then?" the professor asked.

And it was the Nana who answered, as if she could read young McKenzie's deepest thoughts: "Because she'll only come back," Nana said, "if this *joven* convinces her."

So Milagros's Nanny was the first one who recognized the great McKenzie gift, who started him on his career, so to speak. She was the one who convinced Professor Gallardo to beg Cris to try and find, God willing, the vagabond daughter.

Milagros was at the seaside near Cartagena—that ocean Magellan had baptized the Pacific because he came upon it the one day in the last three centuries when it was calm—and what she liked about it was precisely how wild the water was. She had described the site to Cris when they talked at the *asado*, the open beach, *la playa grande*, the way the waves reminded her of something she desired but could never really possess, the spray a suggestion of how everything passes, the harsh light of the sun a hint that maybe something stays in September.

Her future husband and my future dad came up behind Milagros on that beach, touched her unobtrusively on the shoulder, and before she even turned she knew who it was, *era él*. This was the reason she had run away, to force him to follow her, so he could see she had not been lying when she said there was a place in the world where you could smell the sand and the breeze and the crabs scuttling their existence away and not feel sad. She had fled home, she now realized, with the hope that he would come after her.

It wasn't difficult for Cristóbal McKenzie to induce Milagros Gallardo to return home. She was just a lonely kid who tolerated her father and adored her Nanny and wanted some attention, needed someone just out of adolescence to reassure her that this pubescent desolation wouldn't last forever. That was it, that was all.

Except that before he deposited her into the loving arms of her Nanny (and refused any compensation from her father, though he did expect old man Gallardo to correct any future papers and exams with a supremely benevolent eye), Milagros had extracted from Cristóbal a promise. It was on the train they took back to Santiago when she let slip the remark that he would be going back to his other women, and he answered, with utter simplicity, the truth:

"I haven't got any women in my life, not one."

"You'll have lots," she answered, already insanely jealous of the thousands of females he would eventually dazzle and poke. "You're good at this. You're going to spend the rest of your life doing it, finding little lost girls and boys."

Cristóbal answered that he didn't think so. It had been a chance coincidence. "But I'll tell you what," he said to her. "From now on, if I ever get another chance, I'll only bring boys back home. I won't accept to go after another girl. You'll be the one and only. And that's a promise."

And murmured something else to himself, a warning: he'd better stay away from this little lady and her infatuation. It could get him into trouble, statutory rape and that sort of thing. Better to forget the daughter and concentrate on her father the professor, who, after all, held the academic key to his career as a psychologist.

He didn't see her again until seven years had passed, until he wandered into the Alameda, Santiago's main avenue, that night in 1967. But by then he had had occasion to keep his promise to her many times over, had been protected by it—indeed, needed to invoke it not fifteen days after the rescue of Milagros when his phone rang and it was another professor, Enríquez, from Biology, a brawny friend of Gallardo's who asked Cristóbal if he wouldn't mind coming over. It turned out that Armando, his eldest son, age sixteen, had taken all the money in the house and left a note on the dining room table informing the family that he was getting the hell out of there and that they shouldn't come and look for him because at the first sign of a cop on his trail he would make sure all they'd bring back was a corpse, he would take his own life. And if Cristóbal McKenzie had done wonders for Gallardo's daughter, perhaps he could also be of assistance in this case. Cris merely answered, "I'll do my best." And also, "Lucky Armando's not a girl," which must have been taken by Armando's father as a commentary on the dangers a girl in that situation would face: kidnap, rape, prostitution. Dad, of course, meant something entirely different: he had recalled his promise to Milagros and meant to keep it.

"So he really loved you," I interrupted her. It was getting late in that kitchen under that solitary weak lightbulb and I wanted her to get to the night of my conception, Che Guevara, that damn bet.

"Who knows what was going on in his heart, in any heart," Mom answered. "I think he knew that if he started going after underaged girls he was going to end up in jail. Chile was as repressed a society then as it is now."

"But boys. He had no trouble finding boys, right? I mean, he was able to track down that Armando boy?"

No trouble finding him. Retrieving Armando was another matter. Cristóbal McKenzie had gone through the runaway's room, sat on his bed, laid himself down upon it. This was the way, Janice, he did it, how he figured out who the kids were, where he himself would have escaped to if he were that kid crumpled up in that bed. It was only his second case, but he guessed right: young Armando Enríquez was shacked up in one of the whorehouses on Calle Riquelme, spending every last penny he had been able to steal from his parents, drunk out of his mind and ready for another bout with a lanky hooker called Casilda. The problem was that Armando had no interest in returning home; his father was going to beat the shit out of him and . . . "Frankly, Cris," he said to his would-be rescuer, who had just finished singing a tavern song with him, "how can anybody persuade me it's better to be belted with a strap by my old man who has biceps the size of a stevedore's than to be fucking here to my heart's content?" As my father himself was still a virgin and would have gladly mounted sprightly Casilda right then and there, he sympathized with Armando's point of view. "But your father," Mom mused, "had this stubborn practical streak. He knew that as soon as the kid's money ran out he'd be on the street and that if something bad is going to happen it's better that it happen soon so it won't get worse. So he wanted Armando to have some bills left in his pockets when he went home."

Cris told the boy to go up the brothel's blue stairs to Casilda's torrid embrace while he negotiated with Professor Enríquez Armando's peaceful return to the nest. "All is forgiven," he told Armando, and when the runaway was reluctant to believe it, Cristóbal McKenzie assured him that if there was any violence he could come and sleep at the McKenzies' until the squall blew over. The suggestion was well-meaning. Also imprudent, given that Armando knocked on the door that very midnight and Cristóbal's mother, Claudia, gave instant refuge to that sixteen-year-old boy, all bloodied and bruised. A furious and betrayed Cris McKenzie only allowed the victim to go back to the muscled arms of his father once the brute had been through several therapy sessions that Cris asked old man Gallardo to organize, making sure that Professor Enríquez understood that he and his wife would not regain their son, Armando, until physical coercion had been banished from their house. Cristóbal McKenzie had a way with people—he was studying, after all, to be a psychologist—so when Armando returned home again a week later, he was not beaten up, not then, not ever.

That first experience with Armando's parents would end up being central, in the years to come, to how my father developed his practice, well on its way to becoming a full-blown detective agency by the time he met up with Milagros on the Alameda the day after Che Guevara's death. As word spread of his sensational powers, parents—not to mention uncles, aunts, grandmothers, guardians—flocked to him. And before agreeing to take their cases, Cristóbal made them sign a pledge that there would be no abuse of the prodigal runaway, a pledge ensured by a mammoth check to cover board for the child if that trust was violated. My father calculated that the threat of monetary damages would block the hand of the enraged parent more than love for the wayward child ever could. But once in a while his calculations went askew and he found himself lodging the child at home until an arrangement could be worked out.

Problem was, after a few years of boys entering and departing the maternal abode as if it were a merry-go-round, two of them in fact staying for over a year, his mother informed him one day—it must have been in 1962, maybe early 1963—my future grandmother Claudia told him that enough was enough, she had brought up two fatherless children, Cris and Pancho, and was not now prepared to be the nursemaid to all the troubled waifs of Chile. She cherished her eldest son's every footstep but maybe it was time for him to rent an apartment of his own with the excellent money he was making from his runaway-retrieval service. And that is what my father ended up doing, transforming his new residence into a halfway house for the kids he rescued. But no girls.

"What a great love story," I insisted one more time to Mom years later in that 1983 New York dawn. That's how I saw things then, Janice. You yourself told me that what you most liked about me when we first met was my incurable romanticism. "He was keeping himself for you. He didn't want to find anybody else."

"That's one way of putting it," Mom said. "But remember that nobody else wanted him. That's the paradox: the more success he had as a hunter of runaways, the less he was scoring with the ladies. Until it became, well, a pattern, I guess you could call it."

"Or a trap," I said. I stood up and walked to the window. Down in the street a yellow cab was streaking blindly through the New York night. I thought of you, alone in your bed, thought of tomorrow, dismissed the sadness in my own voice.

Mom looked at me, puzzled by my choice of words, maybe puzzled by something else, that word on the night when, according to her, I had made love for the first time in my life. "Yes, a trap. From which I had to free him."

"Well," I said from the window, "he must have loved you or he would have escaped the trap by taking the case of a young girl runaway and then he could have screwed her when he was taking her back home. Wasn't that what you wanted to do with him?"

She ignored the reference to herself. "No doubt about it: the girls would have seen him as a knight in shining armor. They would have fallen for him. But to look for young damsels in distress in order to screw them, well, that would have been a real defeat: to be loved because they were vulnerable and he was their rescuer. Besides, there was another problem. He told me—in fact, told me that very night in 1967 we made love for the first time—that he feared that his skill at finding runaways was only possible because he was himself a virgin. I'm scared that I'll never find another kid again in my life, he said. He was so obsessed with the idea that he repeated it to me one more time, even as he began to find a way into me, tease open my—"

"Mom," I protested.

"Well, that's how it is, Gabriel, that's what it means: a man puts his thing inside a woman, just like you did tonight, boy, and that's why I'm telling you this story, why I waited so long, till you were old enough."

I didn't answer. Let her think I had made love with my sweet Janice Worth that very evening, let her think we'd gone all the way, your vagina and my penis. If I had only revealed the truth to Mom then, told her, asked for her help. But I was too embarrassed. I was, as usual, making believe I knew everything. Top of the world, Ma, on top of Janice, Ma. Or if I had told you the story, Janice, the next night—or told it to you years later when I tried your name on the Internet and there you popped up, ready to start all over again. Instead of making up all those stories. All true. Except that it was my father who had done the fucking and I who had done the dreaming. I told you his life as if it had been mine.

"And now you're old enough," my mom repeated, "to know all the details."

I leaned against the windowpane, striking a casual John Travolta pose. "I'm really not that interested," I said to her. Not true: I wanted to know everything my father did with a woman even if that woman happened to be my own mother. I lied to her like I lied to you, Janice. "I couldn't care less for the gory details."

"No blood," she said. "Your dad was the virgin, not me. I had even been with—well, you know, somebody just the night before. In fact, I was looking for him when I saw your dad. And your dad almost didn't make it that night of the rally. He had been retrieving a runaway kid . . ."

That kid, that runaway kid. I have to tell you how my father found him that afternoon, that evening I almost didn't get a stab at birth, because that kid Leopoldo will reappear in my life, resurface all too soon under the nickname of Polo, that kid grown to adulthood has made my existence miserable ever since I returned to Chile last year. And it's significant, I guess, that he met my father just hours before my parents reconnoitered on the Alameda, almost as if stupid, skimpy Leopoldo had run away from home with the express purpose of blocking my future conception and having my dad all to himself forever and ever. Though I'm being unfair. He was just fed up with his parents like any normal ten-year-old and he had taken the drastic step of running away that hardly any of them dare, hadn't even left a note, so his concerned parents called on the wizardly Cris McKenzie.

After some preliminary and perfunctory questions, my dad climbed the stairs to the boy's room and rummaged around for a while in his belongings, browsed through Leopoldo's collection of books, records, photos, the banners on the wall, the unwashed socks hanging from the lampshade, the unruly pile of underwear, the portraits of clowns, a photo of the steppes of Russia, and after two hours of meticulous sniffing, he parked his rump on the runaway's bed and lay down for another hour staring up vacantly at the ceiling, while the parents stood by, increasingly impatient.

It was the mother who broke the silence.

"Is that all you're going to do?" she asked. And what crept into her voice was the suspicion that they had made a mistake, they should have phoned the police, who knows if their little nomadic Leopoldo was not lying at this very moment, mutilated and bleeding, on a railway track somewhere in the shantytowns south of Santiago. Pity it didn't happen that way, pity they didn't rape him and cut his heart into shreds. But her suspicions were unfounded.

"I'm putting myself in your boy's place," Cris McKenzie explained. "I'm figuring out where I would go if I were your Leopoldo. There's no other way to find him."

And find him my dad did. In the third row of the Teatro Caupolicán (remember that name, Janice, keep it in mind), watching El Gran Music Hall de Moscú, which the Soviet Union had sent on tour through Latin America to prove that all was not gray and drab behind the Iron Curtain. Cris McKenzie sat himself next to Polo and stayed there a good while, elbow to elbow, waiting for the right moment to establish a rapport with the ten-year-old fugitive. It came when Sergei and Yuri, the acrobat-clowns, came lumbering on, standing on their hands, parodying a soccer match. Cris was careful to laugh and squeal one second before the small runaway and then to clap his hands and tap his feet in sync with the kid through the next number, so that by the time the Leningrad puppets were performing a story about an abandoned child, my dad was ready to begin weeding the kid's problem out of him, what was wrong, why he was here by himself; and an hour later, they were munching hot dogs together in a desultory diner on the Calle San Diego, and a couple of Cokes washed it all down, and the kid, looking down at the sawdust under his feet, began opening up to this stranger whom he had begun to trust. That very night young Leopoldo was deposited back home, already planning to return some day—unfortunately for me—to Cristóbal McKenzie's life.

My father was exhausted. To spend a day inside someone else's head, find that person, and then gently steer him back home, talking all the while, making the kid feel he was the center of the universe— whatever it was Dad did or said, those secrets he never revealed to me, it drained his energy. Postcoital drowsiness. That night, he closed the door to Polo's house behind him and remained leaning against it breathless for a few minutes, eavesdropping from outside, making sure the parents were not reneging on their promise and punishing the kid, but also trying to gather the strength to attend the protest rally whose wild cries he could discern cracking open the Santiago air less than six blocks away.

He wasn't in the mood, but he went anyway, like so many others that night, because of Che. "So there's the first link," my mother said triumphantly. "If it hadn't been for Guevara's death, Cristóbal McKenzie would have gone straight home, and you wouldn't have been born."

Dad was more puzzled than shocked by Che's failure, sensing that the news of the execution was the end of something very central in his life and in many other lives of that generation. But he was not quite sure what that something was. "At first I thought I needed to let off steam," he told me later as the white mountains of ice floated by our ship heading North through the mist away from Paradise Bay and the South Pole. "To get together with somebody else, many others, maybe a woman, even if by that time I had convinced myself that I would never bag one, ever, that the same skill that allowed me to track down runaways and get under their skin and inside the compass of their soul, that same youthfulness that I seemed to have preserved when everybody around me was shedding theirs, eager to become adults without ever having really been children—it was that very ability to project myself into the head and heart and sex of an innocent, frightened child that seemed to make the girls avoid me, want me as their best friend but most certainly not as their lover. If it hadn't been for your mother, if it hadn't been, of all people, your mother whom I met that night after not having seen her for seven years . . ."

He didn't recognize her right away.

He was jumping up and down in the middle of the multitude. *"El que no salta es momio"* was the chant that somebody, leaping like a madman, had invented at a previous rally, as a pretext to warm the body during the wintry protest marches in favor of Vietnam and against the Yankee intervention. Now everyone on the Alameda was bouncing in place as they shouted, "If you don't jump, you're a mummy," meaning desiccated, conservative, right-wing, a dusty, infected murderer of Guevara, each and every one of them celebrating life, swearing with their bodies that Che had not died in vain, that they were alive and ready for the revolution. Everyone, that is, except my mom, Milagros. She was ready for something else—at least that night, thank you. The duty of every revolutionary might be to make the revolution, as Che had preached, a phrase that she would continue to repeat herself for many years, particularly to me. But for the moment something else was in the making.

She had seen him, quietly watched his body leap among the thousands of other bodies, and she had known immediately who he was; she had been waiting seven years for him to come back to her. So it wasn't difficult for her to wait a bit more, edge to his side, stand there discreetly, not moving a toe, not joining in the fun, waiting for the moment when he would settle down, when he would stop this hopping and jerking and land right in front of her again and remember his promise. That is how she told it to me when the time came. That is how I remember it through her eyes, the night she spilled the beans.

To think, Janice, how different my life would have been, maybe yours as well, if I hadn't been so anxious to find out everything in that kitchen in New York, if I had learned two days later and not that night how my father had been jumping up and down that other night of October 10, 1967, to prove that he was not a *momio*, to prove that Che was still alive and they were all still defiant. And then he had seen her standing there, her feet absolutely immobile in the midst of the dizzy waves of the crowd, only her eyes and her head moving, following his bounces and his shouts, he saw her there, as if she were a tree and he had pranced up and down a couple more times and then, his heart beating, he had ceased his exercise, landed right next to her, "almost body to body," Mom said. "I was almost touching her breasts when I came down," Dad admitted several years later when it became his turn to tell me what had happened as we navigated the *Galvarino* through the directionless landscape of the Antarctic Ocean.

And then Milagros, instead of saying hello or even reminding Cristóbal McKenzie of how they had met before, said something that really bowled him over and was to have consequences through the night and into the years to come.

"*Está muerto*," she said, and there was something of a dead volcano in her voice, a volcano that knows it will never ever again erupt. "He's dead. He's really dead, El Che. And there's only one thing we can do to bring him back to life. And it isn't the revolution."

It was something my dad had been feeling stirring inside ever since the papers had announced two days earlier that Guevara had been

2 2

captured in Vallegrande. He had been anticipating for some time—even while on the surface he had proclaimed, like most other young people his age, that the guerrillas, urban and rural, would soon overthrow oppression all over Latin America, just as they had done in Cuba and Algeria, just as in Vietnam—that this was not the way, that something was wrong, and Che's death had brought that old misgiving and newfound tiredness to his conscious mind again. He had dismissed it, didn't like to see himself despairing or hopeless, didn't like the image of himself that stared back at him from the mirror if in fact Che was really dead. But the suppression of the truth he felt inside was useless now that this young woman whom he could not identify but who was nevertheless chillingly familiar, now that she was saying to him exactly what he had been thinking. As if she could read his mind now and would be able to do so forever more.

When they made love that night, no more than an hour later, he confirmed it and he shared the thought the next day with his own brother, Francisco—my Tío Pancho—and his best friend, Pablo. He discovered inside Milagros that this was the only truth, the best and last truth available to him in the world when Milagros melted his virginity with a heat that could have dissolved the iceberg itself if it had chanced to float across her horizon that night.

"I don't get it," I said to Mom. I walked back to the table from the window, began playing with some bread crumbs left over from breakfast, still scattered over the worn blue tablecloth Mom had jubilantly brought home from some thrift shop. "Sorry, but it makes no sense. What does Che Guevara, alive or dead, have to do with sex? You guys back then in the sixties must have been really out of your minds."

Dad's answer, years later, was better than the version Mom gave me as dawn approached New York in 1983:

"I saw her naked there on that hotel bed and I began to understand, and understood it even better when I finally got inside her and I lost and found myself there, that this was what life was about, its meaning for me, the only meaning that really fit into this only life that had been given to me."

"It was a discovery he made," Milagros had told me, slapping my hand as if to say, Don't play with the bread crumbs. "Not at the moment when the pleasure he felt began to *acalambrarle la musculatura*, cramp his muscles ready to explode, no, it was me, what I . . ."

She stopped, uncharacteristically reticent.

"The moaning of an angel," my father completed my mother's unspoken admission, so many years later. "And I realized that I was the one producing that sound in her, I was the author of that sound."

"And Che Guevara?" I asked, groping for clues.

"I think, therefore I exist," my dad had said to Milagros a good half hour later, as they lay sweating in each other's arms, while the shovel loads of dirt were being piled on the mortal body of Che Guevara halfway across Latin America. "First there was Descartes. Then Marx: I make history, therefore I exist. But none of that's true. McKenzie's axiom: I fuck and therefore I exist."

"Your father," Mom explained, "had always somehow doubted his own existence. And I gave him, my body gave him, he said, proof that he had been wrong. Guevara was really and truly dead, and Cristóbal McKenzie was alive—but only totally alive when he was making love to a woman."

"And that's when he swore . . ."

"The next day he would make that damn bet, that he would fuck every day of his life, but it was that night he swore to live only for that moment when you copulate," Mom said, and Dad swore that not a day or a night of his life would pass without his finding a way, the only way, to deny the message of death that morgues and cemeteries and history books had been sending him all these years. "The message," my dad said, "that Che's execution and grave in Bolivia were trying to make me accept, that we are born alone and die alone and live alone."

"He wanted to verify, every day of his existence," Mom said, "over and over, in his body and the body of another human being, that they both did exist, even if only in that moment we felt that night, that moment I hope you felt tonight, *hijo*, a moment nobody can take from us."

I thought of you, my Janice, sleeping unfucked in your solitary bed at home and quickly changed the subject. "And that's when he decided to make the bet you've been talking about all these years," I said. "The Don Giovanni bet."

Mom thought that the bet was an accident, an unfortunate co-incidence, his *juramento*, his vow, no more than youthful enthusiasm. He had just lost his virginity, after all, had just realized the difference between the toilet seat and what a woman had to offer. Mom had heard other men bellow out similar vows as the blood pounded in their heads and the semen rushed out of their penises: I want to love you every minute of the day, I could stay here forever, this is the road to heaven, God must feel like this every siesta of his life. She thought Dad was being rhetorical and maybe he was, maybe if the next day he had not met Francisco and Pablo for lunch that insane *puto* idea of his would never have gotten off the ground, would never have been made public. He would have stuck his *pichula* inside her, in and out for a good while, a week or two, and then one night he would have fallen asleep in his own apartment and realized drowsily that he hadn't managed to make love that day, no big deal, like skipping dessert after a good meal, like forgetting to brush your teeth. Life is like that—we swear we'll do lots of things, and then we bypass them, get engrossed in the scenery, take a detour, forget to reach the temple we always vowed we would visit, sleep somewhere else, and think nothing of it. Not everybody is Christopher Columbus, not everybody is that obsessed. No, Mom was convinced that it was the unfortunate lunch the next day that nailed Dad to his oath, turned what had been a passing fancy into a goal for life, made Cristóbal into a sex fanatic who carried out Leporello's *catalogo* in ways that Mozart's hero could never have imagined.

"It was the other men," Mom said, "they're the ones who turned him into a modern-day Don Juan, more than my charms. That's why I'm telling you this now, Gabriel. I don't want you doing something silly, boasting to your macho pals that you'll fuck forever or anything of the sort. Believe me, Gabriel, it'll mess up your life. Because it wasn't the sex that did us in. It was the bet."

Or maybe the fault lay in the fact that the next day was Cristóbal's birthday, his twenty-fifth on this earth. And he went to celebrate it as usual with his best friend, Pablo Barón, who was also exactly twenty-five that October 11.

This was a story that did not have to wait until I had presumably lost my virginity. I knew it by heart. First because my father and Tío Pablo loved to recount it to loud laughter and between swigs of wine in the backyard of Casa Milagros in the time of Allende back in the early seventies, and then because Mom had told it to me many more times in exile. Naturally, she insisted on repeating it all over again.

The two friends had discovered the strange coincidence of their parallel births when, twenty years earlier, in 1947, little Cris had found himself handing Pablito an invitation to his fifth birthday party—which Señora Claudia, *viuda de* McKenzie, had been diligently planning for the past month—only to receive in his other hand, from the selfsame Pablo, a request to come to *his* house at precisely the same time on the same day. It was the first occasion when Dad felt that he was somehow being duplicated, that someone else shared his destiny, though the extraneous sensation did not last long. There were more urgent matters to resolve: all the tots in the kindergarten had two invitations and would have to choose which to honor, whom to scorn. The mothers, when they heard from their apprehensive sons about the overlapping invitations, smiled indulgently, and called each other up simultaneously until, after many busy signals, one of them got through (each mother avouched later that she was the one who had managed to break down the phone barrier) and both suggested in the same breath that the other postpone her party. They argued back and forth for a while, ultimately agreeing, with what each thought was surprising alacrity on the other's part, that the younger child, he who had been born last, would have the right to hold his party on the October 11 in question, both of them making the suggestion like two cheating card sharps who have four aces in their greedy fingers, both of them sure that the other kid had to be older, because Pablo was born at . . . and here, Pablo's mother paused for effect, at 11:59 p.m., one minute before midnight, just before October 12. She was non-plussed when her rival, Claudia, the widow of McKenzie, answered that Señora Barón had better produce written proof, because it was Cris who had been born at that very moment, yes, 11:59 p.m., 23:59, to put it in terms that could leave no room for ambiguity, and that is why she had named him Cristóbal, because he was born almost 450 years after Columbus discovered America. Pablo's mother responded that this was precisely why she had not baptized her son with the name of El Descubridor, and if the Lord had wanted him to be called Cristóbal or Cristófero or even Cristián, He would have prolonged her labor for sixty-one seconds, but had preferred to let the child be born before the Día de la Raza and the Día del Almirante and the Día de la Hispanidad: Pablo was a more appropriate name. There was no "almost" about the Lord's disciple who had seen the light on the road to Damascus. The answer came fast and furious from La McKenzie, that in Spain, from which Columbus had left, it was six hours later, so her own boy had in fact, at least in the only place where it mattered, the *madre patria*, been born on October 12. Pablo's mother told her not to be ignorant, there were no time zones back then. And who are you calling ignorant?—and from there the hostilities escalated and the two mothers threatened each other with all sorts of dire consequences if the other birthday party was not postponed instantly and they hung up at the same time, believing, each of them, that she had been the one to leave the other fuming at the dial tone. Both of them turned to tell their sons, who had been listening to this pitched phone battle with increasing distress, that they were to hold their parties on the assigned day and that under no circumstances was the other child to be invited. We'll see who's more popular.

Pablo and Cris, however, decided to stop the nonsense, to hold their parties together at the kindergarten itself and to flip a coin for next year and to alternate from that day onward. They couldn't have cared less who was younger or who was older: they liked each other, though adored might be a more pertinent term, and theirs was a friendship that was to last for many years, even if it was to be sorely tested by the bet they made on their twenty-fifth birthday and even more by the iceberg that was looming in their future and in mine.

"What happened next?" I asked Mom back in 1983. "Did he brag about his conquest at the birthday lunch?"

Not at all. It had been Cristóbal McKenzie's intention to keep the whole affair a secret. "Understand, *mi amor*, your father is, above all, a discreet man, *un hombre discreto*. Kids knew it just by looking at him, someone who would never betray their confidence."

Except that what had just happened to Cristóbal McKenzie was written all over him, every pore in his body was singing the royal flush of consummation, the fuck happiness of a young man who has just learned on his first night of love that the best way to discover your own body is by exploring someone else's.

"Even so, Pablo and Francisco—"

"Tío Pancho?" I said.

"Yes, your Tío Pancho. He was there, had tagged along to the lunch with Pablo, and they were both engaged in a furious discussion about politics, so they did not look closely at your father. He just sat himself down, ordered a beer, listened to them arguing about Che Guevara. They—"

"Mom, I'm really not too interested in this Guevara guy you keep plugging into the story. And I'd like you to take him off the wall of my room. It's my room. I think I made this clear to you: I'm really not into this *Latinoamericano* politics shit."

"Well, you may have turned your back on your country and your cause and your heritage, but I can't leave Che out of this: it was Pablo and Francisco's disagreement over the meaning of Guevara's death that detonated that damn bet a few minutes later, so just listen. Or maybe you'd like me to tell you all this tomorrow."

I grabbed some bread crumbs, hid them in my hands under the table, played with them secretly while I listened to her drone on for another half hour about the quarrel Dad's best friend and Dad's younger brother had in 1967, as bored, or maybe more so, than Cristóbal McKenzie many years ago. At least he had a pilsener to guzzle and a waiter to bring him another and a satisfied, happy, flaccid *pija* hanging between his legs that had just seen service worthy of commendation, whereas years later in New York, I understood squat about what in hell they were saying. If you'd been there, Janice, if I'd brought you home with me to meet the mother-in-law, so to speak, you wouldn't have cared either. But you can skip a few pages. I only had bread crumbs to play with.

Here's what my mom painstakingly spelled out for me: for Pablo, Che's capture and execution was the end of the armed-struggle alternative in Latin America, the end of an era. This meant that in order to achieve radical change you had to use electoral, peaceful means. And Francisco was steadfast: a battle had been lost, but conditions were ripe. Che's death would galvanize thousands of youngsters, Latin America would be burning in a few years. Now they had a martyr larger than life—had Pablo looked at the photo of *el guerrillero heróico*, lying Christ-like as if on a bed of thorns, his wounds like something out of a Renaissance tableau. They hadn't killed him, they'd given him life. His eyes. Look at his eyes, about to open, about to resurrect.

"And how long is this total revolution of yours going to take?" Pablo asked, polishing his glasses with a napkin.

"Tell you what. By the time you're fifty, October 11, 11:59 at night—before the five hundredth anniversary of the Discovery, the so-called Discovery—I'll bet the whole continent is socialist, I'm willing to bet anything."

"You're wrong," Pablo answered. "As wrong as Guevara was wrong to try and create a revolution in a country he knew nothing about and where nobody, particularly not the Bolivians, wanted him to be, where the Cubans sent him to get rid of his troublesome ideas and be able to cozy up to a totalitarian Soviet Union. With all due respect, he's finished."

"I wouldn't be so sure."

"Come and see me in twenty-five years," Pablo said. "You think I'm going to be in this restaurant, yakkety-yak-yakking about the *revolución* and what others are going to do and how we're going to kick the shit out of the Yankees? You know where I'm going to be, who I'm going to be? I'm going to be the most powerful minister in this country, that's who I'm going to be when I'm fifty. Not the president: I want the power behind the throne. I'm going to be the invisible guy who holds everybody tight in his grasp. I'll sneeze and the country will say, Bless you. *Salud.* In less than twenty-five years. You'll see."

My father's brother answered that prediction with more passion than was warranted, seeing as it was supposed to be a birthday celebration and not a meeting of the Leninist Youth Debating Society. "I'm not going to see shit," Francisco said. "There'll be nobody with that sort of power in this country or anywhere else in Latin America twenty-five years from now. You know why? Because under socialism, the only real power belongs to the people. You won't be a power behind the throne because there's not going to be any throne."

They could have gone on like that forever, and so could my mom, if my father back then in Santiago in 1967, and yours truly in New York sixteen years later, hadn't been rescued by the waiter, who was impatiently waiting for the order. As a real worker—which none of the three beer drinkers were even close to being, although at least my father did toil hard as a detective—the *mozo* had to make a living and didn't much care who was right about the fuzzy future they were auguring for him and his descendants. Did they want steak or chicken? The special today is *congrio frito*, straight from the sea. What will it be?

They ordered the fish, and then the two debaters turned to the other birthday boy. How about him? What did he think?

"*Está muerto*," Cris said, echoing Milagros from the night before. "And no politics—not yours, Pablo, not yours, Pancho—is going to bring him back to life. Not with bullets, not with ballots, not with bullshit. Che is dead."

No politics? Pablo and Francisco could not have been more astonished if Cris had just announced that he was the beast of the Apocalypse. What do you mean, no politics? How are you going to change things, then?

"I'm not going to change *ni un carajo*," my father said, mildly enjoying their amazement.

Well, then, how was he going to spend the next twenty-five years? Doing what? Achieving what?

"Your father should have just answered something noncommittal like, I really don't know, let's hope the *congrio* is fresh, something like that, and our lives would have been so different. He would be here with us in New York, he'd be telling you this story, Gabriel, or another one. Instead, something in him stirred and he told them the truth. He told them what he had discovered when he entered my body."

"I'm going to spend the next twenty-five years fucking," Cristóbal McKenzie said.

They looked at him in consternation. They both knew he was a virgin, knew that he—and then Francisco burst out: "Wait, wait, tell us all. I saw you go off with that girl, you scoundrel, you, avoiding your revolutionary duty. Hey, the two of you fled the rally so quickly that I looked around, thought you'd spotted a police raid about to— but I'm not blaming you, I—" and here Francisco looked deep into his brother's eyes and then he smiled broadly: "*Hombre*, just in time for your twenty-fifth birthday. You got laid, you finally got laid."

"I don't think Dad would have liked having that sort of information spouted around in a restaurant. Were there many people nearby?"

Mom didn't know. She was only certain what Cristóbal McKenzie's reply had been, and Dad repeated it word for word to me when I asked him about it years later:

"I was very quiet," Dad told me, as we crossed icy waters that were anything but quiet, "and then I said, 'Yes, and I'm going to make up for lost time. I'm going to get laid from now on, every day of my life.'"

It was Pablo's turn to intervene.

"She was that good?" he asked.

"He didn't?" I myself asked Mom as she reiterated, there in that kitchen in New York, the words that Pablo had uttered many years before in Santiago.

"That's what Pablo asked. And then he added, 'No matter how good she was, you can't possibly screw, want to screw, every day of your life.'"

"Sure I can."

"I bet you can't."

"What do you mean?"

"Tell you what—I'll make this easy for you, Cris. I'll give you twenty-five years exactly. Till your fiftieth, *ya*? We'll make it a bet. We're betting, right? We're betting who the hell we'll be in twenty-five years, right? I'm betting I'll be a man with so much power it'll make everyone else tremble, you guys will be coming to ask me for favors, and Pancho—"

"I'm betting that it doesn't matter what I am, I'm betting that we'll be free, the collective will be free, that's what I'm betting, no favors, no favoritism."

"And Cris bets he'll have screwed every day for the next quarter century, an impossible task that Hercules and his big godlike *pico* couldn't accomplish. Beyond the means of Humphrey Bogart. Or Rock Hudson, for that matter."

"It's easier than what you guys want to try," my dad answered. "And it depends on me, not on history, things happening in the big world, like revolutions and politics and people being killed. Just me and my sex."

Now it was Francisco's turn to intercede, as if he were the elder and not the younger brother. "Listen, *hermano*, don't bet something that stupid. You don't, well, know about these things yet. Your pecker, you know, needs to rest once in a while. At the moment, you're full of enthusiasm but three months from now . . . *La huevada no está hecha de goma*. The motherfucker isn't made of rubber, you know. And anyway, it's not that easy to find someone every time the little fellow perks up and looks around for—How many women do you intend to screw?

You'd have to find thousands of willing maidens. And so far you haven't been doing great, to put it inoffensively. One fuck in your first twenty-five years—wait, let me calculate, that makes nine thousand one hundred and twenty-five in the next quarter century. That's a lot of women."

"Your father," Mom explained, "is one of the most stubborn men I've ever met. The most stubborn. He said that he wouldn't need to convince that many women. 'I'll just make love to the same woman, over and over again. I don't want anybody but her.' "

"Let me get this straight," Pablo said. "The only woman you're going to fuck more than once is the one you fucked last night. Any other woman—"

"There won't be any other."

"Any other woman, you'll only make love to once. Once and that's it?"

"There won't be any other, but yes, that's how it'll be. If there is anyone else, I'll only screw her once."

"Well," said Pablo, "you can screw any other woman as much as you want or she'll tolerate, but for the purposes of this wager, the second time doesn't count. Let's say you go out with—" He pointed to a rumba-swaying blond window-shopping in front of a record store across the street. "With *esa*. You pick her up right now. Say you like the merchandise, tomorrow you repeat the dish, eat some more of her pussy—you would still have to roll off the damn bed and find yourself another one before midnight. Because she only counts as one score, is that clear? One *mina*, one day. Next day, another one. Are we agreed?"

"Yes."

"And we're talking penetration here, erection, ejaculation, the works," added Francisco. "No mouth stuff counts. I mean you can use your mouth—"

"Well, thanks," Dad said, "I'm glad to have your permission."

"—but for accounting purposes, you have to go all the way."

"At least till she reaches orgasm," Pablo intervened. "Give him a break, he may not have enough *chuño* in him to ejaculate that many times. He's not a horse."

"All right. Till he ejaculates or she comes, whichever is first. And no whores. No paying a woman to reach your goal."

"And no men," Pablo added. "Only women count."

All so fortuitous. All these conditions created out of nothing, rules of a game my dad would spend the next twenty-five years strictly adhering to, terms casually and frivolously hammered out as the waiter snatched away the remains of *congrio frito*.

"But how will we know?" Francisco asked, reaching for a toothpick.

"Because McKenzie here, your big brother here, never lies. If he fails, he'll come and tell us, right, Cris?"

"I'll let you guys know."

And that, my mother explained in New York, was that: they swore, all three of them, to meet twenty-five years hence, on October 11, 1992—just before the fifth centenary of the Discovery—and see which of them was right.

"And what was the prize?"

"The prize?"

"Yes, what did they bet?"

"They bet what Latino men always bet, the one thing more important than their money or their women or even their souls or their mothers."

"And what's that?"

"They bet their honor, their fucking honor, their pride."

By this time, they were ready to leave. Pablo had a final question. Who was the lucky—or maybe unlucky—woman?

My father hesitated, at least that was his version. But he figured if he was going to fuck her the rest of his life, they would end up knowing it soon anyway, so he gave them Mom's name: Milagros Gallardo.

Pablo nodded. "Oh, I know Milagros . . . Good choice." He stood up from the table. The waiter began clearing up immediately: there were people standing by the table, people salivating, maybe a few more tips to be pocketed. "She must have been real good," Pablo said. "Are you going to marry her?"

"Your father says he had already decided to marry me," Mom said. "But I don't think that's true. I think if it hadn't been for the bet we would have screwed a couple more times and then his eye and his gonads would have started to roam. He had just discovered sex, and it would have made sense for him to explore some other options before settling down. Pablo's question pushed him into something he would probably not have chosen otherwise."

I had stopped playing with the bread crumbs by then. I had more serious matters to deal with.

"And how about me? I was already inside you, growing, right?"

"Yes. One of your dad's spermatozoids had outpaced all the others, kicked the living daylights out of them, tripped them up, squeezed them into exhaustion, reached my egg, closed the door behind it—and that was you, *mi dulce*."

"But when Dad . . ." I almost stood up again. Instead I looked toward the window and the whole island of Manhattan still sleeping out there. "If you'd have told him that I was on the way, well, he'd have . . . he'd have . . . I mean, you would have . . ."

Mom looked at me. Behind her, streaks of dawn were starting to crowd the New York skyline. I could hear a garbage truck roaring on Riverside Drive below.

"I probably wouldn't have told him."

"But he would have found out, he—"

"Listen, *hijo*. I was nineteen, I had my whole life ahead of me. If I hadn't married I don't think I could have stood being a single mother. Nana would have fixed things. Do you understand what I'm saying? Is that all right with you?"

I answered yes and meant it. I think I meant it. I had always felt that I had been this far from not existing and now Mom was merely certifying how accidental I was. Now I knew for a fact that if it hadn't been for Che's death Dad would never have gone to that rally or intersected with her again or made the bet the next day. If not for Che rotting in his earth in Vallegrande, Pablo would never have had occasion to suggest marriage. In short, my mother had just told me that she would have aborted me.

"But that's not how it turned out," Mom said gently, placing her hand on my hair, stroking it slowly. "Cris proposed to me that very night and we were married around a week after that. Although the fact that I had inherited this huge house from my dad and that I had this wonderful Nanny who was great with kids and that I loved the idea of turning my house into what Cris called Casa Milagros and giving refuge to—"

"Yeah, yeah, all the kids who had nowhere else to go," I interrupted.

"This I know, this I've heard a thousand times. A place for kids whose parents couldn't pay or didn't have fat wallets. Subsidize the poor with money from the rich, sure. What I don't know and nobody's ever bothered to tell me is why it didn't work out. What happened?"

As usual, Mom ignored my questions and plodded on with her own story, what she thought I needed to know.

"You have to understand, I loved the idea of a Casa Milagros. I knew what it was like to feel abandoned and misunderstood and then to be cared for the way Cris cared for me and about me that afternoon of the *asado*, the way he followed me to the beach. I could see my whole life unfolding in front of me, Cris and me and my Nana. And maybe that's how it would have been, except for the bet."

He hadn't breathed a word to her about it. They made love that night and the next one, and again, and then again, and the night they married as well, and the honeymoon days that followed, which were spent in getting the house ready for all those kids that my father was sure he would start collecting. He had all these people in his debt, appreciative parents, the police commissioner, the undersecretary of defense—to each and all he had returned their children, and they all guaranteed that his establishment wouldn't be shut down or slandered by goody-goody rival organizations. His friends made sure that he'd get the legal papers worked out, the subsidies, especially now that he had a woman acting as nominal head of the newly founded Casa. "He was really overjoyed those first days, that first month," Mom said. My father had been so scared that he would lose his touch once his virginity was gone, that his youngsters would see him as an enemy, an unreliable adult, now that he had crossed the threshold of a woman's flesh and matured, so to speak. But nothing of the sort happened. They continued to trust him implicitly during the light hours no matter how many positions Milagros and he tried out in the dark.

Mom got up, went to the refrigerator, poured me an enormous glass of milk I didn't need.

"Maybe it was my pregnancy," Mom said. "It was bound to happen sooner rather than later anyway. My sex hurt, my back hurt, there was this tiny ulcer developing on the inside of my vagina, I was feeling some nausea. We had been going at it nonstop, thirty-one days since we had been married, plus some—what were they, eight, nine days before that—almost forty days and nights . . . Drink your milk, *mi amor* . . . So that when he undressed that night, I thought, Oh no, not again. Now don't get me wrong. It had been the best sex ever, the first time I ever had a multiple orgasm. In fact, thanks to you—"

I stopped in the middle of a gulp of milk, almost coughed it up.

"Thanks to me?"

"Yes. When you're pregnant, the blood flow increases, rushes to every part of the body, makes the breasts, the clitoris softer, more lustrous than ever, makes them extrasensitive, so that the slightest touch from a man—"

"I really don't need to hear this, Mom," I protested, feigning bashfulness, hoping she would tell me everything.

"All right, all right, maybe you don't. I hope I'm not embarrassing you?"

"Not at all," I lied.

"What matters is that I told your father that we should give it a rest, even God rested on the seventh day, and I had been *dale que suene*, like a happy whore for more days than Noah's ark had been afloat, and the very idea of the ark and the waters enticed me, made me drift off to sleep, because the next thing I remember is being woken up by him, his hand shaking me tenderly. A few hours had passed. He had been watching me all that time."

"I had been watching her all that time," my dad told me years later on board the ship. I thought I heard the mating calls of whales, I thought I heard the whales calling to one another as he told his tale. "Watching her as the minutes ticked by. And knowing that I could not force myself on her, or on anybody, for that matter, that the bet shouldn't be won in that fashion, it had to be consensual, not something stolen from a woman in the dark." And that is when my father decided to awaken my mother. He told her that they had to make love, told her about the bet—not all the details, just the vow he had sworn and that he needed to fill his quota for the day. Mom says that those were his words, Dad would deny it, but they both agreed that Mom had been indignant and had thrown him out of the room and that Cristóbal had found himself at ten-thirty at night without a bed and without a woman and an hour and a half in which to be the first one to lose the bet and he—

"He what?" I asked Mom, entranced.

"He found someone," Mom said, "but you'll have to speak to him about that part, because when he came back, it was one in the morning. When he left, I had started to cry in despair, but when I went to wake my Nanny, she gave me some good advice, so that when Cris walked through our bedroom door and began to tell me what had happened to him, the woman he had picked up at some funeral, I begged him to stop. I didn't want to know anything—*oídos que no oyen, corazón que no siente*, what the ears don't hear, the heart doesn't feel. We talked till dawn, just like you and me tonight, *mi amorcito* Gabriel, and we reached, well, an agreement, I guess you could call it, to cohabitate, continue to live together even if he made love to other women."

"You didn't mind?"

"Remember, I already knew you could screw around and still be deeply faithful to one person. I knew because that's how I had lived my life ever since Cris took me back to my father's home. That day, when I was a twelve-year-old girl hugging Papá first and then my Nanny, I became acutely aware that that was not enough. I needed a man, I needed something physical and deep that neither of them could give me. That something was sex and I began to take it where I could, when I could, generally on Saturday nights, after parties, you know, while the radio played 'Will You Still Love Me Tomorrow?' Things became easier when my papá died—sadder, of course, I missed him, though he had been a distant sort of man, a cold fish, really, only in love with his books. I was lucky that Nana stayed with me, fought off the relatives of all sorts and sizes who came to 'take care of *la niña*,' though I think they were relieved not to be responsible for me. They thought I was a bit *loca*, wild, and they were probably right. And I became wilder as the years passed. I didn't know that what I was looking for in men was Cris. My Nanny would tell me when I came back, That's not the one. She would take my pulse, feel my forehead, sniff me like a dog. You've made a mistake, she'd say, shaking her head, you should be keeping yourself for the one man that matters."

Mom, however, had gone right on doing it, trying out men like other women try on shoes, doing it with abandon, until, that is, the dawn of—by then it was October 11, 1967, when Milagros came home after spending that first night with Cris and Nana said, This time it worked, don't let him go, he's the one who found you seven years ago. She even knew Mom was already expecting me. And when the crisis exploded, forty days later, it was Nana who convinced her that Cris was only making up for lost time, that it was good for him to know some other women so he could realize how special she was, instead of hungering for them in his mind. Nothing destroys a relationship more, Nana said, than unfulfilled desires.

"And I thought to myself, also," Mom said to me in that kitchen in New York as the first rays of the sun crept over the Hudson down below, "Cris has been faithful to me all these years—at least, that's how I explained his long years of abstinence—so I could let him have his fun now, and besides, I was certain he wouldn't be able to find somebody new each day. He's a timid sort, your dad, or he was back then. I forgave him. He loved me and I loved him, he could hump other women as long as he met certain conditions that I set down, my own rules, four of them, to this insane game he was playing. First of all, no bites, I didn't want him marked by any other teeth, and he said that all he could do was try, ask his companion to comply, which meant that he was sort of promising that he wouldn't do to her the same things he did to me . . ."

Mom paused. I must have been looking at her strangely, as if I wanted—and simultaneously did not want—to know in excruciating specificity what those things were. She waited for me to say something. Another missed chance, my silence. Oh, God. So she continued spelling out her rules and conditions.

"And second," she said, "that once he'd failed—and I was as sure he'd fail as Pablo and Francisco had been at that birthday lunch—I made him promise that from the day he lost that silly bet, he would start to live a normal life with me, no fooling around anymore."

"But he didn't fail."

"He liked women, women fell for him like crazy. He just kept on coming home quietly triumphant, accumulating *conquistas* the way postmen deliver the mail, through rain or sleet—"

"Or snow."

"Except it doesn't snow in Santiago. And he would make love to me a lot as well, whenever I felt like it, because he always wanted to. He said that if I agreed, he would make love to me the rest of his life and mine, but I said that I couldn't make that sort of promise. I mean, I was about to have a baby. You're supposed to wait for around six weeks, though Cris would have mounted me in the ambulance on the way to the hospital if they'd have let him. In fact, he tried to sneak in for a quickie the day you were born. I think he screwed one of the nurses instead."

"He screwed one of the nurses who was taking care of me?"

"Or taking care of me. But listen, what matters is that I couldn't agree to his terms, they turned love into something routine and mechanical. I preferred things this way. Okay, okay, he answered, all he demanded was that I tell him in the morning, by the time breakfast was over, if we were going to do it that day or not, so he could make preparations—"

"It does sound pretty mechanical to me," I said. "He can't have been having a very good time."

"You'll have to ask him about that, Gabriel. I didn't want to know anything about what he did or how he did it or with whom. I could even say I was happy, though I would have been happier if he had failed, I think, but he kept on telling me that he would rather fuck me than anyone else in the world but that if I wasn't willing and able, and as the months passed, as you grew inside me, it became more difficult to—"

"I came between you," I said. "Is that what you're saying? You felt nauseous, tired. That night he went off, if you hadn't been pregnant . . ."

"My pregnancy turned out to be a blessing. Not just the multiple orgasms, I mean, your existence, above all, and also it accelerated a showdown that would have come about anyway, forced us to reach an understanding early on."

"What was the third condition?"

"The third condition? Oh yes. That he was not to bring any of those women home. And he accommodated me, he wanted me to feel comfortable about the whole affair, and we could have gone on like that forever—or until his fiftieth birthday, when he could finally cease and desist—we'd still be living our pact if Salvador Allende hadn't been elected in 1970, promising a peaceful socialist revolution."

They would have still been living their pact—and I'd have been in Chile watching them live it—if three years later the *golpe* of the *fuerzas armadas* hadn't come and sent that idea of a bloodless revolution to hell just like Che's death had sent the idea of an armed revolution to hell six years before. And Mom had headed into exile with her son, Gabriel, and Dad, he stayed behind.

"He stayed because of that idiotic bet," Mom said, still as furious in New York as she had been in Chile when she had fruitlessly tried to convince him to leave the country. "He stayed to chase his women and we left."

"And you missed him."

"Terribly. Still do. Though let me tell you a little secret. I miss my Nana even more. Every moment of the day at the restaurant, I think of her. When I open in the morning and when I close at night and when I buy the ingredients at the market and when I plan the day's menu, she's—but the stubborn old witch wouldn't come along. I belong here, she said. Within seven years you'll be back, she predicted. I'll be cooking a *cazuela* for you the day you return. I thought it couldn't possibly last that long—a couple of years of Pinochet and we'd be rid of the *hijo de puta*. I thought we'd be back in a flash. Your father knew that wasn't true, that it would be a long time. 'Most people in this country aren't like you and Pablo and Pancho,' he said. 'Most of them are like me. They just want to live out their short lives and make love as many times as they reasonably can before they die. Most people don't have their heads full of theories that will never come true. They have enough trouble just making an honest peso. No, I have to stay here where the kids know what I'm saying to them, where the women know what I'm saying to them.' His tongue was always his most crucial instrument, in every sense. He wanted to make sure he could use it, not live like a stranger. It's ghostly enough, he would say, just to be on this earth. To leave would be too much. Just promise me, I said to Cris, that if you fail, you'll join us. And he promised. 'On the first plane,' he said, 'the day after I can't find someone to make love to.' "

"So he's fucked every day since then?" I said.

"It would seem so. I'd be the first to know if things had gone wrong. I'm the one who gets him back when his Casanova days and nights are done. That was our agreement, that and the four conditions. The fourth, by the way, was that he was always—except with me—he was always to use a condom." Mom stopped her story here to look at me with a mixture of pride and severity. "Which reminds me, Gabriel, you did use a condom last night, didn't you?"

I lied to her. Of course I had used a condom, I told her. One more of the many lies I would tell her. Lies that haunt me now, that first mother of all lies that haunted me the very next evening, when Mom saw me all spruced up, ready to go out on my date and enjoy with Janice Worth what Mom, jumping the gun, presumed had already been consummated the night before. She smirked knowingly and said, "*De tal palo, tal astilla*. A chip off the old block. Going back for more, huh?"

But I wasn't going back for more, as you know only too well, Janice, because I had never had anything in the first place. And that new night with you I didn't get much either. Remember how auspiciously things began, making out on the comfortable living-room couch that your parents had so kindly purchased on sale a few years back. I had a pack of ribbed condoms in my pocket, and I started to slip down your panties—I know you remember that moment!—and my finger was starting to explore what I intended to explore with another, sturdier part of my being in a few more minutes' time. Except that there was nothing sturdy about it. All of a sudden I was drooping, falling by the wayside. I urged it on, scuttled my hand away from the hot hole in your body and reached toward the appendage on mine that was supposed to go in and out of the hole, and nothing. I know you remember that: it was supposed to be your first time, too. I couldn't get that cold thing hanging down there to obey my commands. I tried to concentrate on you and your exciting little whimpers, but all I could think about was my father thousands of miles to the south—who at that moment must have been screwing his woman number five thousand and forty-something, he interposed himself between me and your body, Janice, he stepped between me and my own dick. He jinxed me, Mom had jinxed me by prematurely telling me the story, fucking Che Guevara had jinxed me by dying and leaving me alive to hear you ask me what was wrong. You were asking it with your lips and your breasts and the muscles trembling in your calves and your toes that were scratching my backside softly, and I had to abandon ship, that night and the next two nights, until I gave up. Until I came up with the lie I'd tell everybody: my father had just died, that's why I couldn't perform, I'd get back to you, Janice, get back to each of the dozens of girls in the future, I'd fuck your eyeballs out when I was over my grief.

I was going to use that pretext more often than I had imagined. Every time I tried, my dad would be there, screwing ahead of me, as if his organ were in her before mine could even begin to rise up, as if I were previewing his ass moving up and down with every girl I wanted, every girl who responded to me. I had gotten between him and my mom, I had placed myself in the one impregnable position that had made his vow to fuck only her the rest of his life impossible, and now this was his vengeance. Not that he knew anything about it, but that's how I saw it. Oh God, Janice, I began to give up before failing. I withdrew before even trying for ultimate penetration so as to avoid ultimate frustration. I spent more and more time in the bathroom with my hand and, yes, even the cold-hearted toilet seat, and the only womb I penetrated was the deep throat of my computer screen, where one day you miraculously appeared, Janice. Now you were full of experience—or so you said—ready to experiment with me, who was also the great screwall—or so I said. And when that happened, when we reunited in cyberspace and I found myself even farther from the outer folds of your sweet wet cunt than when we had tried to make out on that secondhand couch, that was when I decided that I had come full circle and that there was only one solution to my dilemma: to see my father soon, to get him to liberate me from this curse that his *catalogo* life had unwittingly placed upon me. In my mad imagination he was both the rival in bed who had hopped in a moment before I arrived and the ally who would, as soon as I explained what he was doing to me, gladly guide me to the best erotic spot, give me all the tips on how to make perfect love. From his letters I knew he was that sort of guy.

I sat down a couple of times to write to him, once even began to speak my absurd lines into a cassette recorder. But I was a son who hadn't seen his dad in umpteen years—how was I supposed to just spit out from this distant land what was wrong with me, find out how he did it, and take it from there? How was I supposed to trust the mail, U.S. or Chilean, with my most-secret queries?

The most secret of all, the most evident and manifest: my face. The face I didn't want you to see. A face that you'll never see now.

It was not growing older along with my body, that face. It froze back there when you and I were fifteen. The face you last saw floating above you on our third night and thirtieth attempt, as we unsuccessfully tried to make love one final time. That face of innocence had remained where it had been back then in midadolescence, waiting, as the years passed, for a sexual breakthrough to free its features, unable and unwilling to let me forget that I was still a virgin. Oh, I tried to compensate. I told myself I could make everybody believe I was my father's son, even if they had no way of knowing of his exploits. I preened as if I were the motherfucker of the universe, the *putamadre* of the *madrazos*. I assured myself every girl thought I was fucking her best friend, every boy thought I was fucking his girl. But the face I had to look at in the mirror each morning was telling me the truth, would soon be telling everyone else in Manhattan and the Bronx and Brooklyn the horrible truth if I did not fool them as I had fooled my mother. I discovered early on with her that the best way to hide oneself is to become a blatant exhibitionist. It was with her that I rehearsed what would be the lonely years in the chat rooms of the Internet, the perverse positions of cybersex that ended up being the only intercourse available to me, exposing my silent howls of pleasure to disembodied strangers who were themselves afraid of touch and smell and pubic hair, and even the memory of your real body under my real weight was getting more and more remote, Janice Worth.

And with each boast that bolstered my public and later my on-line image, I was drifting farther from being able to tell the truth to somebody like you or my mother, not to mention my dad. Not in the mail, not over the phone, not through E-mail later on, if he had even known what the hell E-mail was. Type out the words on the screen: You got me into this mess, now you get me out, tell me how you fucking do it. He knew the answer, he was probably answering at that very instant a similar query that some lovelorn runaway adolescent in Chile was posing to him. My father was helping that kid find his way into some female heart, promising sexual sustenance and relief, dropping hints, whispering to that boy everything his own parents were too stupid or repressed to let him know. What my dad would whisper to me as soon as I could sit down and have a man-to-man talk. As soon as we could go back.

"When is that going to be?"

As if I didn't know what she'd say. "Once democracy is back, that's when," my mother would invariably reply. "This Milagros isn't going there until it's good riddance to that bad rubbish Pinochet."

So that's how I slowly began, after our fiasco had been followed by similar sexless ordeals, to interest myself once more in the fate of the country where I had been born. Out of cruel necessity.

We need to rewind now, Janice. Why didn't you know I was Chilean? Why hadn't I told you? After all, to be slightly exotic is always a plus in bed, right? Remember how I told my mom that night in 1983 when I had not made love to you that I didn't care a hoot for this *latinoamericano* political shit? Remember? Well, I wasn't exaggerating. Over the previous four years, since 1979, to be exact, I had been desperately swimming away from Chile, attempting to escape the sparkling Latino eyes of Che Guevara, escape the continent he died for and asked everybody else to die for, escape the Chile that was full of that death. I was reacting to those ranting words, Mom's overkill—You owe him your life, back home kids are going hungry, back home Pablo Barón is hiding and your Uncle Pancho is risking his skin, back home horrible things I'm too ashamed to even name are being done to anybody who dares to so much as mention the existence of Ernesto Guevara, Salvador Allende, democracy, bad words back home, words we keep here like a sacred fire (her phrase, not mine: *como un fuego sagrado*). Mom was educating me in the revolution that she had been unable to bring to life in reality but was now bringing to fruition in her poor child's captive brain: the *Venceremos* songs of the Quillapayún and *Te Recuerdo, Amanda* by Victor Jara, whose hands were chopped off in the stadium (Did they really chop them off, Mom? I mean, chopped with an axe?) and the Inti-Illimani, who named themselves after a volcano in Bolivia. (A volcano in Bolivia? A Chilean folk group? Why? Don't ask why. When you're older you'll understand.) Hauling me to rallies where hundreds of teary-eyed exiles and their erstwhile gringo *compañeros* held their fists up high and intoned hymns of hope and imbibed large quantities of Gallo wine, because there was a boycott against Chilean products, and devoured even larger quantities of *empanadas*, brought by my mother straight from her Latino street stand and then from her Restaurant Milagros. Forcing me to attend ceremonies for a dead and dying country that I could hardly remember as I watched the lean Manhattan men eye my mother and wonder if she would come home with them, if she would bring one of them home with her, perturb my sleep with the sounds of their coupling in the next room. It was all too much for me.

One night—it was September 11, 1979, and we were in some loony artist's loft in SoHo, protesting six years of military power—I simply disappeared, headed for the door like all those kids my dad was bringing back home at this very moment over there in Santiago. I couldn't endure another patriotic speech, one more poster of Chile's presidential palace going up in flames. I was only eleven years old and already stuffed with too many Spanish words that meant *nada*, I mean nothing nada to this U.S. boy: *junta fascista, hijo de puta Pinochet, buen asilo contra la opresión*. I headed for the street.

As my perennial bad luck would have it, downstairs, on the sidewalk right outside the building, some black kids were doing something that would soon be called break-dancing. I watched them gyrating, shifting from one hand to the other as they turned and returned just an inch above the ground, I recognized that music blaring from their boom box as mine, gave myself a home in that beat and discharge that had nothing whatsoever to do with the strains from a Cuban ballad that were wafting down to me from the loft in the stifling late-summer air, something about Che Guevera being immortal and not really being dead, *no estás muerto, Commandante*. I managed to blot those sounds out and make believe that I didn't owe Che a thing. Not true that I had a giant poster of him haunting my life. I pretended that I was like these kids, no different from them, just one of the gang. And they must have detected my need, because soon enough they stopped their dancing, gabbed with me awhile. They were getting ready to go professional, they said, they were saving up to try and make it to a TV show—What's your favorite TV show?— and all of a sudden from upstairs I could hear the sounds of the Inti-Illimani singing a song of melancholy victory and some high-pitched male voice shouting "*Compañero* Salvador Allende" and a chorus bellowing back, "*Presente!*" over and over again. I imagined my mom and all her buddies with water dimming their eyes as they swore loyalty to another dead man, tried to pretend he was alive just like they had been trying to pretend for the last decade that Che had not been killed in Bolivia, and something came over me. I had to burn my bridges to that loft and those shouts and those dead men, and realizing full well what I was doing—oh, I felt the delicious tremor of betrayal, I loved the chill of knowing exactly what I was doing and why—my hand descended into the hellhole of my pocket and gave the break-dancers all my money. Well, not really mine—all the money I had collected from the sale of posters, books, records, and delicious food my mother had cooked with Nana's recipes, the cash from all the other etceteras that had been sold in that loft that evening. I handed them the money that came from the sale of trinkets crafted by political prisoners and that was supposed to help sustain their families, I gave those black kids the money meant for the forbidden newspapers and the underground trade unions and the soup kitchens in the slums. I handed them Chile and hoped they would never return any part of it to me ever again.

"It's a donation," I said when they looked at me in astonishment. There must have been a couple of hundred dollars there. "A donation from the Chilean resistance"—as if they knew where or what Chile even was, as if they didn't think that I had gone stark raving cuckoo, as if they were not quickly gathering their boom box and their jackets and getting the hell out of there before the crazy Latino kid repented.

I didn't repent.

I headed uptown, walking all the way, taking my time, absurdly hoping Mom would have fallen asleep before I tiptoed through the door. Taking my time. Maybe that's why I stopped at that Crazy Eddie appliance store, its window brimming with television sets, all transmitting the same program, maybe that's why I allowed myself to dally there for an hour watching the same images repeated on twenty-five fractured screens, those mountains of ice floating on a sea that was black with waves, those caverns of snow and fog that I saw for the first time that evening, that soundless special on Antarctica that I watched, entranced, from the other side of the window. At that moment, of course, I had no idea that the Chile I had just repudiated had any connection whatsoever with that extraordinary forbidden world I was discovering and devouring with my eyes. It is only now that I see how ironic and fateful it is that on the very night I declared my unilateral independence from my country I was waylaid by images of a silent crystal continent that was part of the territory of that country, Chile surreptitiously creeping back into my life through the back door while I stood in front of the house and blindly barred its entry. No, I had no inkling that the iceberg was already calling to me, seducing me, waiting for me to find it in those howling waters. My mind was too interested in my own transgressions, that money I had given away, which instead of liberating Chile was going to liberate me, I was sure, from Chile.

And from ever having to go to any other gathering in solidarity with Chile.

Mom never took me to another meeting. She paid back the money out of her own pocket, sold off my record collection, cut my allowance for a year, stole from me much more than I had stolen from the *resistencia Chilena*, kept eight soup kitchens going in Temuco and five workshops for jobless women in Arica and who knows what peasants' cooperative in Puerto Varas. She left me without a cent for months and months, but it was worth it, ransom money paid out so I would not be her hostage, the hostage of her past, which I no longer wanted to recognize as mine. She understood my message of independence, that I was informing her that I had broken off with the country where she and I had been born, that I was an American from now on, an all-around Boy Scout who wanted to play baseball and never hear the word *soccer* again: *fútbol* was American football, with helmets and game plans and rough stuff. She understood because she placed two conditions upon that autonomy of mine and I accepted them both: first, that I was to speak only Spanish at home—at the slightest sign that I was losing my mother tongue she was shipping me back to Abuela Claudia's in Santiago. And the second? "The poster of Che stays right where it is now," she said. "If you move it, I'll kill you." I think she meant it: she had not yet explained the connection to the man who had made my existence possible, but if I dared to tear his image down, she would personally return me to the land of the dead from where that man had rescued me by his own disappearance from this earth. Not that I was that hot to get rid of the poster, anyway—not until I had been fully versed in why the man with the beret and the star in that beret and the mischievous eyes and weak whiskers was so crucial to my origins. At any rate, why test my mad mom's resolve now that I had obtained what I desired: to unshackle myself from that remote country I no longer wanted to call my own.

"One final warning," Mom said. "You'll come back begging to go to a rally, you'll beg for news and I won't give it to you."

Her words turned out to be more prophetic than she could ever have foretold.

One night five years later, about ten months after my final frustrating bout with you, Janice, by the time I had already exhorted myself to visit the distant father who held the answer to my dilemma—one night, it must have been sometime in 1984, when I was sixteen, I surreptitiously found myself watching the Chilean protests on the CBS evening news. For the last five years, whenever there had been an item on Chile, which was seldom, I had made a point of standing up to get a Coke, yawning ostentatiously, opening the book that was invariably perched on my knees. This time, looking over Mom's head, I caught a glimpse of students fighting the police in Santiago, women being dragged by the hair into police wagons, jets of water knocking down kids my age.

Mom clicked off the screen. "What's this? Let's put on some cartoons." She waited for an answer. "Or maybe you'd like to see some more."

I looked her straight in the eye with all the innocence my face of an angel could muster.

"Yes," I said, "I'd like to see some more."

"Some more of your country," Mom said. *"De tu país."*

"Of my country, yes."

Mom could have mocked me, triumphantly crowed several I-told-you-sos. Instead, she welcomed back the prodigal revolutionary, made up for the five years she had bit her lip, kept her information inside. Now that I was putting myself voluntarily in her clutches she set herself the task of bringing me up to date, indoctrinating me about *el pueblo*, who had found a way of breaking the tyrant's grip. For the last year there had been monthly riots in Chile; the invisible country under the boot was beginning to rise, rise, rise.

I did not tell her that I was hoping that the mythical *pueblo* would help my own wilting penis to rise and rise some more by bringing down a dictator half a world away, that I was hitching its fortune to that imminent fall which would allow me to return to my father. She would not have taken well my certainty that I could not free my poor *pija* until the country itself was free. I couldn't let her know that my reasons for wanting the resistance to purge Pinochet from this planet were not exactly as patriotic as she supposed.

It was sick, I'll admit that now, Janice, and you'll probably agree, once you hear what happened to me when I went back to Chile last July. But at the time I was going on seventeen and I felt trapped, I was at the point where it was no longer only my father who was coming with me on my ever-diminishing dates. He's a nerd, he's a wimp, he's a noodle, he warms you up and then he's a refrigerator—word was getting around pretty fast in high school and had preceded me when I got to Columbia University. I walked into the freshman classroom and was sure that all the girls in Composition 101 had already heard about Gabriel McKenzie, Mr. Droopy, Mr. Likes-to-Pet-but-That's-About-It, Mr. Heavy-Breathing-but-No-Exercise, Mr. Fucks-the-Books-but-Not-the-Ladies-or-the-Gents, because by then, Janice, all the energy 99.99 percent of young men explode into somebody else's hole I was expending on words on a screen or words in a library. I understood why medieval monks sublimated their starving penises into opulent pens, all that excess desire, reading Dostoevsky instead of listening to rock groups, writing caustic essays on the sexuality of De Sade and getting the highest SATs in America instead of seeing Freddy Kruger flicks eight times while a screaming date clutches at your hand and maybe at your crotch. The more I knew inside, the more encyclopedic and intellectually conversant I became, the less my face showed it. I mean, Janice, I was offered an honorary membership by the Just Say No Coalition and the Virgins for Jesus and the Chastity Belt Champions. I mean, I was really screwed—well, not really, not literally, just super-fucked-up, *jodido*. And not only my father was with me each time I spoke to a girl, whispering to me over my shoulder—If I were you I'd say something witty now, I balled someone just like her, with just those boobs, a few years back, in fact, I've fucked several similar specimens—I kept on inventing a facsimile of his voice inside me, taunting me or urging me on. Every night he was making love in Chile and I was abstaining in New York, as if an insane deity had decreed that only one of the two McKenzies, father or son, could insert his organ into an expectant vagina and that it was always to be the father and never the son; not enough that he was my constant companion—*Mi padre es mi copiloto*—but General Pinochet was on board as well, disparaging me as I groped some youngish lass, and Dad at least was a benevolent presence, he wanted me to get it on, whereas the general was a leering demon, like some sort of medieval warrior who leaves his sword on the bed when he gallops off on a crusade, leaves it next to his wife, separating her from the lustful men who might want to savor the lady's honor in the lord's absence.

As if damn Pinochet were somehow guarding the distant virtue of the New York adolescents I coveted.

Trapped, yes, I felt trapped in some evil magic spell, and the protests in Chile were not getting anywhere, no matter how much my mother and I cheered them on from our differing but apparently unanimous positions, and the only way, I told myself as I looked at the lonely Hudson River flow by my virginal eyes one sophomore day in September of 1986, the only way to break out of that trap was for some hero to slay the dragon, kill the bastard so I could go back home and have a good fuck.

And no sooner had I nursed the thought than I walked back to our apartment on Riverside Drive and sat down at my Kaypro and spelled it out as if the mere fact of enunciating the thought on a screen could make it come true, and the phone rang like an insane angel and my ear attended to what my mom was excitedly answering that voice from Chile: Pinochet had been assassinated, a group of urban guerrillas had lain in wait for him in the Cajón del Maipo and dispatched him to the next world and, unwittingly, sent me a ticket back to Santiago. But one hour later, the radio disclaimed that information—the general had miraculously survived, four of his bodyguards were dead, Augusto Pinochet Ugarte was alive and kicking, which meant that he would keep on kicking his compatriots and making life miserable for them and, without knowing I even existed, make my life unbearable and unfucked as well.

Even so, that was the countdown, the moment when I felt that there was hope, even a slight cocoon of it. Never mind, I said to Mom, they'll be back, they're lying in wait, they'll get him next time, only to have the phone ring sometime in 1987, a Sunday eight months later, in the middle of a brunch of sesame bagels and lox and honey-walnut cream cheese and Mom's face growing pale.

"They've arrested your Tío Pancho," she said. "It seems he was involved in the *atentado contra* Pinochet. Your grandmother Claudia's had a stroke, they don't think she'll survive the night." And the next day: "She's died. Your father says they won't let Pancho go to her funeral. That Pancho is—they're giving him a hard time. He claims he's innocent, but . . ." And she didn't add, as she could have, that Pancho's lunchtime prediction of a future socialist Latin America back in 1967 was appearing less and less prophetic with the years—

and that if there was hope of ousting the general and getting me laid, I would have to switch allegiance from those who wanted to kill Pinochet to those who wanted to use political means to organize his ouster. In other words, I started to place my hopes on the other birthday boy, my dad's alter ego, Pablo Barón, who was slowly but surely climbing toward the almighty power he had foretold at that lunch the day after my conception. I watched how Pablo, who had been living semiclandestinely all this time in Santiago, now emerged as one of the leaders of the opposition, I watched how Pinochet made the mistake of agreeing to a plebiscite that he thought he couldn't possibly lose but did—in 1988 he became the only dictator in history to lose a plebiscite. Mom, can we go now? I asked. Why don't you vote in the upcoming presidential elections? But she stubbornly refused—I'm not returning until that *cabrón* is gone forever—and she kept on refusing even when Patricio Aylwin won the election the next year and when he took over from Pinochet, the first democratic president in seventeen years. And Pablo Barón, there he was, a minister, just as he had promised, the éminence grise of the new regime, the mastermind, the man who had known how to market the image of democracy to a nation that was half consumed by fear. Mom, Pinochet is gone. No, he isn't, he's still commander in chief of the army and he's designated a third of the Senate and he can't be removed and all the judges are his cronies and . . . So I watched the country inch toward a transition to democracy that included keeping all those old structures in place, and I began to really despair, Pinochet was going to be around forever, or at least until March of 1998, and after that he would still be a member of the Senate for as long as he could breathe and the bastard would probably live to be a hundred and ten just to spite me, just to make sure I'd be a virgin till then, till the year 2017, unless I decided to go back by myself and see my dad, ask for his help in getting rid of this curse, this face, ask him to guide my dick in its quest for real handling and palpations instead of all the endless words about sex that greeted me for hours at www.allpositions.com., do in reality what you and I, Janice, were trying out in masturbatory solitude. I have to go home, I would say to the anonymous screen, the anonymous nonbodies typing back to me from San Diego and Calcutta and who knows where. You are home, you little fucker, come to Momma, come to Poppa, come and suck my tits, not even knowing if what Sexy Sybille was offering, those tits, even existed on her body, even if there was a her at the other end of the wire or if she was some man pretending to be a woman. I had done that as well, I had made believe I was eighty and infirm, I had fantasized my father's thousands of females on that screen, I had screwed that screen every night for the last two years, probably at the moment when a woman in Chile was opening her legs to my father and I would switch off the computer and the room would be quiet and dark and he would turn the lamp off and he could hear her breathing right there, he could feel the long backbone of vertebrae, one by one, he could go down to that rump and grace his fingers with her warmth, while his son was here so many miles away touching the frigid keys that contained all the potential words in the universe and not one kiss, and I started a more permanent relationship, if it could be called that, with you, my dear Salacious Janice, always so full of good advice and bizarre *Kama-sutra* positions and with similiar intellectual concerns. I mean, you are one brainy lady, Janice—you were the only one who suspected that something was wrong, you kept on saying I have a feeling you're not originally from California, you're not telling me the truth, let's meet, and we—But I couldn't tell you that it was my mythical dad and his thousand and one female nights that I was trying to reproduce with you, though I hinted that I might be going on a trip soon and you said that was good, go on that pilgrimage (that's what you called it, remember?) and then come back to us, we're your real family, darling, I'm the lover you really need, and I could feel myself dipping like a Ferris wheel into depression and perhaps insanity, unable to tell you or anybody and certainly not my mom what was really happening as every week I received my dad's photo and his invitation to return: When will I see you? When will you come back? Come back before it's too late. And Mom, as if she were reading the dementia I was lapsing into in spite of how I kept on telling her I was fine, Mom came home one day in early 1991 and plunked two plane tickets down on the kitchen table. We're going home over summer vacation. A birthday present. I've fixed everything at the restaurants, it's all covered, we'll be there on July 9, the day you're twenty-three, she said.

My hopes were high, I have to admit it, I could not have been in better spirits as the plane took off from Kennedy. I was so sure that everything would be all right that I almost didn't pack my computer and then, as we were going down the elevator with the bags, I thought of you, Janice, I had said a remote goodbye to you that very morning, I remembered I had promised to write the very next day and I pushed the stop button, rushed back up, grabbed my Toshiba and my modem and set off to meet the man who had made me at the precise hour Che Guevara was being buried alone and dead in Vallegrande.

Not knowing that what would keep me in Chile would be an iceberg that was on the verge of being carved out of Antarctica. If it hadn't been for that iceberg from hell that had been emerging out of the sea for the last five thousand years and that had already ravished my eyes that night I had supposedly broken with Chile, if it hadn't been for Antarctica, I would have come back on the next plane, I would never have seen that bastard of my father again in my life.

Been away for a few hours, Janice.

I slipped out, followed Rodrigo de Triana, winding all the way to the expo. Rodrigo de Triana the street, not the man. Though who knows? I may have been following the man all this time without realizing it, dead though he's been these five hundred years. Maybe you've seen those T-shirts: MOM AND DAD WENT TO EXPO '92 IN SEVILLA AND ALL I GOT WAS THIS STUPID T-SHIRT! Well, Rodrigo de Triana could have had one that said: I WENT ALL THE WAY TO THE NEW WORLD, WAS THE FIRST TO SET MY EYES ON IT, AND ALL I GOT WAS THIS STREET NAMED AFTER ME. He died here in Sevilla in the most abject poverty. According to my Andalusian (and I suspect half-gypsy) landlady, Christopher Columbus betrayed him, claimed for himself the ten thousand *maravedíes* that the Reyes Católicos had promised to the man who first saw the Indies. I felt like answering that Columbus had stolen the award from someone else, one of the men or women who crossed over from Asia fifty thousand years before Rodrigo de Triana was even born, but then I thought better of it. Who am I to defend the natives of America, the forefathers of my Nana? I, who went all the way to Chile and don't have a T-shirt to show for it and certainly not a street named after me. But lots of betrayals, Rodrigo de Triana. We're joined in that.

What I was telling you, however, was that, venturing out for a bite to eat, I landed in the rather mediocre U.S. Pavilion. As the world's only superpower, they obviously don't give a shit how they look to the rest of the universe. Not like Chile.

There I was, back home, you could say. Last time, I grunted to myself, I'll have a New York meal in my life. Filled up on a gigantic pastrami sandwich on rye at the deli. Tons of mustard. They even let me pack the remains in a doggie bag, a practice that is frowned on in Chile. Or in Spain, for that matter. They think it's "dishonorable" to be seen taking leftovers home: it might send the signal that you don't have enough to eat back there. Honor! Appearances! Illusions!

Speaking of illusions, I then wandered along to take another gander at the iceberg in the Pabellón Chileno, visit the scene of the future crime, so to speak. Watched visitors stream by the majestic stack of Antarctic ice that brought me here to Sevilla as if it had written the ticket itself, the iceberg that kept me in Chile when I should have left, when everything was telling me to get the hell out of there the very day I arrived.

Yes, Janice, it was the iceberg that did it.

Until I saw it gleaming enormously in the middle of that vast empty room in Santiago, until then, everything that could go wrong in Chile had gone wrong. Everything that afternoon a year and a half ago when we returned from exile, everything was going sour. Then I realized with amazement that my father was just as fascinated with that bulk of living ice as I was and that maybe we did share something, maybe we could contact each other after all. Because let me tell you that in the previous two hours since Mom and I had arrived from New York, I had found myself drifting farther from my dad than in the seventeen years of our separation, farther and farther away the closer I got to him physically. I am sure I would have sailed over the edge of his world, fallen from his sight and his life into some pit of nothingness, lost him forever, if the iceberg had not stolen his eyes, if it had not simultaneously stolen mine.

And our hands. One of my hands and one of his went out to touch it, I could feel that mound of blue-white ice pulling at our fingers like a malignant magnet. The South Pole itself had attracted hundreds of men who had died trying to get there, trudging through the six-month blizzard of night to stand in the one place on earth where only the north exists no matter where you face, and now that's how it was calling to me, to us. There was something vulnerable and hurt in its depths that was asking for protection. Someone had ripped this fragment of a glacier from its home in Antarctica and had brought it all the way here to this overheated, sultry hall in Santiago, only so I could, so we could—

There was nothing there.

"Touch it all you want," *Ministro* Pablo Barón said. He was speaking more to my father than to me, but it was my neck his hand was cordially clasping, massaging my shoulders. "You can both touch it all you want. It's an illusion, a replica, a hologram. Just to give the *empresarios* and the press a feel, a hint, a suggestion of what the damn thing will look like once we've captured it. Even the cold is fake. Now the real iceberg—Ha! That's another story. Wouldn't want you to touch that, Gabriel, *m'hijo*, waste those seventy tons of Chilean ice with the warmth of any human hands. Nobody's going to soil our iceberg, melt the bastard. Right, McKenzie?"

My father looked the other way, as if there were another McKenzie present in the cavernous foyer of the Tourism building and the *Ministro* were addressing that other man. Then slowly, like a ship turning against the wind, he looked at me as if to seek my approval and then moved his head onward to meet Pablo Barón's eyes, the eyes that Mom had said belonged to his best friend.

"*Mira, huevón,* I don't have a fucking clue as to why you dragged me here. I thought you were coming by the Casa Milagros later."

That's my translation. He didn't really say "fucking." He said "*puta idea.*" Maybe "motherfucking" would be a better way of phrasing the affront he was directing at his buddy Pablo Barón, although it was not the word itself that was meant to be insulting but rather the tone with which my dad conveyed it. I didn't like it, Janice. Didn't like him showing off for me, exuding a macho belligerence that he had not exhibited when it was needed two hours ago, when our first meeting in seventeen years had been interrupted. Violated, should I say, that meeting. As soon as Mom and I, exhausted from a flight that had been delayed twelve hours, staggered through the sliding doors of Policía and Aduana to a raucous welcome from a gaggle of unknown relatives encountered previously only through sporadic photos and intermittent stuttered phone calls on birthdays and holidays and emergencies, the remote nephews and third cousins I had never seen born, scurrying between my legs, hiding behind them, playing tag. A little squealing girl who grabbed my thigh with both her scraggly hands as if she was scared that I might up and disappear for another interminable exile, a whirlwind of names and faces and heaving bodies I was being forced to embrace without any idea as to who they were, why these scarecrows seemed to love me so much and squeeze the breath out of me, when the only one I wanted to hug and hold was my father.

But he was in no hurry.

He was looking at my mother, that's what he was doing in that airport arrivals lounge, ready to probe the muscles flowing under that green dress, undressing her in public for anybody to devour who had eyes, and I had them, I had them, I watched him watch her, bend into her from afar, I followed his predator eyes curving around my mother's breasts, he was measuring what seventeen years away from him had done and undone, hungering for every night and every climax of those years, guessing how many other men had curved into her and on top of her, his eyes were asking if tonight he would be able to ask her something else with his hands and another part of his body, whether the sexual pact they had agreed upon so many years ago was still valid, renewable, ready to be renegotiated, whether tonight he would lift the sheets of his bed and contemplate her naked body waiting for him while I listened in the next room.

"Don't worry. They won't fuck tonight, your parents."

Those were to be the first words to greet my return to Chile, the first words I can remember somebody saying to me. They came from behind my back and, startled as I was by them, I did not turn around to identify the owner of that low, urgent, lascivious voice. I did not want to lose sight of my dad, I did not want to lose the moment when he would veer his vision onto me and gather me into his eyes for the first time in almost two decades, cradle me in his gaze. Whoever had spoken must have realized what I was doing and why I was doing it, just as he had surmised my thoughts as I probed my parents' reaction, surmised them because maybe they were his thoughts, and then the owner of that voice and of my thoughts stepped out from behind me and interposed his rusty thirty-something figure between my father and my eyes, thrust his thick hand into mine, shook it, said, "I'm Leopoldo, but you can call me Polo."

Polo. The ten-year-old kid my dad had rescued the night Che

Guevara's death gave me a shot at existence. The kid my dad had guided back home before meeting up with his future wife at the protest rally on the Alameda. The kid who, my mother had informed me a long time ago, had ended up years later running the Casa Milagros and the McKenzie Detective Agency. I knew all about Polo from my father's letters, how he had come looking for work, miraculously making an appearance the very day in 1981 that the Nanny told Dad that she could not continue working for him. She had agreed to keep that house going on the understanding that the military regime would not last forever and her girl, Milagros, and her Gabrielito would be back soon, but it was clear that the situation was not going to change soon—seven years had gone by since our departure. That was the magic number she had given herself for her loved ones to return, so she accepted Pablo Barón's offer of less strenuous employment. The Nanny had gone out one door and three hours later a knock had come on that same door: it was Polo, now twenty-four years old, Polo knocking on that door the one day when he could not be denied the one job he had been dreaming of all that time, assisting my father, following in my father's steps, becoming those steps, proving by the very fact that he materialized on that doorstep at exactly the moment when he was needed that he also possessed a sixth sense, that he might be just the person the agency needed to help in the search for runaways, just the right person to manage the Casa Milagros now that the old and weary Nanny had decided to leave.

And here he was, ten years later, managing me as if I were one of the kids who had sought refuge in the Casa Milagros, giving me advice about how to deal with my elders, supposedly calming my anxieties. "I'd be worried too, Gabriel," Polo was slushing into my ear. "But you shouldn't be. Your father's already had his woman for the day. Early. A plump one. A servant from the neighborhood. I'll try her out tomorrow. If Cris has no objections, that is." Polo smiled, as if nothing could be more natural than to be discussing his sex life and my father's with the returning son here in this airport milling with the fervent Gallardo and McKenzie clans. Polo lowered his voice even more. "By the way," Polo whispered, "your dad wouldn't want you to know this, but . . . as a matter of fact, he screwed early out of consideration for you. He said that way he'd be free the rest of the day, seeing it's your birthday. That's the sort of guy he is. Didn't know you'd be so late. But just in case, he made provisions. He always makes provisions."

I deflected my vision from my father for a few seconds and tried to explore this interloper's face. But I was a stranger in this land and Polo's map was written in a language I had never learned. He was telling me too many things, all of them contradictory. Those mocking eyes of his seemed to say that I had better damn well accept that Cristóbal McKenzie would never love me as much as he loved Polo, even as his mouth spouted how much my father adored me, the charming smile on his lips insinuating that this was all a joke to melt the ice and that good old Polo was tender as a clown inside. Tender, Polo, yes, and cruel as a clown as well, I realized. Polo would mind-fuck me all through my stay, starting right then. Because now my father suddenly came out of nowhere, and his movement toward me had been blocked by Polo's stocky shadow and the sound of his steps by Polo's slur of words—my father's lieutenant had diverted my attention at the precise moment when I needed to be most alert. I felt my father come out from behind Polo like a wave that knocks you over on the beach when you are small, my father surged onto me without warning; before I was able to get a clear view and gain some grip on what was about to engulf me, he was upon me, enfolding me in his arms like a bear. Gabriel, Gabriel, Gabrielito—the improbable warmth of that body—It's been so long, too long. *Porqué tardaste tanto?* Why did you take so long? Maybe he had missed me, maybe Polo had come as a messenger of good tidings, maybe everything was going to be all right.

It was then, as I felt myself begin to relax, as I started to formulate in my mind the film of the rest of my stay, seeing myself ushered by my father into the mysteries of seducing women and becoming a real *hombre*, it was exactly at that longed-for point that I felt a heavy hand tap my shoulder. Not the hand of trickster Polo, not my father's little helper interjecting himself, but someone else, another sort of intruder. I tried to rid my skin of that brawny hand, make believe it was not there, evaporate its flesh and discard its bone. But the hand insisted, tapped again, then again, and when I would not let loose, pulled with a sinewy urgency that I could not deny, tore me asunder from my dad.

Standing in front of us was a swarthy hulk of a man, towering at least a foot above us all.

It turned out I was not his prey, merely an impediment, a dead dog in the road that had to be garbaged. He had bigger game to bag.

"Don Cristóbal," he said. "*Ministro* Barón told me I'd find you here. He said he wanted to see you. Right away."

Dad didn't answer, I'm busy, can't you see I'm busy. He didn't answer, This is my son, Gabriel, and nothing can keep me from him on this day of all days. He didn't answer, You can tell the *Ministro* to go fry snowballs and stick his invitation up his ass. I expected him to, I expected the famous Cris McKenzie, savior of the young and darling of damsels, to put this bodyguard or cop or whatever the fuck he was in his place, maybe even expected something more, for him to nail the bastard right then and there. We could take him on, father and son swinging, maybe with some help from that runt Polo. We didn't need to take any orders from anybody. Democracy's back in this country, *hijo de puta*, maybe you haven't heard that the military doesn't rule anymore and that's why my mom and I came back, you barn door, you lump of toxic waste, you—

My father was scrutinizing me. He looked me through and through with his video-camera eyes, took in my baby face, my horn-rimmed glasses, my puppy love for him; my father registered every cybergeek detail. I don't think he liked what he saw. I was not his spitting image: I was ugly, I was a virgin, I had the hands of a computer nerd, everything about me said, Kick me, kick me hard. He did. He kicked me hard. Worse still, my dad erased what he had just recorded, pushed the red DELETE button, fast-forwarded me the hell out of there. I watched him do it, I watched him turn to Polo, look past me at his assistant, look right around me as if I hadn't arrived, as if I were still back in New York. "Polo," he said. "Can you follow me with the car?" And to the Hulk: "This better be important, Ignacio."

"The *Ministro* said to come right away," came the reply from the hefty scrap of meat called Ignacio, as if he knew no other words. But he did: "Forget the car. One of my men from Investigaciones will bring it along." And he held out a beefy paw for Polo's keys.

Surprisingly, Polo did not yield immediately to Ignacio's authority. "How about him?" Polo asked, nodding in my direction, withholding the keys. "The kid's been waiting seventeen years for this moment."

Ignacio thought about that for a second. "Seventeen years, huh?" he said, without so much as a glance at me. "Well, if he waited this long, it won't hurt him to wait a few more hours now, will it? Right, Don Cristóbal?"

My dad's reaction to this new provocation was to shrug his shoulders. Was that his message to me? I told you to come sooner. I kept on asking you to come back before it was too late. You never even saw your Abuela Claudia again before she died. At any rate, that's how Polo interpreted Dad's shrug. Polo tossed Ignacio the keys to the car. "Sorry, Gabrielito," he said.

Big Ignacio scratched his head with one of the keys. "Oh, that's Gabrielito. Why didn't anybody say so? The *Ministro* specifically ordered me to bring him along. Said something about his birthday, in fact. Said there'll be plenty of champagne." Ignacio sized me up. "As long as Cara de Guagua's old enough to drink."

If Ignacio was looking for an additional reason for winning an unpopularity contest with me, he had found it. The bastard had frazzled out my weakest point, he had called me Cara de Guagua, Baby Face. I had inanely told myself that nobody in Chile would notice the way my face had not aged, could not age. But if this hunk of brawn had nailed me with this nickname just a few minutes after my arrival, then so would every girl in the country. So would you, Janice, if I had ever let you gaze on my mug eight years after you last saw me. Every woman in this country and the rest of the world would guess, as Ignacio had guessed, that the absence of a father from my life had turned me into a walking, sopping milkweed, the very father verifying that intuition now by saying, "Cara de Guagua, huh? What do you think of that, Gabriel? You like that name?"

I said nothing.

"Or you really don't care what anybody calls you?"

"I really don't care," I said.

"Not going to do anything about it, huh?"

"Words don't matter. You can say anything, write anything." I was thinking of his letters to me, his letters full of an affection that had faded as soon as I walked into his life.

"You're right," Cristóbal McKenzie said. "*Tienes toda la razón.* Words don't matter. Smart kid. Smart kid, Milagros. You took good care of him. Congratulations."

"Better care than you did."

Silence. Fortunately, Ignacio was there with the broken record of his usual insistent delicacy. "The *Ministro* said right away," he said. He indicated the waiting limousine.

We all clambered in.

Mom talked nonstop all the way from the airport. She had prepared this trip for too many banished evenings to let it be ruined, had rehearsed every detail with me after hard labor at the Restaurant Milagros, was determined to salivate the gray city and its alterations into my ear, pointing out from the front seat as she twisted her head back to speak to me, how much everything remained the same and how everything had also changed, weighing what seventeen years can do to a person and a country. Look, I told you that old men still take their produce to market in carts with horses almost as old as they are. My God, what have they done to Bascuñán? Is that the new metro station? Gabriel, look. But I was not in the mood. I was too aware of my father by my side, silently grazing his eyes on the drizzling city, only turning to plunder a cigarette from a pack, tap it on his wrist, settle it in his mouth. Instantly Polo's arm slithered from the other side of me and flicked a lighter, lit my dad's cigarette, and then took it from his lips after the first puff to light his own.

The car was soon filled with a foul haze of smoke.

I held back my cough, unwilling to give them the satisfaction of even acknowledging their rudeness, those lips of my father's caressing the tobacco like they had caressed my mother's skin in a hotel bed near the Alameda not a mile away from this speeding car, that night he had found the time to look for Polo, that night he had tracked him down at the Teatro Caupolicán and sat next to him and made jokes and wondered how to anticipate his thoughts and please him, almost inviting the boy to do something similar for him all these years later. Polo rendered Dad service, reminded him of appointments for the next day, asked him if he had signed those checks before leaving for the airport, pointing out how one of the kids was not getting over that rheumatic cold and maybe he should be seen by Dr. Ciruelo again, Polo putting on a vaudeville show of his own for my sake, so I would know who would inherit the agency when my father retired. Polo, who had been lapping up his wisdom for the last ten years while I tried out toilet seats and hot sponges and the ever-closing legs of

6 2

derisive gringo girls like you, Janice. Polo, who had extracted the answer to every last sexual question from his mentor, whom, from my New York banishment, I had been cultivating like a garden. And it was Polo who would taste the plump female merchandise tomorrow that my father had already tried out today.

So what did it matter if my father now, an hour later, here in this Tourism building in the center of Santiago and with only Pablo Barón as audience, was staging a belated revolt for my benefit? Perhaps the fact that we shared something, our coincidental attraction to that iceberg before it had been revealed to be a glowering hologram, maybe that common experience had warmed him momentarily toward my existence, had made him use that expletive, *puta idea*, so the *Ministro* understood just how angry he, McKenzie, was at this interference with his family.

But the *Ministro* also knew how to speak about one thing while supposedly referring to another.

"How's the house, the Casa?" he asked pointedly, his glasses gleaming malignly. He knew that the two of them might be best friends but that my father didn't really need him, could live without him, only had to see him one more time, in fact, on October 12, 1992, to collect on the bet they had made almost twenty-five years ago. The great McKenzie didn't need anything from Pablo Barón. But the hundred youngsters that my father had taken in through the years, they did need official support, they did need the fat hand of the *Ministro* to crawl into his breast pocket and take out a Parker and sign a check a bit scrawnier than the *Ministro* himself but still grand enough to take care of the year's deficit. Those former runaway kids needed that money which four Chilean governments of every stripe had provided: the reformist Christian Democrats of Frei in the late sixties, and the Allende socialists in the early seventies, and the neoliberal fascists of Pinochet for his seventeen long years, and since 1990 the transition-to-democracy government of President Patricio Aylwin. All of them had generously supported the apolitical refuge that my father, with Polo's ardent efficiency, had furnished to Chilean youngsters with nowhere else to go. So my father could swear all he wanted, but he had come when power had beckoned and he was going to stay here for as long as the *Ministro* wanted, freezing all our asses with the cold air that was steaming out of hidden air conditioners, as if trying to materialize a real iceberg out of thin air. Barón would force us to stand in front of this piece of mock ice and listen to him because he held the purse strings and the police strings and the power strings. He was well on the way to winning his part of the bet, you'll have to come to me and tremble and lick my shoes, I'll be the puppeteer behind the throne. We were his hostages. He knew it and we knew it and, now that the preliminaries were over, we could get down to business.

"We're taking it to Sevilla," the *Ministro* said. "Not this hologram. No, we're taking a real iceberg, seventy tons of it, straight from Antarctica. Crack it from the eternal ice, eight, nine meters tall, splinter the blocks, reassemble them in Punta Arenas, lug the thing across the Atlantic to the frying pan of Spain and the last world's fair of the century, give them something to cool their drinks with and wag their tongues about next summer. Expo '92. The other Latin American countries are pissed. They wanted us to be part of their collective pavilion, but we're going it alone. Once this is over, nobody in Europe will confuse us with the other countries in this hemisphere, no sir. Bye-bye, Latinoamérica."

"But they're pissed," my father repeated. "And I'm here—you've brought me here, Pablo, because I take it they're not the only ones who are pissed."

"McKenzie, you are one clever cookie. That is, *ni más ni menos*, why I've brought you here. But how about you and me and Gabriel having some coffee over there." The *Ministro* nodded toward a small table tucked in a corner where a luscious miniskirted waitress hovered over a pot and three cups. "Although I've heard it's the boy's birthday so maybe he wants some champagne. That is . . ." and here Pablo Barón let go of my neck and the shoulder that he had been amicably nuzzling all this while and squinted at me over the glint of his glasses as if some sort of harsh light emanating from my body were forcing him to adjust his vision. "How old are you, anyway? I thought you were . . ."

"Twenty-three, Pablo. He's twenty-three today." My mother, not my father, intervened, defending my honor.

"Yes, that's what I thought, he's older than Amanda Camila by five years, right. And by the way, she'll be here any moment now, she insisted she wanted to come and—"

"I think you owe Gabriel an apology," my mother interrupted, grabbing one of the *Ministro*'s arms.

Pablo Barón nodded his head vigorously. "An apology is absolutely in order. Please pardon me for forgetting your age, Gabriel. Your mom's right: I should remember, if anybody should. *Mal que mal*, I'm the one who suggested that your dad marry our Milagros, right, McKenzie? So, be my guest, *m'hijo*. Guzzle it down by the barrel."

"Polo and I will do the guzzling," Mom answered. "We have so much to talk about; we need to get acquainted." She let go of the *Ministro*'s arm and clutched Polo's, shushed his protestations with two fingers on those thin squalid lips, and carted him away as if he were a frozen piece of dark Antarctica itself, leaving the *Ministro* to steer me toward the table. He stopped on the way to pick up an extra chair, sat us down, shooed away the waitress. Then, from his pocket, he extracted a piece of pale blue paper and placed it carefully in front of my father. Dad took up a napkin and, using the tip, lifted the sheet of paper, read what it said, and then, to my astonishment, handed it to me, perhaps out of courtesy, perhaps in order to give himself time to react. Or maybe he was beginning to understand that he wasn't going to get a bite out of my mother's forbidden fruit unless he treated me with some deference. Or who knows, he might even have been interested in my opinion. You always said to me, Janice—you guessed things about me even while I was lying to you—that I have a tendency to exaggerate. So who knows if I wasn't overreacting, discerning hostility from him where none was intended?

But back to the letter. In crude block letters someone had written: NOS VAMOS A CULEAR TU ICEBERG.

In other words: WE ARE GOING TO FUCK YOUR ICEBERG. IT DOESN'T BELONG TO YOU.

And a bit farther down: WHO AM I? THAT'S FOR ME TO KNOW AND YOU TO FIND OUT.

The note was signed: COMMANDANTE YOU-KNOW-WHO.

"*Commandante El-Que-Sabes*," my father repeated to himself. "This was sent to . . ."

The waitress sidled up to the table to serve the coffee. The *Ministro* motioned her away impatiently and poured the coffee himself, but Dad called her back.

"Sugar," he said.

She didn't know what to do, whom to obey. So she looked straight at me. It was too much. I avoided her dark Botticelli Madonna face, fixed on her bodice, felt or imagined something steamy emanating from her, hoped she would say something to me, anything, ask me what I wanted, pour some more coffee in my cup until it overflowed, pour something hot and liquid down my throat. But she spoke to my father.

"There's sugar there, sir. *Allá*."

"Well," Dad said, "I take two lumps. But if you serve it, miss, I'll only need one."

She fluttered at this compliment, picked up a tiny pincer, and nervously plopped a solitary lump into the cup. A few drops of the coffee jumped out like Mexican jelly beans, one droplet stinging the back of my father's hand. He brought it to his lips, licked it, looking up at her mischievously as his tongue darted out and then in. She grinned back at him and then, submitting to the *Ministro*'s imperious order, left the table. Without giving me any sugar. Or even a delectable thought, for that matter. I would have liked to have said something smart to her, to have imitated my father's peculiar mix of urbanity and lechery, but nothing came out, not even a squeak. It was as if my dad had cornered all the Casanova words in the universe and left my throat dry and empty.

"*Por Dios, hombre*, will you stop flirting?"

"It's your fault, Pablo," my father said, "and don't you forget it. You made the bet."

"Have you had your fuck of the day?"

"You know I have," my father answered. "With Ignacio's men following me around as if I were a criminal."

"Maybe they haven't got around to giving me their report. Or maybe they're not even tailing you. If I'm asking you the question . . ."

"This morning," my father answered. "Only once. So I haven't fucked as many people as you have today."

Pablo Barón laughed at this, took it as praise. "That's what this business is about. Fucking others for the greater good, for their own ultimate happiness. And some people end up loving it and claim they're your friends and others hate it and they think they're your enemies forever, that you've done it for personal reasons. Big mistake. Nothing personal."

"So, which one of your enemies—or your friends—sent you this message?"

The *Ministro* shrugged as if to say, If I knew that, I wouldn't have called for you, would I?

"How did you get it, the letter?"

The *Ministro* lowered his voice.

"This morning. Came to my office. Came through the mail. Here's the envelope."

My father used the napkin to examine it, then handed it on to me. The same block letters on a pale blue envelope. And the return address: YOU KNOW WHO. *El que sabes.*

"So . . . ?"

My father sipped his coffee meditatively, stopped, and looked around for the waitress. Entranced with the iceberg, she had her back to us. I watched her and, for a moment, saw myself as I had been that night so many years ago in New York, breathing through my eyes the images of Antarctica on those twenty-five floating television screens. I saw a child of eleven saying to himself that someday he would have to see the real thing, touch the real thing, make the trek to the South Pole. My father, of course, had no such thoughts, no such memories. He just wanted to make sure the waitress was not aware of how he was suavely slipping another clandestine lump of sugar into the cup.

"What do the police say about it? I mean, Ignacio could probably tell you more than I—"

"Are you crazy, Cris? Ignacio doesn't know about this. Heaven knows who he's reporting to—in the army, in the high command, who knows. And the other policemen, I trust them even less. I found a wiretap on my own phone yesterday. We haven't been able to dismantle the previous regime's . . . No, this needs a private investigator."

"I don't do politics. And I certainly don't do icebergs. In fact, I don't do adults. You know the rules: runaways, male, over ten, less than eighteen. I'm not really a detective, I'm—"

"Yeah, yeah, you're a psychologist, I've heard it all a hundred times. Except now you're just going to have to help out, because this could be very serious, this could be—"

"You could lose your job, huh?"

The most powerful man in Chile after the president looked at the man who had made love to more women than anyone else in the country and gave a rap on the table that shook all the cups.

"You're saying you won't take the case because that way I'll lose the bet? Is that what you're saying? You want me to fail? Have I ever used my power to try and make you fail? And now you're going to use yours to screw me over when I need your help? Is that what you're saying?"

"I'm saying it's a prank, this letter, it's obviously some sort of practical joke." My father waited to see how Pablo Barón reacted to this. Pablo said nothing. *"Una broma,"* my father repeated, as if his friend were hard of hearing. "The sort of escapades my *muchachos* engage in endlessly at Casa Milagros. I'd recognize that sort of insolence anywhere."

"And if it isn't, Mr. Soothsayer? If it's a group of right-wing paramilitary former officers—or active officers, for that matter—who want to embarrass the new democratic government? Or some other minister in the government who wants my skin? Or terrorists who are angry because we're not funneling a horde of weeping widows to Sevilla to tell the world about the human rights horrors of the past? Or some crazy lady ecologist who thinks we're going to rape nature, open the legs of Antarctica and fuck a hole in its white, frozen, unpolluted ocean ass, kill the ice like we killed ten million seals and forty thousand whales last century? Her words, Cris, not mine. This iceberg—there's a loony fringe out there ready to sabotage it, kidnap it, hold it for ransom, melt it to a puddle, pull the plug. Not to mention the Bolivians, who are enraged with us because they say we stole their sea, and the Argentines, who think this will strengthen our rival claim to Antarctica, and the Canadians, who are envious because they were going to take their own North Pole iceberg to Expo '92. But we beat them to it and they don't want to be accused of imitating a poor, backward Third World country. Except we're not, we're not, we're the New Zealand of Latin America. The Brazilians are already green with envy at our economic success and will get angrier still when they hear our whole marketing strategy is that a nation that takes an iceberg to Spain is far from the tropics. They think we're specifically targeting them, not to mention the Saudis and the sultan of Qatar and even the Israelis, who have proclaimed that icebergs should be used to turn their sand dunes into gardens and not as playthings or promotional tools to attract the attention of the rest of the world at the fair. There are a lot of incensed people and countries and organizations out in the wide, wide world and they're gunning for us."

"That's a rather long list of suspects to begin with," my father interjected. "And all of them, I'd guess, with vaster resources at hand than a piece of paper and a second-class stamp."

"In a few minutes," the *Ministro* said, waving aside my father's objections, "every important businessman in this country will traipse in here. Ready to invest in Expo '92, to buy into the new image Chile is marketing to the world. They've begun to understand that you don't sell a product, you sell a whole goddamn country, you trademark and position the whole goddamn beautiful country. They're primed, they're panting for something new, anything that will close the doors of the past and advertise who we are. They're looking at the future with modern eyes, but if they sniff out something that smells bad, they'll back out like this. Whoever is doing it wants us to think it's a prank. But we know better." The *Ministro* snapped two chubby fingers and the sound was more like the crack of a whip. It bounced around the room, went right through the hologram of the iceberg that continued to glisten in fake whiteness, rattled the waitress, who was still gazing into its wounded depths. The poor girl thought the ice was real, she didn't dare touch it. Her head jerked up and she followed the sound as it came back to us. I saw the confusion in her brown eyes, asking whether *el Señor Ministro* was demanding service. "Because you know the one thing businessmen in this country fear more than losing money? They're scared of looking ridiculous. And the deranged mind that conceived this sort of threat knows that."

"*Commandante* You-Know-Who," my father said. "Is there anybody you'd immediately suspect, somebody you know?"

"So you're taking the case?"

I heard my voice speak out before my father could answer no.

"Yes," I said. "We're taking it."

Both men turned in unison to look at me, listening less to my words than to my accent. I myself had never quite heard my Spanish in the way they were hearing it now. In New York nobody had questioned that I spoke my mother tongue like a native Latin American. But then, those who had zero reservations about my Spanish in New York were not themselves natives. Here, thousands of miles away, my edgy twangs were suddenly alien, definitely bizarre.

"What did you say?" my father asked.

They thought I was baby-faced, huh? Cara de Guagua? Didn't know how to fight back? Well, they were in for a surprise. This Gabriel McKenzie was going to show these Chilean hicks a thing or two.

"We'll do it," I said to Pablo Barón.

"Wait, wait, wait." My father stood up, knocking over his chair.

"Papá," I said to him. "*Quieres mirarlo?* Look at it." He turned and looked at the hologram of the iceberg. Even if light was streaming through it, there was nothing transparent about that iceberg. Not clear and open like water might have looked and yet it was waiting to be explored, needing us to explore it and bring it back from the confines of the earth. I knew that he had to be thinking how much more magnificent the real thing would be, he was thinking that we could not let anyone harm it, he was thinking that this was the only territory we shared and that we had to nurse it together. I hoped that this was what he was thinking.

He must have been thinking something of the sort because when he turned back to us, he said, "I'm warning you, Pablo, I don't want to be blamed if this all blows up in our face, if we don't make any progress."

We. He had said *we.* I stood up by his side.

"You won't be blamed, Cris, I—"

"I'll do it for two weeks, Pablo. Two's the limit."

"We'll talk when we reach that limit."

"In writing, Pablo. And while you're writing, you might as well write out something that ensures that Casa Milagros survives for another year."

"Cris, I'm surprised. I'd even say I'm hurt. One thing has nothing to do with the other. Casa Milagros is a national treasure. I already signed a subsidy order this morning."

"That was thoughtful of you," my father said. "That way you can pay my services with something else."

"What?"

"You know what. I've told you what."

"I can't do it, Cris. You know I'm doing my best. If I let him go and not the other prisoners, can you imagine what—"

"Let them all go, then."

"Not yet. We're negotiating, you know that. Negotiating with the military, negotiating with the judiciary, with the opposition. We're— But I tell you what, if you bring me the name—real proof—of who's behind this, and I mean hard evidence, Cris, then I'll get your brother out of jail."

"And that's a promise."

"*En la medida de lo posible*. As far as I'm able, yes. Pancho will go free."

"Well, that's good enough for me," my father said, shaking Pablo's hand.

The *Ministro* heaved a sigh of relief.

"Not a word of this to anybody."

"Only to Polo."

"Polo, of course." Barón snorted as if this were so obvious that to even mention it was a waste of breath. "I'm worried about the press. And the business people."

"And the police," my father added. "But that leaves me with a problem. How do I interrogate people without creating suspicion?"

"I hadn't thought of that," the *Ministro* said.

"I can solve that problem," I piped up, surprising them again. It was as if every time I opened my mouth I suddenly sprang into view. As if I had been invisible until then, their words passing over me like tennis balls over a net. "I'm a journalist."

"Is that right?" Pablo Barón mused. "I thought your expertise was in computers." He seemed to know an awful lot about me. I wondered if he had asked Ignacio to open a file.

"Computers, yes. But I have a diploma from Columbia University in journalism."

"So you work for a paper?"

"I'll start work soon," I said to him. Not a lie, Janice. At that point I was fully prepared to return and start up the *Whatever* project that we dreamed up together, the first on-line magazine exclusively dedicated to gossip about what's buzzing on the Internet. It was your proposal, Janice. And you know what? It'll work. I even have backers. Too bad I won't be around to see our plans come true. "When I get back," I added.

The *Ministro* answered that as far as he was concerned I was never going back—and he wasn't wrong, was he? Though what he meant was that the country was full of opportunities, tons of jobs for anybody who could work with computers. Did I know that Chile had the highest per capita use of electronic dataports in all of Latin America, the most fax machines per inhabitant, the most cyberspace?

I didn't get to tell him that a country can't accumulate cyberspace, that its meaning is precisely its lack of geographical bounds, because my father intervened: "Very interesting," he said, "but that still doesn't answer my question. How could Gabriel's amateur reporting help me investigate without alerting people to the threat against the iceberg?"

"We can tell them," I said, "that I'm here to report on the iceberg. I'll go around asking gringo questions."

"Of course," Pablo Barón agreed, "great idea. You can tell them you're from the *New York Times* or whatever. These people here wouldn't know the difference. Good head on your shoulders, *m'hijo*."

"And I'm supposed to wait for him to tell me what he found out?" my father said.

"You're supposed to come with me," I said. "Nobody will suspect anything: we haven't seen each other in so long, you're accompanying me while I visit. I mean, Polo can take care of the business, right?"

"*Bueno*," Dad said slowly, drawling the word, staring across the room, which was beginning to fill with guests. He looked at Milagros and Polo, who were talking to a few bejewelled ladies thin as stringbeans, their hips jutting out aggressively. "I'll probably need to take Polo along."

"Take anybody you want along," the *Ministro* said. "Just find out who the fuck wants to scuttle this project."

"Anybody we should start with?" Having sunk my teeth into the matter, I wasn't about to let go that easily.

"Start with Jorge Larrea. He's the brains behind all this, been coordinating the whole operation for the last few months. If you wait around, he'll be here any moment now. You can meet him and—"

"I've already met him," my father said.

"You helped him get back his runaway kid? Or did you screw his wife?"

"I'm not commenting on that, Pablo. What I do with my dick is confidential. And whom I work for is as well. Let's say I went out looking for our Amanda Camila, to give an example. Would you want it plastered all over the cocktail circuit?"

"You never went looking for my daughter," the *Ministro* said, and a hard edge crept into his voice. "First, because she hasn't run away and second, you don't go after girls."

Barón was getting more and more agitated. And then, suddenly, something changed in his attitude. He waved his hand in greeting to somebody behind our backs. As he lifted his chubbiness from the seat, his face was—well, you know that I hate to sound corny, Janice, that I pride myself on my writing, that my prose is something I've worked on and polished, even back when we were fifteen it was my use of language that got you into bed or at least onto your mother's couch. I've got my pride, so you'll pardon the cliché. Here it goes: his face was like a rising sun. Okay, a cliché, but not without some truth to it. Now that I've seen how the sun takes hours to loop slowly out of the Antarctic horizon of ice as summer approaches and everything begins to crack and melt, that's what I'd now compare Barón's face to, that sort of boreal sun. In love with light. Or maybe it would be more appropriate to state that for a second his mask of power shattered, his defenses came down, he was being transformed into somebody powerless, seduced. And the reason was the person who had just come in. I turned before he said, "Well, speaking of girls, here she is." I saw her as he added, "Gabriel, meet Amanda Camila."

I had seen that face before. Mom had shown me photos in which I was a five-year-old running circles around a baby. There, that's Amanda Camila, you'll meet her when we go back. But it was not the face that drew me to her now that I was contemplating her alive and robust in Chile, it was her slim body and full breasts gliding up to us, her lips pecking a lipstick kiss on her father's cheek, her trembling fingers alighting on my father's neck as the kiss was repeated, this time much too close to the mouth for my taste, and only then and finally those eyes, monstrously green—you could swim in those eyes and gladly drown in them, I could, I would, I told myself that this was why we had come to this country my mom called home. I had returned in order to slip into those eyes and reach deep into the back of this girl's brain—or maybe what I wanted was to slip into her a bit farther down, smuggle myself in below the screen of the waist, so to speak, and climb up toward her eyes from inside. I was miraculously feeling an erection starting at the base of my groin, wanting to get so deep inside her that I would be the one looking at myself from—

"You're Gabriel," she said, "you've got to be Gabriel."

I nodded idiotically.

"*Hola*, Gabriel," she said. "We've been waiting for you for a long time. Welcome home."

"*Hola*," I said.

The *Ministro* pushed her toward me. "Give him a kiss, Amandita. He's practically your cousin. And it's his birthday."

"We were going to come by Casa Milagros later," she said, disregarding her father's suggestion and staying a prudent distance from my cheek. "But we decided we couldn't wait. There's somebody you have to meet."

"Somebody?" The only somebody I wanted to meet happened to be standing right in front of me, and my stupid parroting of her word was proof that if I was to make any headway with her I'd better get those lessons in seductive arts from my dad soon. She was now taking my hand as if she were going to lead me to a dance. The slenderness of those fingers made my heart ache out of the desire to put each one into my mouth and clean them to the bone and then crunch the bones and the articulations for good measure. They made me forget that I was poison to girls, that I had no chance with her or with any of them until my father saw fit to lift the curse on my unfortunate balls and even less fortunate features. Sensing that some strange thought was making my grip weaken, Amanda pulled me away decisively.

"Outside. She didn't want to come in. Says this place is jinxed."

Having successfully disengaged me from my father and her father, Amanda Camila let go of my hand and headed toward my mother. She left me there, shipwrecked in the middle of that large room, which was filling up with fashionably dressed men and women— suspects each and every one of them!—dribbling in for the iceberg's first *presentación en sociedad*, the launching of the Sevilla Expo '92 project that someone was trying to sabotage.

My mother was pressing the flesh of arcane and bespectacled old beings whom she obviously had met who knows when. As she greeted them, I could see her attempt to find something that hadn't changed in her absence, somebody who had stayed the way he used to be, freezing time so that the seventeen years would be an illusion and she could trick the calendar and return to 1974, when we had left. Then she scooted a glance toward us, toward the man whom she still loved and who was still her legitimate husband. In her eyes I could divine what she was wondering and I was fearing: if the one rock she could count on in this endless swamp of time lost was Cristóbal McKenzie and wondering also what they might do one of these nights to recover years of suppressed lovemaking, the one unaltered pleasure of life taking her back to that moment I had been conceived in the shadow of Che Guevara's corpse. But she dismissed the thought and so did I as soon as Amanda Camila jumped into her arms, laughing like a maniac: Tía Milagros, Tía Milagros. As soon as they began heading for the exit, they both waved at me to join them as if they were going on a picnic. I followed them. I wasn't going to let either out of my sight, I wasn't going to let this godsent hard-on of mine die that quickly.

It was then, as I weaved and bobbed and dickered my way through the crowd of ambassadors and senators and bank presidents, it was then that, for the second time in less than two hours, I heard that voice creeping up from behind me, buzzing in my ear.

"Forget her," said Polo, at the exact moment that Amanda turned, right there by the door, and shook her long hair to hurry me up. Forget her? He was the one I had forgotten. Her breathless presence had helped me joyfully obliterate his existence for these few minutes. Not that he had forgotten mine: here he was again, guessing my thoughts again. He had ferreted out what, translucent as venomous ice, I incestuously desired. "Quite an ass, I'll give you that, but Amanda's only got eyes for your father. Says she'd like to get lost only so he could find her. Says she's waiting for her hero McKenzie to bring back girls. But let me tell you something: he won't do it."

Except my mom, I thought. He brought her back.

"Except your mom," Polo said uncannily, following me to the exit past admirals and ministers, reporters and executive officers, telephone company sponsors and copper corporation advertising vice presidents, all murmuring eulogies to the iceberg and *Ministro* Pablo Barón. "But that was the only female runaway, the first one, and never again. Amanda says she's going to be the second one. A pity Cris has ruled her out of bounds."

I turned on him savagely.

"You," I said, emphasizing the word like a dagger, as if I were typing it on the screen of his forehead. "You—stay—here." As if he were a deaf-mute. "She didn't invite you."

"*Oye*, Gabriel. No way was I going with you. Your father might need me." His clown eyes smiled coldly. "Be sure not to take seventeen years this time."

I watched him disappear into the crowd, heading straight for the prettiest young woman in the room, a dainty brunet dish in a conservative two-piece suit. I didn't wait to find out whether he was going to try and bag her sleek legs for himself or for his boss or for both of them. I bounded up the stairs, up into the lobby of the Tourism building and out into the street.

"Here," Amanda greeted me. "Here's the real Chile."

A hullabaloo of *transeúntes* and street vendors erupted into my eyes and ears, ten thousand smells and calls, a *loquerío* of cries and colors and castaways, a madman selling ice cream in the middle of winter, *el helado, al rico helado, piña*, pineapple, *chirimoya alegre*, chocolate, *refrésquese*, plying the gray men in gray suits who were walking by so gray and calm that they seemed to belong to another dimension. The sidewalks were jammed with wares, imitation Woody Woodpeckers, flashlights from Hong Kong, herbs of all sorts and aromas and names—*Compre albahaca, patroncito, al perejil, al perejil*—a sick sweetness of *maní confitado* filling the air, tiny peanuts wrapped in sticky toffee, and toys assembled in Indonesia, and stolen watches from Peru, and scarves from India, and secondhand records and CDs and cassettes and comic books and fake Wranglers. And this carnival of people—even two tiny beggar boys chanting and dancing to a song on a small radio—all of them were surprisingly well dressed, their jeans and worn Nikes and headbands and inverted baseball caps and parkas practically indistinguishable from what I was wearing. Only their dark faces and short stature indicated that they were not white and American, that their race was—and that's when I saw her, just as my mind fastened on the word *race* and my eyes stopped roving, because there, in the middle of that gentle chaos, was my mother, holding onto an ancient dwarf of a woman, both of them rocking each other back and forth, mother and child, child and mother, clutching each other as if on the edge of a cliff over which they were about to fall.

Who was she? She couldn't be . . . ? She had to be.

I had never seen a photo of the Nanny. She doesn't like photos, Mom had explained offhandedly, doesn't trust them. I had somehow conjured up a Victorian nanny, prim and Mary Poppins-like and cosmopolitan, reading Jane Austen at night through her pince-nez and quoting Beaumarchais in the morning, advising her young charge, Milagros, about life and liberty and men. I had constructed her, quite naturally, as European, pink, debonair. That's how nannies were in my books. I'm sure that when I first mentioned a nanny, Janice, you also conjured up some Dickensian vision, but this woman, she . . . she was an Indian, entirely Mesoamerican, bronze Inca skin, only darker and more yellow, slanted eyes, stringy gray hair, the hint of a moustache browsing her upper lip. Only later did I learn that well-to-do Chileans call their maids Nanas—from *nana*, the word toddlers use for wounds, for pain, for the hurt that only the one woman who is at home with them all the time can assuage. Only later did I learn that all the Nanas, or almost all of them, came from the countryside, were indigenous, had ancestors who had been here before the McKenzies or the Gallardos or the Baróns or the Colóns had ever crossed the Atlantic in search of gold and land and fame. I was to learn soon enough that they absorb the pain of children of all ages, that she would absorb my pain.

There was a sudden flurry in the street—*Los pacos, los pacos*—a hissing alarm of sounds that emerged from around the corner and trafficked from vendor to *vendedor*, and they began to gather together the blankets that were spread all over the sidewalk, folding the four corners into one knot with a swiftness indicating much practice and even more fear. The police were coming, and within seconds they were all gone, scampering past me and Amanda Camila. There must have been four street sellers for every potential buyer, because the street the fugitives left behind became clear and quiet and the view of my mother and her Nanny suddenly pristine and unimpaired. I saw the Nanny uncouple her hands from my mother's resplendent body and come toward me, smiling, her arms open.

Those arms enveloped me in the cold winter air, buried me deep into the folds of her rough overcoat. "*Ay mi niño, mi niño,*" she said, "*mi guagua, mi guagua,*" my child, my baby. I didn't object to her calling me that, I wanted to be called by those names, labeled in love and not in derision, I wanted to be welcomed, I wanted to come home and recognize everything. But she was the first one I really did remember, perhaps because I had killed her memory in me as soon as I had left Chile so I would not feel the pain of her loss. It had been inside all these years, waiting to rush out. I breathed her in and the smell was of the bread that she had baked that morning and had baked that dawn seventeen years ago when we left this country and had baked the morning after Milagros conceived me and for the thirty or so years before that for Professor Gallardo and his family. Here was one person who had kept a place for me in her heart and in her hearth, preparing her loaves day by day, in her fingers whispers of all the *cazuelas* she had cooked, once a week, in anticipation of our return. I was her *niño*, her *guagua*.

I couldn't help it, I started to sob. Everything that had happened to me in the last two hours and in the last twenty years came out of my eyes like a sad river. I had tottered to her as a child of three with my burned finger and now I fell into her as a child of twenty-three with my burned soul. She understood what her *guagua* needed and in her mouth that word meant what it meant to her foremothers in the wilds of Chile before the Spanish ever came to these shores. The word *guagua* had been passed down from mother to daughter and nanny to nana so that she could say it to me, this gringo boy who had been born by accident in Chile and had been received by her hands the day of his birth. She knew what I needed. She knew who I was, her Gabrielito come home.

Again my homecoming was interrupted by a masculine hand and a masculine voice.

"*Andando, andando, qué pasa acá?*"

Like Ignacio, this man was tall and bulky, but unlike Ignacio, he was uniformed, clad in the ugly green outfit of the carabineros, the *pacos*, the Chilean cops. He had roughly broken up our embrace, clasped the Nanny's arm in one hand and mine in the other, and was propelling us none too gently toward a black and white police van that was waiting, its motor idling, by the curb. The *paco* ignored the Nanny's objections that we had been doing nothing, that we were— he didn't want to hear a word of it: Tell it to *mi capitán* at the station, caught loitering, selling illegal goods, smoking dope, you and your grandson, *andando, andando*. It had all happened so fast that I hadn't been able to react, but now I twisted in the *paco*'s grip and saw my mother and Amanda Camila hurrying to catch up with us. They had withdrawn a distance out of discretion, once I had started to cry, but they never got the chance to mediate, because ahead of us, just in front of the police van, Ignacio materialized. He stopped the *paco* and his two captives and flashed an ID.

"Not this time, *huevón*," he said. "Go find someone else to fill your quota."

The *paco* did not let us go immediately.

"*Vamos*," said Ignacio, "she's the Nana of *Ministro* Barón, you idiot."

"How about him? He was harassing her."

"Cara de Guagua? Harmless. The minister's godson. So go chase some *marihuaneros*, a couple of *maricones*."

The *paco* released us. He headed for the corner. I watched the hand that had held my arm reach for a nightstick, ready to make any street vendors he might track down pay with their backs for the recent humiliation inflicted on him by Ignacio.

"You," Ignacio said to me, "are going to have to change your face, boy, if you want to stay out of trouble."

"Don't listen to him." It was Amanda Camila. "*Filo* with him. *Filo* with all the *viejos de mierda*."

It was the first time I heard the expression so current among Chilean youth: *filo*, a word that originally meant razor blade, knife, something that cuts deep. Slit their throats, it means, slit the old bastards' throats.

"You'll get used to being arrested," she went on. "If you're young . . ."

"I thought things had changed."

She laughed. "For some people, yeah. But if you're young or poor . . ."

"Go complain to your dad," Ignacio said. "Inside. 'Cause you can't stay out here. I have to go back. Maybe we can all go and have ourselves a drink?"

"Not that place, Don Ignacio," the Nanny said. "Not with—that thing in there. We're going back home with Milagros."

"Only for a few hours," Mom said to me, as if excusing herself. "You want to come with me? Or do you—"

"I think I'm needed back there by . . . by Dad."

"Good idea," Mom assented. "Go and see your famous detective father in action. I'll catch up with you in time for your party at the Casa Milagros."

Nana nodded gravely. "But you must come and see me tomorrow, *mi niño* Gabriel."

"Tomorrow, Nana," I promised.

"Tomorrow," Amanda Camila added. "I'll be there too." She moved a bit closer to me, finally blessing me with the cousinly kiss her father had urged upon her. I felt her lips quick as perfume on my cheek; they were gone before I could even try to register their touch, like the wing of a butterfly on the day of its birth, on the day before it dies. I was grateful for its flutter even as it evaporated.

I watched all three of my women, all three generations of Chilean womanhood disappear into the crowd. The street vendors were drifting back, they had walked around the block and were setting up their blankets on the wet cement as if nothing had disturbed them. They would be here tomorrow and the next day and who knows how many days after that, as they had been for the many years we had been away. They would be here again when we went back, if we went back, if I decided to return to New York.

As Ignacio and I re-entered the building, he was stopped by a stocky elderly man dressed in a suit that had seen better days and certainly better nights but that, for all its frayed quality, someone had taken the care to press and clean.

"Is he coming out this way?" the man asked.

"You know I can't give you that information," Ignacio said. "Go see him at his office."

"What for? He hasn't had time to . . . I thought if—"

"Can I give you some advice, Don Jacinto?" Ignacio towered above the man, but there was nothing menacing in his body language: it was as if he were shading him from some implacable light, protecting the stooped old coot from the wind. "This is not the way to get the *Ministro* to do you a favor."

"Not me," said Don Jacinto, adjusting the lapels of his suit as if he were afraid it would fall apart right in front of us. "My son. My son, who was Pablo Barón's bodyguard for seven years. Seven years. And what has he got to show for it?"

"That's my advice," Ignacio said, and he gestured to the security guards to let us in. They opened the door, left the man standing there, craning his neck to see what was going on inside. "Strange," Ignacio said. "Ten years ago, I could have killed his son. Now I'm giving his father advice. Democracy."

"What does he want?"

"Don Jacinto wants a *pituto* for his son. A cushy job, in the Ministry of Health or wherever. He thinks the *Ministro* owes it to his son. And his son is too proud to ask."

"Will the *Ministro* give it to him?"

"Maybe he'll get lucky. But there are hundreds like this guy and if he's failed so far . . . He's been trying for over a year, sits in Don Pablo's office every morning."

"Maybe I could do something."

Ignacio looked at me. "You want some advice?" I didn't, but he gave it to me anyway. "Stay out of this."

It was good advice, I decided.

Downstairs, the inaugural launch of the iceberg project was going full blast. A silver-haired man was holding forth about the pavilion, an arklike structure projected onto a wide screen behind him. "Just like the one used by the conquistadores to come to these shores, all made from genuine Chilean *alerce*. Everything will be done here, even the refrigeration technique, and refrigeration, my friends," he said, adjusting his tie—they all had ties, and I suddenly felt how out of place my baseball cap was here, the jeans and sweater that had almost landed me in jail—"godlike refrigeration is what makes our exports grow, salmon, fruit, shellfish. It's ice that allows us to place food tomorrow in Singapore or in Seattle, and it's ice that will tell the world that we are efficient and responsible." He snapped his fingers and on the wall behind him images of black seas and white craters of ice floated by, the same ones, I was sure, that I had watched on twenty-five television screens that night in Manhattan. "And that ice, ladies and gentlemen, is being served right this very moment with your beverages, ice straight from Antarctica, courtesy of our glorious air force, which flew it in this morning. So you drink that ice down! You'll be drinking the purity of Chile, taking into your body an authentic chunk from the last frontier on earth, water that has been frozen since before the Bering Strait let the first noble inhabitants of our continent cross over from Europe and Asia."

There was applause as waiters began to circulate with large vats of chipped ice and all manner of alcohol to wash it down.

I had stationed myself on the steps descending into the room and from there had been surveying the guests, trying to find my dad. For a few seconds, I wondered if he was not shacked up in some nearby hotel room, delving into the delicate architecture of the Botticelli waitress, extracting some more sugar, but I caught a glimpse of that particular *moreno* maiden offering some eager entrepreneurs streams of whiskey, and besides, my father had already fulfilled today's plump quota, according to Polo in order to spend some time with me, yeah, sure, but maybe tomorrow, maybe tomorrow he would . . . My thoughts were interrupted by the sight of Cristóbal McKenzie and Polo standing in front of a stalwart army general bedecked with medals and his scrawny, crumpled wife, her hair bleached an abominable blond so ugly that I inferred that my father could not be trying to set up the harridan for some future date. Maybe he was gathering information about possible dangers to the iceberg.

I was weaving my way toward them when I was accosted by Miss Dainty Dish herself, the gloriously endowed young brunet in the two-piece suit I had seen Polo stalking as I left the party.

"Could I ask you a question?"

All you want, I almost said, ask me what I would do to you if I were my father. Ask me what I'd like to do to you before I leave this country. Ask me what my dick could do if it weren't limp and extinct at this moment.

Instead: "Er—sure."

"It's a question about the iceberg. You're the youngest person here, the youngest by far, so I wanted to know. I'm a reporter, Cristina Ferrer. You may have heard of me . . ."

She waited, ready for me to pump her vanity by telling her how much I loved her work, had listened to her on the radio, watched her on TV, read her last gossip columns. But her reference to my age stung me. I was tired of being patronized.

"I don't give out opinions, Miss. I gather them. I'm a reporter myself."

I saw her delightful jaw drop, whether out of admiration or skepticism was not clear. I decided to pursue my advantage.

"For the *New York Times*," I said, hating my need to impress her with false credentials. "I'm Gabriel McKenzie. Reporting on the iceberg, just like you are."

"McKenzie, huh? We have some McKenzies here in Chile. You wouldn't be related to—"

"He's my father," I said swiftly. "Cristóbal McKenzie."

Something changed in her. Those vivid eyes crossed the room and alighted on my father and I knew they had made love. Here was one of the nine thousand bodies my father had been entering and burglarizing during my sterile years in New York. And I knew something else as soon as she looked back at me with a sudden flicker of interest. This hot little item had had a swinging time with my dad, would have repeated whatever it was they had done together if he had been willing, if he had not been a one-night lover needing to hop onto the next bed and pry open the next pair of legs to complete his daily allotment. And maybe, perhaps, who knows, was that what I was gleaning from her eyes, which looked at me differently now, was she wondering if the son had inherited the father's amatory qualities? Or was it all in my sex-starved imagination? And I had come to Chile for this? To be another Polo, going over territory that my father had already plowed and fathomed?

So when the reporter put her hand in mine and kept it there for much longer than required, under the pretext of introducing herself to me again, when she suggested we might compare notes—and not only about the iceberg, she added, squeezing the palm of my hand suggestively—when she seemed to be making my dream scenario of Chile come true just a few hours after my arrival, a gorgeous woman inviting me into her life and probably onto her mattress, instead of squeezing back, I responded by withdrawing the hand and dashing that dream: thanks, but no thanks. I decided then and there that I would only make love to a woman who had not tasted the fruits of my father's tongue. I would only go where he had not ventured before. I would bed the one person I was sure had not been screwed by him. I would lose my virginity to Amanda Camila, I swore to myself under the gigantic shadow of that fraudulent iceberg, it would be Amanda Camila or nobody. A hasty decision that sealed my fate, that led me, like a dusty dog, to this room in Sevilla.

As if he had been listening in to my secret frequency, who should come up at that very moment but the father of the woman I had vowed would be mine.

"Gabriel," Pablo Barón said, "I want you to meet Carola. My wife, the mother of my two boys, the woman who saved my life."

Carola was a sleek bombshell of a woman dressed in a drastic red, and when she maddened my cheek with a kiss as soft as it was elusive, I wondered if my stern resolve to make love only to her stepdaughter could withstand the overflowing proximity of bodies such as hers.

"Saved your life?" Cristina asked Barón. "When was that? Sounds like a good story."

Pablo Barón turned to the reporter. "Not a story for you, my dear. But I see you haven't lost any time, have you, Cristina? Already met our boy Gabriel, hey? Two reporters, hot on the trail of the iceberg. Can't wait to see who'll get the inside scoop."

"Which reminds me, *Ministro*," Cristina Ferrer said, "that I still haven't found the quote from Generation X I'm looking for—"

"How about Amanda Camila?" Pablo Barón asked. "She's somewhere around here."

"She's gone home," I said.

"How about Carola?" the *Ministro* insisted. Someone in his family was going to get interviewed!

Cristina scrutinized Pablo Barón's wife as if looking for traces of a plastic surgeon's scalpel on her skin. "Maybe some other time," the Ferrer señorita finally said. And turned to leave and then swivelled back in order to hand me her card—her card and one last flirtatious look. "If you're anything like your father," she said, "you'll call me." With that she was gone.

"Bitch," Carola said and changed subject effortlessly. "So when are you coming to see my twins?" she asked me.

"I'm visiting tomorrow," I said.

"Problem is I can't make it tomorrow," Carola cooed.

"We'll miss you," I lied. "But I'm sure Amanda will take care of me."

"You like her that much, eh, Amanda Camila?" The voice behind me belonged—I should have guessed—to Polo. He really had the most remarkable genius for creeping up anonymously, melting out of the shadows to deliver in one's ear the words one least wanted to hear.

"Yes, of course, I like her," I said, not deigning to throw a glance in his direction.

"How much?" Polo insisted. "How much do you like her?"

Pablo Barón narrowed his eyebrows; a dangerous color rose in his pupils as he turned to confront Polo.

"What sort of question is that?" Pablo Barón asked. "What the fuck are you insinuating?"

"*Yo*?" said Polo. "Nothing, *Ministro*. *Nada*. Just an innocent question."

"Well, we'll give you an innocent answer then, won't we, Gabriel?" Here Pablo Barón spun me around by the shoulder, mashing his fingers into it; everybody in this country seemed to feel that my muscles were their property, that I had flown all the way from New York so they could gouge and pinch and shove me. Even in this case, where the *Ministro* seemed outraged at Polo, it was my body that was paying the vicarious consequences. Or was Barón really sending me a message, letting me know that his power did not stem from his ministerial rank but from his butcher hands and what those hands were capable of perpetrating if ever he really got angry? "Before you were ever born, Leopoldo, this boy's father and I, we were like this, this close. *Comprendes?* Gabriel here can't help but love Amanda Camila, because he's like her brother. That's why she trusts him, why I trust him. That's why he's invited to my house tomorrow and the day after. And he'll be received by that girl of mine as if she were his sister. Am I right, Gabriel, or am I right?"

I told him he was right. What was I supposed to do? Tell him the truth while he molded and extorted my flesh as if I were a clay statue, tell him that I wanted to screw his daughter from the moment I saw her and that the fact of her seemingly being the only female in the city whom my father hadn't ravished had only served to confirm that desire and harden my erection? Tell him that he was at fault, he and his moronic bet with my father and Tío Pancho the day after I was conceived? Tell him all of this precisely now that my father had come up and was canvassing the whole scene with his mysterious eyes?

"Good," said the *Ministro*. "He's a good kid, Cris. We should both be proud. And you'll remember this day you came home, Gabriel. Many years from now you're going to remember the day your father here, your *padrecito*, took you to see the iceberg." He clamped his other large paw on my dad's shoulder.

What was there to remember? His daughter, yes; her Nanny and my Nanny and the Nanny of Milagros, yes; the day that was still to come when the true dream of ice would surface like a whale of white out of the mist and madness that gathers whenever anyone dares to approach the South Pole, that day, yes. But remember this phony shimmering piece of nothing destined to dazzle the sponsors and the moneymen and the colonels and recede into darkness—why should I? Though here I am in Sevilla eighteen months later, remembering, remembering, wondering how it is that the day of my arrival it was all written out, my destiny, my future death. And not only mine, Janice. Not only my death.

"I'm tired," I said. "I want to go home."

I meant New York, I meant my warm room overlooking Riverside Drive, I meant the on-line chat room where I would be able to tell my faceless friends my sorrows and hopes, receive questions and advice from you, Janice of the sensual suggestions, try out another position that you said you were in so I could penetrate you from afar and on all fours while my fingers worked at my sex, while your fingers worked at your sex. I was tired and wanted to go home.

The home they took me to was the Casa Milagros in the barrio of Nuñoa and the friends who tried to cheer me up were the hundred or so youngsters who sang "*Que los cumpla feliz, Apio verde* to you," to the son of their McKenzie protector. The gift they gave me, a Walkman, was totally useless, and the room I was eventually shown was cold and damp despite the electric heater glowing in the dark and the hot water bottle that Polo had ordered someone to place under the covers. The time was late, late in the night of an endless day whose minutes were ticking by on a watch that my father had given me as a present and that I did not want and did not need.

And the chat room?

It was there, it should have been there as soon as I hooked up my modem and switched on my laptop, I should have been able to access your E-mail where you and so many others were humming back and forth across the emptiness of digital darkness. I should have been given the chance to tell you how everything had gone wrong in Chile, to confess right then and there that I was a fraud and ask you if it wouldn't be best for me to take a plane back home the very next day and have you meet me in Manhattan. I had never needed your words, Janice Worth, gliding off my Toshiba and into my eyes more than I did that exhausted midnight—except that there was a flash and a crackle and the screen went black and promiscuous smoke began to curl its way out the back of the keyboard.

"Fuck, fuck, fuck!"

I reached down to the electrical outlet and, not caring if I burned myself, almost hoping that the pain would wither this hand condemned to masturbating in yet another bathroom, I yanked out the twisted ruins of the adaptor plug that I had attached to my computer's cable. How could I have been such an idiot? How could I have forgotten to hook up a transformer? And how long would it take me to find somebody who could fix the laptop at a reasonable price, if it could be fixed at all, that is?

And yet, after the initial anger gave itself time to subside, I found myself settling into a more contemplative attitude, wondering if this disaster might not be a bizarre message from the gods, a sign that I had to decipher. Why had this happened precisely at the end of my first day in Chile? What did it mean?

I was being cut off, that much was clear. To re-establish a connection with you, Janice, and other Internet friends, abolishing this too too solid space I was trapped in, had to be easy. No trouble tomorrow in finding another terminal. Wasn't Chile, according to Pablo Barón, such a modern country? But was that what I needed? If I had roasted my computer with such deliberate clumsiness, maybe something deep inside my life did not want me to hear the message you would probably deliver to me, Janice, once I told you where I was: To hell with Chile, to hell with that asshole father, to hell with that iceberg or the forbidden girl you say you're in love with. Come home to me, let's finish what we began back then on that couch, that night. Maybe I had contrived this accident subconsciously so I would be forced to solve the mess and puzzle of my life on my own in the days ahead, maybe being set adrift was the only way to rid myself of this baby face, maybe I wasn't supposed to keep my promise of contacting you, Janice, the very next day. Maybe, maybe, maybe . . .

It was midnight.

I wandered downstairs for a snack. Useless to try and sleep with all the words I had meant to dribble into your ears still boiling inside me.

From the kitchen window, I could see the dormitory building, the annex my father and Milagros had built in those first years of their marriage, investing every cent that came from the thriving agency into bricks and mortar and beds for the kids who could not afford to go back to their parents once they had run away, bathrooms for the kids who may not have had parents to go back to. Now a solitary light shone on the fourth floor of the dorm.

I was drawn toward it and went up the stairs slowly, almost floating on the rhythmic breath of the hundred youngsters sleeping there, guardians of my footsteps, until I came to the one room that was lit up. I stopped at the threshold. Seated at the edge of a bed, my father was quietly crooning lullaby words to somebody, a small urchin it seemed, a boy who could not have been much older than six or seven, though I knew that children were not admitted to the Casa Milagros until they were ten. The boy had been crying—I could hear the residues, the last wisps of his sobs. "It's all right," my father was saying to him. "It's going to be all right, *todo va a estar bien*. Would you rather have monsters in your dreams or monsters in this room? Isn't it better to drown them in your dreams? Isn't it, isn't it?" and now I remembered. I had been that age or maybe a little younger; it must have been a few nights before we were to leave for New York. I had started up from a nightmare and there, above my bed, the great McKenzie had been standing. He must have been there for a long time, watching over my sleep, waiting for the moment when I would wake up on my own, not wanting to intervene as I struggled with some horror, not wanting to leave, just waiting and watching and then holding me in his arms like he was now holding this other child seventeen years later. I stayed there for a few seconds, listening, and then took a step backward as if I had stumbled on a scene that was somehow forbidden to me now, the child I had been and this child I could never again be and the father I had lost. I took that step and my father called out, without turning his head in my direction: "Come in, Gabriel. I've been expecting you."

I obeyed and walked over to the bed.

"Carlitos," my father said to the urchin, "this is my son, Gabriel. He once had bad dreams, he thought they would never end. But look how he's grown. And he never thought he'd make it either, did you, Gabriel?"

"You'll be all right, Carlitos," I said. "Have you got one friend? One friend in the world?"

"Yes," Carlos said. "He's my friend. He found me. He brought me here."

"One friend's enough," I said. "You don't need more than one friend to pull through."

"I have to go pee-pee," Carlos announced suddenly.

"That's good," my father said. "Can I tell Gabriel why it's good?"

"If he promises not to tell anybody else."

I promised and my father explained that Carlos had been wetting his bed, that in the last few nights things had been getting better. The boy had been remembering to go to the bathroom before going to sleep, and this was a secret. The others were not supposed to know.

Carlos slipped out of the bed now and padded into the cold night, holding my father's hand. Then he stretched out another hand for me.

As the boy pissed gently into the urinal, I had the urge myself, unbuttoned my fly and let loose, and was soon accompanied by the sound of my father following suit. There was something so absolutely right about the moment, it was strangely comforting to know that on the other side of the planet screens were being clicked on, words were being typed, people were seeking one another through those words, and I was not among them; it was better to be here, pissing through the freezing air with my father and his little runaway. Everything would be fine, I thought, if only we could stay like this forever, all three of us letting our waters flow together forever.

And that feeling of *bienestar* outlasted the moment, it was still there when we tucked the boy in, switched off the light, lingered by his bed until he was fast asleep.

A few minutes later, down in the yard, we stood, my father and I, under the freezing moon that had abruptly appeared from behind the clouds. He took out his cigarettes, offered me one, smiled when I refused, lit up himself, and puffed deeply.

"He's a bit young to be here, isn't he?" I asked.

"Most kids here have a home to go back to," my father answered. "A home, if you can call it that. That kid Carlos doesn't have anything but the streets. He tried to pick my pocket one day at the Mercado Central. I go there once in a while to see who tries to steal from me. Those are the ones I want, the ones who are the smartest, the most daring, anyone who sees me as a challenge. He'd escaped from the Hogar del Niño, which the *pacos* run, and before that from the Hogar de Cristo, which the priests have set up. Nobody could do anything with him. Now, maybe, who knows, he might stay here, though he's returned to the streets twice since we took him in. Polo found him sniffing glue just a month ago. If the kid goes back one more time, he'll stray into harder drugs and heavy crime to pay for them, and there won't be any way we can save him. So we took him in even if he's young."

"What if you're full, if there's no space for somebody like him?"

"Then he'll die on the streets."

Behind my father, under the sudden moonlight, I could see the expanse of the Andes come into view, the snow on the mountains shimmering back light on him as if he were a ghost.

"I know every kid in that building," he said. "By name, by story, by everything. Your Tío Pancho, your Tío Pablo Barón—they decided to save the world. I decided to save one kid at a time."

"One kid at a time," I repeated.

"The ones no one gave a fuck about," he said.

Like me, I thought. He's going to hug me now, I thought, start from where Ignacio interrupted us, close his eyes and close mine and close the circle and go back to that moment when everything began to go wrong, that's what he's going to do now.

But he didn't. He took another drag, threw the butt on the ground, let the smoke wreathe up toward us like a veil.

"Gaby," he said to me. For the first time he addressed me with that diminutive, called me the name he used when I was a little boy and neither of us knew that I would leave him and the country, that I would return with only an iceberg to join us. An iceberg and the piss of a scamp who was scared of the dark. "Gaby," my father said, "maybe it's time you stopped feeling sorry for yourself."

He turned and went inside.

I stayed there for a while. Then I crushed the hot ember of the cigarette my father had been smoking. I lifted my foot and crushed its glow under my shoe.

And that's where I'll leave myself for now, Janice, on that first night in Santiago. I've been writing since five in the morning of this day that marks the twenty-fifth anniversary of the death of Che. I need some air, some food. If I don't show up at dinner tonight with my family at the Chinese Pavilion, for a Beijing banquet, they'll begin to suspect something. They'll wonder what I've been doing with myself. Especially Amanda Camila. She's got antennae for this sort of thing. But I'll fool her, I've been fooling her for so long now . . . Oh yes, I also have to get some hens I've bought. Yes, Janice, real live hens, the sort you have to kill by placing across your knee and strangling, twisting their necks till they're dead. Just like Nana taught me. Yes. Enough writing for today. Time to start preparing the dinner with which I'll celebrate the birthday of Cristóbal McKenzie and his best friend, Pablo Barón, in two days' time. I'm going to cook them a special meal for their fiftieth birthdays. I'm going to cook them something they'll never forget.

A last supper. Before all hell breaks loose.

PART TWO

OCTOBER 10, 1992

•

Fraud, which gnaws every conscience, may be practiced by a man upon one

who confides in him.

—DANTE, *THE INFERNO,*

THE SECOND CIRCLE OF HELL

've been wondering if you're there, Janice. There at the other end of this long suicide note, I mean, from a man who after all lied to you every chance he got. If you haven't abandoned the ship, so to speak, before reaching the climax and conclusion of this voyage of discovery.

Not that I haven't done my best to keep you in suspense, displayed every narrative trick. Once upon a time, in another existence, pre-Chile, I did dream of being a writer. That's why I thought to myself, as I made my way late yesterday to Sevilla's feria—not the World's Fair, just the fair, the market where they sell the sort of food I'll need to make the *cazuela* for tomorrow night's meal. I thought to myself as I chose the right small round potatoes that are one of America's gifts to the world, This is a mystery story or at least the story of a mystery, so maybe I ought to seduce you a bit more, Janice, my one and only reader even if you'll never be my lover; maybe it's not enough to promise my own death. The death of somebody else should also be offered up. Yes, as in any mystery that prizes itself as such, there is a murder. Murder will make its appearance in this story I am telling.

But first, my dear, the mystery deepened.

Exactly two weeks to the day after Mom and I returned to Chile, exactly when my father was getting ready to quit the investigation just as he had warned he would, a second letter threatening the iceberg arrived at *Ministro* Pablo Barón's office. The same pale blue paper, the same envelope, the same stamp, the same block letters, the same

Commandante El-Que-Sabes signing it. Only the message was different:

IS IT ECOLOGY THAT MOVES ME?

THAT'S FOR ME TO KNOW AND YOU TO FIND OUT.

WHAT IS SURE IS I'M GOING TO FUCK YOUR ICEBERG.

COMMANDANTE YOU-KNOW-WHO.

Pablo Barón was not pleased.

"McKenzie," he said to my father from across the vastness of his ministerial desk, he said it to him in a whisper, because he was still obsessed with microphones that General Pinochet's boys had presumably hidden under the carpet. "McKenzie, you haven't been doing fuckall."

It was true. My father hadn't been doing a damn thing and Pablo Barón knew it. Whether the *Ministro* had called off Ignacio's men or not I cannot say, but I can assure you that he didn't need their reports, because he had another spy to inform him: Gabriel McKenzie, yours truly, assistant and son to the chief detective. Although I had spent the previous week in Patagonia, I had been careful before that to keep the minister abreast of the great Cristóbal McKenzie's extreme laxness about carrying out the investigation. This second letter came to my rescue just in time and allowed the *Ministro* to corner his best friend and demand he keep on the case—and with a bit more *energía*, Cris, *carajo*! What I had not told the *Ministro*, however, in the secret postluncheon conversation where I had double-crossed my father, was that this very selfsame father assumed it was Pablo Barón who had written the threat. I did not tell Barón what had transpired the morning after Mom and I disembarked in Chile, that July 10, 1991, when my father sat me down to a late breakfast with Polo in the Casa Milagros and asked us, "So how do we deal with this iceberg thing?"

"We do nothing," Polo said, buttering a crusty golden *marraqueta*. "It's obviously Barón himself."

I grabbed a piece of that wondrous bread you can find nowhere else in the world and asked him what he meant.

My father looked at me across the tablecloth, tracing with his index finger one of the *copihues* woven into the fabric. Whatever magic we had shared the previous night under the moon of the Andes had dissipated; he was back to being slightly ironic, definitely judgmental, no Gaby mentioned, not even Gabriel. I could feel him itching to call me Cara de Guagua, his cruelty checked perhaps by the image of Carlitos holding our hands.

"He means that Barón has faked the letter in order to screw me over, make me lose the bet. That's what Polo means."

"How can that make you lose your bet?" I said. "I don't understand."

"You don't understand," my father continued, "because like every other gringo in the world, you thought you could come to a country you know nothing about and step into a situation you know even less about and promise somebody you just met that you could solve his problem—which he cooked up in the first place. He's been trying to find a way to get me under his thumb since he was named *Ministro*—"

"But he's your best friend."

"Of course he is and I love him like a brother. But I'll give you ten to one, no, make that a hundred to one, that he's using this as a way of making sure I lose the bet. You watch, he'll dispatch us to Antarctica, he'll transport us down to Patagonia, he'll send us on every wild goose chase he can make up. And I'm not playing along. Two weeks from now, I'm off this case."

"What's wrong with going to Antarctica?" I asked. I shivered, not because of the cold winter air that was hardly being warmed by the kerosene stove sputtering away. I shivered in delightful anticipation: the hidden continent that man had only begun to take a peek at during this century, the place where Scott died writing goodbye notes while a blizzard advanced, the icy flatlands and mountains that Shackleton had never been able to cross from sea to sea. "Don't you want to see the real iceberg?"

Polo was about to answer, but my father stopped him.

"Yes, I do," he said, and something softened in his glimmer, in his voice. "In fact, I'd very much like to see the real iceberg. But I can travel anywhere I want, all I want, after October 12, 1992. Once I'm fifty. A bit over a year away."

"I still don't understand why Barón would want—"

Polo was answering my question before I finished formulating it. "No cunts on board ship," he said. "There'd have to be—let's say the trip by sea took fifteen days—so fifteen girls, one per night, a whole chorus line. And how many women are allowed on board that sort of vessel? Zero, zilch, not a *mina* in sight. Maybe they'd accept one at the most—and there you go, your dad loses his bet, the *Ministro* has the last laugh: one McKenzie brother in jail and Latin America not exactly in the state he predicted, *comprendes*; the other one marooned in the middle of the eternal ice, his dick unused for the first time in almost twenty-five years, just in sight of victory. And why? Because his son fell into the trap that Barón laid for us. Because his son thought he knew best. Now do you understand?"

I understood that I was the one who was marooned, I was the one who was fucked, though not literally, because if hostilities and blunders continued to pile up in this way my chances of getting laid in Chile were becoming more remote by the minute. Life for me would be an endless trip to Antarctica on a journey with not a skirt on board. I'd be like Scott, dreaming of the warm women he never loved as the deep polar night advanced on him and his frozen men. But my father had told me last night to stop feeling sorry for myself, he expected me to fight back.

"What if I make a bet of my own?" I said. "What if I bet that somebody else is out to get the iceberg, that it's not Barón, what then? Tell you what. If I'm wrong, I won't screw for the next twenty-five years. Not a woman, not a man, nothing. Not even a lamb's ass."

Polo had stopped chewing his bread. He held a cup of *café con leche* and it stayed there, midway in the air, wafting puffs of steam into the frosty kitchen, as he waited for me to continue. Maybe he was realizing for the first time that I was my father's son and therefore knew how to use my tongue above all instruments—not to mention that gambling was in the family genes, raging in my brain cells.

"And if you lose," I went on, "no more female flesh for the next quarter of a century. *Nada*."

My father laughed at this bit of bravado. Who knows if he didn't see me as a replica of that young man who had sat so many years ago at that birthday table with his brother and Pablo. Not that he was going to let his dear pal Polo, hyperventilating at the thought of his genitals going into deep freeze until the year 2016, be humiliated. He called a truce: "No bets, you two. We have work to do." Or maybe he said those words to placate Milagros, who had just sauntered into the kitchen, to suggest to her that he repented of that wager he had slapped down on a table so many years ago.

"Where are you off to?" Milagros asked.

"Going to see his Tío Pancho," my father answered. "And then Pablo set up a meeting with Jorge Larrea. You remember him? Pinochet's minister of finance?"

"The guy who married Pocha Alvárez?" my mother said.

"Pochita Alvárez," Polo said. *"M'hijita rica."*

My father frowned at this vulgar revelation of their intimacy with Larrea's wife. Not in front of Milagros, you idiot! he seemed to be saying. Polo's smug smile vanished.

"That guy," my father confirmed. "Well, he's coordinating that iceberg project which Gabriel here is interested in finding out more about. Some article our son says he wants to write."

"Oh, really?" My mother looked at me inquisitively. "I didn't know you had agreed to do some work here."

"Just something," I said, "I might peddle back in the States."

Mom said nothing more. She had long since learned, I guess, that when a woman interrupts a male ritual, a locker room confrontation or a Boy Scout bonding ceremony, the best thing is to let the little boys play. Though that didn't stop her, as I was following my father and Polo out to the car, from taking me aside to find out how this *retorno* had been treating me.

She didn't look all that happy, my mom. She had bags under her eyes the likes of which I hadn't seen in years. I hadn't burdened her with the sorrows of young Gabriel back in New York, when she'd been carefree and sure of herself; now that she seemed so stressed, trying as she was to retain a hold on the country she had lost for seventeen years, it seemed even less appropriate to give her a full blown confession of my whole saga of fathers lost and virginity retained. I could manage on my own as I had all this time.

"How are things with your father?" she insisted. "I saw you both talking last night down in the yard. I was watching from my window."

Had she been watching to see how I was doing or to see if he was coming up to visit her bedroom?

I didn't ask.

"Things are great," I said.

"How about friends? You want me to contact any of my—"

"I'm fine," I said. "Amanda Camila will set me up. I'm sure she'll take care of me. I'll see her at lunchtime."

"She's nice," my mom said. "Don't you think? Attractive?"

"Nice," I said, "but not my type."

"I thought you sort of—well, took to her."

"Definitely not my type," I lied.

"So nothing's wrong?"

She suspected something. I had to give her one morsel, one problem, so she wouldn't feel left out.

"It's just that my computer blew last night. Forgot the transformer."

Ever anxious to help, she offered to take it to Pablo Barón's house. I thanked her and headed for the car, scarf floating in the crisp, clear breeze, ready to face Polo's sarcastic gaze and interrogate my father's suddenly nervous body movements, as if he wanted to scratch, but had no hands. Maybe he worried like this whenever he visited his jailed brother in order to inform him one more time that there was hope for a reprieve that somehow never materialized. Maybe he'd already brought his brother the solemn promise of the *Ministro* to get him the hell out of there and nothing had ever worked out.

Not that Tío Pancho believed a word of it this time.

"That son of a bitch?"

His words echoed loudly in the immense dank room filled with prisoners and their frigid families, huddled on makeshift stools. In a nearby corner an ill-shaven muscular man—young, he was so young—was nuzzling a woman, had seated her on his lap, was practically balling her in front of us all, including a little kid and some guards. They didn't seem to mind; they walked past the couple, went on to other taciturn gray convicts and their wives or mothers or sisters, all uniformly dressed in something drab and dim, as if they knew color would not register anyway in that icy gloom barely lit by dusty sunbeams filtering in through the high gratings. I looked up, caught a glimpse of two sad bulbs ineffectually sputtering high on the rough cement walls, seeming to leak darkness down to us instead of light. This was a high-security penitentiary? With its metal-detector machines on the blink, with its sleepy wardens more intent on picking their teeth than going through our clothes? I could spring my uncle out of this replica of a Dickensian debtors' prison, we could do it in a snap. We didn't need Pablo Barón.

Tío Pancho didn't seem to feel he needed him either. In fact, he had no use for him.

"*Ese traidor*," he bellowed, rousing everyone in the room. The guards stopped pacing, the nearby prisoner and his lover interrupted their jerky bustle for a second, men and women lifted their heads and stared, then everything went back to normal, fogging the frost in the air with their sad breath. They seemed to be used to these outbursts. "That traitor! That neoliberal Pinochet cocksucker. When he was in the resistance, *sobrino*, do you know what he used to say about the economic model, about capitalism gone mad, about Milton Friedman and his free market? When Barón was fighting the dictatorship? Tell him, Cris, tell your son what—"

"I couldn't care less what he said," my father interjected. "He's the best bet I have of getting you out of here."

"I'm not leaving until we're all free," Tío Pancho said. "No privileges. No favors from people who once said they wanted to end misery and now just continue Pinochet's policies. Have you taken him to the hospitals, Cris? Have you taken Gaby to see how patients have to bring their own cotton, their own aspirin, because there's no—"

"He just arrived yesterday," my father said. "He hasn't come here to see hospitals. He's come to see us, to see his family. Why don't you calm down?"

"I'll calm down when I'm dead," came the belligerent answer. "I'll calm down when there are no more people without shoes and without schooling and without jobs, that's when I'll calm down. Gabriel, do you know how many people in the world live on less than a dollar a day? Do you?"

"Leave the kid alone," my father said, but I answered no.

"One point three billion. Almost one and a half billion. In 1960, the richest 20 percent owned 70 percent of the world's wealth. You know how much it is now, after globalization, now that the Pablo Baróns are in charge, sucking imperialist and multicorporate tit? The richest presently have 85 percent. And the poorest? They used to own 2.3 percent. Now they own 1.1. And here in Chile, it's getting worse as well, it's—"

"Statistics say it's getting better," Polo said.

"Statistics." Tío Pancho snorted. "You twist them this way, you twist them the other. Take him to La Pintana, Cris, take my nephew to La Pintana to see if things are getting better."

They began squabbling as if they were both still children. My father told him that politics didn't interest me, or him, or anybody, for that matter, and that Pancho should have listened to him when Che died; and my uncle accused my father of being responsible for the sorry state of Chile, people like him who sat back and didn't care, who hadn't participated during the Allende years and hadn't done anything to stop Pinochet; and my father was glad he'd done nothing, because now he'd be in jail like Pancho; and Pancho answered that Cris was scared of being in jail because he would've lost his bet and couldn't have screwed the brains out of every woman in the world.

Which was when Polo broke the tension. "Maybe you'd like us to smuggle a woman in, Pancho. I think we could get a couple of willing *minas*. Tried and tested."

"Women soften you," my uncle declared. "They tie you down, want to burden you with a family. That's why Lenin never had children. That was your mistake, Cris. Until you met Milagros, you were—"

My father stood up. He had enough. He didn't know why he had even bothered to visit his brother. He had warned him last week that he was coming with Gabriel, had asked him to behave, and they had agreed that they would steer clear of controversy, hadn't they agreed to make Gabriel feel comfortable? He had work to do. Goodbye.

My father started to move across the room. I said to his back, "I'm staying here a bit more with Tío Pancho, Dad."

My father looked at me. For the second time this morning, I was showing an autonomy that must have surprised him, perhaps pleased him. He nodded. "I'll be with the head warden," he said, and went off, Polo hot behind.

"He's not a bad man," my uncle said quietly, once my father was out of range. "The head warden owes him a favor. He was once a runaway himself and Cris brought him back, solved his problem. Now the guy makes sure that I'm well-treated, that nobody—you know, touches me. I appreciate it, don't think I don't. Cris thinks I'm too loud. But I'm not loud. It's the rest of the world that is silent, that's all."

My father had warned me that his brother was moody, given to wild temperamental swings. "They hurt him, you know," my dad explained in the car as we hurtled toward the Peni, drinking in the glorious sun of a day when everybody should have been free to wander under the snow-smothered Andes. "To make him confess. He kept insisting he was innocent, till finally they—broke him, I guess. Ever since then he's . . . " But that had not prepared me for the intemperate explosion of words I had just heard or even less for the peaceful and almost diffident Tío Pancho who now sat in front of me musing about his brother.

"I was rowdy today," he said, "on purpose. I wanted to get rid of him, wanted to be alone with you."

He was cannier than I had been led to believe. Did anybody in Chile ever tell the truth, directly state what they thought and why?

"You wanted to be alone with me. What for?"

"So you can tell me what's really going on. What Pablo wants so bad that he's ready to trade it for my freedom."

I told him about the threat, about Dad's suspicion.

"Someone's out to get that iceberg, huh?" my uncle said. "Well, you can bet your ass it's not Barón. He wouldn't jeopardize his plans for Sevilla just to win a stupid bet. No, it's Cris who's obsessed with winning. I wouldn't be surprised if the *Ministro* thinks that's who's behind the threat: my brother, Cris trying to see if he can make that bastard Barón lose his job—and the bet."

"My father sent the letter?"

"Maybe. Maybe that's why Pablo called Cris in, to keep an eye on him. That's what this country has turned into: all people care about is gouging the other guy's eyes out, rising to the top of the heap. Compete and then compete some more."

"Couldn't it be something simpler," I suggested. "Some of your comrades, for instance, striking back at the government for the reasons you just expressed, protesting a democracy that keeps people like you in jail."

"I don't think so. I would have heard about it. But now that you mention it, maybe that's not such a bad idea, blowing the thing to smithereens. Have you seen it?"

I told him only a replica but that I was already entranced with its wonder and mystery, and he immediately launched into a diatribe against the iceberg, its transparency and whiteness and cleanliness (even though I tried to explain that it was bluish and beautiful). He saw it as a symbol of the whitewashed world that Chile had become, wants to become. With no blood, no smelly old shoes, no military boots, nothing that would disturb the blankness of a country that wishes to forget its pain, shut the door on its past, not see its own reflection in the mirror, rush into a modernity that will make it even less independent.

I tried to reason with him. For all his eccentricity, I had the impression that here was the first person in Chile giving me any real respect, who did not want to use me, who could not, in fact, use me at all, given that in a few more minutes he would be back in a cell a hundred times more dismal than this pitiless room, and I would be free to roam the streets looking for the man who wanted to destroy the iceberg I was trying to describe to my uncle. "You know what I felt? Looking at it, through it, I felt as if it could give me back something I'd lost forever, some sort of paradise that—and I wasn't alone, my father also felt—"

"Right, you're both looking for paradise in a piece of unpolluted nature. Who isn't? Certain objects in nature, in art, I do understand. Engels once said something about how that brought out the use-value of—at least I think it was Engels. But listen, all the ice in the world and all the world's fairs aren't as valuable as an old man who's dying by his sad self in some ditch somewhere and who's worked his whole life and hasn't even got a bed, not even a hand to comfort him. I'd trade all the pictures in all the museums in the world so that old man could die with a smile."

I stopped arguing with him. You don't argue with a man who is in jail because of what he believes in, you don't try to take away what that man needs in order to survive, to convince himself that it was worth it.

"I've got to go, Tío Pancho."

I hugged him, felt his body shaking against mine.

"Let them blow it up, Gabriel," he whispered into my ear intensely, as if this were his last message on this earth. "Help them blow the motherfucker into the sky."

I let go of him and took a step backward. He was a lovely man, he was my uncle, he was out of his mind.

"I don't think I want to see that iceberg die, Tío."

"What if it's me, there, with dynamite in one hand and a match in the other? Would you stop me, would you shoot me down to save Pablo Barón's iceberg?"

"I've never shot anyone in my life," I said, "so I don't think I'm going to start now."

"Never too late to begin."

This was sounding like a bad gangster film. Though given how violently things have ended up here in Sevilla, it turned out to be rather anticipatory, that conversation.

"I'll come back and see you again, Tío."

"One thing, *niño*." My Tío Pancho took out a ballpoint and scrawled some words on a piece of paper. "I'm expecting you to come visit, Gaby," he said. "This Sunday. Without your father and his dick talk, so we can really get to know each other." He crumpled the paper into my hand and was gone.

As I moved toward the exit, a guard blocked my way, wanted to know what I was hiding in my hand. These guys were not as dumb as they seemed. Maybe they just pretended to be asleep to con naive New Yorkers like me into making fools of themselves. I opened my fist, smoothed the creases out of the paper, read it, said to the guard, "It's just a message from my uncle."

"No messages get smuggled out of here, gringo."

"It's something personal."

"Now I can't tell that until I've read it, can I?" He snapped his fingers impatiently.

"IF YOU WANT TO GET LAID IN THIS COUNTRY," the guard slowly spelled out the syllables of my uncle's message, "YOU'D BETTER START LOVING IT." He looked at me. "What the fuck does that mean?"

"Ask him. I didn't write it."

"I'm not going to ask him anything, that madman. If he weren't Cristóbal McKenzie's brother, we'd—"

"You'd what?"

"We'd teach him some manners."

I was thinking about what that meant as I made my way outside, past the pale prisoners and their haggard relatives and their heavy-lidded guardians. My father was waiting by the broken-down metal detector, speaking to a woman in dark clothes, while Polo hovered nearby.

"No," my father was saying, "I'm sorry, but I really can't."

"Just tell me where he is, if my missing Enriquito is alive or dead. Just that. You come to my house, to his room, you sit on his bed, and you tell me where they've got him. His bed's just the way it was the day they took him away, Don Cristóbal."

"If he'd left of his own free will, I'd be glad to accept his case. I think we already discussed this. But given that he was arrested by the secret police—"

"Well, they used to say he had gone off with some girl, that's what they'd say every time I asked about him. 'He's gone off with some girl,' they'd say, 'grew tired of living with his ugly mother.' You could take his case based on what they said."

"Yes, ma'am," my father said quietly, "but we know that isn't true. It wasn't true back then and it's even less true now that the boy has been recognized as officially dead by the new democratic government. So I really can't—"

"Then where's his body? If he's dead, where's his body, you tell me that. Or help me find it, you could—"

"I really have to go," my father said, turning toward me and taking hold of my arm.

The woman looked at us both. Her eyes were dead and yet they burned into me as if they were on fire.

"This is your boy," the woman said. "I can tell he's your boy. If they'd taken him, what would you—"

"I'd be coming up to a detective like me and he would say what I'm telling you: I don't do kidnappings, I don't do politics, I don't do murder."

"You don't love him," the woman said suddenly. "If you loved your son, you'd help me."

My father didn't answer. He steered me out of the prison, left her and her dead burning eyes behind, walked me to the car.

Inside it, he said, "You're shocked."

He had misread the look I was giving him. I wasn't reproaching him for his treatment of her. He had done just what I had done that night in SoHo, he had turned his back, I had turned mine, on this sort of pain, these problems, protected ourselves. What I resented was his attitude not toward her but toward me, the fact that it was true that he didn't give a damn about his son. Even if I was more like him than he realized.

"I can't help that woman," my father insisted. "Nobody can help her. She first came to me fifteen years ago, she grabs me every chance she gets. I always treat her with respect. But I'm not getting involved. You learn to stay out of it, above it, beyond it, away, away, away—as far as you can go. Like you. You went away, you and your mother got out of here as fast as you could."

"I was six years old."

"You could have come back sooner. When your grandmother died, you were nineteen. Nobody was holding you back. So don't blame me for keeping my distance."

It was not clear if he was referring to his distance from that woman or his distance from me now or his general distance from everything and anything that was not the pain of youngsters who had run away from home. To them he gave the same warmth he had transmitted to me in his letters over the years. Or had his warmth drained away like a dead rabbit bleeding into one vagina after another, one dizzy night after the other for almost a quarter of a century, had he exhausted all his tenderness in that endless stream of Chilean pillows he probably could not even recall?

We didn't speak for the next fifteen minutes. We were stuck in a traffic jam. Horns reverberated, taxi drivers shouted insults, the smog and the blue fumes from exhaust pipes seeped into the car, already hazy from the cigarettes that Polo and my father had lit up even before the engine was turned on. Incredibly, I saw a Chevy the color of vomit charging by on our left side, oblivious to a stream of oncoming cars heading toward it. They swerved to the side to avoid it. The driver was hunched determinedly into his seat, spitting words urgently into a cellular phone. He stopped a few yards in front of us, blowing his horn belligerently so the drivers he had passed would open a space for him to slip in—which they were just as belligerently disinclined to do, even if the result was to snarl up traffic even more.

"That guy's crazy," I said. "Doesn't he realize he's just making matters worse?"

"He does it before anybody else does it first," my dad said, as another car followed his example and sped past us, almost bumping the Chevy. "That's what happens when you have a country full of people who don't give a fuck about anybody but themselves."

"So I've seen," I said.

My father looked at me. Did he think I was alluding to him, to him and me, to him and the woman? Did he think I was being sarcastic at his expense? Whatever my intention, Cristóbal McKenzie took it the wrong way. He opened the door of the car. "I'm out of here," he said. It seemed to be one of those days he would spend running away from his male kin.

"You're not coming with me to see Jorge Larrea?"

"Waste of time," my father said. "I'm going to be late—something else I have to do." I could imagine what it was, the waitress, some other syrupy young thing, waiting, another bed to sample, another liquid sliver of heat to ooze out of his body. Or maybe just a pretext to run. "Polo, you take the kid to Larrea's, then come and pick me up at three—you know where."

"Wait a second—who's taking me to Amanda's house?"

"That's taken care of," Polo said. "You'll see."

"At three," my father repeated, half his body already out of the car.

"We're taking the case of the missing twins?" Polo asked.

"We could do with the money," my father said. "The iceberg's only giving us headaches so far, right? See you tonight, Gabriel—you know where."

Before I could ask him what he meant, where was where, he was gone. I saw him weave his way among the jammed cars and disappear into a fog of horns, catcalls, and gas fumes.

"He's having a hard time," Polo said. "I don't think he's making much headway with your mom."

"I don't think that's any of your business."

"McKenzie's business is my business," Polo said without a hint of hostility in his voice.

"You do much business?"

"Tons. We could branch out, bring in new detectives, service a whole range of other issues. You know what's invaluable in this business, in any business? Brand recognition. Parents know that Cristóbal McKenzie delivers. And every year that passes it's getting easier: we've got all these people who owe us favors. But even if we didn't, brand recognition, market position, does the trick. Just like women, you know."

"Women?" I asked. I shouldn't have asked. It was something I had to speak to my father about, my father and nobody else, but I couldn't help myself: if yesterday and today were at all typical, I wasn't going to get much of a chance at playing Twenty Questions or even One Big Question with the great Cristóbal McKenzie.

Polo nodded. "Women, Cara de Guagua." The car ahead of us inched forward; it seemed the traffic might be starting to ease up. Polo pressed his horn with joyous ferocity and accelerated. "Women go for him—well, they can guess that he's got magic, can make them go whooooosh, yesssss, yes, they know, women do. But it's not only that, it's the brand recognition. They've heard he's screwed so many, they don't know how many, nobody really knows that there's a bet on—strange in this country where we end up finding out everything—all they know is that this guy is hot and that's enough. They want to try the merchandise, see what all the fuss is about. So before he even sticks it in, they're ready to come, explode. They expect to be nicely fucked and their expectations are met, not much different from the McKenzie Detective Agency. But it takes a long time to create a reputation, let me tell you." The car was now speeding along and Polo threw out his third cigarette of the ride, barely missing a street vendor who was selling overgrown shiny green avocados in the middle of the avenue. "Once you're famous for doing one thing, that thing becomes *chancaca*—everything flows. And the other men are in such awe that not even the cornuto husbands seek revenge. They want autographs. Advice! Of course, there's a down side to all of this, Cara de Guagua. You know what it is?"

I had a feeling he was going to tell me.

"If you start getting a bad rep, a bad rap—that's it, in war, in business, and with women. It clings to you forever. If you know what I mean."

I knew what he meant.

We had arrived at Larrea's headquarters. The building was made of dark glass, glittering above us in the smog. I didn't want Polo to accompany me up to the seventh floor to the Expo '92 offices. Anyway, he'd be more than happy to leave me alone, glad to spend the next few hours hunting down the woman my father had nailed yesterday, the plump specimen from the neighborhood. But to be courteous I said, "You coming with me?"

"Waste of time," Polo echoed my father's words. "We already fucked Larrea's wife, cute-ass Pochita."

"You fuck everything my father fucks?"

"Not everything. But I get around. If you get close enough to him, maybe you'll snatch some pussy too."

And with that comforting prophecy, Polo was gone.

I came away from the offices that housed the iceberg project with three suspects. No, make that three and a half. Not a bad harvest for one morning.

First of all, Jorge Larrea himself. The silver-haired man who last night lavished ice from Antarctica on the whiskey-thirsty throngs at the inauguration, the very person in charge of the operation and obsessed with separating Chile from a Latin America of siestas, disasters, and bloodshed. Here is a chance, he said, for people abroad to think of Chile as a place like New Zealand or Hong Kong, full of industrious, responsible, efficient people, not swarming with lazy Che Guevara look-alikes bitching about the past, begging for help. Self-reliance. Independence. Prosperity.

He expounded his theories as he wheeled me through the different cubicles where Expo '92 was being designed—400,000 boxes, the sculptures, the sound. He pressed a cassette into my hands, *El Túnel de los Sonidos*, the noises that will greet the crowds as they come into the pavilion on their way to the iceberg, the multiple sounds that contain and represent Chile. He steered me from room to room, down grand expanses of light, curving corridors of pale creamlike wood, ceilings aglow with translucent copper wires, abstract paintings of masks in soft colors and with quiet contours. Until finally, with his enthusiastic hand on my unenthusiastic shoulder (this was definitely the national custom, my shoulder as bait and somebody else's knuckles as hook), we came to the heart of the project: refrigeration, the reason why he had signed up to direct it.

Larrea showed me a model of the system that would keep the iceberg cold, showed me diagrams of wires and contraptions and thermostats and tubes and auxiliary vents, and I should have been paying attention—this was where the saboteur would strike, if at all—but I couldn't listen closely to the bewildering details, because Larrea had extracted from a small wooden box tinctured with the Chilean flag, in order to illustrate exactly where the iceberg would be in the pavilion, at the far end of—what do you think he brought out of that box? He brought out a piece of pale blue paper, the exact size of the one on which someone anonymous had transcribed the threat to the iceberg in block letters, and it was in block letters now that Larrea's hands scrawled the word ICEBERG and then passed the sheet to me and I suddenly remembered that I had kept the original in the pocket of my jeans back at the Casa Milagros. I scrutinized this piece of paper just like I had that one less than twenty-four hours ago, and I was hard put to conceal the beating of my heart. Maybe he had written that letter himself? But why? Without a motive, every detective story always tells you, there is no crime.

And then, almost as if he had read my mind, he spelled it out: What might make Jorge Larrea menace his own pet project.

"When they came to me with this idea, back in 1988, I was no longer the general's minister of finance. I was bored, looking for something to do . . . But first, let me tell you about my family." Larrea looked at me anxiously. I began to take notes, the diligent Yankee reporter. "My dad did something fifty years ago that nobody thought could be done: he started to manufacture refrigerators, our own Chilean brand, right here in this country. Marca Conquistador. Conquistador. You know why? Because my ancestor, twenty-five generations back, came over with Diego de Almagro, 1532, when Chile was discovered. That expedition failed. But he came back for more with Pedro de Valdivia, the first Larrea. They crossed the *cordillera* at the San Fernando pass and the horses began to stumble and die in the cold. Not to mention the Indians, who were used to more tropical weather. And a few months later other conquistadores came down that same pass and ate the horses, were saved by eating the horses that had been preserved by the snow. That's when the first Larrea learned that all power starts and ends with ice, and his sons and grandsons transmitted that vision to their descendants; we all grew up swearing by the gods of ice. My ancestors were the first landowners to think that food could be kept forever if you just had enough cold at your disposal. They would send their *indios* up into the mountains to bring back ice for the wine. Chilled wine in summer. Nothing better. You see this finger?"

He showed me the finger that had worked on my shoulder, that had just spelled out the word ICEBERG, that might have spelled out the words COMMANDANTE a few days ago. There was something smoky and pale about it.

"When I was a kid, I put my finger in the freezer. I bet my eldest brother who could keep it there longer. I won, *carajo*. I've got no feeling in it, it's been numb ever since. But I showed him who loved the ice more, who was the real son of our father, who could have survived that first expedition across the Andes with the Calchaquí Indians attacking them while their feet bled from stones that were like knives. And now, I'm going to take the ice back to Spain. I'll bring back to the Larreas that stayed behind and did not dare brave the oceans and the deserts of America, I'll bring them more ice than they could ever have dreamed of."

And it was here that the revelation came. He leaned forward as if he were ready to share a secret with me, whispered hoarsely across the blueprints and models of the machine that was supposed to keep the iceberg from ever melting. "There's something missing," he said. "It's an adventure, oh yes. We have so much going against us. Can we make it down to Antarctica? Will we be able to capture our white beauty? We're talking about hundreds of tons of ice, about breaking a floating mountain into pieces in the midst of waves thirty feet high. And then there's the question of whether our refrigeration system will work. But something's missing. You know what I'd like? I'd like somebody to try and melt it, that's what I'm looking forward to."

"There've been threats?" Trying to stay composed.

"Not yet, damn it. But I'm hoping, I'm praying."

"You want somebody to destroy the iceberg?"

"I want them to try. I want somebody out there who hates it as much as I love it, I want him to make the attempt. That'd get me going. Let me tell you when I felt most alive ever. Write this down, go on, it'll let your foreign readers understand a thing or two. You know when? When Allende wanted to expropriate our refrigerator factory back in the early seventies. Yes, the socialists wanted to turn it over to the workers. As if they had any idea how to run it. Run it into the ground, that's what they wanted to do. And we fought them, we beat the shit out of them, we won. Chile, *país ganador*, a country that knows how to win."

He looked at me.

"I know, I know. You've got an uncle who's in jail. History hasn't been kind to him. And it can't be easy for your family. But don't forget that if that uncle of yours had had his way, we'd all be suffering under the terror of a communist dictatorship, the Andes would be our Berlin Wall, that's what would have happened if Allende hadn't been overthrown, if people like your uncle had got their way. Allende was a democrat, I'll grant him that much, but a dupe. Like Kerensky. The people who would have used him, the Soviets, the Cubans? Bad people. And our economy? In ruins. No economic miracle, no growth year after year, no dynamic middle class, everybody dressed in drab uniforms, everybody marching to the same tune. But that's not what happened. Your uncle lost and Chile won. No drab, dull uniforms at Chile-Expo. Here, let me show you one last exhibit."

He moved me into the next room.

I thought to myself, Maybe he's delusional. Maybe he wrote the letter to give himself a thrill, wrote it and then forgot he'd done the writing. Maybe he needed to feel under siege, with an enemy out there trying to gun him and his iceberg down.

My thoughts stopped there, because who do you think was waiting for me in that next room?

Amanda Camila.

"What are you doing here?" I asked her, flabbergasted.

"I work here," Amanda Camila said, smiling like a princess, curtseying.

"She's one of our hostesses," Larrea said. "Our happiest hostess. Bubbling with enthusiasm."

"My dad decided it was what I needed," she added cheerfully, "and who am I to disagree with him?"

"Take a look at those clothes," Larrea said, as if he were announcing a fashion show.

Amanda Camila was wearing attire that both was and wasn't a uniform: a white blouse, a short brown skirt that dropped in effortless pleats to her knees, and a sort of blue-black smock that let you guess at her body but not too much, that hid something delicately at the same time. I was surprised because it was so chic, so up-to-date, and yet whoever had designed those clothes had also managed to keep sexuality somehow under wraps, subdued, almost restrained. As if I were being invited to take a peek and then right away were forbidden to go any further, really view what was beneath.

At that moment, another hostess, blond hair flowing, entered. "*Ministro* Barón for you, Don Jorge. Phone call in your office."

"I'll take it there, Laura."

He left me to admire the dresses of both young women. "That's the new Chile, my friend," he said as he sped out the door, "loose, contemporary, individualistic, unified in one common purpose." Laura had a blue-black jumpsuit flowing down her thighs and a brown frock covering it, the colors the same, the arrangement different, everything interchangeable with my Amanda's outfit or those of the other hostesses flitting through the corridors, flagrantly showing and shielding their bodies. Laura herself was about to leave when Amanda said, "Don't you want to meet Gabriel McKenzie?"

Laura turned. "McKenzie? Any relation to Cristóbal McKenzie?"

"His son."

I thought I caught a lewd look emerging like an animal onto the night of Laura's face. Could that look, which seemed to whisper an invitation to come-by-and-see-me-later be for me or was I, once again, merely a proxy for my legendary dad? Something in me began to undress her in my mind, the father that I had inside my brain started to disrobe her. She saw what I was doing, she pressed forward to peck my cheek, and I smelled her breasts and she sighed my name into my ears as if we were already under a hot shower and I could feel her nipples hard against my chest. Or was I making it all up, was I going crazy?

Maybe I would have gone crazy, locked the door, barricaded myself in, grabbed one of Laura's breasts in one of my ripe hands and grabbed one of Amanda's in the other one for good measure, stripped those dresses so carefully crafted to tease me and every male here and in Sevilla, maybe I would have ended up burying my head in their crotches and begging them for mercy, if we had not been interrupted by a fair-haired young man looking like a fashion model, who entered the room in search of Laura, his jacket the same warm brown as Amanda Camila's skirt while his black trousers contrasted with a turquoise blue shirt loosely buttoned at a tieless virile neck. I hated him instantly.

I had dressed up for the morning. Not wanting to have another run-in with the police and determined to play the hip New York reporter, I had shed my backwards baseball cap and faded jeans for a suit and tie, but in the presence of this Adonis and his Armani-like color scheme, his slim buttocks, his absolute composure, I felt painfully inadequate. I'm glad to report that he wasn't with us for more than ten seconds, just enough time to depart through the same door he had entered, towing lovely Laura along, just enough time for Laura to send one last luscious look my way and disappear—from the room and from my life. No problem: Amanda Camila stayed behind and the hug she gave me, tight, more than compensated for the loss of Laura. My fickle heart remembered that I was supposed to screw Amanda Camila and nobody else on this voyage of Discovery.

"Oh, I'm so glad you're here, Gabriel." She let me go. Much too soon for my taste. "This place is *so* boring."

"You don't look that bored."

"I'm supposed to look happy. They all are, the idiots." She waved her ravishing thumb that I would have gladly put in my mouth and sucked for a whole hour, waved it like a wand toward several smart, sexy, swaying girls in the corridor outside who were playing their hostess duties, all of them blond and pale and not really Chilean-looking at all. "I hate this place, this stupid project. I hope somebody fucks that damn iceberg."

Culear. She had used the very word found in the letter. And could have used the stationery from Larrea's office. And seemed angry enough—and mischievous enough, if my father's idea of a prank held any water—to do it. My second suspect!

I probed further. "You sure have Larrea fooled."

"I do. I do and I can. Fool him. I can fool anybody. Years under old Pinochet make for great training. My dad, for instance, my dad hasn't got a clue to what I'm thinking, he supposes I'm Miss Happy Times."

"And you're not?"

"Now that you're here, yes. You're my pretext to escape, taking you home for lunch. You are a darling, Gabriel."

"How long have you been around the project?"

"Since the start, I guess. Dad's been plotting with Larrea for a whole year now. Why d'you want to know?"

"I was just wondering. In the States, if they were working on something this sensitive, that has public opinion divided, there would be all sorts of security measures. I didn't even see a guard."

"There's no need for security. Some people may not like the iceberg much—"

"Like you."

"And most of my friends. But they're not going to do anything, well, violent, Gabriel. People in this country talk a lot of violence, but now that there's democracy, they're not going to do anything, you know. I mean, it took ten years before anybody even tried to kill Pinochet. Talk about patience!"

"But suppose you wanted to, say, melt the iceberg, how would you go about doing it?"

She laughed at this. Much too matter-of-fact for my taste. "Melt the iceberg? It hasn't even been captured. How could anybody . . . ?"

As if on cue, Larrea poked his silvery head through the door. "Time to go, Amanda. Your father's already at home, said you were both to have been there half an hour ago."

"I haven't quite finished," I said. "We'll—"

"It's all right," Larrea said. "Come back in the afternoon. Nobody keeps the *Ministro* waiting. Not even his hotshot reporter *sobrino* from Nueva York. Amanda, get your car and meet young Don McKenzie in front of the building in around ten minutes."

"He can come with me."

"I said you're to meet him in ten minutes."

As soon as she was safely, albeit reluctantly, out of the way, Larrea turned to me and said, just like that, "So you're worried about the iceberg, eh, Gabriel? About somebody melting it, huh?"

Had he been listening at the door? Or was he just guessing? "Not really," I said, trying to sound casual.

He walked me toward the exit. "I think you are."

"Well, you gave me the idea yourself. Maybe you've heard something you'd like to share with me. Off the record."

"I haven't heard a thing. Wish I had." He popped into his office to get his pipe. "In this country, we always end up knowing everything."

Behind him, on his desk, I saw a prominent portrait of his wife, Pochita, of the cute ass.

"Not everything," I said to him.

"Tell you what," Larrea said, accompanying me to the elevator and savagely pressing the down button with that finger of his he had frozen to prove he was worthy of his conquistador forefathers, pressed it as if it were his enemy who had wanted to take his factory away, his iceberg away, his honor away. I hoped he didn't know that my father had made him into the Cornuto of the Conquistadors, though I wouldn't have minded if silver-haired Larrea, who seemed in pretty good physical shape, were to deliver a couple of swift, well-deserved kicks to Polo. "If you hear about anything, you let me know, and I'll do the same for you."

"It's a deal. But you must have somebody you suspect already or you wouldn't . . ."

As soon as we were in the elevator and the doors had closed behind us, Larrea said: "No microphones here." He smiled bitterly. "You know, our project is like the country, it brings together people like me who worked for the military regime with our opponents, people who used to be Allendistas. They form the bulk of the staff, the creative talent, of this project. Architects, filmmakers, sociologists, sculptors, you'll meet the lot of them. They also want a new Chile, like I do. Or so they say. Because I can't help but wonder if it's not all a sham, if some resentful revolutionary hasn't infiltrated our organization. Off the record, right, Gabriel?"

I nodded. My nonexistent paper in New York would never publish his revelations.

"I just don't trust former revolutionaries when they say they're tired of a Chile that feels sorry for itself. So at first I suspected they might want to sink the iceberg. Then I'd be like Columbus, I thought, with a saboteur on board."

We were now out on the street and not even the smog that had enveloped the city, turning its glory of the morning into a sullen over-cast gray, could abate his musings. He went on, obsessively. "Of late, however, I've discarded the idea of an inside traitor. I'm focusing on someone else. I came down here with you so you could meet her." He only stopped talking because at that very moment we were accosted by Cristina Ferrer, my dainty journalist from yesterday, who gave Larrea a rapid kiss on the cheek and then turned to repeat the ceremony with me. "Why, it's Gabriel McKenzie, what a pleasant surprise!" she hooted. Embracing me, she hissed into my ear an invitation to join them for lunch. It would be so boring if I didn't come. Was every woman in Chile really this bored? Her breath was humid and she was almost panting, apparently still in search of her second adventure with the notorious McKenzie genitalia that in my case were feeling rather downcast and depressed.

And more so when I glimpsed a second woman who all this while had stood to one side with distaste as she watched the spectacle of Cristina pecking at male cheeks. She was a tall, angular lady, severe in her features and parsimonious in her dress and undoubtedly both severe and parsimonious in the underendowed body that, as luck would have it, was well hidden inside that spinster's dress.

"Gabriel McKenzie," she said, and the way she repeated my name indicated she had no intention of inviting me to share her flesh; even a lip brushing a cheek would be horribly promiscuous. "You must be the son of Cristóbal McKenzie."

"Yes," I fluttered, hoping she wasn't a relative so I wouldn't have to give her a hug, "and you are . . . ?"

She heaped shame on me. My father had resolutely refused to lend his name to her campaigns. He hadn't, I gathered, participated in the plebiscite against the dictator, hadn't been interested in helping organize the soup kitchens, couldn't care less about the attempt to save the forests down south from the Japanese or to enforce a temporary restriction on whaling more recently.

I finally managed to stop her onslaught by reminding her that I was not my father. Her cascade of insults was replaced by a smile, if what trespassed across her lips could be called that. She suggested I rescue the family name by signing a protest against the defacement of Antarctica by the Expo '92 people.

A protest! So this was the suspect that Larrea wanted me to meet, here she was, heaving into view on a horizon that was already quite crowded. This woman was certainly well suited, if anyone was, to the task of iceberg busting. And if she had an inside partner who had smuggled her some of the stationery of the Expo '92 office . . .

"All they do all day is circulate protests," Larrea mocked her. "That nobody reads and that cost more money to print and circulate than it would take to buy some land and plant some trees. That is, if you're really interested in saving our ozone. Eh, Berta?"

Berta made believe Larrea hadn't spoken.

"There's no other place like it left on this globe," she said to me, her face softening, almost fattening. "Have you been there? To Antarctica?"

"No, but I'd love to—"

"He's going to come with us," Larrea interjected, "to bring the iceberg home."

"The iceberg is at home," our ecological friend answered. "That's where it belongs. And we'll do anything we can to keep it there."

"Anything?" I said, scenting possible violence.

But the violence came not from her but rather, on a day when each new event seemed designed to surprise me more than the previous one, from a paunchy man who rollicked out of nowhere. At least it seemed like nowhere, because I didn't see him advance until he punched Jorge Larrea squarely in the face and sent him sprawling on the sidewalk.

Larrea remained there for a second, blood dripping profusely from his nose, while the man glowered above, his fist still clenched, slopping drunken words at him. "That'll teach you, *hijo de la gran puta*, you and your fucking *conchudo* iceberg. That'll make you think twice before insulting me."

If Larrea was thinking twice about anything, it was not about ceasing to insult the man. On the contrary, he arose with an alacrity that belied his sixty or so years and, handing me his glasses as if I were his manager in the ring, with two swift blows, one straight to the stomach and an uppercut to the jaw, knocked the man to the ground.

It happened so quickly that I hardly knew how to react.

"Who is he?" I asked Larrea, as Cristina applied a handkerchief to the spurting fountain of his nose, while Berta attended to the stricken adversary, who lay moaning at our feet.

"Never seen this *maricón* in my life," Larrea said.

Just then, Amanda Camila's car screeched to a halt right in front of us. She didn't leave the driver's seat to find out what was going on, merely observed us all through the window as if it were a TV screen and we were performing a soap opera for her entertainment.

"Your ride," Larrea said to me, "has arrived."

I protested that we should call the police, take him to the hospital. He literally pushed me into the waiting Subaru. He would be all right, he said. He'd debate Berta over lunch as planned.

Amanda Camila accelerated. From what I could see in the rear-view mirror, the debate had already begun there on the blood-dripped sidewalk, two of my suspects going at each other with gusto while the other one, the sweet third suspect, maneuvered our car away from that confrontation.

"Well," I said, "there goes your theory that nobody wants to do violence to the iceberg."

"You think this incident's related to the iceberg?"

"Isn't it?"

"You know what I love about you, Gabriel? You are so naive, such a perfect gringo. That's why I feel so safe with you. These men here, all they want is to paw you, get you under the blankets or on the backseat, and give you a good poke." Her hand reached over from the stick shift and lightly skimmed my arm. It was like a current of delicate electricity passing into me. A hard-on began forming you-know-where. "But you, Gaby, I knew the moment we met that I could trust you. You can't imagine how wonderful it is for a girl to feel that sort of friendship."

You would have thought that every dismal fraternal word with which she was praising my supposed innocence would have dampened my phallic enthusiasm, but the subject in question was only aching and arching upwards under my pants with greater fury than ever, anxious to unzipper itself and prove her instantly wrong. I tried to tame its impetus by interrupting her. "Wait," I said, "what does any of this have to do with what I just saw? That man attacked Larrea because of the iceberg, you—"

Amanda Camila stopped at a red light, waving at a slender young man who was crossing the street while he jabbered into a cellular phone—obviously some friend, damn him, because he waved back. Over the next few minutes she explained, a bit too conveniently, why the drunken lout back there had nothing to do with the iceberg. It was, she said, no more than a *combo en el hocico*. Chileans are always socking it to you, she said, for no reason you can understand, for reasons they often don't understand themselves.

"That guy back there? Last night he was at a bar, downing his fourth wine bottle, when Larrea appears on TV and drones some innocuous words at the launch ceremony, something about the iceberg as a symbol of how cold and modern we are, and our drunk takes those words personally, thinks Larrea is telling him that his wife's frigid as the iceberg, and then Larrea goes on and proclaims, like my father, that every patriotic Chilean's got to do his duty and the *gallo* thinks Larrea is accusing him of not doing his duty, hasn't fucked his wife lately or didn't call his mother for her birthday, and he spends foggy hours mulling this over and drinks some more and gets all frazzled and his mushy buddies egg him on—he should teach that

Larrea a lesson—and our plastered hero can't sleep all night and he finds out where that *huevón* Larrea works and lies in wait for him, and when our descendant of the conquistador ventures into the street to escort you to the car, wham, *combo en el hocico*. The idiot will wake up and won't even remember why he hated Larrea so much. Or maybe he'll nurse a grudge till the day he dies. Welcome to Chile, land of the envious and the resentful. It's the mountains: everybody wants to cut everyone else down, make them small. That's what happened. I'll give you odds. Ten to one. No. Make that a hundred to one."

God, she sounded just like my father. I made the mistake of telling her so, opening the way for my Amanda Camila to spend the next minutes, her eyes shining with excitement, asking questions about him. How were we getting along? Had I accompanied him anywhere interesting, met anybody special, gone out on the town with him last night to celebrate my birthday? I didn't know how lucky I was, she babbled, to have that sort of parent, always ready for adventure to fall into his lap.

"If we're talking about adventure," I said, preferring to interpret adventure as something that Tarzan risks as he swings from tree to tree, "seeing as my dad didn't move a muscle against the dictatorship, your dad was in far greater danger. I mean, *you* were in greater danger than my dad's ever been in. He was too scared to do anything."

"It wasn't that bad. You know, I shouldn't say this but—*sabes*, I miss those days."

"You liked being in danger?"

"You wouldn't understand, you people who were far away will never—"

"Try me."

She cast a glance at me, listened carefully to the undercurrent of sorrow, of loneliness in that "Try me," decided to trust it.

At the beginning it had been full of dread—that's the word she used. When she was hiding with her dad and mom, before her mom died, before she—

Amanda was silent for a few moments. I let her be.

"Half the time I was scared out of my wits and the other half I was bored to death and I still don't know what was worse. That lasted till I was nine, maybe ten. Then the protests began. I was as frightened as ever, but at least we were out in the streets, I wasn't waiting for some monster to come and take us away. At least we were full of life, we knew why we were doing what we were doing."

She turned her sea-green eyes on me, probed how I was taking this confidence, then veered them back to the congested road just in time to avoid a man pushing a cart full of cardboard boxes. Again, she must have liked what she had fleetingly conjectured about me, because she went on: "That anger was so good, Gabriel. To feel that angry and sure of myself. As a child I used to think I was bad. You say to yourself, If they ever knew, the adults, what I really think, who I really am, they wouldn't love me. And then Mom died as if to—to punish me, I guess. Well, that was all gone, all the doubts erased by the danger. For the first time in my life I felt so—pure."

There was in her voice an emotional sincerity, a nakedness, yes, that startled me. I think that may have been the moment, Janice—don't be jealous—when I came to understand that I might really love her, not the sexuality she was skating by me on her way to somebody else, not the body she kept flaunting at my reproductive organs as she turned away from me toward my father, but love *her*, the stripping of the masks from her soul more important than the moment when she might take her clothes off. I glimpsed her need for one member of the opposite sex on this planet who would rather listen to her than fuck her. She had honored me by impulsively deciding that I was that person and it didn't matter, at least for the moment, if that meant she would never make love to me; it didn't matter that I might have to pay for that unforeseen faith by acting out forever the role of disinterested friend. I almost welcomed the way my penis was shriveling between my thighs, diminishing its urgent cries for relief. I had been where she was, I had been desperate all my life for somebody to share my secrets and had not found anyone. And though I could tell her nothing of what ailed me, though I could not open her heart or her legs and pour my loneliness into her, I was glad to open my own self to her outpouring, let Amanda Camila come inside me.

"How about now?" I asked.

"Now there's no big bad Pinochet, no *lobo feroz* to make us feel good about ourselves. Now everything's sort of gray. Fortunately gray, as my dad keeps saying. Blessedly gray. No danger. No grand projects. And I'm waiting for something to happen, anything to happen. An earthquake, for instance. What do you think about earthquakes?"

I told her that earthquakes scared the shit out of me. I remember as a kid, before we left Chile, there was a major quake, and I thought the ground was going to swallow me up. I had told my Nana that I was sure there was a colossal snake down there growling and it would open its mouth and—

"I love them," Amanda Camila said. "I love the idea that all of a sudden we're reduced to insignificance, shrugged off by God's skin as if we were no more than an ant. I love that feeling, that something is finally going to happen. Finally, finally things will change forever, nothing will ever be the same. Nature's telling us to realize who we are, some poor lonely animals who can barely hold onto this planet by the tips of our teeth. I love the feeling that I'm about to die, that I can't do anything about it, that it's not in my hands. More, more, I shout. I want more, I want everything to explode, I want the apocalypse. Haven't you ever felt like that?"

She was describing what I thought I might feel if I made love to her, she was—I didn't want to go on thinking this. I didn't want to ruin this island of shared peace we had reached. I said, "So what do you do when the earthquake is over?"

"You make your own earthquake," she said, laughing. "You try to fuck things up real bad. I've done some things . . . "

Was she referring to the letter threatening the iceberg? Was she about to reveal herself as the *Commandante*? I waited for further intimacies, but they did not come. So I probed her. "What've you done? Something at the iceberg project?"

She brushed aside my suspicions. She was just there for a while. She had been intent on studying anthropology, archaeology, was obsessed with uncovering the wisdom of the old tribes, what the last survivors brought to current humanity from the beginning of time, but her dad had disapproved, declaring that Chile was full of talking heads, intellectual airbags, and that she should go into business administration. He had said she could do more for her precious natives if she knew how to run a company than if she studied them to death. Carola, her stepmother, had mediated between them, suggested a compromise, that Amanda take a year off, make some money, cool down, and if at the end of that period she was still convinced, they'd pay for her education. And, Amanda added, her parents had thrown in a little gift. They had promised a trip to

Patagonia, two trips in fact. Her dream was to go there, to find a survivor of the hunter-gatherers, the canoe people, aborigines who had been exterminated. Maybe she could contact one person who remembered how it used to be before the white man came.

"Free," Amanda Camila said, enthralled. "Maybe that's why I obsess about them, because they were so free."

"Why don't you just leave?" I asked.

"Leave?"

"Yeah, if you hate it so much, just go. Get a job, rent a room, take out a loan, you know."

She abruptly drove into a gas station, stopped the car, handed the keys to an attendant.

"This isn't the States, Gabriel. Kids here don't do that. Kids like me, I mean. Girls leave home only when they marry. Boys, too, for that matter."

"And that's not changing?"

"A bit. Not fast enough. And I'm—I haven't got the guts to break the trend. I like the comforts. I bitch about what's wrong, but I love this car, a nice house, good food, a powerful dad, my little brothers . . ."

She received the keys back, paid for the gas, gave the dark-faced attendant a tip, got the car moving again. And told me what had happened to her at another gas station when she was about twelve years old. One of the first times she'd gone out with Carola, who had just started up with her dad. They had stopped and a young blond man had come out to put gas in the car. Greasy uniform, his hands covered with oil, checking motors and such. Though his hair was corn-yellow and he had sky-blue eyes. It turned out that Carola knew this golden boy's family. A total reject, he'd split with his rich family, gone off to live on his own. The way Carola spoke about him, it was as if he'd killed somebody, killed his own parents. Amandita, Carola had said, look at him. I want you to take a good look at that kid. He could have had everything and now he's living like a beggar.

Amanda stared straight ahead at the road, flanked by dusty trees. "After that, I'd have nightmares that I would end up at a gas station."

"That's crazy. They don't even have women attendants."

"It's crazy, but that's how they keep you in line. Adults have the money and we'd damn better do what they want. It's easier to fight the police in the streets than your own folks at home. That's why I love what your father does, how he confronts parents, defends the kids, thinks that the ones who run away are the best and not the worst."

We had arrived at a large green gate, which slid open at her beep. "This is where we live. It's a *comunidad*," she said. "We moved here after Mom died, more or less when La Nana came to work for us. Dad needed a condominium where all the owners—there are twenty houses here, more in some *comunidades* in Santiago, less in others— were against Pinochet. So if the military came and dumped weapons in your living room and then accused you of terrorism, or even if they simply came to arrest you, you had lots of witnesses, lots of friends."

"It must have been nice, secure," I said.

"Back then, yes," she said. "It was a real community: we were all in the shit together. Now it's full of idiots who don't know how to mind their own business."

She shifted gears, passed the gate, waited for it to shut behind her. It didn't. She pressed her beeper twice, three times. Nothing. "Gabriel, be a dear and close it. The mechanic came to fix the damn thing yesterday and it's already broken again. We're such a modern country, you know."

As I shut the gate, I caught a glimpse of Don Jacinto, the portly old man who had been lurking outside the iceberg reception yesterday, trying to get to speak to the *Ministro*. He was propped against a tree, smoking a cigarette, staking the place out. He waved at me as if we were old friends. I waved back.

I was about to comment on his presence to Amanda Camila when something else captured my attention: off to one side, behind a canopy of leafless trees, was an empty swimming pool made of con-crete. I thought of the girl next to me in her bathing suit, sunning, tanning everything except her most private parts. I thought of those pale white parts that nobody had seen yet, I thought of her strokes shimmering through the cold water, the pool one more perk she was gaining in exchange for her freedom.

"Well," I said, "at least you've got a pool."

"I don't use it," Amanda Camila said. Her voice hardened abruptly.

"C'mon," I said. "Not even in the summer?"

"If you only—" she began, then bit her lip. "Forget it."

"Forget what?"

"Everything," Amanda Camila said. "Forget everything."

"Hey, it's just a pool. Why're you—"

"Look, I don't want to speak about the *conchudo* pool, okay? Would you mind respecting my privacy? Or are you going to be like all these fuckers that live here?"

Her mood only got nastier during lunch. The food the Nanny served should have cheered her up. Nobody's outlook could stay gloomy long with those wonders wafting into the nostrils and then down the throat—better than what was served at any of the three Restaurant Milagros, better because this *palta reina*, this *pan amasado*, this *pollo arvejado*, this *arroz con leche* were the authentic plates that my mother palely imitated in faraway New York and that the scores of gringos who guzzled it down on Amsterdam Avenue could never fully savor. The Nanny would never cook for them, would never get on a plane, would never leave her country. But Amanda Camila sulked, toying with her appetizer and her bread.

The truth is that her father did not make things easier for her. "How'd things go with Larrea?" he asked and I felt that Amanda needed me to be critical, I felt compelled to present the point of view that she obviously could not voice out loud, in the office or at home. So I pointed out that the image of Chile the Expo '92 people wanted to present was based on erasing any signs of the past, particularly the Indian past, the Indian roots of the national identity. And as soon as I said that, Amanda Camila stood up, took a step back, outside her father's vision, and nodded encouragement vigorously.

"Oh no," Pablo Barón said, "don't tell me you're one of those *intelectuales*. Listen, Gabriel, I know them. Damn it, I used to be one of them. These guys live in all comfort with their VCRs and cellular phones and latest-model refrigerators, and if any of their services ever happen to be interrupted for five minutes, you watch the scandal they make. They can't live without cable TV and fax machines and world-wide webs. And what do they want for the Indians? Those hypocrites want the natives to stay stuck in some mythical, nonexistent, impossible-to-resurrect, impoverished Indian past. They want to be able to visit Indians in quaint Mapuche villages and listen to quaint and fake Mapuche songs. And if you dare to question that, say that the Indians would rather share in the prosperity and progress along with everyone else, the so-called Indians, because there are actually not that many of them left here in Chile—"

I interrupted the *Ministro*.

Since he had launched into his speech, Amanda Camila had, behind his back, begun rehearsing a slow mock striptease, lasciviously pretending to undo, button by button, her expo dress, using the silent body of her language to comment on every word her father was spouting, urging me to rebut his assertions, blowing me kisses, kicking up her heels obscenely. Was she suggesting that if I ever hoped to get her to repeat this ceremony somewhere else, just for me, no tease, just the stripping, I'd damn well better act out her fantasies of rebellion against her father, and she'd reward me by possibly acting out mine? For a second, I had the illusion that we understood each other.

"Begging your pardon, Tío Pablo, but I saw many people yesterday in the streets and they sure looked like Indians to this reporter from New York."

"A mirage," Pablo Barón said. "They look native, but they aren't. Go and ask them. Not one of them speaks a word of Mapuche, not one of them lives in some *ruca* and believes in *machi* witch doctors. What they want is what everyone else in this country wants: not to be screwed over by a bad economy. Jobs, running water, a car, a color TV set, nice clothes, that's what they want. They want their children to have the same chance any other kid should have, to read your magazine on the Internet. The same chance Amanda Camila's got, right, *amorcito*?"

He turned to her and she froze halfway through a contortion, pretended she was scratching a leg, sat herself obediently down at the table again, watching her father pump me intensely about my work, relieved perhaps that we were off the delicate subject of natives. Maybe it was a mistake to mention you, Janice, that there was somebody else involved in my pet project, our pet project, our *Whatever* magazine. I said it not to make Amanda Camila jealous, only to answer her father's query as to whether there really was a niche on the Internet for this sort of product, only to let him know that somebody else, specifically you, Janice, was sure we could get financing for our scheme—a bit of a lie, but I wanted him to think I was self-sufficient. But Amanda's playful mood of a minute ago turned dour and remote again. Maybe she guessed that this female business partner had once been—almost been—a partner in my bed. She liked you even less when the *Ministro* commented "You could learn from Gabriel. You see what can happen if you put your mind to something? You see how business administration would be great? You see how this girl Janice knows what to do with her life? Look at how Milagros made a career for herself with just her cooking skills."

Just then, Nana came in with dessert and placed a big bowl in front of Amanda Camila, saying, "Your favorite." But even that did not make her appreciative of the marvelous honeyed rice, powdered with cinnamon, that her father and I began devouring as if we hadn't already eaten a meal that God might have commanded for the Last Supper.

I made one last effort, however. Sensing Amanda Camila's discomfort, I pointed out that my partner, meaning you, Janice—and I am sorry for using you like this—could learn a thing or two from her. We gringos could all learn something from a girl who had gone through hard times, clandestine times. But her dad wouldn't let her be drawn into the conversation. He grabbed center stage again and, instead of filling my ears with stories of his daughter's heroism, said it had been kind of fun. In fact, it was time to tell the funny side of the resistance, enough somber stories, enough harping on the darkness.

He launched into a long story about how one day he had stood on a street corner, waiting for a *compañero* to take him to a safe house where Amanda Camila and her mother were waiting. There was a password, used by resistance people to recognize one another. Except that Barón had forgotten it. So when a stranger came up to him and asked for a cigarette, Barón gave the wrong answer, that he didn't have any. The man went away and came back five minutes later and both of them made believe they were window-shopping. By now the curfew was approaching. The stranger had to be the contact, but what if the secret police had arrested the original guy and they were setting a trap for Barón? The man took out a pack and lit up and offered one to Barón and Barón said he'd love one, which again wasn't the right thing to say. Nevertheless the man passed him the cigarette and Barón had to smoke it so the stranger wouldn't be suspicious. Barón began to cough, of course, because he'd never smoked and both of them eyed each other suspiciously and then stared at the washing machines in the shopwindow they were parked in front of like two vagabonds. The man started to edge away and Barón watched him turn the corner. He realized that, whether the man was his contact or not, he was dead meat, stuck with nowhere to go on a street that soon would be brimming with military patrols who arrested anything on two feet that looked vaguely human.

The *Ministro* winked at me from behind his glasses.

"So what do I do? What the hell, I break every rule in the book: I rush after him and reach him just as he's driving off in his car and I say to him—Amandita, tell Gabriel what I said."

"'I forgot the fucking password, *huevón*,'" she told me in a perfunctory tone. She had heard the story a thousand times.

"Just like that. And d'you know what he answered? 'So did I, *huevón*.'" Barón laughed, almost choking on a sizable portion of *arroz con leche*. "So did I! Somebody should write the story of the resistance as a black comic epic."

"Weren't you ever scared?" I asked.

"Of course. But fear is boring, fear is always the same. Ingenuity— now, that's different. Listen, let me tell you what happened one night. I was at a safe house—in those first months I was changing houses every other day practically—and the tantalizing woman who had given me refuge—"

"Oh no, Papá," Amanda Camila complained. "You're not going to tell him that one."

"My little girl doesn't like this story," he said. "Children never accept that their parents are sexual creatures."

Amanda Camila stood up. "I'm out of here. Back to the Expo office."

"That's okay," the *Ministro* said. "I'll take him back myself. You go ahead."

She flounced off in a huff. Frankly, I was happy to see her go. I had not been looking forward to the drive back if her present foul mood persisted. And I also felt intrigued by the story Barón had been dishing out. I was beginning to wonder if nature or maybe some jokester god or the ghost of Guevara had somehow played a prank on me by inflicting me with the wrong father, if here was someone who could have guided me.

"So I'm at this house and there is this absolutely gorgeous *mina* hosting me, and let me tell you, there is a certain glow about being on the lam—you learn to play it up. Women like men who are being hunted. They like to feel they can protect you, a mother inside each of them. I've only got one evening to score and I can't figure out how to get her into bed. Because she is saving your ass, if you get my meaning, so you want to make sure she's not pissed off, doesn't think you want to take advantage. Which you do, of course, you want to take every advantage, a handful if you can. Though maybe she'll get pissed if you don't service her a bit before parting, don't live up to your romantic persecuted image. And on this occasion I was doing a bit of both, insinuating something, then receding a bit, when there's a commotion down the street and the maid comes running and says the military are searching house by house. We look at each other, and I grab her hand and hurry her up the stairs to the bedroom, and we start undressing and she says, It's only make-believe, right? And I say, Yeah, of course. And downstairs they're knocking on the door with a rifle butt and we hear the maid opening and the soldiers barging in, and quick we jump into bed and I get on top of her and It's only make-believe, she says again, and I say Of course, but the fear has made my dick—I mean, it was the best hard-on of my life and she starts to get sort of appreciative and I can hear them marching up the stairs and I kick back the covers of the bed so that we'll be in full view when the door opens, and it opens and we both turn, this woman and this Pablo, we had already worked up a bit of a sweat, and behind the captain who storms in is the maid, who is apologizing to us that she told him we were not to be disturbed, and he comes into the room and my ass is still going, heaving up and down, and she's giving little moans that could be real or not and the captain begins to blush and takes a step back and I pant to him, It'll just be a minute, just a minute, and he says, Never mind, it's okay, and he leaves the room and off he goes with his troops."

Pablo Barón stopped, waited for my reaction.

"And did you go on?" I asked. "Once they were out of there, did you go on?"

The Nanny, with a young dark-featured maid in tow, had bustled in to clear the dishes. Pablo Barón waited till they were done and gone and then leaned forward and whispered, "You want to hear something that I've never told anyone?"

I nodded.

"You asked if I went on? That woman—she's Carola."

"Carola? Your wife?"

"My wife. And she'd be furious if she learned I've told you about this little affair. Everybody thinks we met years later, including her mother and her ex-husband. So you can see that not everything the military did was bad, Gabriel. If they hadn't raided her house that day, I would never have got into bed with her and I'd have lost the woman of my life. But there's something you want to ask me. Go ahead. I can tell there's something . . ."

I wanted to ask him to explain how you know when a woman is willing, when her no means yes, when her maybe means yes, when her yes means only this far and no more. But those were questions that I was reserving for the great McKenzie, that I was betting I would someday get to ask him, get to learn by his side. I did have a question for Barón, however.

"Does Amanda Camila know?"

"I told you, you're the first one. I'm glad my daughter had one of her tantrums. When she gets moody I wish she were down in Patagonia studying bones in some archaeological site, anywhere but here. Anyway, if she'd stayed, I'd have unloaded the bullshit sanitized version, how I got in bed with this woman whose name I can't even remember and we made believe we were doing it and of course we didn't and we fooled that stupid captain, though Amanda's old enough to realize that it's more difficult to get out of bed than into it. But she has no idea—nobody has any idea—that I kept on going back for more while her mother was alive, that the woman in the story is the woman I married later, once Marta died. The woman who would give me my twins." He smiled at the thought of his two boys. "C'mon. Let's take a look at them. Then we really have to go. I can keep the president waiting only so long. Even if my *sobrino* has finally come back home."

They were sleeping their siestas side by side in two large cribs, while the Nana kept watch, humming a song I recognized—"*Arroró, mi niño, arroró, mi sol, arroró, pedazo de mi corazón*"—calling them *mi niño*, calling them her sun, calling them a piece of her heart as she had called me, she had called Milagros, she had called the mother of Milagros when, at seventeen, Nana had nursed her as well. Someone just like her had murmured those words into the ear of Pablo Barón when he'd been this small. He smiled at me, tucked them in gently, winked his eye as if to say, Look at how a real father cares for his kids.

As we moved to the door, the Nanny took my hand.

"*Mi niño,*" she said. "Tomorrow you're coming for lunch. I'll make you some *sopa de lentejas, congrio frito, leche nevada.* Just the two of us, in my kitchen. Without him"—she pointed to Pablo Barón—"or them," she added, nodding toward the pictures of Amanda Camila and Carola that hung on the wall next to Mickey Mouse and Porky Pig and the Chilean Condorito, safeguarding the placid sleep of the twins.

I looked at the second-most-powerful man in the country to see how he took this banishment from his own house.

"She's in charge," he said sheepishly. "We do what the Nana says in this house. She's the real *patrona,* the boss."

Maybe. But in the car he became the boss again. He ordered his chauffeur not to brake at the sight of Don Jacinto, who, as soon as the car heaved into view, had cast aside his cigarette and begun waving his fat arms like a windmill. Before I could ask him about the old man, Pablo Barón was plying the phone, fielding any number of crucial questions that had been boiling at the presidential palace. "The Argentines are really pissed about this iceberg thing," he whispered to me after one call, as if they could hear him, "not to mention a secret protest from the Bolivian navy—a navy without a sea, what do you think?" Then he called the president of a labor union to explain why a strike would be highly inconvenient, that *el presidente* himself would appreciate anything that calmed tensions and gave an appearance of normality. Then a call to a colonel. "No, *el General* has nothing to worry about. I can assure him personally that there will be no investigation into his son's bank account." And a wink at me. "Sorry about all this work. You were a bit late."

I was flattered, naturally, and utterly charmed by the fact that he had postponed dealing with these affairs of state in order to have lunch with me, though I was not as naive or innocent as his daughter had suggested or as my face might have led Barón to believe. He wanted something from me. And it emerged when he paused in his urgent calls to ask me casually how the iceberg investigation was coming along.

We had just pulled up to a spacious two-story chalet in a residential neighborhood that had recently, according to the chauffeur, been converted into a computer repair shop. "The best you can find," he confided, "run by a friend of my brother's. Tell them Simón Sierra sent you."

"The iceberg investigation?" I asked, my foot already out the door.

"Yes. I'm in the dark. I've told Ignacio not to report back to me on any of your father's movements. So I've kept my part of the deal but I'm not sure if Cris has, if he did everything he could this morning to find the bastard who wrote that letter."

I told the *Ministro* I'd be back right away. I wondered what I'd answer while the young *morenita* behind the receptionist's desk wrote out an order for my computer with dainty hand and long purple tinted fingernails. What a relief: a woman who didn't recognize my father's name, didn't automatically assume that this McKenzie (or any other McKenzie, for that matter) somehow had to live up to family standards. If I hadn't been worried about Pablo Barón's question, I'd have flirted with her. I'd have taken her existence as proof that there were millions of female Chileans, not to mention billions of women of other nationalities, whom my progenitor had not bedded. But I had no time for this liberating thought: the *Ministro* was out there in the car, waiting to see if I was ready to inform on my own dad.

I was and I did.

I held back, of course, that the great Cristóbal McKenzie was sure that none other than Pablo Barón himself had sent the letter in order to win the bet that was at the accursed origin of my existence. But everything else: how he had refused to accompany me to Larrea's that morning, how he had missed important clues that I could not divulge (no way was I going to mention Larrea's stash of pale blue paper or my suspicions about Amanda), how my father seemed to be absorbed in other things. Female things, I ventured.

"Doesn't matter," Pablo Barón said, as we braked in front of the building that housed the Sevilla-Expo '92 offices. "As long as you keep on working to find who's behind this conspiracy, keep me up to date, we'll be fine. Next week I'm going down to Patagonia with Amanda Camila. A gift for her—she's really been a good girl. Want to come along? Inspect security for the iceberg operation? Maybe we can convince Cris to join us, figure out a way to bring him on board."

Music to my ears. Let the *Ministro* do the dirty work, pressure his best friend into spending time on the iceberg and therefore with me as well. I'd manipulate Barón into helping me bond with my reluctant father.

I couldn't know, of course, how miraculously well my plans would turn out: that in less than two weeks a second letter would come, followed by a third and a fourth and a fifth letter in the next months, every Tuesday another pale blue sheet with another message in block letters threatening the iceberg. I couldn't know that Barón would summon us to his office when the second one arrived and use that new letter to coerce the great McKenzie to start looking in earnest for the guilty party.

But by then, of course, I had already been to Patagonia and had a pretty good idea as to who had sent that letter. I was, in fact, already preparing a trap from hell to catch Commandante. You-Know-Who.

Sorry about the interruption.

I went to inspect the kitchen at the back of the Chilean Pavilion here in Sevilla, where I'll be cooking tomorrow night's meal for the family. Everything's in order, going according to plan. Federico doesn't suspect a thing. Don Jacinto's son. Remember Don Jacinto, the old bulky fellow who wanted something for his son? Well, I got him a job, shamed Pablo Barón into providing one. Lucky for me it turned out to be head of security for the iceberg first, then for our pavilion. Didn't know, of course, that I would be needing him someday, will need him tomorrow to turn a blind eye to what I'm going to smuggle in along with the pots and pans, under the carrots and onions, beneath the clucking hens that I'll throttle and pluck and boil.

If I'd known about how to fool security guards back then, that afternoon, I'd have spent those hours with Amanda Camila rather than walking the grimy streets of Santiago, where cars break down and rallies get broken up, maybe she'd have kept confessing to me and maybe we'd have made love that night.

That's not, of course, how things turned out. Two burly armed guards were at the door to the building that housed Larrea's dreams and Amanda Camila's inaccessible body, and they turned me away. "You can't come in," the taller one said, and the other added, "Not without a special pass." When I suggested they call Larrea, they had a good laugh: Don Jorge was in the hospital with a broken nose—some lunatic had attacked him earlier, that's why security had been beefed up. So the boss could not very well vouch for me or anybody else now, could he? They put me through to Amanda Camila, who was all cloying sugar, her foul mood having passed, for all the good that did me. "Gabriel, you poor thing, I'll call my dad." I would have none of it. The *Ministro* already knew I was a snitch; I didn't want him to fancy that I was also a crybaby. Stop feeling sorry for yourself. Right! Last night I had looked on the bright side of things when the computer blew; maybe this predicament now meant that I was not supposed to spend the whole afternoon inside a glass tower, learning how to remake Chile's image for a bunch of foreigners in Spain. Maybe Larrea's nose had been broken so I'd be forced to face some hours entirely by myself in the unknown city where I was born. Here was my opportunity to explore that *ciudad* and begin to love it and therefore to increase, according to my jailed uncle, my chances of getting laid.

Faced with an array of fantasies to choose from, an entire grid of streets beckoning to me, I thought I'd begin at the beginning, so to speak, go to the place where Santiago had been founded. "The Cerro Santa Lucía, you mean," Amanda Camila said. "I'll tell you how to get there. Try to climb to the top. There's a tiny theater up there, built a hundred years ago. A blind actor used to open each performance by singing a ditty: 'Come, girls, to the Santa Lucía, / Come, girls, to Eden again. / Those without a man will a husband find / and widows will as well.' Though you mustn't go up there if it's dark, not even if somebody offers you a quickie."

"I'm not interested in widows or a quickie," I said to her, hiding my pride at this recognition that I was my father's daring son.

She ignored my answer. "I mean it. Remember that the sun sets really early here in winter."

I shrugged off her warning: "*M'hijita*," I said, "I've survived seventeen winters in New York."

I was in a moderately optimistic mood as I set off on my pilgrimage, let my feet walk me all the way downtown. It was good to be alone, a stranger in that urban sprawl where no one knew me, under no pressure to perform or lie or adjust my features to someone else's eyes and desire. I strolled along at my own pace, mulling over my list of suspects. My dad, Pablo Barón, Larrea, the former revolutionaries working on the project, that ecology woman Berta, Amanda Camila, even the supposedly innocent drunk—it seemed as if almost every person I bumped into had a reason to threaten the iceberg, everyone except me. I had fallen in love with it, would defend its call for a new beginning. It was the one Chilean landscape that promised an immaculate tomorrow.

Perhaps that was what also drew the founder of Santiago to this valley so many years ago, to this hill where my short legs and my long thoughts had finally brought me. There it was, off to one side of the city's center, the Cerro Santa Lucía, where Pedro de Valdivia had, on February 12, 1541, established the city of Santiago del Nuevo Extremo. Established it, according to the Web site I had consulted before coming to Chile, farther south than he needed to, farther from his supplies in Peru than was prudent, because he wanted to lay claim to the disputed territory that was up for grabs thousands of miles deeper south, the desirable and dangerous straits that Magellan had chanced on twenty years earlier and that led to the riches of the Indies. Valdivia had ushered Larrea's ice-obsessed ancestor across the Andes and situated his capital here in this very valley because he wanted to be the owner of famous and mythical Antarctica. He left all his worldly goods and all his Indian slaves and land behind in Lima because an iceberg of sorts had also peopled his dreams, the hope of a new inception. And also, according to nasty gossip, because, being a married man, he wanted to be able to screw his lover, Doña Inés de Suárez, at leisure, far from the cloistered eyes of the Peruvian Inquisition. I understood him: to come all this way just for a good fuck. I hoped it had been worth it for him. No quickies for him on the Santa Lucía.

I stood there, at the foot of that hulk of a hill, just off the Alameda Bernardo O'Higgins, to one side of some majestic Roman steps that led upward into a tangle of rock and trees and columns. I stood there and read a letter carved in stone, a fragment of a letter really, the one that Don Pedro, the conqueror of Chile, sent to Emperor Charles V to convince him of the wondrous land that was being colonized in his name: "So that your majesty can let those merchants and people who might wish to come and settle know that they should indeed come; because this land is such that there is no better place in all the world to live and reproduce. . . ."

Well, old Pedro had been right about that: they sure had reproduced, as I myself was proof, as all the smear of traffic roaring behind me also proved. My parents had taken his injunction to *perpetuarse*, perpetuate themselves, quite seriously, right here on the Alameda, my father jumping up and down while my mother waited for him to stop bouncing and take her hand and pilot her to that nearby hotel room. But that's as far as the reproductive process went. It had all dead-ended with me, this twenty-three-year-old virgin who felt mocked by the conquistador's words and the conquistador's boisterous bouts of lovemaking with Doña Inés on this very spot. Though who knows if I wasn't myself acting like that drunk last night who took Larrea's words as an insult when they were meant more as an invitation. Who knows if Valdivia wasn't just another of the older males in my life proclaiming that if you love the land enough you end up perpetuating yourself, thrusting yourself inside somebody, filling her with child? Maybe what he had written over four centuries ago was still valid for this child who had not yet managed to pour his hot seed into anything more welcoming than a New York sewer system.

I sat down on a bench to consider my next move—up the hill or down here among the plebeians, history past or history present?—when I noticed, to one side, a tall blond man being filmed by a camera crew. Speaking English with a heavy German accent and yet, even so, perfect English.

"This is the Cerro Santa Lucía, known to the Indians as Huelén," the man was saying. "For years, it was a dump, a wilderness of rocks and dust in the middle of the city. Until 1872, when Benjamín Vicuña Mackenna, Chile's greatest historian and at the time the *intendente*, or mayor, of Santiago, turned it into a majestic park. Over here"—and he pointed at something embedded in the rock, half-hidden by draping wet vines—"Mackenna put up a plaque the day he started work. Everybody thought he was crazy, but he pulled it off in three years. When the neighbors complained that the blasts from the Cerro were dislodging rocks, falling on their roofs and children, Mackenna didn't stop. His one concession to public opinion was to pay a bugler to sound a warning before each explosion so the people below could seek refuge. No hard hats back then."

The young blond man laughed briefly at his own joke.

"Give me a close-up of the plaque," he said to the cameraman in

Spanish. As the camera zoomed in, he translated the words into English: " 'To the memory of those exiled from heaven and hell, buried over the course of half a century, 1820–1872.' *Exiled* may not be the best translation, because the Spanish word is *expatriados*, which means without a *patria*, landless. Why this reference? Because this used to be a cemetery." He gave another order in Spanish: "Pan the Cerro during my description." The cameraman did so. "The whole Cerro Santa Lucía," the tall blond man continued in English. "For fifty years. A dumping ground for those who the Church or the state wouldn't set to rest in holy ground. Suicides, heretics, executed prisoners. Murderers. The people nobody wanted, nobody claimed. All buried here. A hill full of ghosts. A sad story."

The blond man was looking straight at me. "Or maybe not such a sad story," he said, gazing right into my eyes as I sat on that bench. "Maybe Vicuña Mackenna, who had been in exile, knew what he was doing. You build a park where the dead and forgotten are buried. You begin again from scratch, you plant trees, you blow bugles to wake and warn the neighbors, you clean the memories of the dead from the rocks. You don't let the past devour you."

He spoke so fervently, with such conviction, that I almost felt as if he was expecting me to answer, as if he were an angel come to cheer me up. Or a devil come to beguile me.

"You don't let the past devour you," he repeated. And then, "Cut."

The cameraman asked him if he thought that was enough and the blond stranger said it was time to go up the Cerro, start today and finish tomorrow. He looked at me curiously, as if waiting for me to invite myself along. Or perhaps as if he recognized me as well, knew me from before, from some other existence.

I said nothing.

He started up the steps of the Cerro and for one last moment our eyes locked as we measured each other, asking why we were drawn and repelled by the other's presence, the other's absence. And then he was gone, I thought forever—though he will return. Like Polo, he would turn up when I least needed him; more than one time in this story will that fair-haired double of mine make his appearance. At that point, he influenced my life by keeping me from the Cerro. Because he almost dared me to climb up there behind him, I did not do so. A serious mistake.

I settled my butt into the bench and was answered by a sharp pain poking at me, the cassette, it turned out, that Larrea had handed me before lunch, the sounds that Chile had accumulated in the centuries since Valdivia founded this city on the edge of nowhere, the sounds that would be taken to Sevilla to entice new merchants, different from the ones the conquistador invited, to come to these lands and perpetuate themselves. What better place to listen to those sounds than here, what better time than today? What better homecoming?

I happened to have with me that small, supposedly useless Walkman that the boys of the Casa Milagros had chipped in to buy for my birthday. I had slipped it into my jacket as I was dressing that morning, hoping the people I was going to do mock interviews with would mistake it for a reporter's mini tape recorder. I adjusted the earphones, inserted the tiny tape, and switched it on: what a visitor would have to hear and learn before he was admitted to the sanctuary of the iceberg at the Chilean pavilion in Sevilla.

I closed my eyes, the better to concentrate, and waited in the semi-darkness under my eyelids. Then I heard, coming out of a ghostly silence, the enchanting melody of an *organillo*, a hurdy-gurdy like the ones whose sounds had swept into my ears from the streets of Santiago as a child. I remembered how I would go to my Nana and beg her for a coin to deposit in the cup that a grizzled monkey held as it tottered on the shoulder of an old man cranking a song of sixpence, a song of something lost and something gained. The music merged into a grave, low voice, as if the speaker were barely awake and wanted everybody else listening to go to sleep as well, as if he were trying to extract words like minerals from the past: "*Sube a nacer conmigo, hermano.*" Rise up to be born with me, my brother. I should have known who that was. I had heard my mother playing a scratchy record of that monotonous voice, but I couldn't remember the name. I had already been born once in this place and wasn't doing too well, thank you, so it didn't seem such a hot idea to try and rise up and be born again, and there was no *hermano* nearby that I could tell, especially now that the next sound made me even more keenly aware of how lost I was—a tree crashing through shrubbery. I didn't know fuckall about that tree; I only knew that it seemed to be gigantic. I could not imagine its trunk or leaves or name its species or place myself in the forest where it had fallen, I had no View-Master to peer inside the mountains where that tree had grown before being hacked to the ground so that someone could capture its death on a tape recorder. And then came raucous screams of fans, probably soccer fans chanting words I could not decode and cheering for a team, Colo-Colo, I had never seen play, and the more I listened, Janice, the less I could identify. As if somebody had compiled the whole collection intentionally to remind me of what a stranger I was, compel me to go through the experience of losing my country one more time, the country I never admitted to you or told you about as we wrestled on your mother's secondhand couch. And right then and there, to make matters worse, overlaid on the sonorous replica of waves breaking on a beach I had never visited—maybe the beach where my father had followed my mother when she ran away from home—intermingled with those waves slapping the wet sand was the sound of angry voices and scuffling feet and slogans being shrieked, and I wondered for one more paranoid instant if someone had indeed targeted me, was inserting this political chanting into the typical sounds of Chile to remind me of the hymns of exile that I had run from in SoHo, but I opened my eyes and took off my headphones and realized that these specific sounds of students shouting did not derive from inside the cassette but from the Alameda itself, where a straggling group of protesters were marching by, raising a ruckus that belied their sparse numbers.

They held aloft red banners and placards demanding the release of political prisoners and a rise in wages and unrestricted access to the university and death to the Yankee imperialists. All of this under the omnipresent portrait of bewhiskered Che in his starred beret, the very picture I had not yet unpacked from my bag, the very one I am looking at right now in this apartment in Sevilla. Fists in the air and defiant voices proclaiming slogans not much different from those that, exactly twenty-five years ago, on October 10, 1967, my mother and father had yodeled into the cold Santiago air, that my mother had valiantly kept invoking in SoHo and other sites of solidarity, that we had heard on TV in the remote United States as the youth of Chile surged into the streets to confront the dictatorship. I felt a wave of aberrant nostalgia well up inside me. If I could only have joined them, if time could only have stood still, if it were merely a matter of standing up from my bench and stepping off the pavement and into the street for time to have been abolished, I somehow imagined I could reconnect with the man my father had been on the night when he first entered a woman. Maybe that was all it took, enough for me to return to the moment when they had met to understand how he had left his innocence behind, just that to follow in his wake and catch up with him. If I could only have returned to those moments in exile when my mother and her fellows in banishment sang their songs of defiance while I watched with apathy, if only I had found the guts or the wisdom to have returned to Chile on my own and fought by the side of Amanda Camila and the thousands of others in these same streets and had gone on to the warm fraternizing that young cute things engage in after they have risked their lives together.

If only this and only that, I thought to myself, but the truth of the matter was that I had not, I was shipwrecked on this side of the mirror of time: it was too late. These were not the protesters of yesteryear, not the ones who had jumped up and down inoffensively, playing revolutionary games without paying the consequences. Nor were they anything like the thousands who had defied Pinochet with their faces to the wind, knowing full well how dearly they might pay for taking to the streets. These twenty-odd youngsters now parading by the Cerro Santa Lucía were isolated fragments of that mass movement, just as much residues of the past as I was, looked upon by the bystanders as a curiosity, almost sidestepped by the citizens of Santiago, intent on catching the bus or eating a sandwich or scolding a child or finding a lover up on Santa Lucía or paying the electricity bill. These dead-serious protesters in the democratic Chile of 1991 acted as if the dictatorship were still raging; they had hidden their faces with black kerchiefs, their rhymed shouts mounting in fury the less people listened to them, watched only by me, their lone witness this solitary baby face who had no intention of associating with them. Though one girl with flowing dark hair snagged my attention and motioned to me to join her. She waved her fist in my direction, our eyes intersected, our dark eyes clinched as if we were making love in midair, and for just one more instant I had the illusion that here was the answer—all it took was the courage to take her hand in the darkness, plunge in. But I said no with my head, my face that would never grow up told her it was too late, and as if that were the sign the marchers had secretly been waiting for, their despair at being neglected turned almost immediately to violence; if the public did not want to hear their voices it would have to acknowledge their existence the hard and harsh way.

One of them picked up a stone and delivered his message straight at a bus. A window cracked and blood splattered from the temple of an old lady inside. Suddenly there was chaos: here came the carabineros swinging their batons, and more stones from the Cerro that had seen Santiago's birth, and I saw the girl who had invited me to participate carted off and dumped headfirst into one of the police wagons that Big Ignacio had saved me from yesterday. I was out of there, running through the tear-gassed air. Time had definitely passed since my mother and my father and Pablo Barón and Pancho McKenzie and throngs of their friends had innocently tried to make believe that Che Guevara had not died; time had passed since Amanda Camila, her fist in the air like the girl who was being beaten inside the police van at this very moment, had waited for me on this avenue, Amanda Camila had waited for me and I had not come.

I darted up a side street away from the Alameda and encountered there proof that other inhabitants of Santiago shared my lack of interest in the misfortunes of my fellow citizens: a youth in a leather jacket and tight pants was pushing a stalled car—a beautiful plum-colored Mercedes, no less—while the driver called out encouragement and a crowd of jowl-faced men and portly women stood outside a grocery store offering sarcastic advice, not one of them ready to soil their hands or stretch a muscle.

I'm sure it's clear to you, Janice, must have been since the day I left you on that untrustworthy couch waiting for my return, that I am, all in all, a rather selfish person, not exactly the sort of guy who thrives on helping folks in trouble—the opposite, in fact, of my famous father. Yet here was an occasion where I felt—what to call it?—outrage, I guess; yes, I began to feel gringo outrage at the hostility those people were showing toward the young man as he strained uselessly to get the car going, their envy because they did not have a car, or certainly not one that luxurious. Their recommendations turned vulgar; it appeared that they were making fun of him because he was gay, or at least so they seemed to think. Stick it in the exhaust pipe, they said. Harder, deeper, they said. You need some lubrication, *mi amor*, they jeered. And I, who had just refused to join that march of protesters, decided to lend my shoulder to that young man, help him to push harder and deeper, just as the spectators were suggesting. The florid-faced driver gratefully urged us on as the crowd began to deride me as well. Hey, you can both fuck Cara de Guagua now. Hey, *maricones*, the police will get you for child molesting. Fortunately the engine started and the youth in the leather jacket and the tight pants wondered if I wanted a ride, could they take me anywhere, and even though this meant even further catcalls from the assembly outside the grocery store—they were calling me *m'hijita rica*, they were calling me a luscious broad—I opened the back door and jumped in, and off we sped.

They wined and dined me, Oscar the driver and Nano the leather-jacketed pusher. They already had reason to like me, but their good feeling quickened into adoration when they heard I was from the States—"the greatest country in the world," Nano asserted—and from New York—"Christopher Street," Oscar sighed in the restaurant they took me to, the Enoteca, on top of Santiago's larger hill, the San Cristóbal, "*qué maravilla*. Not like here, *comprendes*," he whispered. I noticed that he had smothered any sign of affection toward Nano, and his voice had grown more gruff and macho when ordering from the waiter: Chile was keeping them in the closet. "That'll change," he added, pouring me some Antiguas Reservas 1988, gesturing toward the city twinkling below. "People will become more tolerant as the country leaves behind its old traditions. It just takes time. The market, the freedom of the market, will see to it."

Nano immediately disagreed. They were like a married couple. He was sure nothing was going to change, because Chileans—men, women, children, and the Church—all hated gays. Ads about AIDS that mentioned condoms had been suppressed on television. Oscar looked at Nano with tolerant amusement, but when Nano's diatribe ended with a melodramatic "They want us to die," he suggested that his lover was always harping on the negative. Oscar told me how much better things were now than when they met—up on the sinful Santa Lucía, of all places. They now had a gorgeous apartment, which Oscar offered to me. If I needed help, they would provide it. "We'll give you a push in the right direction, just like you gave us one when we needed it."

Another perfectly useless person full of advice. Everywhere I turned in Chile there seemed to be somebody new ready to act as my guide, propose his services—just not the one person I really needed, who at this very moment was probably tracking down a boy he had never met. He should have been here, my father, should have brought me to this restaurant to survey the wide city and its many females waiting by their lonely lamps down there. Neither Oscar nor Nano could provide me with the tips I needed to pick up one of those Santiago girls or those sexy widows who, according to the ditty Amanda Camila had recited to me, might be looking for a husband or maybe a quickie.

"Why don't you leave?" I had already asked that question today, asked Amanda Camila on our way to her home. This time I was really asking it of myself. Why should I stay here any longer, what on earth was I doing in this fatherless country?

"Maybe someday we will," Nano said.

"But first . . . ," Oscar added, rubbing his fingers together to suggest big plans. "This is the land of opportunity, the best place in the world to get rich. We're booming. Highest growth in the world. The Chilean miracle. I started out with peaches and wine around ten years ago, exported them to the States, still do. But that's nothing compared to what we collect here." He pointed to a sleek lothario at a table nearby who was talking energetically into a cellular phone. "See that guy? Well, let me tell you a secret. Ten to one he's talking on one of my phones."

"You make phones?"

"Fake phones," Nano said. "All those people talking on the phone in the streets, in their cars, have you seen them? Half those phones, maybe more than half—they look just like cellulars, but they're not."

"We make them by the thousands," Oscar chimed in. "Sell them to people who can't afford the service, don't even really need it, but are desperate to have others think they're supermodern, make them die from envy. That's what got us thinking. So we branched out. Versace, Armani, Christian Dior."

"You represent all those brands?"

"Sort of," Nano said, smiling mischievously. "We fabricate . . . the labels. Stick them on other products. Nobody can tell the difference. People strut their stuff, show off, feel plugged in. We've made millions."

And were going to make millions more. They were branching out into state enterprises being privatized all over Latin America, real phone companies in Peru, electricity companies in Argentina, all being sold off at a fifth the price. As the conversation turned to their many ventures, I decided to tell them about our magazine, Janice, our *Whatever* gossip rag on the Internet. I thought, Why not pitch it here in Chile? Pitch it to anybody willing to take a risk. And Oscar and Nano were that, modern-day pirates, their fingers in every pie, determined to make so much money that their countrymen would have to accept them, invite them as a couple to parties and dinners. Money— a much better way to force your attention on others than the stones that the protesters had started to throw on the Alameda a few hours earlier. Money would be the great equalizer.

They liked our project, Janice, saw its potential. They were merchants of illusions, after all. Oscar didn't think it could really take off until more customers were on the Net and enough companies were ready to advertise there. Nano felt it was worth the risk. We talked about a budget as the wine kept flowing and the dessert cart came round. And then my new friends and, hopefully, future business partners drove their Mercedes to the very top of the Cerro San Cristóbal, up to where the Virgen del San Cristóbal, a gigantic white statue of Mary, towered above the valley of Santiago. They pointed out the landmarks glittering in the darkness, all those people down there praying to the Virgencita for someone to sleep next to. I was painfully aware that neither the Mother of God nor my own Cristóbal had been interceding on my behalf: here I was, stuck with Oscar and Nano, who couldn't help much, who wound their way down the hill and across the grid of streets we had just contemplated. Oscar signaled enthusiastically in the direction of all the men and women flagrantly spewing words into fraudulent phones in nearby cars, talking to themselves in the solitude of their vehicles, lying so that nobody would know how alone and miserable they really were. Who was I to condemn them? Didn't I lie to my new friends about what I was doing in Chile, didn't I dish out to them the spiel about my being a reporter and doing a story on the iceberg?

It turned out that Oscar and Nano had no opinion whatsoever about the iceberg, had hardly even heard about the project. What a relief! Someone in Chile was not a suspect, though of course in detective novels the character who seems least guilty is the one we most need to keep our eyes on, so I decided to ask them a couple of questions. Proof of how far gone I was. Luckily, we pulled up at that very moment in front of the Casa Milagros.

"You live here?" Oscar asked. "McKenzie? You wouldn't be related to Cristóbal McKenzie, the detective, the one who—"

"I'm his son." I saw Oscar frown. "What's wrong?"

After a moment's hesitation and Nano's attempt to stop him, Oscar suggested that my father—begging my pardon, my father was doing more harm than good with this con game of running after kids and bringing them back home. He was interfering with the natural, healthy conflict between father and son, stopping the kids from learning on the streets how to compete and survive. Just like the state had intervened excessively in the affairs of citizens in the past, over-protecting them like a godfather. Sure, some kids would succumb, some were screwed. But that was life. "When I was seventeen," Oscar said, "I ran away from home. Well, in fact, took off for a night. My dad waited for me to come back, belted the shit out of me—"

"Because he suspected you were *maricón*," Nano said. "You should have admitted it and belted him back."

Oscar ignored this militant suggestion. What he had learned that night the hard way was that nobody was going to come and save his ass, no McKenzie would negotiate on his behalf. It was something that life had to teach him. You make a mistake, you get beaten up. Oscar thought he had been lucky his dad hadn't hired McKenzie. "I wouldn't have had the opportunity to be who I am today," he said. "All those kids in there, coddled and shielded from the rigors of life, d'you think one of them will ever amount to anything?"

We were parked there, the motor running, the heat on, the lights in the Casa Milagros blazing. I thought of six-year-old Carlos in the dorm behind that house, Carlitos last night as we tucked him in.

"But if they're left on the streets," I said, "they'll die or end up in jail or—"

"If your father had left them on the streets," Oscar said, "most of them would have died, that's true. The weak ones. But what of the two or three who'd have made it big? They're the ones who matter, they're the ones who bring progress to the world. The others, too bad. Fallen by the wayside. People like your father are just—"

"Oh, shut up, Oscar," Nano said. "A bit of protection is okay. We sure could use some. Gabriel, what really bugs us about your father is that he hates fags. It's people like him who . . . We've heard that your father takes the kids out as soon as they reach puberty, before they reach puberty, in fact, and teaches them how to fuck women, does it in front of them so they can learn."

For once, Oscar agreed with his lover. "McKenzie's a promiscuous son of a bitch. Sorry, Gabriel. You know what gets me? When somebody like him fucks around, everybody wants his autograph. While we're called libertines. Listen, Gabriel, I'm conservative and monogamous. I love Nano and he loves me and we are faithful, much more so than all these bastards who confess their sins on Sunday and go out to screw their best friend's wife on Monday. And your father—word is that he's fucked everything in a skirt except priests and Scotsmen. Don't tell me that's not true."

"He's done some fucking," I admitted, trying not to show my pain at being excluded from the initiation rites for the kids of the Casa that Oscar and Nano had revealed. "He likes women. So do I. And you don't know what you're missing."

Oscar looked at me. He had guessed, as soon as I climbed into his car, that I wasn't gay, though it was also clear that I didn't give a damn where anybody stuck his dick. If he was puzzled now, it was by the cruelty of the comment, my sudden need to degrade him. I saw the warmth drain from his dancing eyes, I thought I saw them go diamond-cold. Why, he seemed to be asking, did I want to draw a line between us, you over there, me over here?

"You know why your father fucks so many women?" Oscar asked, reaching across my lap and opening the door on my side of the car. "Do you know why? He doesn't dare fuck other men. That's what they're looking for in all those cunts. To contact their buddies, make love to them through the same little ladies. That's why they're running around frantically, hoping they'll screw the woman their friends have just screwed, reaching out to each other through those vaginas, occupying the same space. This country's incestuous."

"Don't listen to this *huevón*," Nano snorted, getting out of the car to say goodbye. I followed him. "It's exactly the opposite. They screw all those women because they hate each other, they want to be the only fathers around, *padres de la patria*. They're scared the other men will treat them like women if they don't."

Oscar had also gotten out.

"Well, they don't know what they're missing, Gabriel," he said. "I've done it with women and I've done it with men—and I can tell you what's better, rougher, no holds barred."

Nano forgave me with an embrace.

Then it was Oscar's turn. He also relented, softened, handed me their card, pointed to his cellular phone inside the Mercedes, lifted his eyebrows suggestively. "That one's for real. You got us out of trouble, we'll stand by you. You need a place to crash, our penthouse is yours. We can show you around Santiago, maybe lend you an ear— or a bed—when you need it. Me and Nano. Maybe do some business. Call me."

"Tomorrow?" I said. "Maybe tomorrow we could—"

"Next week," Oscar said. "Not tomorrow. We're leaving for Bolivia."

He saw my interest, exchanged a glance with Nano. Nano nodded. "Off the record, huh, Gabriel? No telling anybody about this. Promise?"

I gave my promise. It was perhaps the only one I kept. You're the first person, Janice, who'll hear about their plans.

Most people, Oscar explained, were looking for ways to cash in on next year's anniversary of the Discovery. But once the date came and went, Columbus would go back to being one more historical old fart and merchants would be left with millions of commemorative mugs and cheap replicas of the *Niña*, the *Pinta*, and the *Santa María* going for less than it cost to make them. If you wanted to make money, you had to look for someone who was going to grow, a legend whom the media would latch onto and who wouldn't fade away. Did I know whom they were thinking of?

I knew, but I didn't want it to be him, I didn't want that man of all men to keep on haunting me, why wouldn't he leave me alone? I said, "Who?"

"San Ernesto," Oscar said. "Next year it'll be a quarter of a century since he died."

"They killed him," Nano interjected.

"Of course they killed him. What was he doing, Big Mr. Macho Guevara, in somebody else's country, rebelling in the name of peasants and *indios* who didn't want him? They killed him, sure. What would he have done with his adversaries if he'd caught them? What did he do to those prisoners in Cuba? *Al paredón*, he signed their death warrants. Anybody who didn't conform. What d'you think he'd have done with you, Nanito *lindo*? Re-educated you, at the very least."

"Excuse me," I said, "but why are you going to Bolivia then? To visit his grave? It doesn't sound as if you admire—"

"Who cares what he was when he was alive? Somebody dies, and they end up being whatever we make of them. That's what it means to be dead, Gabriel. That's why you should put it off for as long as you can, so people can't fuck you over more than they did when you were alive. Now, San Ernesto de la Higuera—he's up for grabs. He's hot. He represents every rebellion everybody secretly wants, as long as he's safely stored away in death. Question is—only question ever worth asking: Who markets him? Nano thinks we should go into T-shirts, coffee, toy guns. Images? Anybody can reproduce them; they'll end up flooding the market. Whereas land—that never goes down in value. La Higuera. Vallegrande. It'll become a tourist mecca; thousands will stream in to see the place where he was martyred. We're buying up all the available land, huts, stores, even the schoolhouse, every-thing we can get, in La Higuera. Che-Landia. It won't happen right away. Slow growth for the twenty-fifth anniversary, but by the time he's thirty years dead—you watch. The sky's the limit. Che tours, Che wax museum, Ride through His Life, Che restaurants around the globe—imported Argentine beef, Cuban *guajiro* meals, *arroz con frijoles*. Even Che soap, though he was a filthy pig; they called him El Chancho. Didn't believe in hygiene. Would have died of dirt if the CIA hadn't dispatched him so we could make a bundle."

Nano disputed this plan, of course. He thought it would be a passing fad, if at all. Che was so far from the current world that nobody would even remember him. All the more reason to resurrect him, then, Oscar countered, getting back into the car.

I watched their car racing down the street. They were already arguing again, I was already missing them, I should have gone off with them to Bolivia, should have used this opportunity to exorcise Che from my life forever, fervently wished I were gay so they could fuck me up the ass and liberate me from my father. I should have at least disappeared for the night with them and then we'd see if he could track me down, if he even wanted to. Instead, I slipped into the Casa Milagros, catching a quick glimpse of my mother and Polo and the great McKenzie in the living room, drinking some cognac, I guess it was, in front of a blazing fire. I went straight to my room, thinking that maybe I'd join them later, once I'd showered and changed, but in the last two days I had slept three hours, maybe four, and as soon as I lay down on the bed and, on a whim, plugged my Walkman into the hurdy-gurdy sound of my infancy, as soon as the sounds that contained Chile began playing, I fell asleep, simply collapsed into slumber as the country that kept eluding me played and played in my dreams.

I woke up several hours later. Somebody had placed a hot water bottle in my arms as if I were a baby, had covered me with a pair of blankets. Maybe my father had tiptoed in to say good night and his hands had—and then, suddenly, like frost crackling a window open, I remembered that I had an appointment with him, the great McKenzie had told me to meet him you know where and now I did know where. He had been waiting for me, maybe was even waiting for me now, in the dorm where Carlitos slept.

It was five o'clock in the morning, but I still crept down the stairs, crossed the frozen patio, climbed up to that dorm. Maybe my father would still be there.

He wasn't.

It was Carlos who was there, crying into his pillow, scared of wetting his bed, scared of getting up in the dark, that kid who had weathered every street in Santiago that I knew nothing about was scared of the dorm, the monsters that could come and get him now that he was safe in that dorm, now that his defenses were down.

I took him to the bathroom, tucked him under the covers, sang him the song the Nana had hummed to the twins that afternoon. I watched the boy who was the age I was when I left Chile, I watched Carlos fall asleep under my shadow. Next to the tenderness I felt dripping inside me, I was also aware of my cold and calculating mind. I knew that I had done this act of charity primarily because it was expected of me, because I was hoping that my father would hear of it. I'd mention it next day anyway. I was performing for him even if he was not present.

Though he was present, of course. I turned and there he was, my father. How long had he been at the threshold, the great McKenzie, safeguarding us both, Carlos and his son?

We went down the stairs silently, out onto the patio again where last night he had told me to stop feeling sorry for myself. He lit a cigarette again.

"Good day?" he asked.

"I learned something, I think. Maybe."

"Not to be afraid?"

"Maybe."

"Once we learn that . . ." He took a puff. "Rules, conventions, were made to be broken."

"I'll try to remember that."

"How's the investigation? Any suspects?" But there was nothing ironic in his tone—or if there was something, it was gentle.

"Too many," I said.

"Yeah," the great McKenzie assented, "that's the problem with trying to solve a crime before it happens. Anybody in the world could be guilty, right?" Before I could answer, he went on: "Tell me about it tomorrow, okay? While we work on one of my cases. An interesting one. A kid who knows my methods is trying to throw me off his trail. We'll spend the day together. Be ready by eight sharp. But now we need to catch a few winks."

He might, but I was wide awake. I knew what I needed: some exercise. Remember, Janice, how I used to love to jog, back when we were fifteen? I still jog relentlessly, recklessly, joyfully. And it had been several days since I had worked out, so I took a long shower, changed into my gear, did some stretches, padded out into the dawn streets of Santiago, sure that I'd be back in plenty of time to hook up with my dad.

I'll admit I was hyped, I was psyched, I was feeling good about myself for the first time since I had come to Chile, maybe since I had come home that long-ago night in Manhattan when I had shut myself out from your eager legs.

Maybe it was the birds starting to wake up. Maybe it was the intense cold of the cordillera blanketing the valley as I jogged up the street toward it, toward the sun that was breathing just below the mountains, hitting the highest peaks sideways. Maybe it was the promise of the orchards and the sun and the streets where many other men were walking with resolute, strong steps; they were going to work and I was going to make love that night. I knew it, I was sure of it, something magical was about to happen today. My father would reveal his secret and tell me how he found a willing woman when he left my mother the night she rejected him. Tonight I would take Amanda Camila's clothes off with the slow, liquid movements of someone who has done it many, many times. Tonight I would see her green tidal eyes from inside. I ran up the hills past the smell of baking bread and the solitary lightbulbs being startled up and babies calling for their Nanas and toilets flushing, toilets that would not flush my semen tonight, that would see no service tonight.

That's all it took. An invitation from my father, the conviction that I had made a breakthrough, that by fulfilling the riddle of my appointment with him, by understanding where we were to meet and what was required of me, by giving that runaway child who was scared of the dark, scared of the other boys in the dark, a small measure of compassion, I had in some way passed a test, gone through a rite of passage on the other side of which my father and adulthood were waiting for me. Or maybe he had realized that I was not a *maricón* after all. Maybe the passage had come earlier, the temptation to join Oscar and Nano, the line I had drawn between myself and them. Maybe that was what had finally made me a man.

As I trotted up the slope that led toward the sun, as it began to rise behind the Andes, I began to celebrate my existence, to feel the weight lifting from my legs and my sex. I know this is going to sound strange, Janice, especially now that I'm aware that it was not true, now that it's clear that what I was imagining back then was absolutely and entirely false, now that I write to you from Sevilla with death approaching, but what my pounding heart and pounding feet were telling me as I climbed the mountains under which I was born, under which Amanda Camila and my mother and my Nana slept, under which my uncle planned escapes and revolts and Pablo Barón planned a new Chile and Oscar and Larrea and who knows how many others planned to make a bucket of money and Nano dreamed of joining the gay liberation movement, what I thought was that my luck had altered. I thought that the life that exile and history had stolen from me was about to be returned to my control.

My very enthusiasm may have misled me.

I came to a field bounded by a barbed wire fence and a sign that said NO TRESPASSING in rough block letters. Behind it, several horses grazed, and in the distance a small forest of eucalyptus trees swayed in the shivering breeze up on a knoll, beckoning to me. The view of Santiago from there was surely magnificent, flawless; just the right place this morning to inaugurate this new birth of mine, to heed my father's voice inside me urging me to be unafraid, to make every inch of the country mine as he had, as Oscar and Nano never would. When I started to climb the fence, two construction workers who were passing tried to stop me, "No, *joven*, don't do that," or something of the sort. But I wasn't going to mind them. Rules were made to be broken, my father had told me. As they spoke their words of caution, a ray of sunlight from the sun beamed onto the trees as if to set every leaf on fire, and I took it as a sign that God was blessing my trespass and headed farther up the hill. Today was a day when nothing could go wrong.

Plenty of things did go wrong, and the first of them was a soldier who, just before I reached the eucalyptus grove, materialized out of nowhere, his submachine gun cocked.

"Don't you know this is a military zone?" he asked.

I stopped. Drenched in sweat, short of breath, flushed with anticipation of the conquests awaiting me that evening and of the secrets my father would trickle into my ears, decked out in my Nike shoes and my Reebok jogging gear, I did not, fortunately, look like a spy. The young *recluta* did not treat me the way the guard at the penitentiary had the previous day or the way the carabinero had on the street the day before that. Maybe something magical was still about to happen, because instead of threatening me or shooting me or arresting me or giving me a good beating, he must have seen that I was harmless. I emphasized my gringo accent, stammering ungrammatically that I was *desde Estados Unidos*, that I was sorry, demeaning myself and spluttering myself so pathetically that he must have felt embarrassed for me. He said that I had better get the hell out of there or he would . . .—no, not that way, not the way I had come. He pointed in another direction, he pointed to the nearest fence. He was adamant, perhaps scared that somebody else would notice me and blame him for letting me go. He thrust his weapon toward the south, then watched me lope off across the pasture, past the horses, over another barbed wire fence. I never made it to those trees, Janice, never saw Santiago in all its splendor waking to a new day.

The road that I had faltered onto did not lead me back to where I had started. It began to twist perversely, around and down, endlessly winding past streets that said PRIVATE, MILITARY HOUSING. Guards in small booths watched me with pinpoint eyes as they smoked their last cigarettes of the night or their first cigarettes of the dawn. I ended up in an industrial neighborhood, warehouses, factories, fallow fields, and a solitary frost-bitten vineyard: I was completely and absolutely lost.

Until I came to a factory and saw displayed on it an enormous faded sign: REFRIGERACION CONQUISTADOR. Could it be? Maybe my situation was not as hopeless and muddled as I had thought! It had to be a positive development that, of all the possible enterprises, I had stumbled on Larrea's, the factory his father had established when everybody said it couldn't be done.

Outside, a hundred or so workers were waiting for the gates to open, stamping their thick shoes in the morning freeze, exchanging jokes and banter, talking among themselves. They became silent as I approached. I told them I was lost and asked directions. They were divided as to what I needed to do: one pointed me north, another pointed the opposite way; others in the group began arguing and joking about who was right.

I sat down to see if they could reach some sort of consensus. I was winded anyway—I had probably jogged for more than an hour by then, maybe an hour and a half. One of them, an electrician he said he was, came over to me, parked himself by my side, took out a thermos from his backpack, and offered me some coffee. A few others fished into their bags and came out with bread, biscuits, a sandwich.

We talked a bit. I wondered how they were doing, said I was a journalist, and they seemed to think I was telling the truth. Their impressions: things were sort of okay for them, they had jobs and some benefits, though they worried about the future. I should let my readers know that Chileans weren't producing the whole refrigerator here like they used to in the old days. Now this factory only assembled it; the parts came from Ecuador and Indonesia and who knew from where else. China, one of them said, yes, China, they agreed. There were also rumors of some ultramodern foreign machinery that was being imported and that might lead to layoffs.

Then I did something dumb. I stupidly tried to repay their

goodness. There I was, lost and thirsty and lovelorn and late, and this electrician and his buddies were providing me with comfort. And the only way I could return the favor, the only card I held, was that I knew the owner, Larrea, the man who had the right to hire them or fire them, demote or promote each one of them, open another factory or close this one, keep on making household goods or begin to make industrial refrigerators. So I told them that they shouldn't worry, I was a friend of the owner's, I had been with Jorge Larrea only yesterday, and I would put in a good word for them when he got out of the hospital. Did they know a drunk had broken his nose? Why in heaven did I promise to help them, try to prove how important I was? Why couldn't I have just thanked them and gone on my way, back home to my own problems?

The siren sounded in the factory, the doors swung open, and the men began to shuffle in. A few of them looked back at me as if unsure whether to believe the gringo or not. Only the man who had first offered me the coffee took the time to close his thermos, suggest I come inside. If I was such a friend of Don Jorge Larrea's I'd have no trouble getting management to lend me a phone so I could call myself a cab. It was the most logical solution, but I stubbornly asserted my independence. I didn't want my father to have to come to the rescue. I was sure he'd wait for me. I deserved to have him wait for me, damn it. So I told the friendly electrician that I could handle the situation; I left him there to labor away on the wiring that guaranteed that Chilean housewives would be able to keep their meats and freeze their leftovers and cool their cheese and sherbet, I left him in order to confront the immediate streets, where, it turned out, people could not afford that sort of refrigerator, could not, in fact, afford meat.

Just a few blocks from the factory, my running brought me into a rough-and-tumble neighborhood that looked as if it had just been hit by an earthquake and had not had the time to recover: makeshift tin hovels and mud-gouged alleys, impoverished women watching me from dark, smoky doorways, and a gang of small kids dressed in rags who started running behind me, asking for coins, fingering my Reebok pants. Here was the Chile that was two steps down from the workers I had just left, one step down from the street vendors I had seen on my first evening in Santiago, those whom the rising wave of the economic miracle had left gasping and sullen in the garbage. Here was the reason my uncle was in jail, here was the Chile that my mother, her fist waving in the Manhattan air, had vowed to liberate, here was the human refuse that Oscar had suggested just last night should be left to die, here were the men and women left stranded by the death of Che Guevara. And here were the young men whom my father and all the charitable priests and nuns of Chile had not been able to salvage, a pack of eight, maybe nine of them lounging around a bonfire in the middle of what could barely be called a street, a trail of muck between two rows of what could not be called houses either. These were the young who had not been able to emigrate as I had. They had been abandoned, and they knew it, here in a zone of Chile that didn't give a fuck about the iceberg or the Internet or cellular phones or Che Guevara tours; they were simply there nurturing the fire and waiting for something to happen, someone to come along.

And I did. And stopped dead in my tracks. Maybe I should have whizzed past them, made believe they weren't there, as everybody else in Chile had probably done since they were born, run right by them, ignored their existence.

They waited for my next move, and the more time passed, the more I felt the prickle of my danger. I decided to try and go on, skirt the group.

"*Eh, huevón! Dónde vai?* Where you heading?"

I didn't answer. I didn't want them to hear my accent.

"Maybe the *cara de guagua* has come for a fucky-fucky." A tall, gangly kid said those words, *fucky-fucky*, in English. *Vino para un fucky-fucky?* "You come here to screw my sister?"

"The *cara de culo* came here to screw your mother," another of them said, and they all laughed. "Right, Shitface?" he asked me.

"Really?" the tall kid said. He had a scar, livid, deep, just over his right eyebrow. "Is that why you came to visit, Cara de Guagua, Cara de Culo, Cara de Concha tu Madre?"

They were coming nearer.

"What time is it?" one of the other kids said. "Ask him for the time."

"Looks like it's time to ask him what time it is," the tall one said, sidling up to me. "*Qué hora es?*"

I looked at my watch, the one my father had given me for my

birthday. It was, in fact, nearing eight o'clock. Somewhere down in the valley, in the semi-warmth of the Casa Milagros, that very same father was finishing his *café con leche*, he was looking out the window, he was wondering where I was. In the Casa Milagros at this very moment, Polo tapped his own watch significantly.

I lifted my arm, showed the tall kid what time it was.

"I can't see it," the leader of the gang said, squinting. His scar loomed like a sick moon over his eye. "My eyes aren't that good. Maybe I need to see it closer up." He snapped his fingers. I gave him the watch. He looked at it. He shook it. He sniffed it. "Now I have a question for you. And don't play dumb with me, Cara de Guagua. You get a question from me, you answer it. What time will it be tomorrow at this same time?"

"The same time as today," I answered sullenly. So much enthusiastic chatter in my head about being a pioneer and a conquistador and showing these Chileans who was who, my dreams of voyaging to the South Pole, the line I had drawn between Oscar and myself as to who was really an *hombre*, and as soon as I met a real challenge, the only thing to come out of my mouth was this piece of idiotic crap.

"So he's not so dumb. Smarter than I am. Because I won't know tomorrow what time it'll be. I'm sure you're feeling that you want to give me this watch. You want me to know what time it is tomorrow when you're not around to tell me."

"Keep it," I said. "But I have to go."

"Cara de Guagua has to go. But you're all witnesses: this gringo gave it to me of his own free will, right? Now, Leo here has another question for you."

Leo said, "Yeah. What size are your shoes?" He got down on his haunches and began to untie the laces. I let him do it. I let him take off the Nikes. I let him try the shoes on. The mud was cold, my bare feet were supremely unhappy. I sneezed.

"And now Carloncho has a question regarding your pants, Cara de Guagua. You don't really need your pants, do you?"

"I need my pants," I said.

"Well," Carloncho said, "if you're going to fuck Choclo's old lady, you're not going to need your pants. Or are you going to fuck her with your pants on?"

"He'll fuck your mother," Choclo said, "and his pants are going to be off. You can choose, Cara de Guagua. You take them off or we take them off."

As they started to roll my pants down, I thought absurdly of how I had planned the day would end, how the evening would be celebrated, with Amanda Camila peeling off my clothes, going through the same motions these two kids were going through. I thought to myself that this could not be true, this was not where my run or my life was supposed to finish up, with me here shivering in my underpants, and now they were taking those off as well, I lifted one leg up and then the other one, almost as if I were a baby at the beach whose diapers were being changed. One of the kids scrunched my underpants into a bundle and tossed them into the air and the others began kicking them, making sure my underpants didn't hit the ground. The kids were wizards, real geniuses at soccer. I watched them there with my dick hanging loose in the frigid Santiago air, not joining the game, a little boy lost.

"That's enough!"

I turned, the two youngsters who were squabbling over who would be the first to try on my pants turned, and then Leo and Carloncho and Choclo, everybody turned. And there, as if he had come out of a Chilean version of a Terminator film, was Ignacio from Investiga-ciones, Ignacio with a celestial gun in his hand, Big Ignacio who was going to rescue me for the second time in less than thirty-six hours.

The delinquents didn't stick around to argue that I had offered them all this, watch and shoes and pants, of my own free accord. They made off with their booty in the four cardinal directions, leaving only me and Ignacio and the underpants, now buried in the slime. He picked them up with his gun and handed them to me silently. I looked at them, let them fall, decided that it was better to risk pneumonia and butt freeze than to put them back on and contract some filthy chronic Chilean disease.

We both contemplated the underpants for a second. I took off my sweatshirt, wrapped it around my waist.

"We'd better get you out of here, Cara de Guagua," Ignacio said. "Someplace warm."

Sluggishly, I followed him to his car.

"We'll go by my house first," he said, "get you some clothes. I live on the way to the Casa Milagros."

I nodded. That was very thoughtful of him, not to escort me back home with my ass and genitals in full view.

"Nobody needs to know about this," he said.

"How come you knew about this?"

"The *Ministro* wanted me to keep an eye on you."

"So you're not following my father around anymore?"

"Don Pablo thought you might get into trouble. The *Ministro*'s almost always right."

"Well, I don't want you snooping around me anymore."

"When you're *Ministro*, Cara de Guagua, I'll take my orders from you, what d'you think?"

"And what if I try to shake you now that I know you're following me? Now it'll be easier."

"You shake me, I'm in deep shit. But I'm *discreto*. Did I interrupt you when you were with the two *maricones* yesterday afternoon? Did I stop you from trespassing on military property?"

Ignacio braked in front of a modest bungalow with nice winter flowers poking their faces through the grilled bars of an iron fence. A minute later he was back with boxer shorts, sweatpants, slippers, a shirt that said Colo-Colo and had the colored profile of an Indian stamped on it. "They belong to Ignacio Chico," he said. "I think they'll fit."

"How old is your kid?"

"Ten, Cara de Guagua. He's big. Like me."

As I changed, I made a proposal to Ignacio. If he called me Gabriel from now on, I wouldn't try to get away, I'd let him protect me. I'd even consult him before making the sort of mistakes that messed things up that morning.

"Sounds good. But I want you to know that if you try to get away I'll personally break a couple of bones in your leg."

"That wouldn't be taking care of me now, would it?"

"I'd be taking care of you, but not the way the *Ministro* meant."

We laughed at that and somehow the ice was broken. I asked him about his favorite soccer team, which is always a way of making anybody happy, and he extolled the virtues of Colo-Colo and a series of players whose names I had never heard and never wanted to hear, for that matter, ever again. He said that his youngest, the kid whose clothes I was wearing, was a real Maradona and would probably end up being a professional player, which was fine by him. Then we talked about the rest of the family and he passed me some photos of his four kids, the oldest already on his way to a career. Business administration, that was where the future lay. The second was going into art design; she'd be an advertising executive. Life had been good to Ignacio and his wife.

And he didn't want any of them to follow in his footsteps? He said no, he spoke about the hours, the tedium of waiting endlessly outside the house of some big shot he was protecting or some lowlife he was stalking, boring people, all of them. He welcomed the job of following me, he said, because I was so unpredictable, I was so *extraño*. But generally things were routine, not a life he'd recommend.

I felt that I could risk a more personal question. "Not worried about any broken legs, are you?"

"What broken legs?"

"You must have broken a few legs, Ignacio. Those kids back there. If you'd caught them . . . "

"They're *patos malos*, Gabriel," he said. "They get what they deserve. I'm just protecting you, people like you. Your sort complain a lot about police brutality, but if it weren't for people like me, you'd be mugged every day. You enjoy your life? You owe it to people like me."

"How about other people, victims? You know, when Pinochet was around."

"You break what you have to break," Ignacio said, shrugging.

"I would have nightmares."

"It's not good to have too much imagination," Ignacio said. "Too many hours sitting at a desk."

And that was as much as I could get out of him. Whatever he had done, whatever he might still be doing did not bother him. His problem was how to fight boredom, not remorse.

"Remember our agreement, Gabriel," he said, as he pulled up at the Casa Milagros.

I shook his huge paw solemnly and went inside.

My father and Polo had left, my mother said, around half an hour ago. They had waited and waited.

"What time is it?"

"Where's your watch? My God, where are your shoes?"

"Did he leave me any message?"

"Who?"

"My dad."

"Oh, your dad. He was as cryptic and uncooperative and ironic as he's been since we arrived. That you knew where to find him." She looked at me. "Gaby! Where are your shoes?"

"You don't want to know," I said. "I need a shower."

As usual, she had plans for me. I could sense that she was not displeased at my having missed the appointment with my father. How nice, she chirped cheerily, as we drove off in the Casa Milagros van to spend the morning together, mother and son. We bought some prohibitively expensive Nikes—two pairs, my mom was paying, her flourishing Milagros restaurants, "Latino Food for Romantics" back in New York were paying—at the colossal Alto Las Condes supermall up in the hills. It was bigger than anything I had ever seen in the States, a department store where miniskirted young ladies roller-skated through the aisles offering samples of food imported straight from America, which I popped in my mouth and which my mother waved aside with impatience. "What they've done to this country," she said. That became her litany for the rest of the morning. She showed me customers with shopping carts brimming and whispered that just before they reached the cash registers they would abandon the carts and buy only one item, promenading their false wealth for others to see. When I pointed out that if everybody did that Alto Las Condes would have gone bankrupt a long time ago, somebody had to be buying something, she merely said, "What they've done to this country." And repeated the same phrase later when our van passed a corner where, as a child and then as an adolescent and then as a woman, she had bought empanadas that rivalled Nana's, or so she assured me. Now a Burger King, a Pizza Hut, a Dunkin' Donuts had replaced that old *ruca* with its thatched rural roof and white adobe walls. I made the mistake of telling her that I wouldn't mind a late breakfast Whopper washed down with a Coke. She shook her head angrily. "What they've done to this country." "They" were trying to make the deep country disappear, erase everything that made it wondrous and different, turn it into one of those neon shopping strips that line U.S. highways. It was easier to keep the tradition of Chile alive back at the Restaurant Milagros on Amsterdam Avenue in New York than here.

But she wasn't going back that soon. They hadn't defeated her.

Abruptly her mood became positive, almost manically optimistic. Each time we hit a pothole, whacked into it with our wheel and bumped out, she grunted in satisfaction, my crazy mom. "That's good," she said, "it's good to see that the country's fighting back," and when I asked her what she meant, she lapsed into a long hymn to the earth itself, the subterranean Chile that was resisting modernization, breaking the streets up, forcing people to slow down, rush, rush, rush, look at them, what they've done to this country, meaning first Pinochet and company and now the new democratic government that was continuing the same economic project. But Mom thought it wouldn't work, and what she was going to do was to take me and my Nikes to visit some people who were leading the struggle against this sort of exploitation, people who still believed that a nation should be judged on how it satisfied the needs of its own populace rather than the arbitrary fluctuations of foreign markets. People at the grass roots, Mom said, trade unions that were trying to get the dictatorship's labor laws changed, community co-ops, associations of health professionals who were organizing to oppose efforts by the managed-care bosses to destroy what was left of Chile's socialized medicine, training centers for alternative jobs, priests who had not given up on fighting poverty, the *agrupación* of relatives of executed prisoners, a man who was using Swedish grant money to open a center for migrant workers, a group of video makers who brought cameras into the shantytowns so the *pobladores* could film their own lives, therapists who were treating torture victims, the new center against domestic abuse, La Morada, where feminists were challenging Chile's machismo, the female fruit pickers who were responsible for all those peaches and grapes we saw in New York markets, had organized and were protesting the use of pesticide banned in the States, they also wanted child care, and how about an ecology group that was educating factory workers about the effects of pollution on their—

"Wait, wait," I said. "All this today, right now?"

"What we don't visit today we can visit tomorrow. Or next week." She hit me with her full political agenda. "Remember those people we used to watch on TV together? Out on the streets, risking their lives? Some have sold out, think everything's fine, are making money hand over fist. But others, they're still here, just less visible. I've been calling them up, old friends who are disgusted at what's being done to the country. Who still believe that the poor are the final reserve of what is true about us, that they shouldn't be pushed into low-paying jobs and consumerist dreams, rushed into the twenty-first century before we've even had a real twentieth-century experience. This country is still alive, *el viejo* Chile. All you have to do is scratch the surface, Gabriel, and it's there. I'm hungry for it. Aren't you?"

Frankly, no. If I was hungry for anything, it was for a donut, from Dunkin' Donuts if possible, and as soon as possible. I had been given a taste of the poor that morning and was not overly interested in biting any deeper. In fact, I felt I'd be happy if I could simply avoid their fingers and their knives biting into *me*; the farther from them and those who wanted to help them out, the better. Though this did not seem the right moment to reveal that my own enthusiasm for the Resistance Against Oppression and Dictatorship had been, well, sort of a scam all these years, to put it mildly, Janice. Certainly not now that Mom's newly minted rage against what had been done to the country during her long absence appeared to be having a beneficial effect on her spirits. She was definitely in better shape than yesterday.

"Okay," I said. "Where do we start?"

Mom brightened up even more. She'd been thinking about a little side trip to the cemetery. Some bodies of the *desaparecidos* had been discovered in a mass grave, and a group of forensic doctors had managed to make some positive identifications. She had read in the paper today that there was going to be a service for them and she had sort of dated one of them and—

Something snapped. Suddenly I'd had enough. No cemeteries. No mass graves. No former boyfriends who had screwed her. No long explanations of what he had done to her, how he had done it, back when Che Guevara was alive. That was it.

"Drop me off here, Mom."

"Where? Why?"

"On this corner."

"But why?"

"Pull up."

She stopped the van and looked at me with more than a flicker of concern in her eyes.

"What's wrong, Gabriel? If you don't want to go to the cemetery, if you want us to start off at La Morada and—"

I almost told her, I almost spilled my guts. But she was bent on saving the country, my father was bent on saving the runaways, and neither of them seemed interested in saving me. It was really too late to confess everything that had happened to me, not only on this trip but in all the years before, from that night with you to my infatuation with Amanda, from SoHo to Santiago. I got out of the car.

"It's nothing, Mom. I just remembered where I'm supposed to meet Dad. I'll accompany you to the cemetery some other day."

As soon as she was gone, I looked around. Where was Ignacio? It didn't take me long to spot his car double-parked a bit farther down the street. I went over to him. He was munching some *maní confitado*, offered me a few nuggets, popped a handful into his mouth.

"Do you know where my father is?"

"I can find out."

A few minutes and a whole bag of *maní confitado* later, the information crackled through Ignacio's radio.

"Can you take me there?"

"Saves me trouble if that's where you're going. And you can use the taxi fare you save to get some more sweets."

We munched a bit more as we drove. I showed him my new Nikes, he admired them, I handed him the second pair. For Ignacio Chico, I said, so he can train hard, become a real pro.

"You're a generous kid, Gabriel," Big Ignacio said.

"Thank my mother. On second thought, don't. She has no idea that I got them for you. Doesn't know what happened to me this morning. And I'd appreciate it if you didn't tell Barón."

"He already knows."

"What did he say?"

"Said we had to do more for the *poblaciones*, those kids were the children of the dictatorship. Bullshit, if you don't mind my saying so. What we need is more cops, more prisons."

"What did he say about me?"

"I told him that you had beaten the shit out of two of them and that I stepped in when the gang leader took out a knife. He laughed. Said you were a chip off the old block."

"He thinks the world of my father."

"Speaking of your father . . . "

Ignacio stole a parking space from an old gentleman who began to protest until Ignacio flashed an ID, the same one that had cowed the *paco* on my first evening in Chile. He pointed toward a café on the other side of the street. In the window, the great McKenzie was deep in conversation with a rather plain-looking middle-aged woman with a Winona Ryder hairdo that did not suit her round, moonish face.

"He's going to nail her," Ignacio said. "Ten, fifteen minutes, won't need much more."

"She doesn't look too appetizing to me."

"Who knows what she's got between the legs. Once the lights are turned out. Anyway, your father should know, right?"

"He knows," I said, as if he weren't a complete enigma to me.

We watched my father seduce her, take out a rose, smell it, let her smell it, wave the rose in the air, ask for champagne and three glasses, one for the lady, one for him, one for the rose. "That's class," Ignacio breathed, "I've got to remember that one. Champagne for the flower." He passed me his binoculars. "Look at those bubbles."

It was strange, spying on my father with a professional snoop, a man who had probably spied on my own uncle or on Barón himself during the Pinochet years, who had spent his days back then trying to stop me from ever coming home to get laid, and who was now collaborating—unawares, of course—in my attempt to lose my virginity. I listened to him wonder how big the lady's tits were, how purple the nipples, how long it would take McKenzie to make her come, if he didn't ever get tired day after day after day. Why didn't he give it a rest?

"Who's that?"

"Where?"

"That man," I said. "Over there."

I pointed. The man was in a rented Escort farther up the street, with a better view of my father and his *conquista*, a prime spot, in fact. The man, short, squat, pale, was scrutinizing the couple in the window of the café intently. Ignacio's binoculars disclosed his tiny, delicate hands taking notes.

"Oh, him. I wouldn't bother with him."

"Is he one of your men?"

"That foreign fag?" Ignacio seemed genuinely hurt. "You think we'd employ somebody like him?"

"Are you sure? Maybe some other service that—"

"I'm telling you, he's not even Chilean. He's just a nut. Forget him."

I could not. Here was another mystery: my father was being stalked by somebody else. I didn't want Ignacio to think I was worried, so I didn't ask him any more questions and he didn't volunteer any answers. A big mistake, as you'll soon see, Janice.

Things did not seem, inside the café, to be going as fast as Ignacio had predicted. The great McKenzie had ordered some food and it had just arrived. Polo suddenly materialized. Had he been inside the whole time? Had he come in through the back door? He said something to my father, handed him a cellular.

"Boring," Big Ignacio said. "What did I tell you?"

We watched my father speak on the phone; the diminutive man in the car outside stopped taking notes for the duration of the call, resumed when my father hung up.

"This is going to take a while," Ignacio said. "I need to take a crap. I can trust you not to run away, right, Gabriel?"

"I don't want anybody breaking my legs," I said.

I wish he had asked me to promise that I wouldn't get into trouble. I wish I had told him I wouldn't, because then I would not have acted the way I did when I saw the small pale man begin to take photos of my father and the plain-looking lady with the horrible feline haircut. Polo had vanished again, but the two of them were kissing in the window. That dwarf of a spy was snapping photo after photo, and I saw red. Was I angry at him because he was doing what I was doing, monitoring my dad's sex life? Or was it that I liked casting myself as the son who saves the father instead of vice versa? Maybe I liked the idea that I was the one delivering the damsel in distress. I can't exactly recall my motives as I stepped out of Ignacio's car and started to cross the street toward where the man was using a whole roll of film, undoubtedly paid for by some irate husband, some suspicious lover, somebody who would certainly make things difficult for my father once the negatives were developed—make them difficult, that is, unless I put things right. I had been looking for a way in which I could reintroduce myself back into my father's schedule after my dawn jog had gone so catastrophically awry and this was clearly an occasion sent from heaven.

I yanked the dwarf's car door open and grabbed his camera with one hand, installing my other hand on his collar.

"Hey," I said, "what's this? Spying, are we? How much are you getting paid for your dirty business, you pygmy?"

The man spluttered some incoherent words. His Spanish was atrocious. He switched to English and began blubbering for me not to hurt him, please don't hurt me, I'm just doing my job. I hauled him out of his seat and onto the sidewalk. He was as light as a child, with his big head like an egg and his small, hunched body. Your job, huh? Now I was shouting at him in English. Destroying people's reputations, huh? He suddenly went quiet and then, I can't tell why or how, I slapped him. I slapped him because I could do it, slapped him because I was still smarting from my own humiliation that morning, all the humiliations of the last twenty-three years. When we were on that couch together, Janice, you whispered to me, You're so soft, Gabriel, so considerate, I know I can trust you. So you know that I'm not violent; even the S and M masturbation we practiced later in front of your screen, my screen, mere fantasies . . . But I was rough with that guy and would have slapped him again if a hand hadn't held me back. It was Polo, of course, who else but Polo would come up that noiselessly? Behind him was my father and behind my father the lady. From nearby she looked a bit more fuckable, her face as plain as ever, the haircut lamentable, but all in all a more succulent morsel than I had assumed, with lovely hazel eyes, soft skin, slim legs. But I didn't get a chance to see more, because she turned and went back into the café for her handbag, quickly left, and started down the street without my father doing anything to stop her. He had enough on his hands dealing with me.

"Gabriel! What are you doing?"

I explained who the man was, what he had been up to.

My father sighed. "Tell him, Polo."

"*Guinness Book of Records*," Polo said.

"What do you mean?"

"He represents the fucking *Guinness Book of* fucking *Records*," Polo said. "Trying to establish if Cris is the man who has balled the most women consecutively in the world. Not that he's sure he can get his bosses to accept the category. They're still debating the issue. Family values, you know. He's been following Cris around for the last six months."

"But the photos . . . "

"He needs evidence, *comprendes*?"

"Who is this young vandal?" the midget from the *Guinness Book of Records* asked. "Do you know him?"

"Tell him, Polo."

"He's Cristóbal McKenzie's son."

"So this is how you repay my kindness," the man croaked in his broken Spanish. "When I've staked my reputation on getting you into the book. This is how you repay me, you Chileans. Barbarians. You don't deserve to be in our book."

"Fuck your book," my father said. "I never wanted to be in your stupid book. I just want to win my bet."

"Why did you cooperate with me, then?"

"So you'd stay out of my hair. And now look what you've done. You've scared Lila away."

"Your idiotic son scared her away, not me. But that's it. I'm through. I'm leaving for England. The rules are clear: if there is interference, bribery, connivance, cheating, we pull out. You could have made it, Mr. McKenzie. You could have been one of the immortals. The new Don Juan. The new Casanova."

"I don't want to be one of them," my father said. "I have enough trouble just being myself. And you're a pain in the ass. So the sooner you get out of here, the better." In a huff, the man hopped into his Hertz Ford Escort, started the engine, was gone. "Polo, what time is it?"

"We'll have to hurry, Cris. If that runaway kid's trail leads out of town, we could be on the road most of the night and that means—"

"Okay, okay." My father turned to me. "My God, Gabriel. Where the hell were you this morning?"

"I went jogging, got lost."

"You're hopeless. Polo, go inside and pay the damn check, will you? How about the nun? D'you think that the nun—"

"The nun's hot for it, but to get her away from the convent at such short notice . . . What about Hilda at the Mercado Central? She just turned eighteen and she's been making eyes at you for the last—If we can pry her away from her clams for a few hours, that is."

"I'll try Hilda. If you can take over her stand."

Polo left us there on the sidewalk, alone for an instant. My father made a gesture as if to follow him, stopped, looked at me.

"You think I need protection? You think I need you when I can sweet-talk any husband, any father, any brother? When I can call on hundreds of grateful parents, not to mention happy women? Oh, God. What am I going to do with you, Gabriel?"

"I'll meet you—you know where."

"I know where?"

"You know where," I said and turned. I wouldn't have been able to stand his telling me, just like that, to my face, that I could not come along, that if I had made it on time this morning I could have watched the seduction scene from inside the café instead of spying on him from outside, that if some lunatic had interrupted the proceedings by attacking the *Guinness Book of Records* guy, I would have been the one to help him figure out whom to fuck next. We would have feverishly, both of us, all three of us, found a substitute for plain-looking, soft-skinned Lila. I turned from him because if he didn't find that substitute, if he lost that bet with Barón, I did not want to be nearby.

Ignacio had disappeared. I suspected he was around the corner, hiding in embarrassment, and I was right. There he was, looking at me with his old look of scorn, the one I had first seen when he had come between my father and me at the airport. But this time I could not blame him, I could blame nobody but myself, nobody but the chain of circumstances that had begun with that drunken man delivering a *combo en el hocico* to Larrea yesterday at about this time and had ended with Gabriel McKenzie delivering an equally unjustified slap to someone else. One thing had led to another. I was becoming more Chilean, feeling more sorry for myself with every passing minute.

"Now what?" Ignacio asked. And remembered to add, charitably, "Gabriel?"

I was due to have lunch with the Nanny and that's where I went, that's whom I finally poured my heart out to—everything, Janice. My old desire for you and my new desire for Amanda Camila, my betrayal of the resistance in SoHo and my mistake with the *Guinness Book of Records* man at the café, my frustrated arrival in Chile that first evening and my frustrated jogging experience this morning, my fascination with the fractured iceberg in front of that shop window in Manhattan and my horror of women, my encounters with Polo and Carlitos and Larrea, my lies and my dreams, my wilting dick and my rising expectations, everything, just as I am belatedly telling it to you, Janice, everything. Che Guevara and Pinochet, Milagros and Cristóbal and Pablo Barón and Tío Pancho and Oscar. My long exile in New York and my short exile in Chile and my fear that I would be exiled forever, my virginity and boastfulness and sorrow, everything.

There was a goodness in her. I am not making this up, I swear. I am not imagining this; it emanated from her like a wave, something palpable. Like a fruit you could pick from a tree and eat with the tree's blessing. My Nana had given me the only true moments of peace I had experienced on this journey, on that street among the fleeing vendors when I arrived exhausted and depressed, in that baby's bedroom singing her lullaby to the twins the next day. She was there at the origin of each joyous moment in my memory, the hurdy-gurdy swirling its melody in my past, the first bread I ever smelled, my hand in her hand as I toddled down my first street. I had no one else to turn to and her warm body was here now to hold me, clasp me to her, ruffle my hair, comfort me. She was the one person who would not use me for her own purposes, because I felt that her only purpose was to make me happy, to see me fed and clothed and perpetuating myself in this valley. She had waited up all night for my mother the night I was conceived, she had given my mother advice the night my father went off to penetrate some other woman in order to win his bet. She was the one person who would know what to tell this child in a man's body, this man with a child's face, she would make it all right, I knew she would make it all right.

All she said, however, once I was done with my confession and with the wonderful meal she placed in front of me, once I had finished and spared her no detail, all she said was, "I have to do my shopping," she said. "*Cazuela de ave* for tomorrow," she said. "I want you to pay attention."

I asked her what I was to do, and she insisted that certain things can't wait, food for the family, for instance. Someday I'd understand and I was not to ask her anything else until she was good and ready.

I did her bidding. I accompanied her to the feria and watched her buy all the ingredients that I bought today at midday here in Sevilla, the onions and carrots, the garlic and *calabaza*, the string beans and the potatoes. Everything but the corn, she said, which we have frozen at home. But when you make it you'll be able to buy it fresh. Just make sure you peel back the husks and use your thumb to test the yellow consistency of the kernels. And don't forget how to kill the hens, she said, putting one on her knee, stretching its neck till it died, first having asked the creature's permission and thanking it. Don't forget how we pluck the feathers and then scorch the skin a bit above the flames. Just as I will do tomorrow, Janice, when I prepare the *cazuela* for the last supper I'll ever eat, Barón and McKenzie's last supper. It was almost as if she were preparing me for Sevilla, or so I'd like to think, making sure that tiny grits of feather weren't left on the skin, smoking them out with the heat. I watched her grease the enormous pot, bring out the spices. Be sure you have cilantro, Gabriel, and *cuidado con la sal*, always watch out for the salt.

Only when the brew was boiling, once she'd dried her wizened hands on her apron and sent the twins off with the maid to a nearby playground, only then did she say, "*Ese hombre*," she said. "That man. *El daño que ha hecho ese hombre.*"

The harm that man's done. That man. My father immediately jumped into my head as the culprit she was signaling out. But who knew? Maybe it was Polo who had done all that harm, Polo who had taken her place when she left that house and had then taken over mine when I wasn't there to defend it. Or Pinochet. Wasn't Pinochet the one who had screwed us all, sent us into exile, my Tío Pancho to jail, my father to his coldness and businesslike attitude? Wasn't Pinochet the one who had cornered us all, the generation I would have belonged to if I had stayed in Chile, cornered delicate Amanda Camila and filled her with rage? Or was it someone else? Someone only the Nanny knew, someone she would rather leave in the shadows for now, someone who was really harming us all, someone nearer by, Pablo Barón?

She wouldn't say. "I know what I know," she said, "and what you need to know is about women."

It all boiled down to something, it was all revealed in a legend she had heard, she didn't say when. Back when the world was young, women ruled. They ruled by dressing up as monsters, putting on horrible masks and scaring the men, scaring them into thinking the monsters were gods who would punish them if they did not obey the women. They ruled for many years and many generations. Men could not come to the rituals that women practiced, only girls could, when the blood came out from between their legs for the first time, that's who could come into the sacred hut and be told the secret of the monsters. Then they could put on the masks themselves and drive fear into the hearts of the men. But one day a man happened to overhear two women talking, seated in front of a fire. They were laughing about how they fooled the men. "So you can see, Gabriel, how women were always just like women now. They like to gossip, they lose everything they gain by talking too much, and that's what happened back then as well. The man told the other men and they decided to take their revenge. They slaughtered every woman in the tribe, killed each and every one of them—except for the youngest girls, *Dios mío*, the ones who had not yet been told the secret. And then the men waited and made love to the girls when the girls were ready, and the men put on the masks themselves and scared the new wives and new mothers and new lovers. They came dressed as ghosts in the night and screamed in voices nobody recognized and the women had to obey or the monsters would come for them. That is how men have ruled ever since, that is why I make *cazuela* and Pablo Barón eats it, why you have to learn how to make *cazuela*."

The Nana looked at me. I did not know where she was going with that legend.

"Never forget, Gabriel, who is telling you this: a woman," the Nana said, clutching my hand all the while. "Which means that women know. We have the upper hand, finally we hold the keys to the kingdom: babies and pleasure and food. If you make the *cazuela*, you make the world. It's a fight—life, sex, everything. Women mustn't let men know how powerful women really are. And we like you men to be strong and we also like you to be weak. To wear the mask and then to take it off only for us. Do you understand?"

"Not really."

"That's why women make believe they are scared. So you can protect them. They make believe they do not know where monsters come from. Now do you get it?"

I shook my head.

"Someday," she said. "Promise me that someday you will remember this legend. When you most need it."

"When will that be?"

"When you most need it."

And again the Nana changed the subject. It was time to focus on the here and now, she said. She did not like the iceberg, she asserted, thought it was full of evil spirits, but it seemed to contain the answer to my troubles, at least right now. There was a reason I had first seen that blue ice in that window in New York, there was a message being sent to me, to us. If I could solve the problem of who was threatening it . . . She asked me more details about it, about my suspicions, about my investigation. If I had to pinpoint one person who might have done it, who would that person be?

Suddenly I felt—I don't know how to put this, Janice, but I guess the right word is watchful, maybe vigilant. Not because of her—she had already sworn that she would never say a word of this to anybody, "Only to my shadow," she had promised me. No, it was because it dawned on me that Ignacio was probably listening outside, that this house was wired like the *Ministro*'s office was wired, and it was one thing for the secret police to know about my embarrassing life and tribulations, to learn that I hadn't fucked anything fleshier than a toilet seat, and quite another to let them in on my detective work. Though they probably had a better idea than I did, anyway. They might themselves be responsible, as Barón had implied when he had first explained the case to my father and me. I could see Ignacio laboriously writing out that letter so that some iron-fisted officer could sabotage the new democratic government. Who cared if they found out? At this point I had told my uncle, whose cell probably had more bugs than Barón's office, so I might as well spell out my conjectures and weave through the labyrinth of possible motives and felons. I couldn't suggest Larrea and I couldn't suggest Amanda Camila and I didn't even know the name of the drunken *combo en el hocico* guy and I wasn't going to mention my father or the *Ministro*. So I fixed on the ecologist woman. Of all the possible perpetrators she seemed the only one, at that point, to whom I could safely allude.

"Eco? What?"

"Ecological," I said. "People who care about the earth, who think we are destroying the planet with our style of life."

"They're right, those people, those eco people. How do you spell that word?"

And then she took from inside her apron a pale blue piece of paper exactly like the one *Ministro* Barón had received in his office, exactly like the one I did not yet know he would receive ten days later, and she painstakingly wrote ECOLOGICAL in the same block letters that I had already seen and would see yet again in the months to come.

That proves nothing, of course. It proved nothing then. It occurred to me that she might be the one, the Nana, who had written those threats. She had as much of a chance as Larrea himself or Larrea's left-wing associates inside the project or Amanda Camila or my father or Barón or ecological Berta or the Argentines or the Bolivians or my uncle's comrades or Big Ignacio or so many others who would prove suspicious as the investigation continued. But she had no reason, no motive. So I got rid of the thought, told myself I had got rid of it when I was really storing it away.

I need a rest now, Janice. I was sick then, became dizzy and sick almost as soon as I talked to the Nanny. I feel faint now as well. Or maybe it's that this evening, in a few hours' time, I have to go out and meet someone my uncle has set me up with here in Sevilla, a man who will be able to provide me with the explosives I'll need to carry out my plans. Twenty-five years to the day after I was conceived, after Che Guevara was buried in Vallegrande.

It's not enough to celebrate the birthday boys with food, you see, Janice.

I have other plans. But you don't have a chance in hell of finding out about them until it's too late to stop me.

PART THREE

OCTOBER 11, 1992

·

Couples that do well are those that rest, not on love but on friendship.

— M O N T A I G N E

·

Today there came to the ship a canoe with six youths in it, and five came

aboard. These I ordered held and am bringing them with me. Afterwards I

sent some of my men to a house west of the river, and they brought seven

women, small and large, and three children. . . . Tonight there came to the

ship the husband of one of the women and the father of the three children, a

male and two females. He asked that I might let him come with us, and it

pleased me greatly, and all the people on board are now consoled, so they must

be relatives.

— F R O M   T H E   L O G   O F   C R I S T Ó B A L   C O L Ó N

Well, the day's come. It's dawning, the last day before America is five hundred years of age, the last chance birthday boys McKenzie and Barón have to lose their bet. My father must be fucking my mother in their room at the Príncipe de Asturias hotel, just to make sure nothing goes wrong on this day of all days. Pablo Barón, across the hall in his own suite, must be sucking up to the president, just to make sure he doesn't lose his job on this day of all days, giving him a call in Santiago to ask for instructions on how to proceed, how to announce that the Chilean government has decided to cart the damn iceberg all the way back to Antarctica, dock in Punta Arenas, where they set out from, and head back to Bahía Paraíso and let it loose, let it join its brother and sister icebergs in the cold waters one year after its capture. A publicity stunt. As if that majestic blue mound of ice could ever go back, as if what it has lived during its captivity could ever be erased. As if I weren't going to blow it up tonight.

There. I've said it. You probably guessed it anyway.

But I am getting ahead of myself.

This will only make sense once you have followed me down to Antarctica, once you discover what I discovered on my trip to Patagonia.

To think that I almost didn't go, to think that I could have been saved if I had listened to my body. It was telling me to stay, it was fighting for its preservation like a madman, it had made me feel as sick as I'll ever feel in order to force me to remain behind, to not join Amanda Camila or her father on that flight to Tierra del Fuego, to not end up here in Sevilla about to commit suicide in front of all the nations of the globe.

I didn't hear what my body was screaming.

I interpreted the dizziness that came over me after my long confession to the Nana, the five bedridden days of retching that followed, in an entirely opposite way: as a cleansing. Cause and effect. I threw up almost as soon as I finished depositing with the Nanny the sordid and humiliating details of the story I had been unable to tell anyone for eight years. I had not, after all, been sick throughout my adolescence, not since your hot little turntable, Janice, failed to excite me into virile action. It was almost as if my baby face came equipped with its own immune system, every germ on earth fleeing this fallen angel, giving me wide berth. That's how I saw it: the untold story of frustration and repression, deception and longing had been sustaining me all these years, a spiteful, vengeful spider of an obsession keeping the microbes at bay along with the ladies. And now there was a sudden vacuum where the story had been. Now I had vented the story, now I was open like a vagina into which the sickness could spill and then congeal.

Though there's no need for so much idle theorizing. There was a medical explanation for my ailment.

Dr. Ciruelo came to see me. In Chile, doctors still make house calls—what do you think of that? They make the rounds in the evening after their regular hours, house by house, sipping some sherry with the rest of the family. So you can see that Chile still keeps a few old customs that we could imitate in our rush-rush New York. Ciruelo was more than glad to take another gander at the body he had helped to give birth to twenty-three years ago. As he probed and tested, he talked about what a beautiful baby I'd been and his warm hands comforted me with their knowledge. The immediate culprit, the doctor said as the *Ministro*, Amanda Camila, my mother, and the Nana hovered nearby, was the jogging. Even that early in the morning there were enough fumes in the air to knock out a regiment, particularly if our Gabrielito was not used to the sort of smog that plagued Santiago and had half the school-age population gagging. The mountains dammed up the gas and left it nowhere to escape: the curse of the Araucanians upon those who destroyed their glorious valley. I'd get better in a day or two, he assured me, closing his satchel. Nothing to worry about. He turned to Barón. "The real culprit, Pablito," old Ciruelo said crisply, giving the impression he'd pulled the *Ministro* himself into this world, "is the smog. What you're looking at is what will happen to us all if we keep on burning the atmosphere with millions of cars we don't need. Here lies the future."

The future—meaning me—did not intervene in the discussion that followed. The *Ministro* defended the push to modernize and catch up to the industrialized nations as the only way to provide prosperity to the many in need. Dr. Ciruelo insisted it was suicide; we'd end up with the pollution of the industrialized nations without any of their advantages, the worst of both worlds, no matter how much we fooled ourselves. Like that iceberg publicity stunt, Ciruelo said, pointing his stethoscope at Barón. The very people who were contaminating the country with their development-at-any-cost attitude, they were the ones exporting an image of pulchritude and purity to the world. Your pet project, Pablo, it's a scandal, spending so many millions on that iceberg when there's so much to be done here at home, so many hospitals to be built. And the *Ministro*: Blah, blah, blah, how're you going to pay for your hospitals if we don't sell more abroad and that's what the iceberg—Ciruelo interrupted with the words, the very undoctorlike words, That fucking iceberg, it gets me so angry at times I'd . . . I'd blow the damn thing to smithereens. And as for me, Gabriel McKenzie, junior detective, I was prostrate or I'd have smuggled my giddy hand into the bag of that doctor who had helped deliver me into this world to see if there wasn't some pale blue paper inside, if he couldn't be trapped into confessing right then and there that he had scribbled that threat and with that confession deliver me from this chase, transform me into the hero who had saved the day, protected the iceberg, liberated his uncle, impressed his father, and got the girl. But I didn't have the strength to lift a glass of water to my lips, let alone creep into Ciruelo's secretive medical bag. All I wanted was for these men to cease discussing the atmosphere and the ozone layer and the hole that was growing over Antarctica and the new buses imported from South Korea that would emit less particles. The Bolivians could have our old buses and screw themselves, Pablo Barón exulted, they had trouble breathing way up there in the *altiplano*, anyway. I wanted the *Ministro* and the doctor to be discussing me, cooing over me, trying to make my dizziness, or at least my loneliness, go away. I wanted some medicine that would allow me to sit up just enough so that Amanda Camila could slip her pretty lap and her endless crotch under my head, feel the back of my head so close to her sex and the source of all relief, dream of turning that head around and burying my mouth there, between her legs, so I could show her why the McKenzies live and die by their tongues. What I needed was to be cured, what I needed was to stop this pounding in my chest, this drumbeat in my brain, this dullness in my dick. I needed to be loved back into sanity.

That ended up being the only advantage of my fainting spell: staying in Amanda Camila's house for the next few days in that guest room the Nana had improvised for me. I could have gone back to the Casa Milagros; I wasn't that afflicted. But I dissembled, I fooled everybody—almost everybody, that is—into assuming I was infinitely worse. I saw my chance to be near my love and far from Polo. True, far from my father as well, but I said to myself, as I drooled and emptied everything I drank into a pan that Nana loyally held to my face, if the great McKenzie wanted to bring this refugee home, he could do so. Here was a test, a veritable test of what he felt. He did come, once, that same Friday, a few hours after I passed out. I hoped he was no longer angry about my snooping, prayed that my new suffering might blot out the memory of the indiscriminate smack I had administered to the midget from the *Guinness Book of Records* that very morning. When I heard him approach, I closed my eyes and waited to see what comfort he had brought, my forehead waited for his touch, my sweat waited for his handkerchief, my pecker waited for his advice—but nothing. I thought, Maybe he's standing guard over me, preventing the demons from invading my dreams like he does with Carlitos, like we both had done the night before.

That delusion was soon shattered.

A few minutes later he was gone and, straining my ears, I could hear him tackling my mother in the next room. He was telling her that I was obviously okay, it was all a fake playing for sympathy, just like the former runaways at the Casa after they'd done something wrong. Either that or the boy was too soft, *un marica*; you've spoiled him. She asked if he really meant that, that I was making this up, this sickness, and my father said yes, I'd been hamming it up, I'd been squirming for pity, feeling sorry for myself ever since I arrived. Mom told him he, Cris, ought to try to understand how hard it was to come home after so many years, try to give his own son this much, *así*, of the compassion he was showering on every other man-child and grown woman in the universe, even if he hadn't expended an ounce of energy to get rid of Pinochet. His answer—You wanted a hero, you should have married Che Guevara—was countered by, Che is dead. And he said, Yeah, so you told me that night on the Alameda, and I believed you. It was just a way to get your attention, she shot back, I didn't know it would turn you into a coldhearted bastard. And he: You didn't think I was cold back then, you wouldn't find me cold if you gave it a try now. And she: I'd rather fuck a corpse.

I didn't have the strength—or the guts, for that matter—to bark at them to shut up, go fuck each other if that's what will keep you both quiet. My body didn't have the defenses to ignore those voices; they filled me with a venom far worse than the Santiago air. I was relieved when he left, when the great McKenzie, who was supposed to be my ticket to cunt heaven, had tramped down the stairs and my mom was back with me, soothing my brow, taking my temperature, feeding me baby teaspoons of broth from another sort of heaven, from the Nana's heavenly hands, drop by drop of the *caldo* of the *cazuela* that the Nana one day wanted me to cook, that tonight here in Sevilla I will be cooking for everybody but her.

"Milagros," the Nana said, "I think you should go to the Casa to get your things, Gabriel's things."

Mom looked at her, nodded. This was the woman who had told her she was pregnant, who had warned her who was wrong for her over the many years before that, who had counseled her to stay with Cristóbal McKenzie when he had come home with the funeral smell of another woman on his groin.

"Gabriel," Milagros whispered, "we're going to be staying here, at Pablo and Carola's house. Until you're better."

She meant: I'm leaving your father. I've had it with him. This trip has been a disaster.

A few minutes after Mom announced her decision, I heard Amanda Camila coming home from work, heard her ask from the bottom of the stairs how I was feeling, heard her running up to see me, and saw her traipse through the door just as I had dreamed she would. My magical girl knew just what would give me some strength. "You're much too *fome*, Gabriel, stuffy and humdrum. What you need is some music." She went on to play me her favorite American and British pop artists, not one of whom I could identify. "My God, Gabriel, where have you been spending the last five years?" I told her that of course I knew every last song (Nirvana? Who the hell was Nirvana, a man or a woman?), even if the whirling in my head, I explained, did not allow me to concentrate. As if I could fool her about that (I could fool her about other things), as if she hadn't guessed that only classical music had been part of my bookish existence so far, no rock radio, no parties, no dancing, even no weed. She'd teach me to light up and lighten up, smoke and dance, as soon as I could stand straight; she'd make me twist and shout and boogie and mosh. In her adorable Chilean accent, she was mouthing words she did not entirely understand and asking me to translate, which I couldn't have done even if my head hadn't been such a muddle that the words seemed babbled in a foreign tongue. But as long as she kept holding my hand and caressing it, following the veins and the bones and articulations in the fingers with her own finger, I had no complaints. I could feel her energy vaguely floating into me, and not only *her* energy; other Baróns, it turned out, were on their way. Soon Carola pranced in, resplendent and full-bodied in yet another red dress, and brought me still more company—her naughty twins were ready to visit their cousin. Look at your *primo, pobre primo*, he's yucky-sick. The two boys romped on top of me and made me even queasier with their soft smell of shit, but I was sorry to see them go, sorry that the Nana firmly carted them away for a bath. Their silly exploration of my teeth and my earlobes made me feel somehow welcome, so that I was already half propped up by the time Mom returned with our luggage from the Casa Milagros. She proposed a card game to perk me up and things got even livelier when Pablo Barón made a late appearance, straight from a cabinet meeting, and ordered that food be served up here in my room. Not that I ever again wanted to see anything solid, but "It'll do you good to watch others devouring Nana's *cazuela*," the *Ministro* said. It was true. I couldn't hold up a card or a fork or even a noodle, but I loved to watch them so happy, Carola and Pablo and Milagros and Amanda Camila playing poker as the soup and drink went down the hatch, cheating one another and hiding the cards under my covers and making me their accomplice. By the time each of them had kissed me a chaste good night on the forehead, I had accepted that my grogginess was a blessing in disguise, the twisted way destiny had maneuvered me toward a safe landing in the one place in Chile that perhaps—who knows?—I could finally call home.

Yes, really like home, a space where a family lives. So what if my father was at that moment drilling into some unknown female body what my mother no longer would allow him to drill into her? I had loved ones nursing me back to health. And not all was indulgence.

On Sunday, after two days of pampering and coddling, Pablo Barón decided it was time for some tough love, time for me to abandon my bed. If only for a few minutes, I needed to shape up, use my legs again. "On Wednesday," he announced, as I took my first staggering steps in forty-eight hours, about to collapse when his iron fingers dug even deeper into my left armpit and hoisted me up as if I were a toy. "On Wednesday; we're all leaving for Patagonia. I have to meet my counterpart from Argentina, smooth some things out, take a look at the security arrangements for the iceberg. Crazy Carola's invented some business of her own to meddle in down there, and she's offered to stay on a few days after I'm gone, chaperon you and Amanda Camila, make sure you don't get into any trouble."

"How about my dad?" I managed to exhale the question. "Weren't we going to get him on board?"

"He says he's too busy—following a lead on the iceberg. Is he?"

"He's not following shit," I said. "Skirts, maybe."

"Plenty of skirts in Punta Arenas. He doesn't know what he's missing. Patagonian ass, huh, Gabriel?"

"How about my mom?"

Milagros wanted to keep the Nana company. And the Nana couldn't come along. Somebody had to stay behind to take care of the children. "I told you Nana was the boss," Pablo Barón grunted. He sat me back down on the bed. "I told you that she's the one who makes things run here."

Not really, I thought to myself. If she were really the boss, then Carola would be the one to stay home with her twins and Nana would accompany us, a solution I would have much preferred, though I wasn't going to say so to Barón, particularly as at that moment -

red-dressed Carola herself flounced flamboyantly in with a cordless phone. The first call I had ever received in Chile. Absurdly, I wondered if it might not be you, Janice, if you had tracked me down to ask when we'd go all the way. But it was my Tío Pancho, from jail.

Today was Sunday, visiting day, and where the hell was I, what was I doing at Barón's house, anyway? Why was I sleeping in the house of the enemy?

"I'm sick, Tío," I said. "They're taking care of me."

"You're the only one," he answered. "They're not taking care of anybody else. The country's getting deeper in debt every day, people buying TV sets they can't afford to see advertisements for products they don't need. And your buddy Barón's responsible. Back when we were fighting Pinochet, he used to say that the country had to produce for the majority, not for the rich. Ask him, ask him if that's not what he said back then."

The room was spinning. I lay back down on the bed and let my head plummet against a pillow, clutching the receiver in a clammy hand. I mouthed my uncle's name to Pablo Barón, who shrugged his shoulders. I shrugged back: I'm not to blame for my relatives.

"I'll try," I said to the phone.

"When are you coming to see me? Thursday?"

"I'll be down in Patagonia. Tío Pablo's taking me."

"Ha! Going to see the scene of the crime."

"What crime?"

"Ask him, ask Pablo Barón what the Baróns did in Patagonia. Tell him that what his great-grandfather did yesterday his children will do tomorrow. Tell him he's not to blame: he's just being loyal to his family, his class, his blood. Tell him I said so. Tell him to read his Lenin."

"I don't know what you're talking about, Tío Pancho."

"You'll know, you'll know. One last question, *sobrino*. How are your lips doing?"

"My lips?"

"Are they chapped from kissing, Gabriel? Huh? Or are they chapped from the cold? The cold and no company? And talking about the cold, how's that big flab of ice doing? Still floating? Have you found Commandante You-Know-Who?"

I looked at Pablo Barón. Fortunately, he could not hear that I had told the *Ministro*'s worst enemy about the secret. I decided to cut the conversation short. Who knows who was recording our words? His jailers or the men supposedly safeguarding Barón or Ignacio trying to keep tabs on me—there was a wealth of guardians crouching in the nooks of this newly democratic Chile.

"I can hardly hear you. I'll come visit when I return."

"You can hear me. But you're scared my good friend Pablo will hear me as well. Fear is what's fucking up this country and now you've caught the virus as well. You still want to know who Commandante You-Know-Who is? I've got some information that might interest you. Ha! Didn't expect that one, did you? I'll tell you this much: it's an inside job."

The phone went click and then there was a long sustained buzz. Pablo Barón took the phone from me, turned it off, told me how much he still loved that crazy son of a bitch my uncle, even if he was a dinosaur, still clinging to his old Marxist beliefs, unable to adapt to the new world, the new order. Too bad it wasn't possible to let him go. A few months ago, an eminent conservative senator had been murdered by left-wing terrorists, probably from the same group that Pancho belonged to. The senator's death had given the pro-Pinochet forces the moral high ground, allowed them to harp on terrorism as the main problem of the country, erase their own past human rights violations, claim the crime rate had gone up since democracy returned. If Tío Pancho had been loose at that point, justifying the murder, that would have been it: the *Ministro* who'd set him free would have lost his job. And his bet. Not that he didn't intend to keep his promise if we solved the iceberg case . . .

"He said something about you and Patagonia, that I should ask you about the Baróns and some crime."

"Oh, that," the *Ministro* said. "That's no secret. I'll tell you all about it, I'll seat you next to me on the plane. Though I'm going to have to spar with Amanda Camila every inch of the way. She says she wants you all for herself."

"There's plenty of me to go around."

"You wouldn't be falling in love with her, would you?"

I surprised myself with the quickness of my response: "There's a girlfriend back home. Janice. She'd tear my eyes out."

"At times we do foolish things, we think it's worth it, even if we end up getting our eyes torn out."

"Amanda's like a sister, just as you said. No chemistry between us."

"How about her? Do you think she might be falling in love with you?"

What was he trying to get at? Why did he keep harping on these themes? Was he that jealous of his own daughter? I decided to try a little experiment, see how he reacted. I might be nauseated, but I could still spin a plot or two.

"She's interested in my father, I think."

Pablo Barón snorted. "So I've heard. I love it. I hope she stays infatuated with Cris till she meets the right man, a few years from now."

"But aren't you—"

"She doesn't stand a chance. I'm going to tell you why. Turns out only Cris and I know this—promise you'll never tell Amanda, or anybody else."

I promised. Words are cheap.

"When she was born, not two hours had passed and there he was, the great McKenzie, in the hospital ward. 'Pablo,' he says to me, he says, 'Before I even see the little girl, I've got a present for you and for her,' and I tell him the hell with the present, he should come and take a look at his new *sobrina*. Strange, now that I think of it, you had already seen her, you were a tiny tyke of, what was it?, three, four—"

"Five," I said.

"Milagros had brought you—you must have been the first one, besides me and Dr. Ciruelo—to see Amandita. How's that for long-term relationships?"

"My father," I reminded the *Ministro*. "The present."

"An envelope. He hands it to me, a thin envelope. I open it and a condom falls out into my hand and 'Is this a joke?' I ask, 'because if this is your idea of a joke . . .' But Cris stopped me in my tracks. 'It's the one I'll never use,' Cristóbal McKenzie says. 'I just want you to know that there's no way I'll ever screw your little girl.' 'She's a bit small and sort of young for you to be even thinking about—' 'Once a man's daughter is born,' your father says, 'his relationship with the entire pubescent male population changes drastically, and I don't intend that beautiful baby to come between us, destroy our relationship. I'm swearing to you right here, on the day of her birth, that you can rest assured that I'll never touch her. I'll preserve her and look after her as if she were my own. Just like you'll always be there for Gaby.'"

"What did you do?" I asked.

"I said to him, 'Well, thanks,' I said, 'but I don't want your fucking condom. Here, take it back.' 'Keep it, I'm telling you,' Cris says, closing both his fists. 'It'll bring you luck.' And you know what? It did. Ever since then it's like a magic star has been watching over me. Or maybe it was Amanda Camila's birth, like some angel was born along with her. But I'm superstitious, Gabriel. I keep it on me at all times. Here. Take a look."

He extracted a folded little yellowing envelope from his wallet and made me look at it, what would never cover my father's erect penis, what would never be placed inside Amanda Camila's vagina, the guarantee that, in this one field, my father would not be there before me, would not be blocking the way. Unless there were other women he . . . ?

I asked Barón. "And that was the only time he swore he wouldn't touch a woman? As far as you know, that is?"

"The only time."

I felt that we had reached a level of intimacy, almost of friendship— the most powerful man in this country making me his confidant, his buddy, over and over again. If I could only have confessed to him what ailed me, not the air pollution but what really plagued me like a pestilence. I felt that I could ask him something that I had been wondering about.

"Do you mind if I, I mean, you won't be bothered by a question that I—"

"The only thing that can come between us, Gabriel, is if you ever touch that girl, if you ever try anything funny with her. But as long as you stay away from my baby you can do anything, say anything. So go ahead. Shoot."

I asked him how he could be sure of his women, Marta first and then Carola, with a best friend who was perpetually on the prowl.

"First," the *Ministro* answered, "friendship is more important than sex. Sex passes—a few thrusts in, a few thrusts out, a spasm of pleasure, and then it's over. But friendship. That lasts, that's what we live for. Lasts longer than anything we have with women, with their big breasts and their small brains. Don't quote me, don't go quoting me. But to answer specifically: Marta didn't like him. I think she was jealous of Cris. Thought I loved Cris more than I loved her. And she was right. So she'd nag on and on about how he was a bad influence and it couldn't help my political career to be around that sort of womanizer and cynic and so forth."

"And Carola?"

"You know what, maybe he's screwed her—or tried. I wouldn't put it past him. But somehow I think he'd steer away. With so many other women around, why pick on mine, huh? If he valued my friendship so highly that he gave me that crazy condom when Amanda Camila was born, well, would it make sense to poison it? Because your father is right. That is something that can destroy the best relationship. Like the one we have, you and me."

"Like the one we have?"

"Like ours. Tell you what I want, Gabriel. I want you to swear, swear the same oath your father did."

"Swear what?"

"You'll never try and fuck my little girl."

"Tío," I said, "this really isn't necessary."

"It's necessary. Believe me it is."

He had me cornered. I lied my head off, crossed every mental finger in my brain, swore I would never try and make love to his little girl.

"Fuck. Use the word. Never fuck her."

"I'll never fuck her."

"If you do, may all hell break loose. Say it."

"May all hell break loose."

Heaven and hell did break loose when I finally fucked her, Janice. And they began by breaking loose, as if in anticipation, during the next few days. Maybe you'd have perversely enjoyed the sight, my pain: to have the girl I loved suckling me back to health, the body I couldn't hold in my arms holding me as if I were her sister. The sweet pain of hearing her say words that, in another context, would be a valentine: "You're a dream, Gabriel, somebody with whom I don't have to pretend, somebody with whom I can be myself."

You'd probably suggest that she knew of my passion and was playing with me. It's what I asked myself during those hours I would spend alone in bed or hunched in an armchair, while the Nanny knitted by my side and the twins somersaulted nearby. I wondered if she knew what her father had made me swear and was tormenting me on purpose, if she had been giggling in the closet while he made me vouch I would never mount her golden body. Because let me tell you, Janice, she flirted as if she had learned the technique at Vamp University.

After work on Monday, you know what she did? She came into my room with ten different dresses, ten of them. What did I like most for Punta Arenas? It would be very cold there, the southernmost city in the world in the dead of winter, but still, we'd also be inside a lot, visiting museums. She had come to try on her outfits in front of me, ask me which colors suited her best, slip in and out of them as I averted my eyes, catching only glimpses of the cup of her breasts budding inside that bra, the curve of her perfect ass filling the panties, the wisps of pubic hair bristling out and calling me in. You can look, silly, she said. Then on Tuesday evening she invited me into her room to help her pack, handing me each piece of clothing so I could feel it first, what would soon be on her body, what I would gladly have ripped from her body even if it meant Pablo Barón's ripping my heart out. When we had finished packing, the Seductress sat herself down in front of her mascara and makeup and perfumes and made me decide what was right for her. She lay me down on her bed because I was feeling dizzy again and unbuttoned my belt. "Not good for you to have it that tight," she breathed, and then traveled back and forth to my side, leaning her wares over me each time so I could tell her what I thought. "It's great to have a brother," she said. "You're the first one I can ask about these things. Carola's tastes are so passé and tacky, Dad has no taste at all, and Nana says all this artificial stuff is the work of the devil. So that leaves you, Gabriel. Come and comb my hair."

I didn't know whether it was paradise or an inferno to be so close, but I gathered enough strength to totter up again and apply long, vigorous strokes to the head I had first seen hairless when I was five. Maybe I had secretly desired her since that childhood moment, murmured to her quietly, back then, to grow up fast so we could play together. Maybe now she was returning the favor, playing this game as a way of giving me strength and dispelling the demons of my disease, because there, below, sure enough, in the hanging space between my legs, I could feel the stirring of my *pija*, a cocksure sign that blood was flowing back into me. Maybe Amanda Camila grasped that this was the only way to make me well. But if she knew that, then she had also guessed at my muscle's contraband desire for her, though that was impossible, given her adamant repetition of how we were only friends and nothing more. She emphasized it so often and so relentlessly that I could not even envisage an approach. Unless that was the biggest come-on of all. If only I could ask my dad about it, have him say, Of course she's monkeying with you. What you need to do, Gabriel, is grab her wrist and look into her eyes and say—what? What should I say? What could I say that would not make me lose her forever? What would he have said?

Well, to begin with, he'd have fucked her at the first chance, that's what he'd have done if he hadn't taken that oath to spare her and her alone—I mean, fucked her or her equivalent, as he'd fucked many a girl like her whose father was not his best friend. And here I was, one week after having met her, trapped in the sweet terror of her presence, the sweet frustration of her available and forbidden body, the sweet madness of her dad who would kill me if I did and my own hand that was ready to kill me if I didn't soon, soon, soon. All of a sudden, that Tuesday night, it was too much. I decided that under no circumstance was I taking the plane to Patagonia the next day. I didn't think I could stand one more glance at the dimple of her belly button, one more minute of her lungs in the same room. What would happen when Barón went back to Santiago and Carola took off and left us by ourselves, left me to advance upon her and withdraw, left her to advance upon me and retire, left me unrestrained?

The next morning when she came to wake me up, I told her I was staying behind. She answered by tickling me—my God, Janice, she was tickling me as her nightgown billowed open with all the smells of sleep still seeping from her body—and I pretended that I was falling out of bed—anything, even something foolish-looking, to escape those fiendish hands.

"I can't," I said. "I'm sick. I really can't."

"You have to," she answered, "because I'm not going to Patagonia without you."

"Patagonia! Patagonia! What's so great about Patagonia?"

That's where my education began. Not Patagonia as the threshold to Antarctica, as I had been conceiving it all this time. Patagonia as the land where the first and last Indians had become extinct. That's why she was so stubbornly determined to study the Onas, the Alacalufes, the Fueguinos. She grabbed a world map, pointed to the north. The Bering Strait. Over which, fifty thousand years ago, the first inhabitants of the Americas had trudged across the ice. The ice, there at the beginning of the world, there at the end, the ice I will shatter into fifty thousand pieces tonight, one piece for each of the years those Asians who were to become the natives of the Americas were to spend in their new home.

"Now look at this. Down here." She pointed to Tierra del Fuego. "You can't go farther south, can't go farther from the Bering Strait and the northern lights. That's where they ended up, the first ones, the ones who passed over initially, who kept on being pushed southwards. Some would say that it's because they were the weakest, that the stronger tribes coming from behind forced them to move south. But I think they were the most adventuresome, the pioneers. Forget the Vikings and the Polynesians and you can certainly forget motherfucking Columbus and your Massachucha pilgrims and Magellan. My Indians, my men and women, made love for the first time on the soil of this continent that did not yet possess one human inhabitant, Gabriel. They were the foremothers, the forefathers of the people who forty thousand years later, after migrating again and again, finally reached the land where there was no more land, reached the outer bounds of ice again, Antarctica, out there where not even they could venture, though who knows if they didn't explore it in their canoes in the summertime, when it's day all night long, my Indians."

Something sad crept into Amanda Camila's voice as she spoke. Spoke about the extinction of those Indians. Not just any extinction. When they died, she said, what died with them were the eyes that had been repeated through thousands and thousands of generations and had first seen the aurora of the north, then headed south to see the australis. And the legends, their stories, their languages, containing the echoes of the first visions, the first time anybody in the species saw what they saw. Amanda had a special idea about those myths: rather than understand them as adaptations to the cold and the winds, stories of how you survive in the worst climate in the southern universe, she thought their makers might be returning to what they once knew, when they had been in the farthest north, repeating the ice legends they had in the deepest part of their brains, that they had sucked in with their milk. They'd come full circle, pole to pole.

Only to be exterminated. I pointed this out, that their odyssey had ended in death. Worse than death, she said: their extinction was a warning. It was the reverse of the Discovery. The genocide they suffered is the prelude to a northward thrust of death that will someday exterminate or assimilate every other culture, every other tribe that came after them. Their disappearance foretold something more drastic, not just for the other original inhabitants of the Americas. It foretold what will be the fate of us all if we let this happen, if we continue to live as if they had nothing to tell us. She paused, then said, "Gabriel, not only did they see it all for the first time, they named it."

She paused to observe what effect that had on me.

"Don't you realize? The ancestors of the Fueguinos, the first ones, saw that ice up there in the north and gave it a name. Then Alaska and then Saskatchewan and Oregon and then Tenochtitlán and then Guatemala and then Bogotá and then Cuzco and then this valley in this place called Chile, the end of the world. And then down to the real end, the extreme south, and they named each object for the first time as if they were gods. They named the *maíz* and they named the *tomato* and they named the *cerros*. So what's being lost is what those things were called, what the million faces of nature were called at the dawn when men and women contacted it. And my dream is that one of those descendants is still left somewhere, just one of them, and I could ask questions of that last one, the one who survived. Because if he dies, then what is being foretold is that we'll all die as well."

She was out of her mind with her apocalyptic scenario. But I was out of my mind in love with her.

"And that's why," I asked, drawling each syllable, pretending I was in pain, "you need me to get up and vomit my way all the way to the South Pole, so you can look for someone who doesn't exist?"

"There are worse ways of spending your day."

I looked at her. If anybody could save me, it was her. If anybody could inject faith in humanity into me, it was her.

"I'll come," I said.

I shouldn't have. I realized it was the wrong promise less than three seconds later when Mom pranced in and let me know what was in store for me. "Hurry up, you guys," she said, excited. "We have to go by a police station before the airport. They've found the kid who stole your watch."

"That kid whose ass Gabriel kicked?" Amanda said.

How had she ever learned about that? Ignacio! Ignacio had given Pablo Barón that false version and he had passed it on to his daughter and now she thought I was a hero. Would think it, that is, until she heard the humiliating truth from Leo or Carloncho or whatever the tall kid's name was. Choclo! Motherfucking Choclo. Was it too late to crawl back into bed, cover myself with a blanket, forget the quest for the ultimate Ona, and return to New York and your invisible embrace, Janice?

It was too late. I would have to show extra cunning, make sure Amanda Camila never learned what had really happened, bluff my way out of this mess. Though it wouldn't be easy: Mom was coming along, she said, to accompany us to the airport, though I suspected that it was to snoop, to ferret out the real story of how I had lost my watch and my clothes.

"I hope you won't be too hard on that kid," Mom said. "Whatever he did, it's really not his fault."

"Oh? Whose fault is it?"

"The system's," she said. "He's Pinochet's stepchild, just remember that. He's had no privileges, no education."

"No mom like you, huh? I'll try to remember that."

"Gabriel," Amanda Camila chipped in, "will always do what's right."

I hoped she knew what that meant, because I sure didn't.

Before we left, the Nanny slipped a small, smooth white stone cross into my hand. "May *la Virgen* protect you, *mi niño*," she whispered. "And don't worry. We'll fix everything."

I asked her what she meant by "we." She'd promised she wouldn't tell anybody about—Nana lifted her fingers to her mouth and made a turning motion, as if she were closing it with an invisible key. "Only to my shadow. I told you, only to my shadow. My mouth is sealed. I swear on my dead mother's grave, the mother I never knew."

"You don't need to swear. Just don't tell anybody."

My own mother, very much alive, interrupted us from the threshold. "What are you two up to, conspiring? Come on, Gabriel.

Before the police station you have to go get your computer. We'll be late for the flight."

The computer, of course, was not ready. One technician had taken it apart and by mistake another technician had put it together again without fixing it. Now they had to start over. The receptionist tried to calm me down, waving her long purple nails, offering to return it to me, no charge.

I left my computer with them. What else could I do? I had survived so far without communicating with you, Janice, or with my other Internet friends. Maybe the gods of underdevelopment were still insinuating that I should navigate Chile without help from anybody. Though I'd need divine intervention to avoid the tall kid waiting for me. Yes, it was him at the police station, there was no mistaking his gangly looks, his pimpled complexion, that scar like a putrescent half-moon over his eyebrow. Next to him, holding his hand, was a young woman. His sister, his girlfriend? She had been here before, holding his hand on other occasions, dressed in her Sunday best, she had dressed in those clothes over and over to accompany him to this station. She turned to me and I could see it all, I could read her fierce determination to stand by him no matter what he did or whom he hurt or where they sent him, I could see that she expected nothing from me, was not asking me, as my mother had asked less than an hour ago, to go easy on him. She knew that I couldn't care less what happened to him or her or any of them: I was from far away and would return there someday soon and she would be left dressing herself again on another morning to come to this or another police station to hold that same hand, hold it until one day there was no hand to hold, no tall kid to reach out with his hand to her, only his body to bury.

"This is your watch," the sergeant said.

I took it from him. I looked at Choclo's girlfriend and all of a sudden I remembered—who knows why?—that girl who a few days ago had thrown a look at me in the Alameda, that girl with the floating black hair and a bandanna hiding her nose and mouth, only the eyes inviting me to join the march. Even if it couldn't be her, the girl who had been brutally cast into the paddy wagon. My eyes went back to the watch. I returned it.

"No, sir."

"It has your name on it," the sergeant said. "You are Gabriel

McKenzie, born July 9, 1968? A birthday gift from your loving father?"

"I'm Gabriel McKenzie, but it's no longer my watch. I gave it to him."

The tall kid chimed in. "I told you he gave it to me of his own free accord, *mi sargento*. I told you I had witnesses. But who listens to us, right?"

"Shut up," the sergeant said. "Mr. McKenzie, you have nothing to fear from this delinquent, Salvador Salazar, known as El Gangrena. Also Choclo. Or his band. You can tell us the truth and press charges."

"I'm not afraid of him," I said. "I kicked his ass once, and I can do it again. Right, Salvador?"

Choclo saw what I wanted from him, saw what the trade-off was, and played along.

"He kicked my ass," the tall kid said. "And then he handed me the watch."

"And why did you hand him the watch?"

"Let's just say it was an old debt. I felt sorry for him. It wasn't his fault he's deprived."

"So you don't want this watch back?"

"It belongs to him, to Salvador Salazar."

"Yeah," Choclo said, "so hand it over."

Back in the van, speeding to the airport, I offset my new bout of dizziness by basking in the glory of my mother's admiration, Amanda Camila's gushiness at my having first kicked the kid's ass and then saved it. I was feeling pretty good about myself. Not, of course, because of my fraudulent rectitude and magnanimity. I had turned a disastrous situation into victory: I had closed Choclo's foul mouth, avoided the possibility of anybody's finding out the truth, received the adoration of these two women, even collected a thankful, surprised glance from the girl at the police station, who expected nothing from me or anybody in the world. All I had lost was a watch that I didn't want anyway, that was not what I needed from my father. And I also felt relieved—what I had told that sergeant was not entirely false. I did owe a debt. I had stolen money from the Chilean resistance. Maybe Salvador could unwittingly take my watch as part payment in the name of the Chilean people.

"There's just one thing I don't understand," my mother said, as we pulled into the departure lane at the airport. "Why did you give him your clothes as well?"

"It was a bet," I said quickly.

"A bet?"

"Yeah, I gave him the watch and then—I know you won't be embarrassed, Mom—but maybe Amanda?"

"Go ahead," she said. "I'm a big girl."

"He said I had whipped him. Then I'd humiliated him even further in front of his friends by giving him the watch. But it didn't matter, because he had a bigger thing than I did. So I bet him and we both stripped. The other kids stole my clothes."

"Men," my mom said. "You really are your father's son."

"Who won?" Amanda Camila asked.

It was a question that, for the first time since we had met, allowed me to express my sexuality openly, and I jumped at the opportunity. Two birds with one stone: also to probe her possible participation in the iceberg caper.

"That's for me to know and you to find out," I said and she looked at me in a strange way. Because she recognized the phrase she herself had written in that letter? Because of what my roving, desirous eyes were displaying through the words? Whatever the reason, she decided to ignore my allusion, cradle me back to an innocence I was so eager to abandon.

"You *are* your father's son," she said. "You like to save kids just as he does. I'm sure that Salvador Salazar has learned his lesson. You've saved him from a life of crime."

I didn't share her rosy optimism. Just like the kids who had break-danced in SoHo the night I gave them all that money, this street kid in Chile must have thought I was a basket case. I'd bet a couple of more watches that at this very moment he was pawning my father's gift and buying himself a big long knife with which to commit his next felony; he'd give me the fat Chilean *filo* next time we met. But if she wanted to see me as some sort of charitable priest out of *Les Miz*, so be it. Women like to be screwed by heroes, perhaps even by saints.

I was not to feel cocky much longer.

As we crossed the crowded airport lounge, whom did I see but the *Guinness Book of Records* dwarf, standing in a line at the British Airways counter, returning to his homeland to report not that the elder McKenzie had broken all records for stamina in the pursuit of a fuck-a-day but that another McKenzie, a younger member of the brood, yours untruly, was a barbarian. In fact, if that man had known the truth about me, if he had followed me around for the next months of my stay in Santiago, he could have invented a new category for his book that I would have won hands down: the Biggest Fuckup in the Universe. But now he noticed me. He hesitated whether to assault me right then and there. I could tell he had been dreaming of thrusting his elfin hands into my windpipe. I used that moment's lull and dashed away. "I'm feeling a bit giddy," I said to Amanda Camila and headed one way, then, cowering behind a pile of bags that was being pushed through by a swarthy porter, changed direction and darted into the nearest rest room.

As I was unzipping, pale at the thought of being confronted by someone whose ass I had in fact kicked but who would not provide Amanda Camila with a noble or honorable version of my motives, I heard a voice: "You're the *Ministro*'s son, aren't you?" It was Don Jacinto, the fattish old man who had been hounding Pablo Barón for a job. He was standing by a dripping faucet, smoking a cigarette, contemplating my efforts to piss. Needless to say, that stopped me in my tracks—the organ I had not compared with Salvador's, the organ I had not inserted into the folds of your vagina, sweet Janice Worth, the organ that was peckering to get inside Amanda Camila simply froze its functions under his stare.

"No," I said, "I'm Gabriel McKenzie."

"Why are you living at the *Ministro*'s house, then?"

"Look, I don't see this as any of your business. And by the way, don't any of you people know how to read? Look what it says there: *No Fumar*."

"I know how to read. You want me to read you a letter that Don Pablo Barón sent my son? You know who my son is? My son's Freddy Gutiérrez, the man who risked his life for someone who back then was a fugitive son of a bitch. My son's the man who dropped out of university to shield him, worked so hard he burned out. Started to feel fear. Have you ever felt fear, little man? Have you?"

I was feeling it right then, with the Guinness midget wandering around outside and me stuck there, beginning to feel sick again from the bitter smoke of this father intent on helping his son, intent on making me vomit.

"All it takes is for the *Ministro* to call up the head of Municipal Health, that's all, just thirty seconds, thirty seconds to pay for seven years' service. Not that much is it? Eh? Little man? This letter." He took out a pale blue envelope and a pale blue piece of paper. Again, again, I was being followed. Was there anybody in Santiago who did not have access to that stationery? Was this father irate enough to blow up Barón's iceberg in revenge? He waved them in my face. " 'My dear Don Jacinto. Thank you for your patience. We will let you know if we are able to help your son. The *Ministro* sends Federico his greetings and recalls his services with great warmth. *Ministro* Barón is also sorry that he did not see more of him in the last few years.' And that's all. He won't do it. That's what he means. He won't do it. Because my boy only spent seven years protecting him. Because he only ruined his whole life serving him. And now . . . and now . . ."

Don Jacinto came up to me, almost spat the words in my face. I could breathe the stale, hopeless nicotine of his lungs. "You're his son. You tell him what he should do. You tell him."

"I'm not his son and there's nothing to tell," I said and rushed out of the rest room, walking back in just as quickly. Right outside, the Guinness man was lurking, his back to me, but he would undoubtedly see me if I ventured further. The bulge in his bullneck told me that while I had been sinking into the despondency of pollution-induced infirmity he had, minute by minute over the last five days, with the single-mindedness of a man dedicated to pursuing and evaluating records—the longest-haired male in the world, the most teenagers in a phone booth, the biggest apple pie this side of Mars—and with the determination that only dwarfs can command, he had been obsessing about me, praying that the God of Guinness would, before he left Chile, deliver me unto him for one final farewell where he could give it to me, a piece of his mind, maybe a piece of his fist. It looked, though, as if he might have his retribution without even touching me, because unless I managed to squirrel past him I would miss my plane and my chances to get to Patagonia and near the sainted iceberg that I kept hoping would solve all my problems. Amanda and Barón would be up there in the sky while I was marooned forever in this bathroom, as Don Jacinto exhaled his son's lost cause down my spine. I turned to confront the old man and then I realized that we each had something the other wanted. I had the *Ministro*'s ear, which might bring advancement to Don Jacinto's son and God had endowed Don Jacinto with a tall and portly body behind which I could advance toward my plane. That was it! If he hid me from the sharp stubborn eyes of the Guinness man, I would champion his boy Freddy. I was getting good at this, trading favors. Maybe Chile was teaching me something after all, maybe this is the way you bag a lady.

Don Jacinto smuggled me past the dangerous Guinness midget unscathed and I kept my part of the bargain on the plane heading south as soon as I woke up from a long nap I had collapsed into after takeoff, relieved that my dwarfish enemy must be somewhere over the Amazon, on his way to some dreary place like Manchester. Pablo Barón was in the seat next to mine, diligently working away at a mountain of papers. "Feeling better?" he asked. "Look out the window."

There below us was a sea so blue it blazed into my eyes—El Golfo de Penas, the *Ministro* said, the Bay of Sorrows (had everything in this country been named so as to remind me of my sad condition?)—and, heaving into the distance, a stretch of majestic glaciers and multi-colored cliffs. "Darwin saw them on his way up to Valparaiso," Pablo Barón said, "but he missed the Ventisquero Colgante, ice falling continually into the sea, crashing like a waterfall of ice. Oh, Gabriel, this is such a *país maravilloso*. If those of us who have power were only as beautiful as our country, as pure." He paused fervently. "Maybe we'll finally give our people the government they deserve."

I saw my opening and pounced, told him about my chance meeting with Don Jacinto, fulfilled my obligation to the old man by suggesting that something be done for his son.

"You've got a good heart," Pablo Barón said. "Just like your dad. I'll tell you what the problem is. We made a deal with Pinochet. It's that simple: we get democracy back, people vote, no more censorship, no more torture or killings, but we don't retaliate. That means no trials, primarily, and no recriminations, but it also means that all the employees appointed by Pinochet, hundreds of thousands of them, stay just where they were, screwed into place. The result? Not enough, not even close to enough, openings for all those who expect some reward for what they did in the time of the dictatorship. So you can't create new jobs; in fact, international pressure, financial pressure, forces us to cut the budget. The few posts you do have at your disposal, Gabriel, must be used to hire the best. We're not an employment agency. This guy Freddy, Don Jacinto's son, he was an arrogant son of a bitch. The truth is he was sort of a fuckup. I don't want to tell you the mistakes he made . . ."

Barón went ahead and told me anyway. Freddy had screwed the wife of a naval officer in Concepción, an intelligence officer, and never told the resistance. And then one day he had simply disappeared, dropped out of sight in the middle of an operation. And when Barón and company had won the elections, Freddy's father had come whining for a job. The *Ministro* knew that he owed Freddy his life, but he couldn't play favorites, turn the government into some sort of mafia family thing.

I thought of the old man outside the Tourism building, outside Barón's house, outside the airport rest room, waving me goodbye. I said to the *Ministro*, "What about a job with Larrea? After that stupid attack, they'll need someone who's good at security."

And Barón reluctantly said yes, he'd do it because of me. Not knowing that it would be Freddy who many months later, tonight to be exact, would be the one to let me into the Chilean Pavilion through the back door, guide me, with my food and my explosives, past security. Certainly not knowing, Pablo Barón, that it was his own death that he was setting up. He was worried about something else: that my good heart be reined in. "But no more, Gabriel. Got it? No more solicitations on behalf of any other victim. No matter who it is. Have we got a deal?"

I nodded. Sleepily. Pablo Barón reached across me, adjusted my blanket, and I slumped back into fitful dreams.

I was awoken who knows how much later by a shuddering shake of the plane, as if it had been slapped by a giant. The sound of crashing dishes and glasses came from the galley.

"No need to worry," Pablo Barón said, "it's just the wind of *Magallanes*. We're delayed a bit, circling the Punta Arenas airport until some fog clears."

"Isn't it great?" the voice of Amanda Camila piped up as the plane looped downward and the engines roared into double action to rise out of the turbulence. She was standing right next to us, swaying with the deranged bump and rattle of the aircraft.

"Get back to your seat!"

"D'you think we'll crash, Dad?" Amanda Camila said, holding onto her father's seat for dear life as the plane made another dive and another thrust upwards. "D'you think this is our last trip?"

"It'll be your last trip for sure if you don't return to your seat. And be sure to fasten your seat belt."

"Yes, sir!" She saluted in military fashion and staggered back to her place on the other side of the aisle, next to a pale Carola, whose eyes were closed and whose lips were quivering, perhaps praying.

"Look at that."

Though I would have preferred to imitate his fearful wife and close my own eyes and not have to watch myself dying, I obeyed him. I looked down on Tierra del Fuego, the Isla Grande, jutting into the middle of a black sea. It was a wide plateau nestled below a range of ice-capped mountains, and on its reddish-brown-tinged plains thousands and thousands of small white bodies were moving, a slow multitude of—

"You know what that is?"

"Sheep," I said, for once getting something right.

"Sheep," the *Ministro* agreed. "The best wool in the world. Takes to dye like . . . Used to be the mainstay of the region before we discovered oil. Do you remember what your uncle said to you about the Baróns, the crime? Well, there's the cause. If it weren't for those animals and what my great-grandfather did to defend them, I wouldn't be who I am today."

I thought to myself that this was not the moment to learn about the past. This was the moment to pray like hell there was something called the future. But who can resist a good story before he dies? Or why have you remained out there reading, Janice, if not because I have promised to deliver my death in your Seattle mailbox? In fact, what Barón told me as the plane creaked and skewed and madly swiveled did manage to distract me. Which may have been his intention all along. Unaware that his story was another nail in his future coffin.

The Indians, the gigantic Tehuelche and the large Ona and the smaller-bodied Yahganes, had been left alone to roam this most inhospitable of places on the globe for ten thousand years, some of them hunting guanacos on foot and others living in canoes and chasing down seals. The first European explorers had only limited skirmishes with them; there were no massacres, just a couple of kidnappings to cart a few of them to Europe to show off. Darwin himself stole one of the savages, and even when the whites started trickling in toward the middle of the nineteenth century, during a minor gold rush of sorts, things didn't change much, didn't change really until sheep were introduced to Patagonia. Then the aboriginals, the Onas in particular, preyed on the herds and slaughtered them, at times for food, often simply to harass the intruders and force them to leave. They'd plunder hundreds of them and drown them, let the climate refrigerate the carcasses, come back later to eat them. The same ice that was allowing the mutton to be exported! That was the final stroke: the Sociedad Explotadora de Tierra del Fuego, losing too much money, put a bounty on the heads of the Indians. Not really on their heads: on their ears, on their genitals. One pound sterling for each little bundle of flesh.

"And that's the crime my great-grandfather committed."

"He killed them?"

"He paid the bounty hunters. He sat at a table day after day and paid them. Just a man behind a desk, an accountant who had come to make his fortune in the New World. In fact, your uncle is wrong—he wasn't a Barón. He had an English name, Wendell; on my mother's side, lots of English, Croats, Scots came here. No, no McKenzies, as far as I know. It would have been funny if Cris's great-grandfather had been working here in the last century next to my ancestor, one of them in charge of the killing and the other in charge of the counting and accounting, but no, I don't think so. Cris knows all about his family history and didn't make the connection when I found out. Because I did find out. I stumbled on the name by chance one day in a history book. I must have been eighteen, maybe nineteen, doing an assignment for a history class at the university, and I can tell you I was floored. Those were feverish times back then, Gabriel, what with the Cuban revolution and Che already proclaiming the need for a new man, and Vietnam, and I was pretty fiery. I've always been a political animal. I felt so guilty, I felt that I had to atone, you know, make up for what Joseph Wendell had done to the Indians. Here I was, lifting my fist on behalf of the poor, the dispossessed, the great unwashed of the world, and in my own family . . . My mother's grandfather had helped to exterminate one of the last nomad tribes of humanity. Well, I would help liberate them. Well, if not them, the other forgotten people. Che Guevara complex—we all had it back then. Not that I don't believe in liberation now, in building a new society, in protecting those without a voice. That's why I feel it's unfair when people like your uncle or Dr. Ciruelo criticize me."

"Or my mom," I chimed in.

"Or Milagros. Right. People go into exile, come back, want to find the country just the way they left it. But we stayed behind, we learned what you can and can't do, the difference between dreams and reality." He was warming to his subject, oblivious to the wild upheaval and trauma of the plane as it bucked and swooned, getting ready to land. I fought the desire to vomit, valiantly concentrated on Barón's words. "I have nothing to repent of. It's easy to change things in your head. But when you have to deliver, not in the blah blah of big talk, but day to day, when you have to build enough schools so that we get rid of the causes of poverty, when you have to convince the members of the Manufacturers Association that it's good for the country to raise their taxes, when you have to dictate a new law protecting indigenous peoples, you need to be pragmatic, realistic, flexible. I can't give life back to those Onas whose genitals were cut off and slapped down on that desk in front of my great-grandfather, but I can make sure that their descendants have a chance, whatever blood of theirs is still beating in somebody. It's to them I can pay back a small part of the debt."

The plane banked and then dipped and Amandita let out a whoop of joy. She was enjoying the ride more than an earthquake.

"Does she know any of this?" I asked.

"Amanda Camila? I don't think so. I've tried to keep it from her, though with people like your uncle screaming about it, who knows if . . . Maybe she does. Maybe that's where her obsession with Patagonia comes from. She's told you, I suppose, how she'd love to take down the stories, the oral tradition, of the Onas, of one of the Tehuelches. She can't and she knows it—they're all dead, there are none left. But we've never talked about it. I've steered clear because I—well, you know, Gabriel, it's crazy, but I still feel . . . guilty. I mean, I just have this sense that I could have done more, that history trapped us, my generation, didn't let us do everything we should have. But if I were to say that to Amanda Camila, the problem is she—I guess she doesn't understand me, Gabriel. But I have this feeling that you really do, that I can trust you."

What was it with this family, with this country, that I kept on receiving people's confidences? What was wrong with me that everybody came and squirted their secrets in my ear? Everybody, that is, except my father. What was I supposed to do with so much emotion, so much information, such intimacy when I could not retribute, when I had no one but the Nana, a powerless eighty-year-old woman, to commend my soul to?

"If I told her my doubts," Barón went on, "Amandita would just tell me to resign then, to quit the government, and that's not the point. I'm proud of what we're accomplishing. She wouldn't understand that there are moments when her father has these questions, wonders if there couldn't have been another way to . . . But there isn't, there wasn't, that's the point. There's no alternative to what we've done, given the hand we were dealt. It's a miracle we can even do this much. Three years ago I was in jail, damn it."

"You were in jail?"

"Just for a few days. Inciting rebellion, that sort of crap. Didn't touch me. But five years ago they roughed me up, came to our house, threatening to expel me from the country. And ten years ago they could have killed me if they'd known who I was, where I was hiding."

The distance he had traveled since those moments of danger was underscored by the military officers who were waiting at the foot of the wind-ravaged airplane stairwell, the honors they showered him with in the airport's VIP lounge, the armed escort into town. I rode in a second limo, with Amanda Camila, and her words of disgust indicated that her father had been all too right about her lack of sympathy. She was prudent enough, considering that the driver was some army sergeant with long ears and inquisitive eyes, but she couldn't entirely restrain herself. "Why does he have to give them a hug, why does he have to tell them jokes, why does he have to smile at them all the time and ask them to show him photographs of their children?"

"He's just doing his job," I said, feeling that I had to defend him. The rapport he'd established with me on the plane had somehow transformed me into his unofficial representative.

"Doesn't need to lick their asses," she said. "A shake of the hands should be enough."

"I don't—"

"You'll understand. If they've given us the rooms Dad promised, I can show you as soon as we get to the hotel."

The rooms were what Pablo Barón had promised, on the top floor of the swanky Hotel Cabo de Hornos, but I didn't have time to even topple onto my bed before Amanda Camila made another of her whirlwind appearances and stood me in front of the window and drew the curtains. There were the straits that Magellan had navigated on the first trip around the world, the winter sun setting early—at three-thirty in the afternoon!—on their green cliffs and white mountains and dark waters. She pointed to a peninsula, or maybe it was an island, that fifty, maybe sixty miles away thrust itself aggressively into the waterway. A last ray of sunlight smacked one of its promontories with red and rose and yellow.

It was Isla Dawson, where her dad would have been sent if the military had caught him in the days after the coup in 1973. That was if he'd been lucky, she said. Those same men whom Barón had enthusiastically embraced at the airport had turned the island into a concentration camp, filled it with the ministers from Salvador Allende's government, the representatives from congress elected by the people, the undersecretaries like her dad, made them build their own barracks, their own prison camp, jailed them without trial. She was indignant that now her father sucked up to those men, never mentioned the past, didn't want the *milicos* to feel uncomfortable.

I thought she was being too harsh and told her so. He was doing it for the good of the country, to give her and everybody else stability, and besides, her father was the kindest man I'd met in Chile. She didn't know how lucky she was to have a dad who cared for her, who coddled her. She should let up on him.

Amanda Camila sighed, planted a soft kiss on my forehead. I waited for that mouth to descend a bit, slip down to my own mouth. It did not.

"Okay," she said. "For you, Gabriel. I'll try and be nice to him. He really has gone overboard to make us happy, hasn't he? And I've been so looking forward to this trip. Even got Carola to promise she'd leave us alone. You'll see. We'll have such a good time, just the two of us together."

Except that we weren't going to have such a good time and it wasn't going to be just the two of us. *El tercero en discordia*, the third discordant member of the trio, made his dashing appearance at dinner, or rather at dessert time. Amanda Camila had noticed the man in question when we sauntered into the dining room later that evening, when her father had nodded in his direction. She was the one who asked Pablo Barón as the so-called Cabo de Hornos parfait arrived at our table, who that young man over there was. I looked across the room and recognized him immediately: the blond man who had been lecturing about the Cerro Santa Lucía and its cemetery for a movie camera, the man who had given me that mysteriously intent look.

"Who?" asked Pablo Barón.

"That one," Amanda Camila said. "The handsome one."

I didn't think he was that handsome. Good-looking, let's say, rugged features, wavy blond hair, a straight and strong nose, all right, yes, he was handsome, Janice, in fact had movie-star fucking radiance in his blue eyes. But nothing warned me that I would need the advice my father had never sent my way to fend him off during the next few days. I could have done with some heavy counseling from the moment the man who had caught Amandita's eye answered Pablo Barón's waving hand and crossed the room in our direction.

"Max Behrends," the *Ministro* murmured as the guy gracefully wended his way through the labyrinth of tables toward us. "Chilean filmmaker, incredible story of grit and determination. I've been trying to get him to film the iceberg, but he has his own plans. He'll tell you about them, I'm sure."

Max Behrends did tell us about them, he sure did.

In the days to come I was to get to know him far too well. Have you ever met anyone whom you admire and detest at the same time, somebody whose every movement, every gesture, very existence seems an insult, a challenge, a reminder that you could have been different, you could have been that person if you had been luckier or more blessed or simply had the guts to make the right choice at the right time? Max Behrends was that person, he had been put on earth for the express purpose of making me aware of all the mistakes that plagued my life. He had done excruciatingly well everything I had done wrong. Every time I had hesitated on the road and taken one turn, you can be sure he had taken the other one, would have taken the other one given the chance. Max was a carbon copy of me. No, scratch that. Max had stolen my life.

He had just celebrated his twenty-third birthday, two days after mine, in fact. July 11. This matters, this date. You'll see. The day after I saw him at the foot of the Cerro. Like me, he was an exile. Born in Austria, he had arrived in Chile at the age of six, the very age when I had left: we might have intersected at the airport, he might have touched Chilean soil at the symmetrical moment I was departing, his life in Chile beginning just as mine was ending, picking up where mine left up. And that's not all, Janice. For the next five years, he suffered what I suffered in the States: the feeling of being a stranger, the experience of having one parent, in this case his father, insist on remembering Austria, just as my mom overwhelmed me with the memory of my faraway country. And at more or less the same time, September 1979, I couldn't believe it when he mentioned that date, the very month and year when I decided to break with Chile and become an American, Max, in Chile, was reaching the opposite decision.

Kids in Chile make fun of foreigners just like kids do everywhere. They call people of Teutonic origin Otto, Fritz, portray them as slow, dumb. They imitate their accents. "Hey, Otto, Don Otto," the Chilean kids had jeered at Max in the schoolyard, in the neighborhood. "Hey, Fritz, you wanna see my wiener?" And Max had taken five years to counterattack, but when he did, it was devastating. That day in September 1979, he stated to his tormentors, "I bet you I know more about your country than you do, than all of you together."

Good at betting, Max was—like me, like my father, like Amanda Camila. And then Max surprised his schoolmates with a couple of questions that they couldn't answer: "Know who the first woman murdered up on the San Cristóbal was?" "Know what herb the Mapuches use to rub on a woman so she gets in heat and wants to screw the first man she sees?" "Anyone ever heard that the Santa Lucía was once a cemetery?"

The Chilean kids were silent because they were absolutely ignorant about their land, and Max had spent the previous years devouring the story of the country and its people, its animals and its architecture, its heroes and its villains, and now was ready to enunciate every lavish detail. There was the *marqués* in 1820 who cut the throat of the lover he falsely suspected of having betrayed him with his best friend, he did it with a cutlass on the San Cristóbal, then hid her body and ultimately got off without so much as a prison sentence, merely having to pay her mother an annual sum of blood money. A typical story Max would tell to the kids back then and to Amanda Camila and me as he guided us through Patagonia for the next four days, always emphasizing the erotic, the spectacular, the bizarre. They had been as fascinated as we were, as eager as we were to know about the amatory herb of the Mapuches, the *huenangue*, eager for Max to get them some of that love filter from a stand he had discovered in the Mercado Central. Not that I could admit that I was, too, though Amanda had no such qualms. "I'd love to try some," she said as he crunched his Jeep through the snow to Puerto Hambre.

"No better potion than what your own glands produce," Max answered, "but you should try it, by all means."

"So the kids fell for the superstition," I said.

"Yes," Max answered. "It doesn't matter what you call it. If it helped them get over their adolescent timidity. And helped me to survive: I went from being an outcast to a leader. I ceased to be a foreigner."

Another sort of survival was in store for him: four years later, when he ran away from home, it would be that infinite information about Chile that pulled him through. Again, almost the same day I failed to fuck you, Janice Worth, the day my father McKenzie came between us and began to haunt me, Max Behrends was breaking with his own father.

"Do you know who Walter Rauff was, Gabriel?" Max asked. He was always firing off questions I couldn't answer; full of names I should have had at my fingertips, he was always answering his own questions: "A Nazi war criminal, responsible for the direct extermination of hundreds of thousands of Jews. The Chilean judiciary, back in 1963, refused to extradite him. Left him here in this country, scot-free. Which allowed him to offer his services to the military when they launched the coup, show them a trick or two they could perform on defenseless bodies. I met him. A few days after we arrived in Chile in 1974, my father came down to Punta Arenas, introduced me, let him shake my hand, take me on his knee. A nice, kindly old man."

"What was he doing here in Patagonia?" I asked, curious in spite of myself.

"He came here after the Second World War. Got a job inspecting lamb carcasses in a *frigorífico*."

"Dead meat," Amanda Camila interjected. "Rauff had good job experience. Like some of the men in Patagonia who hired him. They'd done some exterminating of their own just a while back." I couldn't tell from her voice if she knew that her own forefather Wendell was one of those men, working on these very haciendas we were passing, which Max had visited as a child. Not knowing back then, Max, what he would find out later, that Albert Behrends was Walter Rauff's financier, the conduit for money that neo-Nazi groups were sending him now that he lived in a country where—and here Max quoted one of his father's letters—"the ideals of the Third Reich could again find an incarnation, where the military was not afraid of spilling some blood in order to cleanse a corrupt, sick, womanly society."

Max had read that letter and a series of others his father had written and then had confronted him, insulted him, and walked out the door, determined at fifteen years of age to survive without any help from his family. The same day that, a hemisphere away, I was hitching my sexual fortunes to my own dad.

"I disowned him," Max said. "Whatever I did from that moment on would be due to my efforts and nobody else's."

"But didn't your dad come after you, send someone to look for you?" It was the only heartfelt question I asked during the drive through the snow that afternoon in Patagonia, wondering if perhaps our lives had coincided in yet one more fantastic intersection, if the great McKenzie had not received that morning a phone call from a distraught Herr Behrends asking him to retrieve the—

"I never heard from him again. I think he left that information, those letters, lying around in 1983 so I could find them. I think he realized that I was on the way to becoming somebody entirely different from him. So he tested me, tried to get me to accept who he was, tried to keep me under his boot forever. I think he hated my exuberance, that I cared about the Chilean Indians, even as a child. I think I reminded him of my dead mother and he hated her, I'm sure he hated her. She was a woman, after all. She was soiled, he kept on saying, dirty. He meant her menstruation. I think he hated himself for desiring her, hated me for being her son. He wanted me to die out there on the streets."

But Max had thrived, not died. He told it to both of us exhaustively as we visited the jackass penguins and the Estancia San Gregorio and the Paleo-Indian artifacts in the Pali Aike cave. He had survived because he knew history.

"I went to the Cerro Santa Lucía—I have a feeling that Gabriel's been there . . ."

"I wonder how you guessed," I said, neither of us willing to acknowledge that we had already crossed each other's paths, exchanged that glance of recognition.

"I talked up a couple of German tourists," Max went on, "gave them a guided tour, got some money for my efforts, snagged some Irish who were delighted to hear that so many Catholics of Irish descent had contributed to the independence of Chile—O'Higgins and Mackenna and so on and so forth—and by nightfall I had enough to pay for a small hotel room."

For dinner, he'd served himself a nice banquet of leftovers in the back alley of Chez Henri, a restaurant in the colonial Plaza de Armas. He shared it with other youngsters who, after eating, had gone to sleep under the bridges of the Mapocho, kids who were probably still sleeping there to this day or were in jail or were dead. Whereas Max . . . Max prospered, saved his money, never did drugs, never stole anything, never got raped. At a time when most Chileans still had not woken to the wonders of the free-flowing market, Max turned one peso into two pesos and two into eight, Max knew how to invest, Max was always on the lookout for ways to make his money work, Max was an Austrian pirate out to make a killing.

At first, it had been no more than intuition that he could sell the tourists something pricier than information. He began demanding a fee from the restaurants he steered his clients to and taking a small cut for each souvenir he recommended they take home. It wasn't long before he realized that if he provided folkloric objects directly to his tourists the profits would rise. And with those profits he set up a small restaurant of his own, like my mom did in Manhattan, Chilean food cooked according to the recipes of the past. And when money began pouring in from that source, the capital went into buying directly from the Mapuches themselves in the south; in fact, Max provided them designs so they could produce what tourists wanted.

By the time he was eighteen, he had accumulated enough cash to set up his own small film production company. Initially, the footage he shot was for tourist videos like the one he had been making for some company the day I saw him in Santiago. But as politics in Chile started to heat up, he specialized in protests and everyday life, selling selections to foreign TV stations. I had watched Chile through his eyes, he had been the one who had secretly been feeding me the country during the years when I hoped the Chilean people would oust Pinochet and bring me back home to my father and a warm bed. He had filmed the whole damn plebiscite, winning an award for best documentary in some stupid mountain film festival and had been nominated for a Golden What's Its Name Something or Other. A large grant from Germany had followed, providing him in turn with seed money to write and then direct a first full-length feature in the States. You may have seen it, Janice, *Into the Body*, about one of these forensic experts, an American, who falls in love with a woman whose husband is missing, presumed dead in Chile, and of course they have to track down the body and find out if he's really dead. Well, I don't know if you remember, but that earned him accolades as the "hottest" new Latino director south of the border—and north as well—the one to keep your eye on. And now Max Behrends was down here, back in the Patagonia he had known as a child, back to pay a debt, he said. Scouting his next motion picture. Pay a debt! Scouting! He had come to steal my girl!

That night he met Amanda Camila in the restaurant of the Hotel Cabo de Hornos, he teased us with bits and pieces of the film he was planning. He sat down and grabbed my parfait. "You don't mind, Gaby, do you?" familiar the bastard was, from the word go, and no, I didn't mind. I hoped he'd get indigestion. "What do you know about Patagonia?" he asked me, as he wolfed down my ice cream. "I mean, journalists read before trips, don't they? What? Chatwin? Pigafetta? FitzRoy? Bridges?"

"A bit from all of them," I said, hiding my ignorance behind what I hoped they would all take for modesty.

"What does the name Sarmiento de Gamboa mean to you?"

I searched my memory banks. Sarmiento. Sarmiento! I had that name on the tip of my—"The Argentine president," I blurted out triumphantly. "He wrote a book in the nineteenth century about Latin America, proclaimed it would never progress unless civilization beat barbarism, the city domesticated the wild countryside."

"Facundo," Amanda Camila said helpfully. "That's the name of the book Sarmiento wrote. *Civilización y Barbarie.*"

Max, however, was talking about another Sarmiento, de Gamboa, who in 1581 had tried to colonize the Straits, close them down to the English and the Dutch. Setting out from Spain with fifteen ships, he had taken three whole years to reach the Straits, and by then all he had left was a frigate. After founding two forts, he headed back to Spain for provisions, new people, everything needed for a colony. Leaving everybody else there, men, women, children, without a ship in which to escape, with just enough food to last till he returned.

Max paused for dramatic effect.

Sarmiento de Gamboa, he said, never came back for them. They waited and waited. When the English pirate Cavendish passed by one of the forts a few years later, he was only able to rescue one of fifteen survivors, a man named Tomé Hernández. The rest were left to die. Then Cavendish went on to the other fort and there nobody had survived. From a gallows, the skeleton of a man was hanging. The king's justice was still being doled out in the midst of ruin. Cavendish called the place Puerto Hambre, Port Famine.

Max paused again in his tale, all blue-eyed innocence. "If you want," he said, "you can come with me and take a look at it. I'm scouting locations before I write the screenplay."

"I don't think we have time," I intervened. "We have lots of other things to do, archaeology and things, natives, you know. Museums. Right, Amanda?"

"Right," she said, but her voice quavered and it was not clear if she really intended to carry out the promise of good times she had been advertising to me not less than an hour ago in my room. The two of us together, she had said.

"What happened to Sarmiento de Gamboa?" Carola asked. She also seemed taken with handsome Max, leaning forward so as not to miss a word.

"On his sea voyage back to Spain, he was captured by Sir Walter Raleigh and hauled to England, where the queen took a fancy to him and let him go. Then on his way home the Huguenots in France put him in prison for two years. Lucky guy, huh? He was finally ransomed by Felipe II but was never able to convince his monarch to send an expedition to rescue the people whom he thought were still waiting. They had starved, of course, by then. For that matter, the Spanish never tried to colonize Tierra del Fuego ever again."

"That's a pretty depressing film," I said, eyeing the ice-cream plate he had licked clean.

"Well, it's really a love story," Max said. "I've invented Catalina, a woman whom Sarmiento de Gamboa loves and leaves behind. The same Catalina whom Tomé Hernández then seduces and also abandons. They both promise her eternal love and never come back."

"That's even more depressing. You want audiences to watch her die of starvation in Puerto Hambre?"

"Oh, no. She survives. She does the only smart thing a woman could have done: I have her joining the Selknam."

"The Selknam?" I asked.

"The real name of the Onas," Amanda Camila said. "What they call themselves."

"Used to call themselves," Barón said, correcting her.

"It'll be a beautiful film," Amanda Camila said, ignoring her father's reminder that the Onas were extinct. "That woman starting a new life among the aboriginals, turning her back on the Spain that deserted her."

"Well, her two lovers would like to come back," Behrends said. "Only they can't. In fact, there's not much of their lives they finally control. You know what my movie's called?"

"*Getting Lost*?" I ventured.

Behrends brushed aside my ironic suggestion. "*Blame the Wind*," he said. "Because the wind's the real villain in this story, that wind out there. Listen to it." We dutifully listened to it. I'd been listening to it, suffering it, since the plane had started to shudder and dip. "Sarmiento never even said goodbye to his friends or to the lady love I invented for him," Behrends continued, "because the wind blew him out to sea, out into the Atlantic, all the way up to Brazil. He kept on trying to go back for several months but the wind kept on sending him in the other direction. Finally, his men mutinied and forced him to head for Spain. As for Tomé Hernández, years later he was on board Cavendish's ship. While his fourteen compatriots on shore were debating whether to accept a rescue offer from a heretic, save their bodies or save their souls, a favorable wind came out of nowhere and the English buccaneer set sail right away. So Hernández never got a chance to say goodbye either."

"Poor woman," Pablo Barón said.

"Not really," Behrends answered. "I think at the end she's finally, well—glad, this woman. I think she finds life among the Selknam to be more peaceful, much more satisfying, human, I'd say, than life among the Europeans."

"Fiction," snorted the *Ministro*. "I'm glad nobody's sticking me in a film or a novel, twisting my life for the entertainment of people I've never met."

"As long as it makes sense," Behrends said, "you can do anything with history. This Catalina, I've made her up, but her experience, that's based on captivity narratives. So many women were abducted by the Indians and it turned out most of them didn't want to return to civilization, didn't want to be rescued. So Catalina's men pine for her on the other side of the Atlantic and she ends up not missing them, hunting with the male Ona, heading for Antarctica to hunt a whale. She disappears into the whiteness with a smile on her face. The End."

"Beautiful," breathed Amanda Camila.

I didn't like that breathlessness, those adoring eyes, I didn't like the way this arrogant Aryan was playing around with my Antarctica, my discovery, the domain I'd fallen in love with.

"And you're not scared that the wind will destroy your movie," I said, "the way it destroyed your protagonists?"

"As long as the people who have invested in the film aren't scared," he said, "why should I be?"

"Well, if your backers don't come through," Pablo Barón said, "think about our offer: the iceberg needs a great artist to chart its trip to Sevilla. After all, it's the trip that woman you made up never took, that very voyage back home. The circle of your story completed."

"A woman's not an iceberg, *Ministro*."

"Some women are," Pablo Barón answered. "Fortunately none of the present company. But think about my offer."

"I'll think about your offer when the government starts thinking about a new law to develop a film industry, *Ministro*. It's a shame that I have to make this film with foreign money, that no profits will remain behind in our country."

"We're working on it."

"Yes, that's what the king said to Sarmiento. It was like that back then, it's like that now. Back then, people were blind, unable to see, let alone exploit, the riches and wonders that were right there within reach, there for the taking. We always arrive late to everything, we *latinamericanos*. If the Spanish had decided to listen to Sarmiento de Gamboa, three centuries wouldn't have been lost. Who knows what marvels this region would have given us if it had been colonized a long time ago? Maybe the Fueguino tribes might even be alive today, like the Eskimos near the North Pole."

"Or have died before, been exterminated before anybody could even photograph them," Amanda Camila said. I took this as a criticism of Behrends, the first one that had slipped from her lips, and used the opportunity to stand up, perhaps a trifle brusquely, because everybody else seemed surprised at the suddenness of my movements.

"It's been a pleasure, Señor Behrends," I said. "Call me if you happen to come through New York next year."

"Oh," he answered, "I don't think it'll take that long."

I didn't think he meant it, I deluded myself into believing he wouldn't turn up again, not ever. He wasn't there at breakfast, wasn't there when the navy limo came to take us to the dock from which the *Galvarino* would be departing in November to collect the iceberg, wasn't there when we inspected the Simunovic *frigorífico* that would serve as a depository first and then as a studio for Armando Jorquera, the sculptor, to reassemble the blocks of ice, wasn't there as I received a detailed answer from an admiral about security measures. Max wasn't in sight at the one place I had feared finding him, at lunch in the hotel dining room as we toasted Pablo Barón and said goodbye to him and lied to him about how much we were going to miss him. And he certainly was not there, the Behrends rival, as Amanda Camila and I tramped through the snow across the Plaza Muñoz Gamero to the Museo de los Salesianos, taking almost half an hour to negotiate the block and a half, having to steer sideways first, then zigzagging back and forth to make progress. I hoped that our Max had decided to take a ship out to Cape Horn and that it had met the fate of Sarmiento de Gamboa's many shipwrecked companions, I fervently wished him to be sinking at this very moment with his film crew to the bottom of the deepest fjord off the Beagle Channel, I wanted his camera to keep on filming him even as he sank to his insolent death in those icy waters, filming a documentary that would have earned him an Academy Award if anyone could have seen it. But nobody would. Nobody would ever see him or his image ever again.

No such luck.

Max Behrends was already at the Museo de los Salesianos, waiting for us. Or rather, waiting for Amanda Camila.

All the previous afternoon and half the night I had been boning up on the museum and on the Onas, Amanda Camila's favorite Indians. I had raided the hotel's ample library, reading myself silly. Next time someone came along with all sorts of tidbits of information and anecdotes and stories, I'd beat him to the punch. My tactic had seemed to be working. On our way to the museum, Amanda Camila had tried to explain that it had been founded by—I interrupted her, Yes, by the Salesian fathers, the same order of Catholic priests that had set up a mission on Dawson Island. Yes, the very Dawson Island that served as a prison camp so many years later. The government had given the Salesians, who spoke only Italian and knew next to nothing about the natives, the right to protect them from the bounty hunters. The Salesians first recruited the Tehuelches and five years later some of the Onas, a twenty-year concession that ended disastrously. By 1911 the good fathers were forced to shut down their mission because most of their so-called protégés had died of pneumonia and other diseases. This museum was all that was left, full of artifacts and weavings and photos.

I have no doubt she was impressed, would have been even more impressed if Max Behrends had not decided to give us a tour of the museum with the benevolent agreement of the father who was its curator. Max had been here many times; this was his fifth trip to Punta Arenas. He had spent half his life, not half a night as I had, studying the region and its inhabitants. Whatever I said, he corrected; whatever I knew, he appended more information to; whatever I commented, he put into perspective.

There we were, standing in front of a sort of tableau depicting the mission, with a severe priest and a forbidding nun overseeing the work of a native woman who was spinning by a stove, spinning the sort of textiles that covered several walls of the museum, spinning without legs, because the life-sized model was not complete. The bottom part of her body had been left in concrete, as if she were stuck there forever, legless.

"They didn't want her to get away," I said, "so they made her without legs."

"There's another interpretation," Max said gently, because he was never aggressive, never overbearing, always exquisitely polite. "Sex. Whenever you can't explain something, if you look for the sexual connection, things tend to fall into place. When Mayorino Borgatello, the Salesian father who was horrified at the extermination of the Indians, went to Italy in 1889 to get funds for the mission, funds to save them, what do you think he brought back?"

I did not say a word. I thought food, medicine, something to do with sex. Maybe condoms, beds, who could guess what the damn priest had brought back with him?

"Clothes," Amanda Camila said.

"Right," Max agreed. "Clothes. Tons and tons of clothes, because the word of God couldn't be preached to the naked. The indecent bodies had to be covered up, the souls couldn't be converted until the bodies had been saved. The Indians had survived for thousands of years out in the open. The sleet slid down their oiled bodies. Their whole bodies were like our faces, able to withstand the worst temperatures, but the priests made them wear clothes and that was it—the Indians grew sick. Twenty years later, 1911, to be exact, most of them were dead. Disease wiped out what the bounty hunters hadn't killed. So that's the pattern. First you kill people with guns, you terrorize them. And then you kill them with civilization. Think of them dying, one by one by one, their language dying with them, the cemetery expanding, their souls off to heaven, the rugs they were weaving off to the museum, their skulls all that is left."

He indicated a row of skulls that grinned at us from a murky corner.

"And that woman?" Amanda Camila asked, gesturing toward the figure of the legless spinner.

"They endowed her with no sex, no bottom part of her body, no genitals with which to sin. But of course they also cut her off from reproduction. Maybe the priest who sculpted her was expressing his subconscious desire to keep her as the icy innocent child of the supposedly sexless and virginal Salesians. Not that they were really able to stop their wards from having sex, even babies. There was a child born just before the mission was closed, eighty years ago. If she'd survived, she'd be the last Ona. But none of them did. Strange how the best intentions can lead to the worst consequences: the priests came to protect the Indians from the sheep farmers and they made matters worse. At least we have this museum. I guess that's a plus."

"You don't think they would have died anyway?" I asked.

"Maybe," he said. "If they'd been left out there, what harm would it have done? Just leave them alone, maybe we could have learned something. But we didn't, we won't, we never do. Look, come and see the school notebooks. There's a scrawl, a hundred times, 'I will earn my bread by the sweat of my brow.' That's what they were taught. As if they hadn't earned their shellfish and their meat and their berries for ten thousand years. Before Italian was even spoken, or Spanish for that matter, they were speaking a language that had a vaster vocabulary than Shakespeare had at his command. Come on, I'll show you."

I'd had enough. Enough of maudlin, extinct Indians, but especially enough of the robust presence and opinions of Max Behrends. I let him take Amanda Camila's brown arm, his fingers delicately guiding it along, I let him continue his tour and wandered off to another room, ending up in front of some photos.

It was then that I made a discovery, made my Discovery with a capital *D*.

Looking at me, straight at me, her eyes boring into mine fearlessly, a small Ona child between her mother and her father, was the Nana. It was her, that full mouth, those slanted eyes, the intensity of that expression, the straggly hair. Not really her, of course, because that photo had been taken several decades after Nana's birth, but a group of painted Onas just back from the hunt in 1931, looking at the camera as if they did not know that time was already against them, the camera was against them, the men who were snapping the photo could do nothing to save them, could do nothing but develop the image and leave it for my eyes and other eyes to contemplate at this museum sixty years later, to tell me that maybe the Nana was a member of the Selknam race, a sister or an aunt or some relative of that little girl in the photo, maybe our Nana was the last of the Onas.

I called Amanda Camila over and Max came with her, of course. I showed her the photo silently, waited for her reaction, wanted to make sure I was not hallucinating.

"My God," she said. "That is incredible."

"Isn't the resemblance uncanny?"

"Yes. Unbelievable."

"Who? What?" Max Behrends was at a total loss. For once he had not a clue as to what was happening.

I would have left him in the dark forever, but Amanda Camila filled him in, how the child in the photo was identical to her Nana, the spitting image. Though of course it couldn't be Nana, because she was eighty years old and anyway the old woman was a Mapuche, she was sure of it.

"How tall is she?" Max sounded like a prosecutor hot on the trail of evidence.

"Tiny," Amanda said, "almost a dwarf."

"Well, she can't be a Selknam, then. She'd be tall. They were all enormous."

"Not all of them," she said. "But wouldn't it have been great if my Nana had been the last one, if the last of the Onas had been taking care of me all this time. It would be my dream come true to find the last one."

"They're all dead," Max said. "All we can do is reconstruct them in our imagination."

"Much good that will do them," I said.

"At least to tell their story," Max replied.

"Right," Amanda said, "that's what you'll do in *Blame the Wind*: try to show viewers how the Indians used to be, back when the Europeans came here and couldn't survive, when those Fueguinos were the owners of Antarctica, still would be if they were alive. That woman you've invented, she'll be our guide into their past, she'll bring them to life again the way they gave life to her when she was abandoned."

I was defeated. The woman without legs spinning eternally under the gaze of that priest and the nun had a better chance of having sex than I did. Amanda Camila was floating away from me as if the damn Punta Arenas wind were blowing her into the horizon. This Max was serious trouble. He had stolen my life, he was stealing her heart, he was unknowingly saving my own heart from being slashed out and eaten by an irate Pablo Barón. Unless I did something quickly, he would be the one to swim into her eyes as green as the sea, get there before I could, ravage that body I had sworn would be mine.

I looked at the photo again.

And then, suddenly, I knew it was the Nana. You'll think that it was because I was looking for one area where I was right and my handsome Teutonic adversary was wrong, wanted finally to beat him at something. But that's not all; that savage male rivalry was merely the driving force behind my interpretation. There, looking straight into the eyes that looked just like Nana's, I remembered what I had been reading last night just before falling asleep. As my eyelids drooped, I had chanced on the description of a *kloketen* in one of the books I had purloined from the hotel library: an initiation ceremony for Selknam males in which they donned masks and scared the women, reenacting the dominion of male over female, exorcising the male-eating woman, the vengeful moon deity, the women who had once ruled over them by hiding behind these same masks. I had been too sleepy to think further about the matter, had not given it another thought till now, when I realized that here was the origin of what the Nana had told me after I confessed my life to her, the enigmatic legend she had asked me never to forget.

Later, this revelation about who Nana was would change my life. But at the time, cracking the true and remote identity of the woman who had brought me up did not help me to stave off Behrends or stop Amanda Camila from eating out of his hand. Indeed, unless I figured out how to turn my superior knowledge about the Nana into a means of defeating him, soon he'd have that hand of his groping other parts of my love's sacred body.

That was what I was thinking on that Sunday, there in my hotel room in Punta Arenas, thinking it as my own hands were poised upon my own solitary anatomy. It was late morning and I had locked the doors so my Amanda could not enter the room unannounced. I was lolling naked in bed, depressed and deprived, with my dick up in the air demanding service: it had been too many days since I had left New York, since my hands had done the relief duty that no girl was willing to provide. In other words, Janice, I was masturbating, just as I did in front of the screen while your words crawled onto it from your Seattle loneliness. Even as I stroked my genitals slowly, rubbing this way and that, closing my eyes to conjure up the image of Amanda Camila's tight little ass inside her panties, those pubic hairs she had Little-Bo-Peeped at me, I felt that I really didn't want to be doing this. What a tremendous defeat, to jerk off here at the end of the world, my great mission and exploration finishing in my own sad gurgle of semen. I anticipated that at the moment of my pleasure's spluttering into the Kleenex handily kept by my side, at that very divine and infernal moment I would be berating myself for this failure, I would be leaving the field to the enemy. Behrends would be coming by for us in half an hour's time to take us up toward Puerto Natales and I had decided to let him go alone with her. He had vanquished me. There was nothing I could do to prevent him from culminating the day with Amanda's seduction. By evening his hand would be opening the knob to her room and her hand opening the sheets to him while I listened next door. It was written that I was to be the spectator to their lovemaking. The previous day had written it: the guy was brilliant, he was everything I wasn't, knew everything I should have known about the Onas and about ice and about Chile and about women. The slightest opinion I voiced on any subject whatsoever was met by one of his theories. "To think it's summer in New York," I said, hoping to turn the conversation to an area where I could at least be his match. And his commentary: "Not only the seasons are changed, you know, Gaby, Amanda. Everything else is as well. Topsy-turvy, that's what we are. The great Western myths, stories—when they're transferred here, they don't fit, they turn into something else. The quest for Ithaca, for instance, the Oedipus myth, Electra, Antigone, all of them are exaggerated and then become twisted out of recognition, people live them differently." And Amanda: "How about Don Juan?" He smiled at her. "If Latin America is hell, then Don Juan can't very well be taken to hell by the father of the woman he's raped, can he?" Smiling at her as if to say, I can take you out of this hell, I can transport you to heaven, try me. And she would, this very Sunday night she would. Not that far from the Cape that had been discovered the day of Saint Ursula and the eleven thousand virgins' martyrdom, she would lose her virginity to him, and even if I managed someday to finagle my way into her private realm, he would have been there first, he'd have plowed that territory, done some planting and maybe some harvesting before I even got the tip of a shovel in there.

So there I was. I had decided that if I could not block that affair, I would at least not force myself to witness it. There I was playing with my dick, watching it in the mirror, making believe a woman was the mirror watching me, and as I grew toward my climax and I felt my mouth begin to water, something totally unexpected happened.

I stopped.

I didn't know I had that sort of willpower. I stopped when I was about to come; when the ache in my organ was creeping toward an explosion, I stopped. This was not the way my first orgasm in Chile should be, not in this solitary bed facing Dawson Island, where so many political prisoners had themselves masturbated in despair into the wind. How could I discharge my seed in full view of the Strait that Magellan and Captain Cook and Darwin had traversed in better times? Had I come to the end of the world in order to jerk off?

I stopped and let my dick wilt and then reached for the phone, dialed my dad in Santiago. I'd speak to him directly, I thought, just tell him the whole fucking truth, just like that. *Papá, necesito tu ayuda*. I need your help. No beseeching with my eyes, hoping he'd understand. Direct communication, man to man. The one advantage I had over Max Behrends: *my* father wasn't a Nazi. He brought boys in from the rain.

I got Polo, of course. He was his usual helpful self: my father wasn't available and, just in case I wanted to know, Cris wasn't with my mother, that didn't seem to be working out as well as Polo had thought it would. How was I feeling, less dizzy? Not that Cristóbal McKenzie had expressed even once, according to Polo, the slightest interest in my health. "Maybe he's pissed," Polo said, "because you didn't hit that *Guinness Book of Records* man hard enough. Or maybe he blames you for something else, blames you for Carlitos. Yeah, he ran away. When Cris went off after him, finally found him, you know what the kid said? He said he'd left and wasn't coming back, because of you. You promised him you'd visit him. So he figured we don't keep our promises. Maybe that's why Cris is angry. What do you think?"

"Tell him to give me a call, will you, Polo?" I said, knowing that even if he relayed the message my dad wouldn't heed it. My intuition was confirmed by Polo's final pleasantry, "Tell Amanda Camila that her Uncle Cris says hello, wants her to have dinner with him when she gets back." He probably had rehearsed that lie, meditated what sort of parting shot would nettle me even more than the dismal news of Carlos's escaping the Casa Milagros. Polo could not know that in fact he was handing me the answer to the question that had really been annoying me: how to deal with the bothersome Max Behrends. Polo had handed me the perfect antidote, and a plan began to form in my mind.

I was hurriedly getting dressed when the phone rang. For a second, my heart leaped with the possibility that it might be my father. Maybe he'd found Carlitos, maybe both of them wanted me to come home, both of them were waiting for me. It was a McKenzie all right, but the wrong one, my uncle calling from jail, another Sunday visitor's day with nobody to see him. He had tracked me down. When was I coming back? Had I found any suspects?

"Tío, I have something to ask you."

"You want to know why it's an inside job?"

"What I need to know, Tío, is when you want something impossible —I mean, you have experience trying to do things that nobody thought could ever be done. What is the one thing you need, Tío, to attain a really difficult objective?"

"Patience," my Uncle Pancho said. "Whatever it is you're trying to accomplish, give yourself all the time in the world, because when you try to do it too fast, it'll invariably go wrong."

It was that advice that would inspire me in the months to come in my campaign to get Amanda Camila into my bed. A long-term strategy. Patience. But I began with something more concrete: I sent her my father's greetings, just as Polo had phrased them. I did it to separate her cunningly from Max Behrends on our way to Puerto Natales that Sunday, while more great sheep haciendas where her forefather had made his fortune slipped by. And then I brought up the great McKenzie every chance I got. You might think that was a silly thing to do, arouse her with my dad, her soft sex beginning to juice over with the thought of his interest. But remember that I was aware that he had sworn never to seduce her, he was the one man I could inflame her with, the condom reserved for her safely folded in Pablo Barón's wallet. To rekindle her enthusiasm for him was to give myself time, driving a wedge between my lady love and the *cineasta intruso*, the intruding Behrends. That's what I did at the Casa Menéndez Braun and at the lone marker to the dead Onas, surrounded by the enormous mausoleums of the sheep barons, and everywhere we went later that day: feed her fascination with my dad, nourish her fantasies, make her desire some male McKenzie, hoping that when that father of mine proved inaccessible, she would eventually realize that there was another McKenzie nearby who was more than willing to provide consolation. It worked. There were not only three of us as we toured that Sunday afternoon, my father had joined us as a phantasmagoric presence. I quoted him unceasingly, praised his amatory abilities, thrust him into the middle of every comment Behrends threw out, made Amanda Camila lust for him, finally found a way to get my unwilling father to help me.

Dangerous, of course, to get rid of Behrends by putting the great McKenzie in his place. The only way I would be able to vanquish the shadow of my father in the eyes of Amanda Camila was if I managed to get help from that very father. And that called for a long-term strategy, as my uncle had suggested, a plan full of patience that I embarked upon during the weeks and months that followed the second letter.

It was then that Nana became the principal pawn in my plot. Two days after I postponed Max's assault on Amanda, on Tuesday, July 23, to be exact, back in Santiago since the night before, I was summoned to the *Ministro*'s office and found my father and Polo waiting for me, gazing glumly at the second letter. It was then that it all came together for me. To begin with, the postmark. Friday morning—the very day I was journeying down to the ruins of Port Famine in the backseat of Max Behrends's jeep, glaring at his head and the swaying head of Amanda Camila; Friday morning, so my principal suspect, Amanda Camila herself, was eliminated, unless she gave it to somebody else to mail, creating an alibi for herself. But that made no sense: she didn't need one, didn't even know she was a suspect. She wouldn't have risked giving that pale blue envelope to somebody else; she would have deposited it herself in a mailbox the Wednesday before we left. No, she was not the culprit.

And then there was the word ECOLOGICAL that I had spelled out for the Nanny on a pale blue piece of paper just like this one on Barón's desk. So our Nana had the means, she had the information; but above all, thanks to my trip to Patagonia, I knew now that she had the motive. Revenge. Maybe all these years she had known she was a Selknam, she might in fact be that little girl born on Isla Dawson eighty years ago, the last Ona born on that island—and she had decided, for reasons I still did not comprehend, to hide herself, make believe she was a Mapuche. Then she had discovered, maybe recently through my uncle, that her *patrón*, Pablo Barón, was the great-grandson of Joseph Wendell, the accountant who had paid one pound sterling for the flesh of her tribe. And now Wendell's descendant was pillaging an iceberg from the continent that rightfully belonged to her, to her dead people, the first ones to have sailed into those mists, to have named them.

I had, of course, no proof, and there were too many questions left dangling. Every hint that I dropped, every query I made about her childhood was met by Nana's stolid stonewalling. I'm an orphan, she would answer, and there's nothing to tell. What if she didn't know that the Baróns, whose male offspring she was cuddling in the crib and cooking for, had paid the money for the ears that had listened to the wind, the testicles that had contained her as a half seed? How could I square my suspicions with her amiability, her loyalty to the family? Or was this all part of the famous dissembling of the Indians, what they discovered from the first clash and loss, to bow your head and never let anyone with power perceive what you are really thinking, to seek refuge in a silence more stubborn and unyielding than the glaciers? Was that it?

These questions didn't matter, finally, because in the months to come I accumulated irrefutable proof that she was guilty.

I laid a trap for her and she fell for it: every week we would have a private lunch, each Thursday she would cook her famous *cazuela*, making me pay excruciating attention. When we finished eating, I would elaborate on the latest suspect in the iceberg caper, each lunch someone different. And that person was invariably implicated in the next letter, always postmarked Friday. One Thursday I told her, for instance, that I was sure that the author was the Bolivian consul, and that's who was pointed to in the letter in Pablo Barón's infuriated hands: AM I FROM BOLIVIA? THAT'S FOR ME TO KNOW AND YOU TO FIND OUT. Or an artist whose exhibition was not being taken to Sevilla. Sure enough, in the following letter: AM I ANGRY BECAUSE MY ART IS BEING EXCLUDED FROM SEVILLA? THAT'S FOR ME TO KNOW

AND YOU TO FIND OUT. Over and over again, the letters symmetrically and systematically echoed what I was divulging to the Nanny and nobody else.

I kept her culpability to myself, of course. I stuck to the decision I had reached in a flash that day when I read the word ECOLOGICAL and guessed it was her. I wasn't going to mention my discovery to my father and certainly not to Barón: why end the investigation at the exact moment when I had received the gift from heaven that I had been hoping for since I arrived in Chile, to spend several hours a day with my father. The *Ministro* had extracted from the great McKenzie the definitive promise that he would henceforth devote every morning of the week, five days a week, to tracking down the person who insisted on mocking us. If not, Barón might not renew next year's subsidy of the Casa Milagros.

The truth is that even if I hadn't stood to benefit by keeping Nana's secret, I wouldn't have denounced her anyway, not then, not ever. Why should I? If she was the culprit, she was obviously harmless, unable to carry out her threats, not even realizing, naive woman, that I had caught her and was using her. At some point, once I had bonded with my father, once I had made love to Amanda, I thought, I might take the great McKenzie aside and tell him that there was no need to continue our detective work. I had solved the case a long time ago. It might not even be necessary to ever tell him or anybody else. There was something satisfying about the idea of keeping it all to myself, an intrigue only I knew, only the Nanny knew, without realizing that I was onto her, a way in which I was collaborating in her task of seeking revenge, no matter how rhetorical, against the men who had stolen her clan from her and who had, for good measure, stolen Antarctica as well. Doing a service to the Onas—that was far more gratifying than anything Max Behrends could cook up with his cameras.

Just in case I'm sounding too righteous, don't worry. I was in it for myself. In fact, the first person I indirectly inculpated and got even with was none other than Max Behrends. "You know whom I'm really worried about, Nana," I said to her a few days after my return. We were alone in the house, the twins taking their siesta, the maid watching Mexican soaps. "There's this *cineasta*, this hot-fingered filmmaker." I didn't give his name or too many details, and all she asked me was how you spelled that word, just like she had asked about *ecological*. A few days later, there it was on Barón's desk. I could see him frown at the riddle: AM I A CINEASTA WHO LOVES PATAGONIA AND DOESN'T WANT THIS ICEBERG FILMED? THAT'S FOR ME TO KNOW AND YOU TO FIND OUT. I could see that I had threaded the worm of a foreboding into the *Ministro*'s mind, I could see him wondering whether to withdraw his offer for Behrends to film the iceberg, whether it wouldn't be better to rethink the government's help on *Blame the Wind*. Yes, in the weeks to come he would close his house and his ears to my rival. Barón would instruct the Nana to tell Max that Amanda Camila wasn't in when he called. I made sure that his messages ended up in the garbage, torpedoed the chances of the man my father, without lifting a finger, without ever having seen him, had already defeated in the field of love down in Patagonia. I also arranged things so my father would meet him, so I could flaunt the great McKenzie in Behrends's pretty face. I did this by playing the innocent when commenting on the *cineasta* letter to Barón, asking him if his office had a list of Chilean filmmakers. "The only one we know wouldn't be involved, that Behrends fellow we ran into down in Punta Arenas," I let drop casually, as if I didn't know that this would make my dad perk up and ask about this man whose innocuousness I certified, just to spite me he was sure to go off and interrogate the one person I was vouchsafing as innocent. A couple of weeks later I amused myself during the hour of their confrontation, watching Behrends try to puzzle out the reason for our visit, my father and my alter ego Max face to face.

The session over, I popped my head back into Behrends's office. "You want me to send regards to Amanda Camila?" I asked, a malicious afterthought. Yes or Why bother, I hoped he would answer—anything forlorn, in the tone of voice I had used when sending a message to my dad through Polo.

He did not give me that pleasure. "Not really," he said, furrowing his brow, no gratifying pain in his response. And surprised me even further by changing the subject entirely. "Do you know who Lautaro is?"

Lautaro? Lautaro?

An Indian, I had come across that name, I had it on the tip of my tongue—then decided that he was playing games with me again, trying to turn the tables, defeat me in the Who Knows Chile Better game he had practiced with such fervent success with his derisive schoolmates.

"An Indian," encyclopedic Max told me. "Must have been the age I was when I left home when he became Valdivia's page. You know, Pedro de—"

"I know, I know."

"Lautaro learned the language, learned the military tactics, though many natives think he knew those tactics already—they'd been using them for centuries against the Incas. A matter of dispute. But what nobody disputes is that Lautaro ferreted out all the secrets of the con- quistadores and then deserted them and led his people to victory after victory, killing Valdivia, though not by pouring molten gold down his throat. That's just a stupid story, a metaphor, if you will."

"Listen, Max, it's good of you to be giving me this history lesson, but you don't need to show off anymore. I don't give a fuck who Lautaro is."

"I just thought," Max said, "you might be interested. That is, if it's true you're an expert on the Internet."

"What does the Internet have to do with any of this?"

"For some people, some natives, Lautaro is the model for how natives can deal with the modern condition: you learn from the invader, you appropriate his weapons, you defeat him. Yesterday the *arcabuz* and the horse, today the Internet. But you're not interested, right?"

"I don't know what you're talking about," I said.

"No," Max said. "You really don't."

"Well, my father's waiting for me." Only, I purposely emphasized the word *my*, *mi padre*—to remind him that I had a father and he didn't. I stepped out into the corridor, then stepped right back into the room when I heard Max say:

"Kill him."

"What?"

"Kill your father, if you want my advice. Which you don't. Even if you'd die to be just like me. But you never will be, Gaby." He was speaking to me as if we weren't the same age, as if he were my damn grandfather. "You'll never be like me unless you do what I did. Leave home. Look at Lautaro, even if you don't give a fuck about him. He forced himself to leave home twice: first he left his Araucanian home, then he left the Spanish home, finally killed his adopted father, Valdivia. Look at Valdivia himself. He left Spain, then left Peru, then left Santiago, because he wanted to go beyond. Take it from me: kill your father or you'll never be free."

"I'll remember your advice when I'm fucking Amanda Camila," I said.

And left those drastic words floating in his ears.

"I hope that creep stays away from Amanda Camila," my father said when I joined him down in the street. I nodded enthusiastically.

It was probably the only thing on which we had agreed in the last couple of weeks. The relationship between us was not going well, to say the least. He still seemed to be angry that I had failed him. He demanded of his many kids absolute devotion and responsibility, was a bit of a tyrant, in fact, my dad. He paid back that adoration with total benevolent commitment, but when you got it wrong, as I had with the Guinness guy, he cut you dead.

Nor had our prescribed morning outings helped iron things out. He hated them, wanted to be out chasing his runaways, couldn't wait to go off to lunch and some expectant maiden or *matrona*, and never once thought of inviting me to come along, neither to the food nor to the foreplay. And his resentment was, naturally, infected even further by the omnipresent Polo. "What a waste of time," Polo snorted, and the great McKenzie would snort back, as if the two were high on cocaine, he wouldn't be doing this if Pablo Barón didn't have the Casa Milagros by the balls, have his brother in jail.

I did not, however, despair of attaining again the intimacy he had offered me those two nights when we had met as twin guardian angels of Carlitos in the dorm at the Casa Milagros. I knew there was one place where I could resurrect the hope that had flared up in my heart back then, before Carlitos had gone, before Carlitos had escaped into the streets of Santiago to be somebody's victim or somebody's mugger. I had realized it the last night I was in Punta Arenas, the night I had perfected my plan for the future. I had looked southward from the docks where we would return with the eighty tons of blue ice dissected from the submerged floating mountains of the crystal continent. That's what I needed. To be with him by myself on the high seas. To get him away from Polo. To dislodge him from the stress of looking for a runaway during the day and a woman every night. If I could just voyage alone with him toward that magical ice which had enchanted us both, which had promised me something wondrous as I fell in love with it the night I had betrayed my country in SoHo. Yes, that was it, I was sure. The ice would melt his anger, soothe his distance. He would open his heart to me, he would complete the story of his life that my mother had been unable to tell me: how he had conquered the first other woman in his life, what you do to convince a stranger to go to bed with you when you only have an hour and a half till midnight and no experience.

You'll have to admit, Janice, that my chances looked slim. Everything was against me except for the one card I held: Milagros Gallardo. She was the real key to my father's heart. She was the one who could push him onto that ship to Antarctica.

It turned out to be less difficult to enlist her cooperation than I had anticipated. With the Nana's advice, I mapped out my strategy. Before anything else I needed to convince my mother to stay in Chile for a few more months, let the three Restaurant Milagros flourish without her hovering eye. I gave her to understand that my reasons for remaining were primarily financial, told her that I had found work.

It was the truth, Janice. Oscar and Nano, back from their Bolivian real-estate wheelings and dealings, had set me up as a consultant to any number of companies that wanted to get wired up at any cost, executives who simply had to be able to boast to their colleagues or rivals about how up-to-date they were, companies that were set on establishing Web sites whether they required them or not. I insinuated to my mother that all of this could lead to a lucrative contract or maybe even an investment in our *Whatever* magazine. Emotional blackmail, Janice: what better way of keeping her in Santiago than implying that her departure would sabotage my career, precisely now that for the first time in my life I was making good money? I expected to have to twist her arm, but she agreed almost immediately, didn't even suggest that I stay behind without her. The manager could take care of daily operations in New York and send us enough to keep us living royally in this country where people were paid twenty times less than in the States. "I could even think about staying indefinitely," Mom said with a sigh, "if things worked out, you know."

The next step, *niño* Gabriel, the Nana said, once I had reported to her that my mother wouldn't stand in my way, was to accompany

Milagros to her afternoon events. "Go with her to the people and places and organizations she wants to visit," Nana suggested. "Praise them and make her happy."

I have to admit that those afternoons were strange, Janice. At 3 p.m. teach some midlevel bureaucrats in an insurance company how to use programs on their computers to downgrade and block legitimate claims and two hours later, at 5:00, follow my mother into a cavernous and dirty hall for a gathering with injured workers whose compensation was being denied by the same financial group I had just been training. Strange, yes, but miraculous also, those lefty alternative sessions I attended, miraculous because they made her feel that I was beginning to see her point of view, to learn from her, softening her up so that when I finally implied one day that the only favor I wanted from her in the world was for her to come along on the trip to capture the iceberg, she was ready, she was willing, she was able. The only woman my father could fuck, according to the rules of the bet, over and over and not forfeit the prize that he and Barón were disputing, the only bait that could entice the great McKenzie onto that ship. That was my blueprint for sexual success; like in some crazy porno Disney film for kids, I had to get my parents back together again, make their marriage work out.

It was not merely, of course, a matter of warming my mother up to the idea. How about my reluctant father? How to get Barón to force the great McKenzie to walk up the gangplank of the *Galvarino*? What arguments could I feed Barón that would help him carry out my scheme? The mere authoritarian order, "You have to go, Cris, and that's that," would be answered by his friend's ironic, "I know you want to win the bet, Pablo, but try to think up something a bit less naive. There's no way in the world I am getting on board a slow, womanless boat to Antarctica."

No, I had to find something irrefutable, something that my dad would at least deem valid, that he would not dismiss out of hand. Only when he was in the right frame of mind, only then could I suggest to my mother that she spring the news on him that she'd love to spend some time chugging toward the ice at the beginning of time. How about a honeymoon in the coldest climate in the world? How about scorching each other after seventeen years of separation?

Again it was my uncle who provided me with the answer.

On my first visit to his jail, a few days after my return from Patagonia, I asked him what he had meant about an inside job, secretly wondering if on his own he might not have uncovered some hard evidence that the Nana was involved.

Nothing of the sort. He said he knew—Sources, he whispered conspiratorially, can't reveal who, why, when, but this is what my sources inform me. They say that somebody from inside the iceberg project itself is involved. "They're all turncoats," he said. "All of them used to be people on the left."

"Larrea?" I objected. "Pinochet's minister of finance? He owns a factory."

"Not him. Everybody else. Quiñones, the man who designed it; Armando, who's going to carve the damn thing; Jacobo, who's going to film it; and Gerardo, I used to know him before he went into exile. He's the engineer. He's thought up how to refrigerate it; he's going to surround it with six columns, phallic columns, people have told me who have seen the drawings."

"Like six big towering dicks," I said. "But what does any of this have to do with Gerardo's supposed animus toward the iceberg? It's his masterpiece."

"He's a traitor. He used to be an Allendista, spent ages in exile, got back a couple of years ago. Now he's collaborating with the very people who exiled him. And then there's Lalo Goic, the worst of all. Used to preach armed struggle. Now he's the PR man. The one I most suspect could be behind it."

"But why, Tío? Why should any of them want to destroy their own work?"

"I know these people," Tío Pancho said, rubbing his hands together nervously, looking at the guards who were making their sleepy rounds. "They're dedicated to the iceberg, want to take it to Sevilla. Their life depends on it, but more important than that, as Marx would say, is the material fact that their livelihood depends on it. They pull this heist off, they're sure to have work for years to come. Even so, deep inside they know it's wrong, their consciences gnaw at them. They feel guilty, and that's when they sit down. One of them sits down to write the first letter. Just as a joke, he says, and that night they sleep well—one of them does, the one who wrote it. But as the days pass by, remorse surfaces again and the guy's like a drug addict. He needs his fix. He has to send a second one to stop his beating heart and throbbing head, to stop the voice inside that tells him, You schizo son of a bitch, you sucked up to power, you secretly hate this transition you say you love so much."

"So this is not the last letter?"

"There'll be more."

He was right that there would be more, each of them sent on by the Nana with the insane information I was funneling her way. And he was wrong, of course, about those five suspects from inside the project. Which did not stop me from using his hunches to further my own agenda.

I incriminated those people, Janice. I slowly layered in their motives in the conversations I held with Nana, directed her hand to write them out in the letters Barón kept receiving every Tuesday. First AM I INSIDE THE PROJECT? THAT'S FOR ME TO KNOW AND YOU TO FIND OUT. Then, a few weeks later, I'M CLOSER THAN YOU THINK. HOW CLOSE? THAT'S FOR ME, etcetera, and then, after the next weeks' diversionary allusions to some Indian rights group and a Catholic bishop who denounced the iceberg's materialism, more jabs at the inside conspirators—WHO WOULDN'T LOVE TO GET THEIR HANDS ON THAT ICE AND CARVE IT INTO NOTHINGNESS? and still later, CAN YOU MELT AN ICEBERG THAT HAS BEEN PHOTOGRAPHED?—enigmatic allusions to the wonderful sculptor, the wonderful filmmaker, wonderful, I say, because I got to know them, Armando and Jacobo and the others, got to spend many days with them before the trip we all took down to Antarctica. Got to betray them.

Let me confess that I felt a slight—very slight—twinge of regret at what I was doing. My uncle's theory was preposterous: my new friends had suffered under the dictatorship, some had been exiled, some had lost their jobs, some had even been jailed. But they felt, as far as I could see, no guilt at moving on. They didn't want to stay locked into their past sufferings. They had matured with the experience, they said, saw the iceberg project not as a betrayal of their ideals but as a revindication of them. Gerardo, to mention just one example, was using the iceberg to return triumphantly to the Spain that had received him a few years ago as a banished beggar. They all felt that way: the world that had grudgingly listened to them stutter mispronounced words in unpronounceable languages, that world would have to recognize their capacity. They were also full of humor, saw this as a way of liberating Chile from its solemnity, its tight collars and gray ties. They were tricksters almost to the man. Time to stop sniveling and complaining, time to bring the country that had been so divided in the past together around a project that was totally mad and ball-busting. They became my friends, as close to friends as I ever had, ever will have.

Which didn't stop me from using them, subtly indicting them, playing on Barón's paranoia, squeezing my father. The letter that was postmarked Friday, October 11, 1991, their forty-ninth birthday, conveyed the very message I had fed the Nanny: WILL I STRIKE BEFORE THE ICEBERG REACHES ITS FIRST PORT? "I think it's an inside job," I had said to her. "I think Commandante You-Know-Who is going to strike before the iceberg reaches its first port." And she had done my bidding, she had created the conditions for the great Barón to warn the great McKenzie, "He's on board, there's a chance he's on board. I need someone I trust on that ship." Before Barón could even say another word, get ready to put the pressure on my dad to be that person, the great McKenzie responded that he'd love to go to Antarctica. The *Ministro* was so surprised that he had no alternative but to agree to Cristóbal's condition, anything to get him on that ship. Barón thought he had bamboozled his best friend, maneuvered him into losing the bet. But Barón went pale when he heard what my father demanded: "Milagros will be coming with me." Barón wasn't even able to say, There's no space for her, they don't accept women on those trips. He was totally nonplussed. After all, my mom was still sleeping at his house along with me; his spies must have told him that things were not working out between the two of them. What the spies could not have known was that my mom, at Nana's suggestion, had dined with her husband just the night before and had popped the Antarctica question over their favorite wine, that my father had answered, drinking her in with total adoration, Does this mean that you, that we . . . ? Barón was shocked, though perhaps not as shocked as Polo, who suddenly found himself having to stay home and mind the store. Poor Polo: his first fateful words to me upon my arrival in Chile about my father's not fucking my mother that night had come back to haunt him. Cornered he was, Polo. He'd lost his own little bet, that he would be rid of this upstart Gabriel, that I would soon be heading north, unfucked and unloved, to New York.

It was then, Janice, in that office, when I heard Barón agree to my father's terms, that for the first time since I had gone jogging up to the mountains animated by the certainty that I would possess Amanda Camila, it was then that I felt sure that time was working for me, finally, finally, on my side.

The rest, I said to myself, watching these two men and all the other men I had manipulated into serving me, will be easy: I'd conquer Antarctica and then conquer Amanda Camila. I would replace my father in her heart and sweep my love off her feet in spite of her own jealous dad.

I knew it would work.

What's incredible is that it did work. Or almost. My plan was perfect. Except for one thing I hadn't planned on. I hadn't planned on my Nana's death.

She died and everything went to hell.

We set sail to capture the iceberg on November 1, *el Día de Todos los Santos*, All Saints' Day 1991. I set out with my mother and my father from the southernmost city in the world with the secret purpose of lifting forever—I thought it would be forever—the curse that had been weighing upon my northern life. Bahía Paraíso was our destination, a particularly calm inlet nestled in the hook of the Antarctic archipelago, where securing that floating mass of ice would not be overly hazardous.

"Which does not mean it will not be hazardous at all," the captain announced to our assembled group that afternoon in the mess hall as the island tip of America disappeared from sight, the last land of the Americas, which had meant the end of the line for the tribes descending from the Bering Strait, the end of the line for so many shipwrecked sailors who had not needed to venture any farther to die in a sea famed as the most treacherous in the world. Our captain knew what he was talking about. "This has never been attempted before. Most ships that go past el Mar de Drake are trying to avoid icebergs, not bring them on board. All of them thus far have considered ice to be their main enemy. Not just the icebergs that can gash into a ship but the ice that can rain down from above and the ice that can immobilize from below and the ice that can sleet sideways like a hurricane and capsize you. It would have been better to have left a few months from now, in summer, when even tourist ships navigate these waters. But our orders are to have this iceberg back by mid-November so it can arrive in Sevilla on time. And I follow orders. Just as I expect my orders to be followed by everybody on board this ship. And everybody, including our guests, may in fact be called upon to help in an emergency. Everybody."

The captain, a member of the Chilean navy, looked disapprovingly at me, with my baby face. Who else would he express his anger toward when he was really furious at the imposition of a woman? To bring anything female on board was to court disaster, even if this one was hitched, romantically head-over-heels involved with the great McKenzie, who was doing his best not to hold her hand too tightly, making sure—my father, discreet as ever—that he was not provoking the envy of the surrounding *machos*, not rubbing it in that every night he would be entering that splendid *ejemplar de mujer* while they would be entering nothing more attractive than their bunks heaving under the ten-foot waves. I wasn't worried. My father would charm them, he would try and disguise the glow of sex dawning on his face every morning, he would tell them stories and keep them entertained. As for Milagros, she had cut her hair short so it could fit under a ski mask, she had dressed like a man, hiding her breasts beneath layers of clothing, implying that she was ready to pitch in like any member of the crew. They'd end up accepting her presence as well.

My strategy was to leave my parents alone, talk to my father only when necessary. Let the adventure talk for me, bond with him slowly, through the collective, one more face in the crowd, one more mouth at breakfast, one more pair of eyes scanning the mist to make sure that the raging, swelling bulk coming out of the white ocean was not going to crash into us. The radar takes care of that, but even so, if you are on the seas and know that there is no land for hundreds and hundreds of miles and that instead of sailing toward it you are heading straight into a quantity of ice so vast that if it melted (and it will, it will, Janice, and then goodbye, Chile, goodbye, New York, goodbye, Sevilla) it would equal all the water in the Atlantic Ocean, you look to the horizon, you trust your own senses more than any inhuman blipping instrument, you are always vigilant for what could sink you like the *Titanic*, down, down, down, into killer waters, heartbreak waters, my father and I both pursuing the same danger, locked together by the landscape.

On our way south, we were lucky. Seas so quiet that First Mate Puertas began to worry. He wondered if something ill might be brewing, if nature would not tip the balance back and eventually make us pay for such tranquillity. "The weather can change in an hour," José Puertas said to us, a group in the bow enjoying the spray of the sea, hardly even getting drenched the water was so calm. "So be prepared. Though the *Galvarino*'s a good ship. Been through everything—well, almost—this continent can throw our way. The *Galvarino* will get us there and back."

The silence was broken by Lalo Goic.

"Not the name I'd have chosen," Lalo said. "*Galvarino*. I've been wondering, Don José. D'you think the captain would object if we changed the name of the ship?"

"Change the name?" the first mate said. "What's wrong with *Galvarino*?"

"Bad publicity," Lalo answered. "A name associated with mutilation, blood. Of all the ships, they choose one named after an Indian chieftain whose hands the Spanish cut off, first the right, then the left one. Bad PR."

When the first mate spoke, it was as if he were wielding an axe himself, as if Lalo Goic should be wary lest his own hands be transformed into stumps.

"Bad PR, Señor Goic," the first mate said, "is if this ship sinks trying to carve that iceberg out of the shelf of ice it's been clinging to for thousands of years. Bad PR is if that ice falls onto the deck and mutilates our hull and you have to swim in waters so cold that you'll be begging to crawl into a refrigerator just to thaw out. Bad PR is if you get so frozen there's no blood to spurt and you can't blink because the cold will dry out your eyeballs. My job is to make sure that doesn't happen. Your job is to make sure people think Galvarino is a hero, a man who insulted the bastards who cut off his hands. A man who insulted death because it would stop him from killing more invaders. A man who would have been proud that his name is on the ship that's defying death. I think it would not be prudent to mention your idea to the captain. Good day, gentlemen."

First Mate Puertas left us to ponder his words in that feverish twilight that lasted, it seemed, forever, the sky and the sea confused in a hue of red and yellow.

"I don't know," Lalo said after a long while, "whether to admire a man like Puertas or to pity him. That story he's telling about Galvarino—insulting his murderers, all that. Probably not true. Sure, they killed him or somebody like him, they probably cut off one of his hands, but no, we need more. It's got to be both hands, we need him to recite verse while blood squirts from his stumps. Like Victor Jara. It wasn't enough that they broke his hands in the stadium and then shot him. No, some idiot journalist in exile had to write that they cut them off—the Galvarino image, you know. Not enough that they killed almost five thousand people. We had to proclaim that the military had killed a hundred thousand."

"That's because," a voice piped up. It was Armando Jorquera. He was looking southward to the shroud of Antarctica, peering into that brightness at the tip of the ship so as to be the first one to see the cap of ice from which we would carve the blue transparent material of his masterpiece. "That's because people insist on forgetting, insist on covering up the past, not letting it show its face. The military says they didn't kill anybody, we answer that they killed many more than they actually did—back and forth. It's the process of forgetting that gets us into trouble." He pointed to the floes floating by us. Every possible shape had been sliced by the wind and the water; it was his paradise, his dream come true. "That's what I love about the iceberg. You see in it whatever you want to see. Some people see progress, some see amnesia, some see the rape of nature, some see the love of nature, some see it as the most Latin American thing we could have done, others insist it is so cool and Nordic and European. I see—a chance. A chance to start over. Nobody's ever touched that piece of ice, ever. Not one hand, not one finger, not one memory. We can make of it anything we want, I can organize it any way my imagination desires."

Armando was a challenge to me. Not because I had incriminated him—I mean, I'd done that with all the expo people on board—but because he reminded me, somewhat as Max had, of the roads I had not taken. With this difference: Armando was my friend, or at least he thought he was, he thought I was a soul companion, someone who understood him, and I did, I did. I just was more in love with Amanda Camila, more in need of a father. I had to choose between my loyalty to him and my loyalty to my dick and I didn't hesitate, making Barón suspicious of him, almost getting him thrown off the expedition. Almost thwarting him in achieving the dream of his life: capturing the iceberg.

Let me backtrack here, Janice, by explaining that Armando had gone to New York about the time my mom kidnapped me into exile. He was a bit older than me, it's true, a few years my senior, but he had also lost his father, to cancer and not to the coup, and just like me he went to college in the States. To keep the parallel cooking, he had also turned his back on Chile at more or less the time I had, tired of the songs and the empanadas and the solidarity marches his mother lugged him to as if he were a walking doll. Though that's as far as the similarities went. He had come back to Chile before Pinochet's defeat, brought his award-winning sculptures and his MacArthur genius grant, the youngest artist to ever get one. And do you know why?

Antarctica! Not just Antarctica but a certain TV program on Antarctica. He revealed to me on board the *Galvarino* that he had seen those same images that had so captivated me on their twenty-five floating screens that night on my way uptown from SoHo, he had been watching in his house that precise travelogue, right there in our New York, Janice, on the Upper East Side, not more than half a mile from where I was standing in the street drinking it all in. That's right. He had seen those phantom icebergs and he had decided that if this was his country he wanted to go there. Whereas I had seen those icebergs and had been just as entranced and yet had leapfrogged over that initial enchantment and not even connected it to Chile; I had rushed on to a life of increasing Americanization in New York that had culminated with our fiasco, Janice, our cold waters. One TV program, leading in my case to a dead end and in his case to a new life, a determination to go back, a certainty that in those waters he would find the material from which to shape what was inside his eyes bursting to come out, the mystery of America, the mystery of life on a planet where ice had once been supreme and would be supreme once again, the chance to foreshadow in his sculpture the freezing embers of the future, when the earth would have cooled down and the universe would be hurtling into nothingness everywhere and in every direction. His chance to carve a monument to a humanity destined to die.

If I could have had one inch of his passion. Not for the iceberg, Janice. I was as fascinated as he was, just as bewitched. The talent for beauty that he had, still has, for forms and movement, the sharp points of things, the round, soft belly of things. Maybe that would have saved me. Maybe if I had not directed all my cleverness to out-smarting others and screwing a woman, maybe if my energy . . . But I am superimposing on that past my present despair. Not the right way of telling this. Because those were, undoubtedly, the best two weeks of my existence. Armando could see the future in the iceberg and so could I: it would draw me closer to my father.

Yes, it would, it did. I knew my strategy was working on the second day, when we steamed into the last outpost on the Beagle Channel to load up on water, the most precious commodity in Antarctica. You can die of thirst, Janice, in the midst of the frozen salt of the sea: there is more water in the Atacama, the Gobi, the Sahara than in that continent of dead liquid coldness. Water was to be rationed, First Mate Puertas explained. We would have to be careful how much we washed—and like the captain, he looked at me when he said that, looked at me so as not to pin my mother in his gaze, not be caught accusing the sole woman aboard of wasting precious H_2O in long showers and deep baths. I could see in his eyes that he was imagining how she would rinse shampoo from her hair, how she would demand that her clothes be spick and span, how he hated the fact that this female body was on deck, how he wanted to fuck her himself.

I saw all that, but it didn't matter. My first deep contact with my father had come a few minutes before, as we watched the water being transported onto the ship. Armando said jokingly that we'd all have to wash together, use the same water over and over for every member of the expedition. "Like when we were kids," he said. "As long as we arrive clean, purified, before we steam into Bahía Paraíso." His words had awakened in me and in the mirror of my father a memory that had been waiting many years to emerge from the darkness of the void where we had consigned it.

It had happened a few days before Mom and I left Chile. The screeching whir of a helicopter had jarred me out of my sleep. I had been dreaming that it was cutting me to pieces, clawing my hands into shreds; the sound itself was grinding each arm and advancing toward my heart. I ran to my parents' room in the Casa Milagros and

Mom was asleep alone in that enormous bed and I almost climbed into it, was about to shake her, force her to save me from the scissors that were coming for me, coming into me, when I saw a sliver of light lilting from the open door of the bathroom and heard the smooth patter of the shower. It was my father. I didn't know then, of course, that he had just come back from having intercourse with another woman, that he was ritually rubbing himself clean so he could share Milagros again, her bed if not her body. I had yet to be illuminated by my mother as to my origins, Che Guevara, the bet. All I knew was that if I chose not to wake my mom up I would win praise from my father, that he would comfort me, that soon we would be leaving and would never see him or the helicopters again, never, my mother promised, see any of the *malos militares*, the bad soldiers, ever again.

So I went into the bathroom and there he was, my naked father singing softly to himself in the shower, his eyes closed as if he were receiving sun in his face rather than that drenching storm of water. I waited for him to notice I was there and a few seconds later he did, turned his head, shaded his eyes, tossed back his mane of hair, and smiled.

"*Chiquitito*," he said. "My little one. You had a bad dream, huh? Come in, come on in. This water's magical. Flushes away every bad thought, every sad thought."

"*Papá*," I said, but he hushed me.

"Let's just keep it down. We wouldn't want to wake your mother up, right? Men take care of women, they make sure they can sleep without being disturbed."

I stripped off my pajamas and joined him under the steaming shower. I must have seen him naked before but this was my first, and in fact my only, memory of his genitals, the first and last time I ever saw them, I was that close.

"*Pichula*," I said, pointing to his dick, so near my eyes, his dick that had seen service inside a woman not more than an hour ago. Maybe I knew something special had happened with it—it was thick and long and even pretty, like the neck of a doll, not erect, Janice, just sort of large and not entirely hanging and in repose. I called it *pichula* because that was the term I had picked up from the ruffian-boys at the Casa Milagros.

He laughed.

"*Pico*," I said, wondering if I'd get another laugh, "*Penca, plátano, pistola, pinga, porongo.*"

"Enough," he said. "Don't go around saying all those words. Your Nana will get upset. Just around men. Call it *pene*, okay? You have it, Dad's got it, Mom would love to have it. Nothing more important in the world, Gaby. Say it: *pene*."

"*Pena*," I said, mispronouncing the word.

"No," the great McKenzie said. "*Pena* is sadness, when you feel like you want to cry. *Pene*, Gaby, is the opposite. One tiny letter difference. But if you know how to use your *pene*, believe me you'll have less *pena* in this world."

He didn't let me touch it. Just handed me the soap, the same soap he had been using to wash away whatever female was still clinging to his pores. He let me froth myself with it as if I needed to clean out that smell as well. We stood like that for a long time—who knows how long, Janice. When you're a kid, a few minutes seem like an eternity. But it was really a while—I mean, the skin of my toes began to wrinkle from the water, my dad simply let it wash over us as if he wanted to disgorge all the warm rivers of the cordillera on us, holding me close to him, taking me up in his arms, making believe I could lift him, the river from above absolving us, saying goodbye for us, each minute an hour and a year, parting and departing and converging us. And then even that water ran out, even the enormous cauldron of the Casa Milagros grew gradually cooler, and he showed me how to turn the faucet off. And then stepped both of us out of the stall and dried me in a long towel the color of the blue sunrise of Antarctica, even if neither of us knew that we were already heading in that direction to find each other seventeen years later, helping me into my pajamas again and carrying me into that flowing bed where his wife and my mother dreamed of some day in the future when he would not have to drain other women from his skin and he would be hers, only hers, we fell asleep, the three of us, that night, immersed in one another as if we were drowning in love. I would never again sleep in their bed, never again wake in the morning and see his arms around her, one of his hands holding my tiny fingers as if I were a kite about to take off, about to fly away and never come back to earth, that was the last time.

And now, he was remembering it as well, here on the deck of the *Galvarino* as we streaked southwards with just enough water to last us fifteen days. We delved into the water of our past and saw there the same blessings and the same bodies, again the three of us on another and vaster bed, the three of us together one more time, hoping that this time we'd get it right, that this time the water that had been congealing for all those years since Columbus had set sail would baptize us as it had been meant to do when the snow had first fallen, was falling that very day so many years ago that he showered and invited me in to rid me of my nightmares.

We didn't mar the moment by speaking of it, pinning it down like an insect in a collection. We just let it hang there between us, as if the memory were Milagros herself, the woman who joined us, the point of our encounter, her deep interior where I had been and where the great McKenzie always returned. As the sky was just beginning to darken at 11 p.m., we allowed the memory to linger in the air like a sun that knows it will come back sooner than you expect, whose faint color under the horizon tells you it has never entirely abandoned you. I did not puncture the memory, he did not refer to it, we allowed it to wash us again, promise us that it would care for us, the communal water, as it had loved us that night of the helicopter and the bed so many years ago.

The memory stayed with us through the next days, though not because my father came any closer or even spoke to me directly. He was obviously so content and my mother so deliriously happy to have him to herself, with a joy that was contagious, that had everybody in a great mood. Even the grouchy, glowering first mate played checkers with Lalo Goic and Lalo let him win almost each time. Milagros told me one morning after breakfast as we strolled on the deck that she had come along to satisfy my craving for her company but that she was being rewarded by the gift of her loved one. Maybe, she hinted, they'd be able to continue this relationship once the ship returned and the iceberg was packed away in its seven container boxes.

That night I stood outside their cabin and listened to them make love, I listened to their shuffling sighs, their hushed laughs, and it was as if I were being bathed again in the moon of my past innocence. I felt not a twinge of jealousy: they were making me again, giving me a new lease on life. He knew that I had arranged this, that if I had ever come between them in the past, I was changing it all now, I was allowing him to win his bet and his woman.

I didn't need him to tell me this. I had confirmation when, on the fourth day, we arrived at the last Chilean bases on the South Shetland Islands, wrapped in a faint snowfall. We descended onto the soil, if that is what you could call that vast wasteland of ice with gnarls and knolls of gashing rocks here and there, and found ourselves in a mini-city occupied by a hundred or so men and their officers, who had camped out the whole winter and were delighted to see us arrive. They showed us the post office and the bank (with an ATM machine—I'm not kidding) and were displaying their entertainment center when a *teniente* came up to the great McKenzie and waved a piece of paper in front of him. A message, an urgent message via E-mail for Cristóbal McKenzie. "And I'd like you to know, sir," the man added in his boots and fur and frost-bitten moustache, "what an honor it is to deliver this to you. You once rescued a cousin of mine who went on to a profitable career in banking. If not for you, he'd have ruined his life. So here it is, the message, sir."

My father didn't take it immediately. "Who's it from?"

"Someone called Polo, sir," the *teniente* answered.

My heart sank. I had dug my own grave. I was responsible for teaching the ineffable Polo the delights of the Net, a way of showing off, really, proving to him my worth. I hadn't given him lessons on my computer, which continued its abandoned slumber in the repair shop, where one promise followed the other like dead birds. Instead, I had wired the Casa Milagros with some old computers that Oscar and Nano had passed on. And now Polo was using the knowledge I had given him—like Lautaro!—to screw me again, intrude from behind one more time. He probably had invented some crisis, would force the great McKenzie to make a hurried retreat from this base, undoubtedly had already contacted the military so they could fly him out on a helicopter that would be a distant relative of the one that awoke me sweating that night just before I had left for the States. That helicopter was going to cut me off from my father, leave me marooned on a ship heading into the Antarctic Peninsula in search of an iceberg that would retract its promise to bring me and my father together.

"Do me a favor, *Teniente*," my father said. "Tell Polo, whoever he is, that his message arrived too late. Tell him I already sailed. Right, Gabriel?"

"Right," I said.

That night—if you can call it night when only four hours are barely darkened—I was slipped out of my sleep by my mother, though not only her, because under the seven membranes of her clothes I could scent the sprinkle of my father's semen. I could celebrate that their bodies had played with each other in the way in which the heavy waves were playing with the ship and the peninsula we were fast approaching, I could accept that it was good that they had made me out of nothing and that before I returned to that white darkness of death, I myself would have played with a body of my choosing. They were healing me, I could sense it. And my mother coming to me now with the whiff of my father remotely cohering to her torso and legs was proof that a time would come when he would no longer use the water with which we had washed together to rid himself of other women, a time was approaching like the Bay of Paradise when we would all three bathe together in the same river.

"There's something you have to see," she whispered, and others who were asleep heard her and started dressing rapidly in the shadows, caring not at all that she was a woman. All of us rushed up on deck, where the great McKenzie and the captain were staring forward and upward and sideward.

In front of us loomed an iceberg the size of a city, a quiet, colossal meteor of ice larger than a football stadium, larger than the largest block of skyscrapers in Manhattan, a floating, shimmering horror that beautifully blotted out the line of the horizon—less than a mile away, a Himalaya of peaks and crevices gliding in our direction.

"We'll go around," the captain said, whispering as if it might hear us, as if God might be eavesdropping and decide to send it in cold pursuit of our ship. "If a bird should land on it, the monster could tip over, that's how unstable it is from the work of the wind over the centuries. If we're caught in its wake . . . "

It was blocking our way. It was telling us not to go on. It was telling me to beware and turn back.

It was guarding the mouth of the Bay of Paradise.

And yet we did not heed that warning, almost did not need to divine what it might be saying through the fog of Antarctica, because we would have had to make a detour anyway, it turns out. A ship was caught in Bahía Desolación, or Deception Bay in English though *desolation* is a much better word for the landscape we encountered as we went to its rescue. Several miles away, there it was, its mast sticking out, trapped in the ice since the winter, waiting for the thaw. A German man and his wife were there, inside that ship. They had sailed into the bay at the end of the summer with their two children and had been caged in by the pack ice, ensnared by the slow coil of what is cold and cannot get colder and then does get colder and wants to get so cold that nothing will ever again move. As the darkness of the polar night descended and ascended and surrounded them, they decided to evacuate the children and remain behind; the German and his Frau had been more than ready to spend the seven months of winter here, with only their bodies for company and a dwindling supply of water. All this we gleaned when we trudged across that ice to the ship and brought the two of them back for a meal and supplies, my father and I and the first mate and Armando and two other members of the crew slushing for several hours across the great white waste. My father nodded when I said that they were like Adam and Eve because they refused to return with us to land. He smiled when I said there was nothing better than to spend a night that lasts six months with the woman you love. It was almost as good, he answered, as spending a day that lasts six months with her because—and here he stopped in midsentence and I knew that he would tell me the rest when he was ready, when I was ready.

On the seventh day of our journey, at four in the morning, as the sun was falling up into the sky of the end of the world, we slithered into Paradise Bay as if we did not want anybody or anything to know we had arrived, as if we wanted to take the iceberg by surprise.

It would not allow itself to be captured that easily.

Armando knew exactly what he was looking for: *hielos negros*, the famous black ice of Antarctica, baptized with that name because it was old ice and had been able to grow transparent with the centuries, had devoured its own imperfections, sterilized its past, operated on its memories, waiting for someone to look straight through it, blue as the sky it wanted to join, blue as the waters it would someday pass through. But that was not enough—age, transparency, diamond depths. Armando had dreamed how each fragment had to be twisted, how the parts would fit, what gigantic edge and sheer cliff and small canyons he needed in those floating corpses of ice in order to bring them all together in Sevilla, sever the legs from the body so they could dance in the light of Spain, grow a new body under the electricity of the World's Fair, he knew what he was looking for.

We set out, two boats of us, into that graveyard of *escombros*, the floating debris of millions of years of blizzards and winds that blew out of the south as if they wanted to announce the end of time and not only of space.

"Down this street," Armando called out.

"What street?" asked the first mate.

"There, there, the streets of ice. See the ice in the streets, see the blood of the ice flow through the streets!"

It was not a mirage. Two days before, we had seen a mirage in the ocean, an iceberg where there was nothing, surging out of the waves like a whale and disappearing, we had seen a caravan of ghosts crossing the waters as if it were a desert of blue sand, we had pinched ourselves and pinched one another and seen islands of green and white palms, we had heard women calling to us from those islands. I am not exaggerating, Janice, this is how that continent defends itself, drives you wild, tempts you to forget your navigational instruments and go into the white blindness and lose yourself before you die. It is the ice that plays tricks. I who have tricked so many say so, I who have ended up here in the city of *el burlador* Don Juan, who tricked many more than I have and ended up like me in hell: we are nothing compared with the specters that the ice throws up and then suffocates and reflects from some mirror in the sky of clouds what is happening thousands of miles away, the ice calling you from its infinite screen. And yet that is not what Armando was seeing, not a delusion of streets but a labyrinth of ice urging our boat into the breach and between the cracks and inside the gorges and hissing fissures of what nobody had dared to touch since the start of human memory, the ice that had killed most of the men who had ever stepped on it, built a fire, walked across its waste.

And we were going to cut off sixty, eighty, a hundred tons of that, not even a finger, not even the sliver of a sliver of skin. But it would resist us, it was alive, Janice, the ice was alive and hiding. "Listen," Armando said to me and my dad, "it wants us to come for it, it's been waiting. You've been waiting for me, you want to travel, you want it, baby."

That first day we worked almost until midnight and came up with
. . . nothing.

"We'll find her," my father said, shivering. Before my mother took
him off to beat the clock, less than an hour left to make love to her, to
keep his wager and his manhood alive. "Tomorrow."

"How do you know it's a her?" Milagros Gallardo asked.

"Because it takes forever to find her," my father said. "And when
you find her, she slips away."

"No," Milagros said. "When you find her, it's the man who slips
away, who can't stand staying by her side."

"Tomorrow," the great McKenzie said, "you come with us."

"I'll find him," she said. "I'll find that iceberg."

And she did. Or her presence allowed it to materialize. I would
swear it was the same spot we had passed ten times, new dirty ice the
color of white nothingness through the previous perishing passes, and
then suddenly there it was, the main core. Armando knew it right
away, saw it with the eyes of Milagros Gallardo, saw it with my eyes,
saw it as my father had seen it that evening of my arrival in Chile
when the fake iceberg had stopped me from taking the first plane
back to you and Manhattan, Janice. Armando simply pointed our
boatman toward it and we glided into its real and royal presence, the
ice that had been forming when I was conceived, when my father and
mother were conceived, when Columbus was conceived, the ice that
had hardened in the wait for our eyes and invaded the mind and
hands of the sculptor so that he could find her, find him, find it when
it was ready to appear, ready to travel.

It was too late to operate on it right then and there. We needed
the light of dawn, a whole day to make sure we did not cut off any
essential parts. Armando had to be able to behold it through and
through as he coaxed it from the mountain out of which it had
grown, coaxed it as one would a child that must be weaned, must be
convinced that outside is life and not death. We had to face it as the
sun came up and not as the sun began to flatten itself into sadness
behind the monumental cathedrals of ice that protected that bay.

"We'll find it in a snap," said the first mate, watching approvingly
as the *motosierristas*, the operators of the ice saw, rubbed their gloved
fingers, gnawed by the chilling wind, in anticipation.

It snowed during the night.

It snowed and the early light of the bay revealed an entirely different vista: everything was covered and hidden again, every abyss had been filled and every passage had cracked open wider. The wind began to move the floes of ice as if they were crumpled paper ships, pushing them against one another. All through the brief night interval of polar summer I had heard the icebergs groaning, grinding at one another, heard the wind that night as I could still hear the monster in the helicopter so many years ago, mocking me, mocking us, the wind giving out a sound like a wounded animal, exactly like the sound I expected to hear the iceberg emit when we sliced into it, gashed it from its mother mountain. I scrambled out of bed and the others had already left. Stumbling from exhaustion, I knew they wouldn't find it. We had lost our iceberg under the camouflage of the snow. Everything looked identical. It was hiding again under the mantle of white that the Antarctic night had sent to save it, keep it fixed there: more thick snow than would ever thaw in the four days we had left, that might take a decade to be turned once again into crystal blue. Unless we could wipe the landscape clean, find its womb in the midst of the garbage of snowstorms and white rubble swirling around the ship as the wind whipped into us with fury, unless we—

The *Galvarino* turned almost imperceptibly. A flare was shot into the distance to call back the two rafts. We were heading out of the bay. It was getting perilous. Any of those drifting glaciers could sink us, crush us, and freeze us into the middle of those waters, could leave us to be visited by the winds and the albatrosses just as the iceberg was meant to be visited by tourists in Sevilla, the End of the World's Fair, the Fair at the End of the World. We would be the exhibition and the wind would carve us, and the wind had been dreaming us for five hundred years and, with its hands and with its blizzard eyes, could turn the hunter into the captive.

"If the snow keeps falling," the captain informed us that evening as we despondently slurped soup that had none of the restorative qualities of the Nana's magical *cazuela*, "that's it. We'll have to grab the first piece of icefucking—hope nobody in present company objects to my language."

"Motherfucking ice," my mom said. "Cold shitface cunt-dead ice."

"Right," the captain said, a bit taken aback but still determined to be the commanding officer. "Well, I've said all I need to say."

We had seen it. Understand, Janice, we had been near enough to touch it. The Sevilla iceberg—the same one I am going to blow up tonight, before America's birthday, before the birthday of Cristóbal McKenzie and Pablo Barón, that one—had shown its face to us, her face, his face; the iceberg had waited till it was late in the day so that we might always know it was there but could never be caught and would never reveal its secret. It had only separated the mists that surrounded it like a valley no one has ever visited, had only done so because it knew in the shudder inside, the creaking of its deep blue underside, that a storm would cover and defend it the next day. It wanted us to see but never touch, to dream but never fuck, to spend the rest of our days looking for it, that's what it wanted.

It wanted to be a virgin forever.

I did not sleep that night. Listening to the wind as it died down, I crept on deck as the snow thinned so I could catch a glimpse of the remote sun at four in the morning starting to sorrow over the ruins of our expedition, to reveal a landscape buried in white, formless, overcast like a sky of nothingness on the flat surface of the waters. *Bahía Paraíso*. An empty paradise that held no paths we had crossed, no markings we had left: erased.

I went to the cabin my father and mother occupied, knocked on the door, waited for the great McKenzie to emerge, his hair tousled by the night's combat, his wife back there on the narrow bunk with her close-cropped head buried in a pillow.

"You're needed," I said.

He was the only one. I knew he could do it. His specialty: finding runaways, following their desires to the one place where the kids thought they could hide. Why not an iceberg?

"You're crazy," he said. "I bring kids back home. I don't invade their homes to take them away. I'm not some fucking police agent who wants to kidnap the runaway, I—"

"The iceberg wants to be found," I said. "You know it. It doesn't want to spend the rest of eternity here."

"I can't do it."

"Feel it calling," I said. I was the one calling and he knew it by then, he knew that I needed him to try.

He found the iceberg at noon that day, November 9, it was, or maybe the tenth. Time ceases to exist at the edge of the world.

Cristóbal McKenzie pointed to a mound of snow in the middle of nowhere and the giant fan that Armando had commandeered from the captain blew into action, a human wind to counter the wind from the South Pole that had buried Scott and almost killed Amundsen and nearly shielded the iceberg from us for another five hundred years. After that fan, three members of the crew managed to hoist themselves up on top of the iceberg as if it were a gargantuan elephant, sweeping the snow into the sea as they crept toward the edge, sweeping delicately as if it were music they were brushing off, its face starting to shine beneath, the same depths of pain and vulnerability that I had tried to touch with my father's hands the evening I had met Amanda Camila and been rocked in the arms of my Nana. There it was, blue as the beginning of the universe, ready to risk a journey through the heat of the tropics to the Europe that had sent Columbus forth in search of spices and gold, ready to return the gaze from the eyes of millions of tourists who would never understand its mystery but would, at least, understand that there was such a thing, that a mystery still existed somewhere on earth, a continent that man had not yet covered with his steps and fingerprints and maps and machines.

It did not cry when we guttered it from its home. There was no other sound than the saw and the instructions and the drip-drop of the sweat and imprecations as we fought against the sun, no other sound than its slow crash into the waters of Paradise, the waves lapping us, licking its edges as we towed it behind us toward the ship, no sound that night as it nestled next to the hull, no sound as it was sliced into the jigsaw scraps of Armando's design, no sound but the grind of the hook and the net, slipping over and over each fractured hulk back into the sea, and the scraping scar of those metallic ropes strangling it, no complaint, no haunting melody, no mirage. Just men the next day cursing and straining and celebrating, chaining the many sharp faces of the iceberg into captivity, landing each one on the deck with a gentle thud of joy, maneuvering it into the dark container, the slight scratch of thermal blankets to keep intact the deep cold it carried inside until we arrived in Punta Arenas at the refrigeration chambers that would protect it during the months to come. Finally, making sure each container was well latched so that someday soon six phallic columns in Sevilla would breathe frigid air around the encroaching heat.

Those sounds and no other sounds accompanied the start of its journey, the end of mine.

We watched it all with my dad as he smoked his cigarettes and looked at it with the eyes he had reserved for Carlitos, looked at it with tenderness, looked at me that way.

This was why I had wanted to extract the iceberg from the blue floating mountains of Antarctica.

Ever since I had arrived in the land of my birth, I had been buffeted like a skiff on a windy sea, this way, that way. My uncle said something and I agreed and then Larrea said the opposite and I also agreed, and I frowned when Amanda Camila frowned and I smiled when Pablo Barón smiled, putty in their hands, modeled by their voices and their desires. As if there were no core to this Gabriel McKenzie who had spent so many years away supposing that when we came home to Chile everything would be settled. But my personality had proven no more than a mist that could be blown away and that was fixed by camouflage into the semblance of an identity but that had no center to it, as if I were—yes, ice floating in a hot sea, ready to dissolve, far from any land that could disclose where north was, where south, how to anchor myself to something that endured, something less evanescent than interwords on the interface of a screen. You know the sensation, Janice, we've talked about it, even joked about it. I had come to Chile, I realized, searching for that *tierra firme*, land ahoy, searching for the beach of my father onto which I might alight—or even the shoal of a father to wreck myself on.

That's why I had come to Chile and Chile, so far, had not answered my call.

"Dad," I said suddenly, "I'm a virgin."

"I know," my father said.

"And I'm sorry I didn't make it back before. I'm sorry Abuela Claudia never got to see me again before she died."

"I think you are sorry," he said. "I think you really are."

We waited while Jacobo and his camera went by, we moved away from the iceberg quietly sleeping in its seven containers.

"I need help, Dad," I said. "I really need help."

"Help is on the way," he said. "All you had to do was ask."

He wanted to know what lucky woman I had set my sights on and I lied to him, of course, told him it was Cristina Ferrer. I was worried that his vow to Pablo Barón, the condom he had given Amanda Camila's father upon her birth, extended to Gabriel McKenzie as well, that Pablo's daughter would be deemed off-limits for any of the male genitalia of the tribe. So it turned out that, at the very moment when I was asking him to open up to me, I didn't take him into my confidence. One more fatal mistake. Though it was okay, I said to myself, because almost immediately he lied right back to me. "Not a bad choice," he commented about Cristina, and I probed him, "You haven't . . . I mean, she isn't one of . . . " And he said, "No, of course not, she's not my type," even though I was to discover quite soon that one of the secrets of his success was that there was no such thing as type. He liked every woman he came across, found something and often more than one thing absolutely redeemable and irreplaceable in each one. But what matters here is that we were quits, both indulging in our separate little deceptions.

"Tell me then, what's the problem?"

"You are."

"Me? I haven't been around you. It's your mother who's been in charge of your education, and in her letters she claimed you were screwing half New York. And if it's the absent father that's been bugging you, I know thousands who've managed without a dad, including me and your Tío Pancho."

I told him what had happened the Manhattan night I came home from your unsoiled couch, Janice, and Mom unloaded his Casanova example onto me. I wasn't fucked up from his absence. I was fucked up by his excessive presence.

"Oh, Milagros, Milagros," Dad sighed. "Women. But that still doesn't answer what I'm supposed to do for you."

I told him the question that had been burning up my sex—or rather, wilting it—since I first heard the story of my conception, the question that Mom had been unable to answer and that somehow seemed to have jinxed me. "What happened that night, the night you left Mom and only had an hour and a half to find another woman?" That question.

He said, Not so fast. First he had to fill me in on his courtship of Milagros, insisted on repeating what I already knew. It took him awhile but finally, as the ship weighed anchor and set sail northward amid cheers, he came to the episode I had been waiting for since I was fifteen, during these eight years of virginity. How had a young man whose only sexual experience had been forty nights with a woman who had been preparing for his presence since she was twelve, how had that young man who had never tasted any female flesh before that night when Che Guevara was being shoveled into the earth, how had Cristóbal McKenzie become a *putamadre*? Because if he could do it, so could I. I had sworn it was possible as irate and dissatisfied women pushed me out of their beds, I had sworn it as I watched other men take every promising skirt and flirt away from me, and now I was about to learn the secret.

"No secret," my dad said as we watched the Antarctic Peninsula recede, an albatross following the wake of our garbage, eating the refuse that we were showering into the sea. "Just luck, I guess. There I was, ten-thirty at night, an hour and a half to go. And I decided that there was no way I would be able to find someone, that if this was to happen I had to let that someone find me, whoever she might be in that vast, dark, drizzling city. It was the end of August, Gaby, rain had been falling steadily since morning. I decided that I'd wander and that fate would take care of me. Though the truth is that I knew that, a bit more than a month after I'd made the bet, I was on my way to becoming the first loser. And the sadness in my face must have shown as I walked there in the rain without an umbrella, the water streaming through my hair. The sadness is what saved me, because five, maybe ten minutes after I'd left Milagros, somebody saw that face, a man in the door of an apartment building on Avenida Irrarrazaval. He was holding it open and when he saw me he nodded as if he knew me (I'd never seen him before in my life), thanked me for coming, said how sorry they all were, and then turned to greet a couple who were limping in from the rain, telling all three of us that we knew where it was, and he stayed behind, holding that door open while I followed that man and that woman up to the second floor. I thought to myself, This is the only invitation I'm going to get tonight, I might as well spend the next few hours here, rescued from the deluge. Until midnight came around and I could go back *con la cola entre las piernas*, defeated, to my Milagros. I went into that apartment and what do you think I found?"

"An orgy," I said.

"A funeral," my dad said. "They were holding a wake. I was so forlorn that the relative in charge, the dead man's brother it turned out, had confused me with one of the mourners. There must have been fifty people sitting around in that small living-dining area, the body exposed in its coffin, candles, flowers, the works. Everybody was sniffling, red eyes, coughing, low voices, already gossiping about the stiff. I wanted to back out, but the man and woman I'd come up with insisted that I go first, convey my condolences to the widow, who was dressed in black, sitting rigidly by the body, trying not to look at it, trying not to look at anybody. They sort of pushed me forward and there was nothing I could do, I had to go up to her and say, *Mi sentido pésame*, something stupid like that, as if anything we say at wakes is ever smart. I gave her my hand and she took it and asked, 'How well did you know him?' It would have been the moment to have muttered another inane nicety and beaten a retreat. But I felt—I don't know how to describe it—so dejected by her pain. Compassion is the word, I guess. Gabriel, I wasn't trying to seduce her, I did not have the slightest inkling that in less than an hour I'd be fucking her in the adjoining bathroom."

"Was she pretty?"

"You don't understand, Gabriel. She was, in fact, more on the ratty side, nondescript, matronly, I suppose you could call her, a real dog compared with Milagros. But that's not the point. When you start measuring how a woman looks, the first thing you have to ask is, are you choosing her because of how she looks to you or how she'll look to the men who surround you? Do you want to fuck her because of her or because she'll make other men jealous? If she'd been dazzling that night, I'd never have made it into her arms, because I'd have immediately thought of giving her a good poke and that would have been the wrong tactic, that would have been precisely what was not needed. I ended up making love because I did not intend to, because nothing could have been further from my mind. I was wasting valuable time, the clock was ticking, seventy-five minutes till my deadline, and even so, I stayed on with her. I answered her question about how well I'd known her husband with the truth. I don't know why I said it, I just felt that she was probably fed up with lies; as soon as someone dies everybody starts lying about the *finado*. I said, 'Not at all, ma'am. I just needed to come out of the rain. But I'll leave right away, leave you to—' She reached for my hand. 'Stay,' she said, 'please stay. You're the only one I can tell how much I hated the bastard. Please don't go.' "

"She hated him?"

"It wasn't that he cheated on her," my dad said. "It was that he beat her. He'd beat her because the food was cold and he'd beat her if it was too warm, he'd beat her when he was drunk and then he'd beat her again when he sobered up, just to show that he really meant it. I had to listen to her murmured complaints, interrupted every few minutes by somebody in tears coming up to commiserate. I should have used the first interruption to exit, but I just couldn't—she was so alone, had not one person on earth—so I lingered on. There was a grandfather clock in that room. I watched the minutes go by, was already thinking of the story I'd tell Milagros that night, the story I'd tell Pablo and Pancho the next day when I reported that the future would be carved out between them, whether Latin America would be socialist or whether Mr. Barón would be the most powerful man in the land, no place in that future for a man who thought the only thing we'd been sent into this world for was to make someone happy for the snap of time it takes to share a bed, share a body. Enriqueta—that was her name—must have sensed something in me that was breaking, because all of a sudden she stopped talking about how much she hated that bastard, how she couldn't wait for the corpse to be a thousand feet underground. She looked at me and asked, 'If you didn't know him, then why are you so sad?' "

"And you told her about your bet, you told her you loved her—God, what did you tell her?"

"I wasn't going to burden her with my troubles, Gabriel. I just said it was a long story not worth the telling. But the fact that she had stopped worrying about herself for the first time since we'd met did allow me to stand up—it was eleven-thirty, she saw where my eyes were pointing—and ask her where the bathroom was. A slight vibration of alarm crept into her eyes. 'You'll be back?' she asked. I had wondered, in fact, if this was not when I should make my escape, but I said, 'Of course I'll be back.' "

"And she followed you into the bathroom."

"She followed me into the bathroom. She was waiting outside when I tried to come out. She slipped inside quickly and locked the door. She grabbed my dick, just like that. 'Man-fuck me,' she said."

"Man-fuck me? What did she mean?"

"Maybe that her husband had never really fucked her, I don't know, I didn't ask. 'Do it for me,' she said. 'I know you want it, I know you do, but do it for me.' So I did. I pushed her against the bathrobes hanging from the bathroom door and screwed Enriqueta, the second woman in my life, for the first and last time. Barely had time to put on a condom—"

"You had the presence of mind to—"

"I hadn't promised your mom yet, but I didn't want to start populating the globe with children—thousands of them if I carried out the bet—so better seek protection right away."

"And you always used a condom from that moment on?"

My father paused, turned from Antarctica toward the ship, toward the north and Punta Arenas, where we were now heading with the cargo we had rescued from the mask of its eternal ice. He smiled. "Always," he said. "I keep my promises."

"So what happened next?"

"It was quick for both of us, we both came almost immediately. Somebody knocked discreetly outside as I was spurting into her, as she was panting in my ear, I killed him, I poisoned the son of a bitch . . ."

"She poisoned her husband?"

"So she said. Maybe she was saying it to turn me on, maybe it was what she had hoped she had done. Women say the strangest things during sex, some begin to laugh, some begin to cry, some whisper something really perverse to keep you going. It's hard work, believe me. But it makes it sort of enjoyable, not to know how she'll react, how her face will change when she opens up to you. It's always sweet, Gabriel, but let me tell you that except for the first time I ever did it, with your mother, the night we created you, except for that time, this was the best even if it lasted no more than a few minutes, the sweetest because it was so unexpected, because it saved my ass and allowed me to meet all those other women and continue my exploration. And I had done nothing to deserve this prize except to listen to her, stay with her when she needed me. So your first lesson is—"

"Don't worry about looks."

"And the second lesson is that you have to know how to listen. Women spend most of their day listening to men or listening to other women talking about men. A man who knows how to take in a lady's words won't find it that hard to be taken into her body later."

"It always happens like that?"

"Oh, no. There are no formulas. It's not an equation: you listen, she fucks. You can fake it, after all, you can make believe you're interested in what she's saying. She may not realize you don't give a hoot for what comes out of her mouth. Or she may realize it and not care, want to screw anyway."

"But that's not the right way, that's what you're telling me."

"Not the right way. You'll lose out from time to time—women who don't pay back with sex your sincere interest in them, but those may turn out to be the best ones, the women you would want to marry if you could marry them one by one."

"And you've lost out?"

"A number of times."

"So how did you . . . ?"

"By then I'd learned a few tricks. To begin with, every morning I read the obituaries, and if, by ten, ten-thirty that night I haven't scored yet, I go to the wake. Believe me, there's always some woman who wants to do it. It must be the proximity of death, the feeling that you'd better have a good time because it's later than you think, the fading rose, all that shit. But that's seldom necessary. I've found that the surest way to fuck a woman is to approach her without the idea of fucking her. I'm not saying that in the back of your head and at the tip of your *pija* you're not hoping that things will work out. I'm human, not a saint, but I start out by keeping my distance. You can trust me, I won't hurt you, I don't even want to touch you, that's how much I respect you. Then, once their guard is down, natural instinct takes over, your sexual drive begins to surface so slowly even you don't realize it, she hardly knows it's creeping out into daylight, calling to her like an insect on a hot summer night. But both of you do end up understanding. There's a moment, the most marvelous moment, some men would say, when you both know what is going to happen, what she'll do to you, what you'll do to her."

"And if that moment doesn't come, when do you call it quits, head for the address in the obituary?"

"Not right away. That's why I generally try to meet women at midday. Because when she refuses, when she turns her back on you, that's when things begin to get really interesting. You don't give up right away. She senses—like Enriqueta—that you're about to lose everything, that your whole life depends on her saying yes. She senses that you're not joking when you say, Unless you fuck me, I'm lost. She senses that you've fallen in love. No, I mean it, Gaby, you have to fall instantly in love and then you can fall out of it just as promptly. She grasps that her indifference—the cardinal sin, Gabriel, indifference to someone else's suffering, much worse than outright cruelty, because cruelty doesn't hide itself, cruelty gnaws at your conscience—yes, make her feel that her indifference is going to destroy you and even so you're still loyal, you're still there for her. That's when she really breaks down."

The waves were growing, swelling up, hacking downward, the *Mar de Drake* was not going to treat us as well now as it had when we had crossed it going south more than a week ago: the stormiest waters in the world were going to show us the worst they could do.

"I've got to go," my dad said. "Your mom isn't feeling too well and I—"

"It's late," I agreed, knowing what that meant.

"You want to see it?"

"See it?"

"I mean, if it would help. I could sneak you in, you watch, maybe you'd understand it's not such a big deal. Milagros wouldn't even realize you're there, she's so dizzy from these swells, and even if she did I don't think she'd mind. That's how crazy she is about you, would do anything, and I mean anything, for you, to make you happy."

"You won't tell her about . . . ?"

"Not a word. A secret between men." He punched my shoulder gently. I punched him back. "So—is that what you need? Is that how I remove my curse from your life?"

"It's great of you to make the offer, but—"

"It's no big deal," he said. "You were there at the beginning, from the inside, so to speak. You might as well take a look from the outside. Maybe it would—"

"No, thanks, Dad. All I need is to know what happened the next day, the day after the widow and the funeral, I mean, who you screwed next, that really should be enough. If you could just fill me in on . . . You know."

"You want me to go through every woman I ever made love to or only numbers three and four and five? It could take us a few years. Where would you like me to stop?"

I didn't know the answer. I had thought that the mere enunciation of his first extramarital adventure, the fact that he could complete for me the story that had been left suspended since I came home from our catastrophe, Janice, that this would free me. I had muttered this hope to myself so often in the last eight years, it had kept me going after each frustrating sexless entanglement, like a pilgrim who thinks that, when he reaches Jerusalem or Mecca or some temple on a hill, all will be forgiven, all the past laundered away. Except that what my dad had given me so far was worthless, might have helped me if I wanted simply to get laid but, given the current hole I had dug myself into, contained no magic formula. What I really needed to learn was how to convince a girl who was treating me like her brother to have sex. And if he also had a hint as to how to convince that girl's father, who was treating me like his son, not to murder me, I'd welcome that advice as well. But this was, of course, not something I could reveal to the great McKenzie. All I could hope was that sometime during his confessions one case would approximate mine, one story would act as a thread through the labyrinth, one word of his would finally hit the nail on the head.

"Everything," I said. "You remember everything, don't you? Every woman?"

"That's the one thing I swore to them. I swore I'd never forget them, and so far I've been true to that promise. Yes, I remember every last detail."

"I need to know everything."

"If we had a year on a desert island . . . ," he said. "But even if we had all the time in the universe, I'm not sure that would solve your problem. Tell you what. Let's meet tomorrow after breakfast. Will you be able to make it?" He pointed to the sea. We were being chopped and mixed as if inside a gigantic blender. I nodded. "We'll try a little experiment. We'll talk to some of the other men."

"You're not going to tell them what we . . . that I . . . ?"

"Your secret is safe with me. I'm just going to ask them what's the best thing about being with a woman, no more than that. See what they answer."

Next morning, I managed to collapse myself out of my heaving bunk, managed to crawl up to the mess hall, which was almost empty, whether because everybody was sick or busy I could not tell. My dad was waiting for me.

"You know, Gabriel, in this business if you want to conquer women it's not enough to know how their minds work. You also have to know what goes on in the predatory heads of men. I've been doing some observations on board. Always size up the competition, even when you're with a surefire date. Always take the measure of your potential rivals. Let's start with him."

It was Armando Jorquera. He sat at a nearby table, staring vacantly into space while his hands, as if they were autonomous puppets, toyed with a *marraqueta*, molding the dough into blocks, unconsciously assembling the whole mess into a replica of the iceberg to be built in Sevilla. So deeply inside his vision was he that my father had to repeat the question twice before he answered it. But when he did, when Armando did give an answer to that question—What's the best moment in a sexual relationship?—it fit perfectly into the story of the wake my father had told me. The best moment for Armando was when he saw a woman across a crowded room and they exchanged glances and both knew that soon they would be exchanging something else. It's all in the head, Armando said: once it's happened in your head, everything else is a letdown. Not that I'm complaining about the rest of it, but nothing like that flash when you see the future unfold like a naked lady slowly letting the bedspread roll down her body.

"Next," said my father. "Our filmmaker. Boy, am I glad it isn't that asshole Max."

We visited Jacobo in his bunk. He wasn't feeling too well. He was discovering that the seas that had allowed him to capture the iceberg with his camera so that the eyes of the world could see what he had seen, that ocean was not going to let him get home without exacting a heavy toll on his body. I thought the great McKenzie would leave him alone, rolling and sweating, poor Jacobo, but no, the same question, it'll do him good to try to answer. And in fact it did perk him up a bit. Jacobo had no doubt about what the best moment was: penetration. "The moment when you go in, all the way, the moment you inch into her and there's no going back, that thrust. She's agreed to open up and give you refuge, accepted that you're inside and won't leave. Even if you do leave soon, if she expels you, if you withdraw, if it's quick or if it's slow, nothing compares to that instant when the world changes, when you've changed everything, after so much imagining, so much Will she, won't she, will I, won't I, just the relief of knowing, that moment."

"We're following a sequence," my father said after we had thanked Jacobo for his confidences and hoped he felt well enough to join us for lunch—at the mention of which our filmmaker headed for the lavatory to rid himself of whatever might be left inside. "Maybe you can guess what the engineer will say."

Gerardo was outside, inspecting the containers that enclosed those hundreds of tons of ice. His response—shouted to us as he made sure everything was latched tight, as wave after wave pounded the deck and we held onto the thick cables that held the containers in place— was, predictably, that what he liked best was plumbing the inner works, everything that comes just before orgasm, the possibility of prolonging that love for as long as you can, all the tinkering and discovery, the ins and outs, the holding back. "It's more than a moment, if you can manage it," he howled into our ears. "If you can make it last forever, more power to you. That's the best part."

And then we went to the radio room, where Lalo was doing his midmorning PR, feeding information to faraway journalists who wanted some report on the progress of the expedition, something about this *Galvarino* growing hands to bring the ice home. He paused long enough to help my dad complete his inquiry, thought it was some sort of informal quiz. There was nothing like the pleasure, Lalo announced and the radio operator assented, of letting go. That's what it was all about. The hell with imagining ahead of time or penetrating or playing around inside—nature had organized things so that there was nothing that delighted more than emptying yourself inside a willing or unwilling vagina. It was all keyed to that moment, everything else at its service, everything else second-rate compared with the real fireworks.

"The captain," my father said, "completes our survey."

Our captain passed the helm to his first mate and took us into his cabin and poured us some water—the most precious commodity on board—before answering that the best moment was undoubtedly after it was all over, when you could fall asleep in somebody's arms, that postcoital rest, that fondling of a clitoris still aching for one last touch, that hand on her breast, that falling into forgetfulness of yourself and her, that was a moment to savor, when your duty was done and the ship was safely home, the journey over.

"How about our journey," my father asked. "How're we doing?"

"We'll be in Punta Arenas by tomorrow. This storm should be over in—give it three, four hours. Not more."

"Time enough," my father said. He went back with me to the mess hall, where the first seating for lunch was being served. While the cook was heating up some broth for Milagros, he turned to me. "So," my father asked, "which of them is right?"

"I don't know," I said. "I've never—"

"They've had the chance," the great McKenzie interrupted, "and they've all come up with a different answer."

"What now?" I asked. "Whom do I believe?"

"Too much advice," Cristóbal McKenzie said. "I'm giving you too much advice, and that's not good. That's what it means. I could tell you the seduction and orgasm of every woman I've fucked in this country and you still wouldn't understand. Worse, the more I told you, the bigger my shadow would grow, the more you'd try to be who I am when your problem, Gabriel, is that you haven't learned how to be you. You keep on trying to perform up to standard, up to my standard, and women know that. I mean, if they can choose between you and the man you admire, if they can choose between the real thing and the imitation for the same price, what d'you think they'll choose? So I'm stopping all this talk. When we get back to Santiago, you'll accompany me."

"The night we get back?"

He laughed. "The next day," he said. "The next night. You and your mom will get your stuff, settle back into the Casa Milagros, and we'll meet up for lunch. Spend some time together. Look for some runaways, then a couple of broads. Do some work."

"Work on what?"

"That face of yours, Gabriel. We're going to teach you how to love and use that face of yours. You'll see."

I won't see, I glumly said to myself then, and said it again during the day and a half left on board, even while things got ever more buddy-buddy with my dad, even as Mom joined us and for the first time since I was a child of six and we left Chile in 1974 the family of three was together and laughing, even as we left the Straits of Drake and headed for the Strait of Magellan. I won't see a thing, I repeated to myself one more time as the plane took off from Patagonia. We were going back to Polo-land without the breakthrough I had been praying for. As soon as I saw Polo at the airport waiting for us, I was sure he would find a way to see that the great McKenzie changed his mind, I was even more sure when Polo embraced me like a brother returned from the grave, when I said goodbye to all my friends to whom the captive iceberg, silently wailing for its mother back in Punta Arenas, had bonded me forever. I was absolutely sure when I found myself alone at Barón's house that night, telling Amanda Camila and her father and Carola all about the iceberg's capture, exuding an optimism I did not feel, falling asleep at dawn after listening at her door all night to the way she breathed, the way my lost love would never breathe in my ear in that bed. Tomorrow I'd move out of there without having felt that breath heaving under my chest. We were never going to get to work on that face of mine, my father and me. Something would come up, it always did, to frustrate my expectations.

Something did come up, of course, but it was not Polo.

It must have been near noon the next day. I was packing. My Nana, somehow anticipating that I would be moving back to the Casa Milagros, had ironed all my shirts and pants, washed my socks, put all my books in a box, the unused computer on the bed, inside its case. "You see, *mi niño*, I told you we'd fix everything." And that's where Ignacio found me.

He had bad news.

An hour earlier, my father and Polo had been arrested. They were being held for interrogation. Ignacio didn't want to tell me why, no matter how much I insisted. He was already putting his job on the line by even divulging that much. Something to do with the iceberg, he said, that was about all he could say. And that Inteligencia Militar had requested that Investigaciones pick them up, Military Intelligence was involved in some way.

"*Dios mío*," the Nana said, making the sign of the cross on her thick torso.

"Where's my mother?" I asked her.

"She's gone to Talca with Carola," the Nana answered. "Carola wanted her to see some project, a *cooperativa campesina*, I think she said it was, that she's been working on. They won't be back before tomorrow."

"Has Carola got a cellular phone?"

"She hates those modern things," the Nana said.

I dialed Pablo Barón's personal number. The *Ministro* was meeting with the president, his secretary said, and was not to be disturbed. I had the same luck when I called Amanda Camila at the iceberg project: she'd gone out to Farellones, up in the nearby mountains, where there was some sort of fashion shoot going on, the hosts and hostesses of Expo '92 against a backdrop of snow and rock, as if they had gone to Antarctica themselves, braving the winds and storms and ice in their skimpy repressive clothes. The receptionist didn't know when Amanda Camila would be back.

"Ignacio. Can you get me in to see my father?"

He was willing to do that for me. They weren't being held incommunicado, he said, in fact they would probably be released tomorrow. Tomorrow! My heart sank at the word.

"And does the *Ministro* know about this?" I asked Ignacio that question as we sped away from the house, leaving the Nana behind to field phone calls from her boss or Amanda Camila or anybody else who might help.

He shrugged. "I think you should speak to him."

"And why are you helping me out?"

He adjusted his dark glasses, looked at me over the tops of them. "D'you remember you asked me some time ago if I minded doing what I did, breaking a few legs, you said, back when General Pinochet was president, back then? I answered no, I didn't mind at all. And I don't. It's kept the country clean. I'm proud of what I did. Would do it again, Gabriel, if I was asked to. But this is something different. People here are using their positions for personal gain. I don't mean money, that's okay, that's part of the deal. But you don't use your position to steal another man's wife or blackmail your lover or help your kid get into college when he doesn't deserve it. You know what I'm saying, Gabriel? You kill so people will be safe, you kill someone before they kill some innocent citizen or they set off a bomb, you kill if you have to so as to protect those who are too weak to defend themselves. But you don't hurt somebody else just because you want to win a bet, if you get my meaning, Gabriel."

"Are you telling me that the *Ministro* is doing this to screw up my dad, force him to lose his bet?"

"I don't know what bet you're talking about. I don't know anything the *Ministro* has done or hasn't done. I never had this conversation with you. But I just wanted you to know that it's not fair, it's not what a man does, if you know what I mean."

"You're on my father's side."

"He asked me to call you, bring you, could I do that for him? He helped a nephew of mine once. It's the least I could do for a stud like McKenzie. He makes me proud to be Chilean."

My father wanted to see me, he saw me as the one person he could trust, who could get him out of this trouble.

That was an optimistic way of putting it.

"You," Cristóbal McKenzie said to me when I was finally talking to him across a glass partition, pressing buttons that allowed us to hear each other, "get me the fuck out of here. You got me in, get me out."

I didn't understand. Why was I to blame? What had I done that—?

"It was all a setup," my father said, his bitterness increasing with every furious minute ticking by, ticking toward midnight, when, for the first time in almost twenty-five years, he would not have screwed a woman that day. "And you fell for it, just like Polo said. Barón writes the first letter to get me involved and you agree to take the case, against my better judgment. Then he writes the second one to make sure I'll accompany you and make the rounds, that Polo and I will visit all these people who might possibly be suspects, keeps the letters coming so I'll be forced to go to Antarctica, be stuck on that *Galvarino* boat without a single cunt, and when that fails—"

"He didn't write them," I interrupted him. "It wasn't Pablo Barón who wrote those letters."

"Stop, Gabriel," he said, "just stop all the delusional bullshit. He wrote them and then handed little tidbits of information to Military Intelligence, mentioned how all these people seemed to have a problem with the iceberg—the Argentine embassy; the ecologists; the artists who were left out of Sevilla; the No More 1492 movement; the

$70 billion Ice for the Deserts project; the Canadian Iceberg vodka people, who were jealous; the Israelis and their Ice for the Coming Era, who wanted to corner the Antarctic water supply. The whole list. And where do you think he got the information that they might threaten the iceberg? Who do you think gave him that information?"

He paused. And that silence of his, Janice, hurt more than any of his words as he waited for my response.

"I did."

"Right. You gave him the information, so that he could then go to the authorities who have my brother in jail and say to them, Look, have you noticed who's visited all these people? If it isn't Cristóbal McKenzie and his friend Polo and his stupid son with that face like a baby. Why don't you bring them in for questioning, one night will do, that's all, just find out by what strange coincidence everybody they've gone to speak to about the iceberg ends up wondering if it wouldn't be a good idea to blow the bastard into the stratosphere. He tells Military Intelligence that this McKenzie is probably giving ideas to all these organizations, may be sending the letters himself, doing it to settle scores on behalf of his dangerous brother Francisco McKenzie, anything to humiliate the *madre patria*. But the motherland won't stand for it. A good scare should be enough, Barón says, a day is more than enough to make sure that McKenzie isn't doing anything that will spoil our image. After all, he has helped many officers find their runaway kids, so let him go tomorrow once he's learned his lesson. Make sure he cools his heels for one night, that's all."

"He's your best friend," I protested. "How can you just accuse him, without any proof, without—"

"That's what's great about his plan. Pablo can claim he's innocent. He didn't do anything, he tried to stop them, but if the army wants to ask me some questions . . . It's his job, after all, to keep them happy. And if they happen to help him win his bet, well, he wasn't looking for that. My best friend, Pablo Barón, gets what he wants and when I come to him, when you go to him, he'll look you straight in the eye and assure you, just like he'll assure me tomorrow, that he's innocent."

"But then why didn't they arrest me?"

"Because you weren't in the country yet when the first letter arrived," the great McKenzie answered. "So you couldn't be behind it, couldn't know who was sending it. You've been corrupted by me, that's what I think Barón told the men who came to arrest me this morning, who've just interrogated me. Or maybe it's because you look underage. Ask Barón, ask Barón why you're free to roam around Santiago looking at all the women you'll never fuck, at all the women I've fucked. Uselessly, it turns out."

The guard had come for him, touching him lightly to indicate our time was up.

"What if I were to tell you," I said as we both stood up, "that I know who really sent those letters, that I've got proof, what if I were to tell you that?"

"Don't tell *me*," was my dad's parting shot. "Tell Barón."

That is just what I did.

I called up the *Ministro*'s secretary again—he was still with the president—and told him to come home immediately, his daughter needed to speak to him right away, it was something very serious, really serious. I then called up the Nana and told her that if her boss called she should say that Amanda Camila needed to speak to him, that she was locked in her room and wouldn't come out. Oh yes, Nana, and don't go out yourself either, I need to talk to you, I'll be right there.

I sat Nana down in the kitchen.

"The *Ministro* will be here any minute, Nana," I said. "And before he comes, I want you to know that I know everything."

She looked at me calmly. "What is it you know, *mi niño*?"

"I know what you did."

"And what might that be?"

"The letters, Nana."

She didn't say anything for a while. "Cristóbal's arrested because of the letters?" she finally asked.

"Yes, and if the person who really wrote the letters doesn't come forward, he'll lose the bet."

"And you're going to save him?"

"I'm going to save him."

"And you've never thought, *mi niño* Gabriel, that maybe nothing better could happen to him than to lose that bet, to stop playing that game?"

"I'm going to save him, Nana."

"And you want me to help you."

"I want you to confess."

271

"Confess what?"

"That you wrote those letters."

She stood up slowly, almost painfully, as if her back hurt her. She went to the sink, filled the kettle with water, put it on the fire.

"And can I ask why I wrote those letters?"

"You were angry with Pablo Barón."

"I was angry with Pablo Barón. You're sure of this?"

"Because of what he did to you." I was hedging, cautiously letting her reveal herself, just in case my theory of the Last of the Onas was wrong. Maybe she had a different motive.

"And you want me to tell him that? You're sure you want me to tell him that I wrote the letters?"

"I wasn't going to tell anybody, Nana. It was a secret I meant to keep. Believe me, if my dad weren't in jail because of the letters you wrote, I'd never—"

"I believe you. A boy must always choose family, a woman must always choose her child before anything else, a father will always choose to protect his children. That's the way things are."

The kettle began whistling. I motioned to her that I would take care of it, I would prepare the tea she wanted, but she laboriously got up anyway, fixed the brew herself, one cup for me, one cup for her, another empty cup that she set up on the other side of the table. "For the *Ministro*," she said. "So he can listen to me carefully. That's what you want? For him to listen to me?"

"Yes."

"And you're sure this is what you want? You're sure he'll believe me?"

"It's the truth," I said. "He has to believe you."

"Yes," she said, "he has no other choice." She sipped the tea, grimaced as it burned her tongue. "And you're not worried about what will happen to me when he finds out?"

I hadn't thought about that; the truth is, I had not given a moment's consideration to whether she might be punished. How would the *Ministro* react to having a traitor in his very home, how would he feel about leaving his twins with a woman so devious and full of hatred toward him? How would the military react if he kept her on? What message would that be sending them as to his weaknesses, his resolve to defend the image of Chile?

I said, "He has no choice, like you said. He can't live without you.

Carola can't live without you. I mean, I couldn't live without you."

"*Niño, niño*, you can live without me. You'll see how easy it is."

"Do you think he'll—Nana, if that means . . ."

"I did what I did," she said, "and now I suppose I have to pay. Everything has to be paid for in this world. Before you pay for it in the next. But don't worry your little head. You're right. He won't do anything to me."

"Nana, you're sure you—"

"You're the one who has to be sure," she answered. "I did what I did and you have to do what you have to do."

At that moment, I heard the screech of tires, the braking of a car, Pablo Barón's heavy feet pounding the pavement. I rushed to meet him at the door.

"Amanda Camila?" he puffed. "What's the—"

"It's not her, Tío Pablo," I said. "I had to tell you that something was wrong with her to get you to come. She's fine, she's in Farellones doing a photo shoot. No, it's my dad."

"You made me come here to get your father out of trouble? You almost gave me a heart attack so you could—"

"My dad's blaming me. Please, have them set him free, please, Tío, I've never asked you for—"

"There's nothing I can do, Gabriel. My God, I can't believe you made me come all the way here to—I've tried to reason with them, but the army's got steel in their brains, cement. They only want him for a night, they say, to find out if he's involved with these threats to the iceberg. How do you think it makes me feel to win this bet with their help? I mean . . ."

It made him feel great. Cristóbal McKenzie was wrong about who was writing the letters but was absolutely right about Barón's intentions: he had used those letters by the mythical Commandante to beat his adversary, used me to pass information along. Cristóbal McKenzie was right and Ignacio was right about the *Ministro*'s strategy. There would be no convincing him to get my father out of jail: he was the one who had put him there.

"What if you were to tell the military that you found out who wrote those letters, that you have a confession? Would they have to let my father go?"

Pablo Barón took off his glasses, rubbed them, put them back on, looked at me as straight as he could, right into the swirling pool of my eyes.

"You're a great kid, Gabriel," he said. "But nobody will believe you sent them. You weren't here when the first one arrived. They won't accept your confession. They'll see it for what it is: a son trying to save his father."

"I'm not talking about a phony confession, Tío. I'm talking about the person who really wrote them."

"Who?"

"If I tell you, do I have your promise that you'll have them set my father free?"

"I'll do what I can, if—"

"No, Tío. That's not enough. I need your promise. On your daughter's life, on the life of your children. You will get him out before ten o'clock tonight."

"How can I guarantee that?"

"You will threaten to resign. You will threaten a scandal: they are holding an innocent man, you will not accept a return to yesterday's violations of citizens' rights."

"You have the culprit? You know who it is?"

"I need your promise."

"You have my promise. Who did it? Who wrote those letters?"

"I need one more thing. The promise you made to my father. About my Tío Pancho. You have to set him free."

"I can't do that. You're meddling in matters of state."

"You promised my dad, you promised me that if we found the person who was threatening the iceberg, you'd do it. I expect you to stand by our agreement. It doesn't have to be today. Before the end of the year. But you'll do it."

"And if I don't?"

"I'll go public with the name of the culprit."

"And that is going to make me comply?"

"Yes," I said. "Promise me. Both brothers go free."

"I promise," *Ministro* Pablo Barón said. "I'd love to have a reason to set them both free. But if you're playing some sort of crazy game with me . . ."

I led him into the kitchen. "Nana," I said, "the *Ministro* is ready to hear your story."

"What is this?" Pablo Barón said. "What sort of sick joke is this?"

"Sit down, Don Pablo," Nana said, indicating the chair. "Let me pour you some tea."

"I don't want tea. I don't want to sit down. I want to know why— what the hell is going on?"

"She wrote the letters," I said. "Nana wrote them. From the first to the last. The first one on her own, the rest with information she got from me, suspects I was investigating."

"What?"

"She did it," I said. "Ask her. Go ahead."

"Nana, has Gabriel gone mad? Have you—?"

"If I didn't write them, Don Pablo," Nana said, "who did?"

Pablo Barón sank down in the offered chair as if it were a grave.

"I wrote the letters, Don Pablo," Nana said quietly, pouring him some tea. She might have been speaking about the menu for the evening meal. "The first one because I was angry and the other ones because I thought it would help Gabriel in his work, it would make things easier for him."

"Angry?" the *Ministro* said. "Why were you angry?"

"I have my reasons, Don Pablo. Would you say I don't have my reasons?"

"This makes no sense," he said. "Gabriel, you should be ashamed of yourself: convincing an old woman to take the blame so you can get your father . . ."

The Nanny's voice rose sharply. "I wrote them."

"Who gave you the paper? How did you get the paper?"

"Amanda Camila brought that paper back home all the time," the Nana answered. "I thought it would be good to put my message on the paper that was being used for the iceberg. I never liked that iceberg. I wouldn't mind seeing it blown up."

"Amanda Camila gave you that paper?"

"She didn't give it to me, Don Pablo. I took it from her without her knowledge."

"I don't believe you."

"You have to believe me, *Ministro*, because it's the truth. By now I thought you would have guessed. From the start the letter told you it was someone near to you. You know who. Commandante You-Know-Who."

"Commandante You-Know-Who. *El que sabes.*" Barón mechanically reached for his teacup, downed a scalding-hot gulp, muttered the words over and over below his breath.

"If you wish, I will take my things and go, Don Pablo. You just have to say the word."

He looked at her in a daze, as if he weren't listening to her. Then he stood up. "No, of course not. Of course not. It was just a prank, like McKenzie said, just a silly joke you were playing on me. Then you wanted to help Gabriel, that's all."

"And do you think we can keep this from Doña Carola and Milagros and Amandita? I would feel very embarrassed, Don Pablo, if they were to know that I've done something this foolish in my old age. I think they would never forgive me."

"Nonsense." Pablo Barón went over to her, gave her a quick kiss on her head. "There's nothing to forgive, nothing. It's best forgotten. But no more letters from now on—right? No more letters?"

"Do you think I will have to speak to the authorities, Don Pablo?"

"No, of course not," he said. "I'll take care of that. They don't want to embarrass me either. I've done some favors for them, this is one they can do for me."

"Like letting my father go," I said. "Right away."

"Of course, of course. As soon as I can—"

"Our agreement," I said, "was right away."

He was visibly shaken, clearly afraid somebody would find out that the threats had originated in his own household. I remembered what he had said about Chileans, how the only thing they really feared was looking ridiculous. He stared at the phone I was offering him as if it were a creature that would bite his hand. He took it, began to dial. "Nana," he said, "are you sure . . . ?"

"I am sure, Don Pablo. This is the only way to save the family. I did what I had to do. Now you must do what you must do."

Pablo Barón finished dialing. Into the phone he barked a name, and when that person materialized on the other end he said, "I need Cristóbal McKenzie free. Yes, I know what I said last night. But now I need him free. I'll explain later. Yes, I can vouch for him. It's that— or my resignation."

I tapped him on the shoulder.

He gave me a wild look. As if his eyes were going to migrate right out of his face.

"Hold on," he said to the phone, and then to me, "What the fuck is it now?"

"I wouldn't mind if Polo were kept for an extra week," I said.

"A week?"

"Our agreement only concerns the McKenzie brothers."

He looked at me with his devious eyes, those eyes of his full of malice. He smiled, he nodded. "Only Cristóbal McKenzie," he gave his order to the phone. "The other detainee—Leopoldo What's-his-name?—there's no hurry with him. I can't vouch for him. Yeah, he can wait till next week. Yes. Thanks."

Pablo Barón hung up.

"I find this hard to believe, Nana," he said. "I really find this hard to believe."

"It's always hard to believe that the people you trust will not be worthy of your trust," she said. "That's always a hard lesson to learn. A *Ministro* should know that, but at times it takes us a long time to learn, to accept that life is like that. Look at me, Don Pablo: I'm eighty years old and I'm still learning, I'm still surprised at what people will do, whom they will betray."

"You're a good woman," Pablo Barón said. "You're a good woman and whatever silly thing you've done, it's all right. We need you here and no place else."

"Do you think I'll have to speak to those military people, Don Pablo?"

"I'll make sure they don't bother you, Nana."

I followed him out to his car.

"What a fucking mess," he said. "You don't know what a fucking mess you've stirred up, Gabriel."

"Me? I don't see what I've done, why I'm to blame."

"Yes, yes, you're right, of course, you're not to—"

"I could have gone to Cristina Ferrer," I said, "and spilled the whole story. You know how close we are."

"I know, I know. You've acted very responsibly. You really have. I'm sorry I said that. I'm just upset, naturally, to think that someone who lives in my own house could—enough said. Let's try and turn the page on this whole incident, get on with what really matters. I mustn't forget what really matters."

He got into the car. "You're a good boy, Gabriel. The best. You really are. Mum's the word. Mum has to be the word."

Late spring in Chile is hot and dry. The sun was melting me there on the sidewalk. I looked around for Ignacio and sure enough, there he was, down the street a bit, waiting for me, allowing himself to appear as soon as Barón had gone.

"He's going to set my father free," I said. "Thanks."

"I don't know what you're talking about. Want me to take you anywhere?"

I almost went inside to speak with the Nana, to thank her for having confessed and saved my skin, but I wanted to be there when the great McKenzie came out of that jail, I didn't want to lose that moment for anything in the world. And five hours later, when he did come out, when he hugged me in his arms like he had never done before, holding me so tight I felt I would go right through him, with no Ignacio to tap me on the shoulder and cart him away to see the *Ministro*, no Polo to murmur obscenities in my ear or contempt in his, nobody between his body and mine, when we finally ended that embrace which had been interrupted at the airport and he was saying to me what he had said then—Why did it take you so long to come?—I knew, Janice, that everything was going to be all right. That's when I realized that I had done the right thing by choosing him over my Nana, getting her to confess so he could be free. That's when I felt . . . I tell you, I physically felt this happen to me, Salacious Janice, I felt my face begin to change as if it were being sculpted by the warmth emanating from the great McKenzie. Not become older, that face of mine, merely fall in love with itself, accept that it was wonderful to look so innocent. That's when I knew again what I had known that day I jogged up to the cordillera and filled my lungs with polluted air, I knew that within a week Amanda Camila would be mine, that's when I knew it.

It was nine-thirty in the evening.

"Two and a half hours," the great McKenzie said. "More than enough time. How did you do it?"

While he was signing his release papers, I said, "I found the culprit. Made him confess. Barón had to let you go."

"He didn't write those letters himself?"

"No. It was someone else."

"Who?"

"I'm afraid I'm not at liberty to give any names. You're just going to have to trust me."

He thought about that for a moment. "Good," he said. "Secrets are good. Make you a bit more mysterious, desirable."

"Barón also agreed to free Tío Pancho. Just as he promised if we cracked the case."

"You're kidding me."

"Before the end of the year. You'll see."

"Good for you, Gaby." He turned to the detective behind the desk. "Where's Leopoldo Gómez?"

The man flipped through some papers. "He'll be released later."

I waited to see my father's reaction. Would he create a scandal? Wait for Polo? Insist on seeing him? Say he was not leaving till they released his protégé as well?

"Could you give him a message?" my father said. "That I'll come and see him tomorrow?"

I imagined Polo in his cell when he heard that the great McKenzie was out there on the streets. I imagined Polo's face beset by a palencss that would be anything but ordinary. More like an old photo that was beginning to fade right there in the mirror in his cell, right in front of his fading eyes. I imagined how he would look in a week, when we came to get him, when he would see that I had reconquered my dad while he had been counting the days and the nights. Yes, especially the nights, the seven nights of my apprenticeship that he would never be able to take away from me.

"So," my father said, as if I were Polo, as if I had already taken Polo's place, "where are we heading?"

I showed him the day's obituaries that I had cut out of *El Mercurio*. He thought that was ingenious of me, indicated quite a bit of sophistication: I wanted to start where he had started, follow his steps as closely as I could.

"You said something about my face," I said to him once we were in a taxi heading for a wake that my dad, knowing each neighborhood, was sure would be right for our purposes, filled with female relatives awaiting consolation. "About working on it."

"You don't know how to use your face," he said. "If I had a face like yours, I'd be shouting hallelujah to heaven."

"You would?"

"Whatever God gives you, Gaby, use it. The problem isn't your face. Women should be falling all over themselves to mother you, bring you back to the womb, cuddle the hell out of you. But you're telling them that something's wrong with your face, that you don't like yourself. So why should they like you?" He scrutinized me, gave me the once-over. "But you know what? Something's already changed. I don't know what it is but you've . . . Maybe I won't have to teach you a thing."

It was his love, his enthusiasm. That was all I had really needed. In the next seven days, his advice turned out to be superb; his stories, amusing; his instincts, unerring; his pickup methods, amazing; but none of it mattered as much as the fondness in his voice, the kinship he established, passing on more than the wisdom of his twenty-five years of chasing skirts. Passing his whole self on, injecting his affection into me, taking me into his confidence with the ferocity with which his arms had enfolded me when I had come to free him from that jail.

The women we picked up really didn't matter that much. He fucked them and I didn't. "I want to keep myself for Cristina Ferrer," I told him. "I don't want to make love until I'm ready." He understood, he taught me to use my mouth, to finger-fuck them, to tell them I was studying for the priesthood and could not betray my religious vocation, to tell them that I had sworn an oath to my dying mother that for a year after her death I would not penetrate a woman. Just make sure you fall in love with them, he told me, learn to fall in love with them at the drop of a hat, learn to do it sincerely, deeply, see in each one the one thing she has that no other woman will ever have and love that one thing, go straight to her core and put your hand on the heart of that thing, love it for as long as you're with her. And make sure that you never betray her memory, that you polish it each day. I could recite my women one by one. And they know it—the proof is that not one has ever complained, not one has ever come to my doorstep to bug and chide and harass me, not one has anything but fond thoughts. Be true to them for that hour, that hour and a half, that day.

It wasn't the words themselves, Janice, but the fact that he was bequeathing them to me. Women want two things from men: they want a father to protect them and they want a son to protect. You can play one card or you can play the other or you can play them both. But if you play them wrong—offer vulnerability when you should be looking strong or come across as too cocky and overbearing when they want somebody helpless—that's when things begin to go sour. Good advice, but not as good as his presence. Advice and positions and cues and pointers I could have picked up from a sex manual, from Henry Miller, from Casanova or Frank Harris; most of it I had memorized already and it had made as much of an impression on me as a leaf on a pond, sucked into a pond after the first rainfall of the season. He was the one I was swallowing, he was the one I was making a place for inside me. I could tell by the way Amanda Camila began looking at me that she was aware of some transfer going on. She looked at me and noticed a change that very night when I came home to her house.

I had gone there to pick up my things for the move that had been delayed by Ignacio's arrival and the ensuing crisis.

She was waiting in the dark at the top of the stairs.

"Amanda Camila!" I whispered her name. "What are you doing up?"

"Where have you been?"

"Out. With my father."

She turned a flashlight on me. I blinked at the sudden flare. "There's been a blackout," she said. "I looked for you. You weren't here. I've been waiting for you."

I let her flit her flashlight all over my face, did not avert it, did not place my hands in front of my eyes.

"You shouldn't do that," I said. "Stay up, I mean."

"It's what any sister would do, worry about her—"

"I'm not your brother," I said. "I don't want to be treated like a brother."

Her flashlight stopped moving around. Her ocean eyes were peering at me from behind that flare, she was wondering what had altered in me like a tide. The light went down my neck, down my chest, down, down, stopped at my crotch.

"Where have you been?"

"I told you. With my father."

Her flashlight was still on the same spot, joining her to me as if we were having sex, as if we were speaking through the beam of light.

"Have you been a bad boy?" Trying, Amanda Camila, to make me a baby, trying to return to some innocence that was fast disappearing, that had never been there to begin with.

"I'm a virgin," I said. Just like that. It came out. My father had said, Women like nothing more than the truth, told brutally, with utter simplicity. Or if you can't manage the truth, the appearance of it, that you are giving yourself to them. You give them the words, they will probably give you their bodies. Where your words have entered, your penis cannot be far behind. I said now to Amanda Camila, "I've never made love."

"I don't believe you."

Kiss her, my father said. Two days ago I wouldn't have, two days before I would have said something like, You'll believe it when we make love or You'd better believe it or I was just kidding. Kiss her, the great McKenzie said inside me, pushed my lips toward her, kiss her as an answer, let your lips answer, let her lips understand that you're telling her who you are.

I kissed her and she understood.

It was a quick kiss. I withdrew right away. My father was telling me not to overdo it. I had seen him that very night seduce two twenty-year-olds. Choose which of these mourners you go for, he had said, the older generation or the luscious younger one. Neither of them care about the uncle who's been dying of lung cancer for three coughing years. Only that he's screwed up their chances of going out on a date tonight. I had seen my father inflame them and then play hard to get for just the right ten minutes, feign indifference, force them to come after him. First you hunt, then you become the prey, he had said later to me. First you're on top, then she's on top. First from the front, then from behind. First from below, then from on high. Variety, Gaby—knowing when to say no, when to say yes, when to say maybe.

"Maybe," I said now to Amanda Camila. "Maybe."

"I thought you . . ."

Don't let them tell you too much, my father was saying inside, he was saying it inside me without having said it to me, not that evening, not ever before, not ever again, I was inventing his words in my heart and under my skin. Don't let them waste words on you. Gestures are always better.

I put my fingers to her lips. "You should get some sleep." I took the flashlight from her, took her hand, led her to her room. "I'll see you tomorrow," I said.

"Here?"

Don't go too often to the place where you intend to make love, my father was murmuring to me from afar, from nearby. Don't waste the novelty of the place, so that it will seem an adventure when you finally do it.

"Meet me at Restorán La Casa Vieja," I said.

"You don't want to have lunch here?"

"La Casa Vieja," I said. "Two in the afternoon."

"You're leaving for the Casa Milagros? Nana said you—"

The last words are always the most important, the ones that will echo during the night, echo in her sleep till the next time you meet.

"I'm leaving so I can come and visit you."

I closed the door, waited outside her door just as I had the night before. This time she knew I was there, she knew I was listening to her breathe, she knew she could sleep well, she knew that my face was being altered from inside even as she slept and I waited.

I took all my things down the stairs, left them on the front doorstep, called a cab.

Then I went upstairs for one last time.

To Nana's room. I went to her door. Was she asleep? Was she praying at the foot of her bed as she did every night? Was she awake in bed, waiting for me to come and say good night to her? I listened for her breathing, just as I had listened the night before and tonight to Amanda Camila's. I didn't hear anything. I almost knocked on the door. Maybe it was consideration for her, not wanting to disturb her sleep. Maybe I thought about the hard day she'd had. Or was it that I wanted to avoid what I imagined might be a glance of reproach? Or something worse: avoid a much more humiliating alternative, that she had forgiven me for choosing my father over her, her nobleness in the face of my betrayal too much for even my clueless soul to resist.

I wish it had been shame and not fear that made me pause at her door, not open it, decide to go down those stairs as the cab pulled into the driveway, lift my bags, and trundle them into the waiting car instead of crossing the vast desert of her room, reaching her bed, reaching for her gray hair, giving her one last caress as she slept, I wish it had been shame that kept me from doing that.

If it had been shame I would have been saved, saved if I could have felt shame then, could feel shame now.

I moved out and did not see her again.

I never got to say goodbye.

I fucked Amanda Camila the night our Nana died.

Not that I knew she was dying. I was dying, my Amanda seemed about to die, first me on top of her, when I came inside her, quickly, without warning, and then she was on me, and I held on and let her use me as I had used her and then there was no more me or her, and in the silence of the night we had to quiet our united heart for fear that it would awaken the living and the dead, but it did not, it did not stop the Nanny from going from one to the other; our love could not stop our Nana from dying in the same house, a few rooms removed.

I don't want to indulge you with a bad description of good sex, Janice. Sorry if it wasn't with you. Sorrier if you've been waiting for this part of my story to warm you up there in Seattle. Hell, I'd been waiting for it since we both almost did it together: more than eight years. But the camera will have to discreetly pan away. Besides, it wasn't any of the things those five men at sea had pinpointed as wonderful about sex, not anticipation, not penetration, not perpetual motion, not ejaculation, not relaxation, not even all of the five together, as my father had suggested. No, what I enjoyed most was our chat, the lazy conversation with Amanda Camila afterwards, the way we shared each other in a different way, her fingers lacing through my hair and making curls of it, my hand nuzzling her breast but not because it was a tit but because it slowly rose with her breath and her words. That's what mattered, that's what I miss now. Lord knows, if there were one thing that could keep me on this earth and make me desist from my plans for suicide and murder, it would be the promise that such things might still come. False promises. They'll never come back again. The Nana was dying nearby, and even nearer by, Amanda Camila was telling me things about herself she had never told anyone. We explored what the other had felt, we wondered at the possibility of a life spent in that exploration, a world where the other is more important than you are. I had that paradise in my hand like a bird, I had it in my hand and I crushed it to death, it was dying as she spoke, as I listened.

What had sex meant to her, what did it mean to have . . . ?

"The rage," she said. "I thought I'd explode, I thought—and now, it's started to drain away, seep away. No, that's not it. It's still there, inside, but it's a good anger. With somebody like you, somebody to tell things to, it can do what anger is supposed to do. Because now I have somebody to speak to. With my body. With my mouth."

She told me what she had kept to herself in the car that intimate noon when she'd driven me to her home for the first time. How full of hope she had been at what democracy would bring. "I guess I believed in a miracle. Now I realize that we were dreaming, but you don't know what it is to have had faith, to have put your trust in all those men, in my own father to begin with. They promised us—do you know what the slogan of our campaign against Pinochet was? *La alegría ya viene.* Joy is on its way, it's almost here, it's around the corner. Except it wasn't. I'm not saying things didn't change, that wouldn't be fair—a bit more freedom, a bit less fear, but not joy, not *alegría.*"

She sat up in bed and my hand slid down her body, rested on her thigh. Only the slightest light from the bathroom glowed in the room, dressing her nakedness in a soft glimmer, only for my eyes. "Do you want to know when I knew it had all been a fraud? The exact moment, Gabriel?"

The pool had done it. The pool that everybody used together at her *comunidad* and that had put her in such a foul mood the day I visited this house where we had just now made love, the house where she was telling me how, during the years of struggle against Pinochet, they had all shared not only the pool but everything else as well, the dread and the risks and the banging on pots and pans and the food. It had been like a small enclave of heaven, an island that functioned in precisely the opposite way from how things worked in the outside world of the dictatorship.

"We built a space," Amanda said, "where things were different, an anticipation of how everybody in the country would live once the terror was over. All of us built it. Not just those of us who were the owners of the houses, Gabriel—all of us. Each house had a servant, some had two even. But those women were part of it. They also participated in the protests; not one of them betrayed the dissidents living here. We were like a family. Including, especially, the caretaker, Eduardo. Caretaker, I say, but he was basically everybody's friend, gardener, handyman, soccer coach for the younger kids, you name it. And his son, Alvaro, was one of the gang, treated like any of the others, even if his dad hardly knew how to read or write, came from the countryside, was darker, you know, more Indian in his blood. I'd be lying if I said Alvaro was the best friend I ever had in the world, but he was a buddy, you know, he'd been around since we came to live here. And Nana—it was as if Nana had adopted him, saw in him some long-lost son she had never had. She absolutely adored that boy."

As the years went by, the relationship of the adults of the *comunidad* with Alvaro had grown strained. Alvaro had become more resentful, more difficult as he began to realize that he would not be given the educational and professional opportunities that the other kids took for granted. Things had come to a head this past summer.

"Alvaro started bringing friends with him to the pool, just like other kids, except that his friends weren't well-to-do, they didn't look like we did or dress like we did, the sons and daughters of the owners. Alvaro brought them home because our parents had always told him, You're one of us, we treat you like our own son. He did drugs, sure, but then, we all did. And he was insolent with adults, like all of us. I mean, he was a teenager. A bad influence, Carola said, and my father agreed vaguely. He was so involved with the coming transition— heading the transition team, setting up the incoming president's cabinet, negotiating with the military whether Pinochet would be a senator for life when he withdrew as commander in chief, the ceremonies, all—that, so he hardly had time to follow what was happening back here at home. But Dad should have, he should have cared. The week after the new president took power, the owners of the *comunidad* met to discuss what to do with Alvaro and voted to ask the caretaker to move out, not to live with his family on the premises anymore, and my father, naturally, voted along with them. 'It's what's best,' he said that night. 'Alvaro's brought it on his head, he's been told over and over that he's got to shape up. It's him or us, him or our kids. That's the way of the world.' The bastard."

"But don't you think he has a point?" I asked, as usual defending the generous *Ministro* from the savage attacks of his daughter, not only because of the hospitality he had shown me but also because I genuinely understood his point of view. More than that, I felt I could risk contradicting Amanda Camila. By making love to her I had somehow been freed of my fears—it was to be a short-lived freedom, Janice. I felt I could now tell her what I really thought, didn't need to bury my opinions, could give myself to her like she was giving herself to me. "This Alvaro you're so fond of should have been more careful. Your dad is right. When you make a mistake and then you make it again and again, and you don't call the shots, you're not only stupid. You're fucked."

"Gabriel McKenzie," my Amanda said, her voice rising. I hushed her. We didn't want anybody waking up, finding us in bed. "You should be ashamed of yourself. Alvaro's only sin was to be poor. His father was employed by us, didn't own a house. If he had been an owner, his conduct would have been tolerated. They tolerate me, no matter how obnoxious I am, because I'm the daughter of the *Ministro*."

"But that's how it is everywhere," I objected. "If I come home drunk to our apartment on Riverside Drive, the porter helps me into the elevator. If some bum wanders off the street and begins to puke in the lobby, he'll get his ass kicked by that same porter. That's how things are."

"That's not how things were when we were trying to get rid of Pinochet," she answered, getting heated up. "It was supposed to be different. A country where everybody has the same chance, where you don't decide how you treat somebody by how much money they earn."

"There's no such country in the world," I said, enjoying my side of the argument.

"Well, there ought to be," Amanda Camila answered. "And that's the country they promised us. And that still doesn't explain what happened next."

"What happened next?"

"Eduardo and his wife and Alvaro and the other kids—five of them, Gabriel—moved out. He kept coming back to care for the lawns and clean the pool. You know: You can work here but you can't live here. Your hands are good enough to prune my trees but not good enough to stroke my ass."

"I should hope not."

"It's a metaphor, stupid," she said. "Anyway, for me, everything had been ruined, that was just a symbol of how things were turning out. You can't build a free country with no freedom at home, you can't proclaim justice unless you're ready to exercise justice in your private life. Because that's where it's difficult: to be fair in your own backyard, not in somebody else's. But of course I didn't do anything. I had enough trouble with Carola and my dad, you know, my career and all that. None of the kids who had grown up with Alvaro did anything. We just said goodbye and went on with our lives. Except for one person."

"Nana," I said.

"Nana," Amanda Camila confirmed. "She staged a little protest every day. Every day she went to the pool and took off her *alpargatas* and put her feet in the water, cooled them off in the water."

"That's it?" I asked. "That was her protest?"

"That was it. Did I tell you that at that same meeting of the *comunidad* where they banished Eduardo and his family, the owners decided to make new rules about the use of the pool? Remember, Gabriel, that these were the people who had been the protagonists in the resistance against Pinochet. These were the people who had been jailed for protesting, been sent into internal exile, thrown out of the country; some of them had been severely beaten and worse. These were the people who were essentially in charge of the new government, who were going to lead us all to the promised land. Do you know what they voted? They voted to restrict the maids from using the pool. It wasn't as though the *indias* took a dip all that much, but a couple of them put on old bathing suits and paddled around a bit, especially when they were in charge of babies like Nana was. Not that Nana ever so much as put her little toe in the water. She's far too much of a prude for that. Flesh is not to be shown, she always says, what you can imagine is always better. Nana had never shown any interest in the pool. But from that day on, she very deliberately stuck both her feet—dusty, they were, almost as if she had got them dirty on purpose—plunged them both into the pool. Day after day after day. And nobody dared point to the regulations that somebody had painted on the board next to the pool. I think they were afraid of her, still are. I certainly am, wouldn't have dared. So they voted to prohibit Nana from entering the pool area ever again."

"Your father agreed to that?"

"He said he had to. As *Ministro* he had to uphold the democratic process, the voice of the majority, all that bullshit. He took Nana aside, explained to her what the decision had been, why she could not use the pool again. Nana looked at him and said, 'I should go, Don Pablo, pack my things and leave. Except that I don't have anywhere to go. So I'm staying. Is there anything special you want for dinner tonight?' And my father answered that he'd love some *cazuela*. And that was that. Except it wasn't, Gabriel. That did it for me, that drove me up the wall. I socked it to my dad real hard. 'It's all right for the husbands to fuck the maids,' I said to him, 'but it's not all right for the maids to be in the pool with the wives. And it's all right to wipe the shit from the ass of the kids, but it's not all right to bathe with the kids. And—' My dad held up his hand. 'Hold it right there, young lady. If you don't like the way we do things in this house, you can find yourself a job and move out. But I can't deal with your constant crabbing and complaining. I have a job to do. People who appreciate me. If you stay here, you will smile. You will make us glad you are living with us. That is what you will do.' "

"And what did you do?"

"I obeyed him and waited. I waited for my chance to get even, to really teach him a lesson. Fantasies of revenge, you know. Silly, I guess, looking at them now. Though one of them—Gabriel, I did one really infantile thing."

"What did you do?"

"It was a few days before you arrived. I was really pissed off about my work at the expo and Larrea's idiotic ideas about there being no Indians. Here was Nana and a few million other Mapuches—"

"You were sure she was Mapuche, huh?"

"According to her birth certificate she was. But that's not the point. The point is I couldn't stand all those fraudulently happy faces and those chic fashion uniforms and the iceberg here and the iceberg there and my father preening about how it would change Chile's image, show everybody how cool and far from the tropics we were, and I thought to myself, I'll give the old bastard a scare, slap him with at least one sleepless night. So I wrote a letter. I wrote my dad an anonymous letter threatening to fuck the iceberg, melt it."

"What?"

"Hey, no need to be so upset. It was just a prank, something to let off steam. Signed it Commandante You-Know-Who. My dad probably threw it in the trash."

"Hold it, hold it. You wrote that one letter. And that was all, no more, no more letters after that?"

"Of course not. Why should I? Though I might have if you hadn't spoken to me that day, remember? About who in Chile would want to melt the iceberg. That's when I realized how ridiculous my threat was. You want to bring down the system, you don't go around blowing up symbols. You blow up people. And that's certainly not for me."

"Why didn't you tell me you'd—my God, Amanda, why didn't you tell me?"

"Why should I?"

"Because you said you trusted me. You promised to tell me everything."

"If I'd told you everything, *mi amor*, we wouldn't be in bed right now, I'd never have captured you. I've been after you all these months. Women always have to keep something back. Just following Nana's advice. She told me to be patient."

"Nana! Oh God. Nana!"

"But what's wrong?"

Plenty was wrong. The Nana had lied to me, to Barón; she must have known that Amanda Camila was responsible. And the *Ministro* must have realized it too when Nana made the false confession. They had both covered up the girl's tracks together. That's why he had accepted Nana's version so readily, why there had been no consequences, why I had been able to get my father out of jail so easily. Barón was protecting his daughter. And himself. Because it was one thing to have an eighty-year-old cook and nursemaid who sends insane letters she knows nothing about and quite another for the *Ministro*'s own flesh and blood to engage in such destructive behavior. He might have had to resign, he might have had to celebrate his fiftieth birthday in disgrace instead of coming here to Sevilla, where I am waiting for him, he would have lost the bet and his career.

Even if Amanda had written the first letter, she couldn't have written the second one, because she was in Punta Arenas with me when it had been sent. Nor could she have written the ones that followed, because she didn't have that list of my suspects. But if not her, then who? The Nana? Or had the Nana, who was obviously better at lying than I ever thought—had she even forged her birth certificate to hide her identity?—told somebody else, who had then written the letters that carried out my plan, written the letters to help me. Who could possibly have done that, who—?

And then, suddenly, I knew the answer. The person the Nana most loved in the world, the person she had devoted her existence to and had brought into this world and had tended to when that person's real mother died and had waited for the night that person was pregnant and had counseled to stay with her new husband when he went off to look for another quick woman in the night. There was only one other person whom the Nana would take the blame for, the person she had whispered my secrets to in spite of her promise of silence, the person who had realized as the Nana transmitted my story to her that she was responsible for the mess in her son's head and the bigger mess in his sex life, the person who was beginning to comprehend how she had screwed him over worse than Che Guevara by burdening that son with a life of exile and then a life with a mythical father with a dick that never flagged, had filled him with stories that kept that son captive, the person who suddenly understood that she had to make amends for having been blind all these years to his pain and loneliness. And she proceeded to write letter after letter, all the letters he needed to force his father to come on board the investigation with him, the letters that maneuvered his father into going to Antarctica. The person who wanted that father on the trip to Antarctica anyway, her strategy and my strategy, her interests and my interests converging, both of us wanting him on the *Galvarino* steaming south to the archipelago—only one person in the world could have written those letters to save her son and save her marriage and save herself:

Nana's shadow. Milagros Gallardo. Lying, conniving, deceitful Milagros Gallardo.

I scrambled out of bed. "Wait, wait, where are you going?" I didn't listen to her. I slipped into my clothes and padded down the corridor to the Nana's room.

And found her dying. Unable to rouse her, unable to awaken her, hardly hearing her breath, hardly a pulse. The blood in her body was slowing down, starting to cool, a harsh rushing sound crawling out of her mouth.

My Nana was dying, but I did not immediately raise the alarm. I was too aware of Amanda Camila in my bed three doors down, too aware of the smell of cunt and congealing semen on my prick and groin, too clear that our hidden sexual encounter would be written all over me, all over us, if I got Barón and Carola up. I ran back to my room, told Amanda to take a shower. "Why? Why?" I'd tell her later, soon, I promised I would, she just had to trust me. I took a shower myself, carefully blew my hair dry, and then, and only then, did I venture back into Nana's room.

She was dead.

Could I have saved her?

Wrong question, Janice. Not the point at all. Not then, at least. Maybe a speedy call to an ambulance might have helped her, though in Chile, believe me, it's not like they're falling all over themselves to rush to an emergency. They would have taken at least an hour, if not more, to screech up to the house. And by then she would have been dead anyway. Dr. Ciruelo had declared, *Derrame cerebral*, nobody could have saved her, it was a painless stroke, she hadn't felt a thing. But let's say for argument's sake that they'd have made it there in five minutes and a respirator would have revived her. The question remains, is this what she would have wanted? The real question: why did she die that night, choose to die—if there is such a thing as choice in death—precisely the night she saw her two virgins come together, the two children of the two families she had served for her whole existence finally make love. Hadn't she died because her mission in life was accomplished?

Anyway, that's how I explained it to myself as I hurried to the shower, as the water cleansed from me the evidence of the love our Nana had made possible by taking the blame for those letters, that's what I understood as the hot water washed the smell of Amanda Camila's blood from my testicles: she wanted her soul to enter ours, she died as we were creating new life, that's what I told myself, she was dying at the very moment I was discovering the lies she had told that had saved my father and saved me and Milagros and Amanda Camila. She had died when I began to live, I thought, she had died so life could go on without her. Just as she had predicted, giving of herself till the last, not the vengeful old woman out to humiliate the men who had killed her ancestors, not the Indian sorceress who would not let the past be obliterated, not the voice of that past filled with forgotten words that harkened back to the beginning of human existence and the Bering Strait and the Americas seen and named for the first time. No, on the contrary, she had played her role of servant to her loyal last, she had served her masters and mistresses till her final breath and beyond that final breath, she had loved Milagros Gallardo and the child who came from that womb and then had loved another child, named Amanda Camila, who had been just as motherless as Milagros, and perhaps had even loved the manly Cristóbal McKenzie, who cared for so many other children who were abandoned and needed a helping hand. And at the uttermost end of her existence, after having brought all her loved ones together, she had been able, with one closing breath, to serve them all, us all. That was the hidden reason, the symmetry in her death and our lovemaking, Janice. A message I told myself she was sending me: It's all right, I don't want to live anymore, there's nothing more to accomplish with my life, I don't want you to ask me why I lied to you. I don't want you to ask me about the last Onas. I want to take my secrets to the grave so nobody can force them out of me. This is my blessing on you and your offspring.

Not that I didn't mourn her. Sort of. I sobbed with them all, each of us sobbing for a different reason and a different Nana. But here's the sad truth, Janice: I didn't care enough about her death because I was too much in love with the life I had discovered. That's the real reason why we—we humans, not just the McKenzies and the Baróns of this earth—do not mourn what has passed and will never come back. I was too enthusiastic about making love to Amanda each night and each afternoon and each morning, too deep inside the conversation that followed each session of body into body with words into words. I repeated the joy the great McKenzie had experienced when he first entered Milagros Gallardo the night Che was being buried. The two of them ultimately didn't give a damn about his death except inasmuch as it had brought them together, just like I finally didn't care that much about Nana's disappearance from this world. I watched the shovel loads of dirt on her coffin in the Cementerio General that November day while the sun clawed into shoulders like a hawk, and a hand descended on my neck and it wasn't Ignacio and it wasn't Barón and it wasn't my father McKenzie and it wasn't Polo but my Tío Pancho. He had just been freed in time for the funeral of this woman who had given him his liberty even if she would never know it. He held me to him and then broke away and threw a flower into the grave. I followed his example, threw my own *corona del indio* into the soil that was covering the woman who might be the last Ona or might be just any Mapuche but was, in all certainty, the only person to really and entirely love me in this world, to love me enough to die for me. I threw that sacred flower of the Indians into that grave to keep her company for all eternity. And then went home to fuck Amanda Camila one more time.

Following in the footsteps of Cristóbal and Milagros twenty-five years earlier.

Literally echoing what happened to them, Amanda took the same forty days and forty nights it had taken my mother to tell my father that she was pregnant. Three days after Christmas, on December 28, 1991, the *Día de los Inocentes*, the day when Herod ordered all the babies slaughtered, that's the day Amanda Camila chose to inform me she was expecting my child and that we had to call it Mercedes as the Nana had been called—and I did not stop to think that I had never known what Nana's real name was. I only thought to myself that if Barón found out, I was dead, he would kill me, he had said so, if I so much as rubbed his daughter's breast with the round hot touch of my thumb. I had been inside her. I had broken my promise.

I panicked. I could not seek support from my parents. I had lied to them, the great McKenzie to begin with. How to tell him that I had screwed his goddaughter, done it because she was the one woman he would not have screwed first, tell him that I had lied about who my love was in order to enlist his help, tell him that I was a conniving bastard and that he had been right from the start to have kept me at a distance? I had seen how savagely he had turned on me in that jail when he felt I had thwarted him, how he had cast me out of his life like you throw away a wrinkled condom.

Or my mother—how to speak about what I had never revealed to her all these years, the story that the Nana had already told her but that had never come from my mouth? How to look her in the eye and let her know that I had left the Nana to die? How to tell either of them, my father or my mother, both of whom had failed me so miserably, anything deep and distressing? Wasn't this the one message Nana was transmitting to me with her death? You're old enough to face this yourself. You're no longer Cara de Guagua, you've grown up—this is what growing up means, being able to take on the burden of the world because the older people can't do it for you. That's what it means to be left without a Nana to listen to you in the funeral of the night, to hear your confession when all else has foundered, that's what maturing means. That she will never come back and you have to figure it out by yourself forever like the orphan that you are.

It was then that I first tried to talk to Nana in my mind, began to feel her absence, began to realize what it means that somebody has died. You can't speak to the dead. You can't get advice from them. You can't go to their bed and put your head in their arms and let them cradle it for a minute, for as long as it takes to get your energy back. I would never again hear Nana sing me to sleep, sing me back to wakefulness, cook me into adulthood, give me a coin to deposit with the hurdy-gurdy man. She was gone, perpetually gone without a trace, taking my childhood with her. It was then that I began to ask myself faintly what I had done, the connection between my happiness and her death, how I could bring her back; the hint of the idea came into my mind and then left in a daze because I didn't want to admit a guilt that might devastate my exhilaration at having become a man, a daze because she wasn't there to save me again—this time I'd have to puzzle out what to do on my own. She wasn't by my side as she'd been by the side of my mother when Milagros had returned pregnant with me, she wasn't here to order me to go straight to Barón and tell him I was the father and let him do the worst because we were going to have that baby no matter what, she wasn't here to say that he wouldn't kill me, he had reasons for not wanting to kill me that she knew.

Would she have told me not to be afraid? Would she have stopped me from hysterically demanding that Amanda Camila abort the child, would Nana's presence in the room have persuaded Amanda Camila to go and see her father with me instead of trying to protect me, like all the women in my life have always done? Could the Nana have hushed Amanda Camila when she nobly proclaimed that above all we had to avoid Pablo Barón's finding out that I had made that child inside her? She would tell him, she said, that it had been conceived in early November when I was away in Antarctica; my Amanda wanted to make sure that when the time was right I would be alive to claim my place by her side, my place as the child's father.

"It'll be a girl," she said, "and I'll name her Mercedes, because she'll have Nana's soul inside her. And nothing, Gabriel, nothing in the world, can make me lose it."

She was wrong, Janice, there were things in this world that she didn't know about and that would lead her to that butcher of a doctor, there were things that would force her to erase from this world the child conceived the night Nana left us for good, things I would tell her.

I found out myself about those things the next day when Barón stormed into my room at the Casa Milagros and by his face it was clear that Amanda Camila had told him, and by his rage I was sure that, of all the men in the world, in spite of his daughter's protestations of my innocence, it was me he suspected of that rape, as he put it.

He looked at me with his eyes full of malice, full of cunning and malice and fatherly love.

"Gabriel! Swear it to me! Swear you're not the one. I won't be angry, I won't—I promise, I won't—but I need to know the truth."

Everything hung in the balance for a few seconds that lasted longer for me than the darkest winter of Antarctica and it was during those eternal seconds that I decided to tell him the truth, face up to his rage and my lies, grow up once and for all. A hum of Nana's words inside urged me on, almost boiled over into the world. But I never got the chance. I never got the chance to change my destiny.

I took too long.

And Pablo Barón filled the void with his own truth that came spilling out for the first time in over twenty-three years, he had his own secret and his own lies to bring into the open. He spoke and silenced me, left my own lies, my own secret, to fester in my mouth and in my heart. He came closer to me, inched his glasses up to my glasses, then receded, desperately whispered the words I did not want to hear, yet still can hear even now in Sevilla on this last day of both our lives. Even then he was afraid of somebody else's knowing, still afraid of microphones, of other men listening to him tell me in a hoarse voice . . .

"She's your sister," Pablo Barón said. "Tell me you didn't do it, damn it. Not to your sister."

"My sister? My sister?"

"I made love to your mother the night before she met your father, the night before Milagros met Cristóbal. We've kept it to ourselves all these years. I would never want him—promise me you'll never tell him a word of this. It would kill him to think that I fathered his only child."

"This is crazy," I said. But it wasn't. It all made sense, horrible sense—how Barón had cared for me since my arrival in Chile, admitted me into his home, treated me like a prodigal son, praised everything I did like a proud father. It explained why he had warned me off his daughter, why he had taken such pains to bring us together and at the same time separate us. Perhaps it explained why I was attracted to her, why I had ended up in his house, in her bed, seeking refuge with my true family. It might even hold the key to why my father McKenzie had automatically rejected me, why it had been so difficult to get him to love me. Because Cris understood somehow, with the animal instinct of the species, that this bespectacled wimp was not really his boy. It made sense, but I still fought the idea. "I don't believe you," I said.

"Because you screwed your sister? The truth, Gabriel. I need the truth."

I was drowning, drenched, sucked into the cesspool of his disclosure. It wasn't the moment to come clean, fill the air with all my noble intentions. I needed time to think.

"No," I said. "You know I wouldn't touch her."

"Good boy," Barón said. "You don't know how proud, how glad, that makes me. Because now you can help."

"What do you mean, help?"

"She wants to keep this idiot child and I can't convince her to get rid of it. But a brother can say things that a father can't, and you two are so close, I know she loves you so deeply, with such affection that I—Gabriel, we can't let her ruin her life."

"Her life?" I asked. "How about my life? How about me?"

"You haven't been hurt by any of this," he said. "You're not the one about to have a baby at nineteen. She's the one we have to worry about. She's the one we have to save."

"I'm going to speak to my mother," I said. "I need to find out if this is true."

"Speak to her," he answered, "certainly. But not a word to Cris. Promise me that."

"You're asking me for promises? God, how could you just keep this a secret all these years, play with me like this?"

"All I've ever done," Pablo Barón said, "is try not to hurt you. Try not to hurt any of the people I love. I did it for the best. And now I'm asking you to help your sister, help your father."

My mother conceded that Pablo had fucked her the night before Cristóbal McKenzie had appeared on the Alameda. Pablo Barón had made mad love to her the night they were executing Che Guevara in Vallegrande. It was always Guevara, always Che at the origin of my story. They had sought each other out in despair, had fallen into each other's arms without either of them knowing that one was the best friend of the man she had been waiting for over the years, that the other was to be the future wife of that best friend. But he hadn't ejaculated inside her, Milagros Gallardo was absolutely sure of that. Something had warned her. Something had told her, when she felt his organ harden and begin to pulse and his thrusts became longer and deeper and dislocated, to expel him from her vagina; she had banished him to the sheets of her bed.

"You made love in the Casa Milagros?"

"It wasn't called that then, but yes, of course, I used to bring lots of boys here."

"So the Nana knew?"

"She might have," Mom said, her eyes clouding over with pain at the unwanted thought of her dead Nanny. "She knew everything there was to know about me, about us. But what matters, Gabriel, is that Pablo isn't telling you the whole truth. Who knows why he's decided to bring this up now. After all these years. Maybe it's because we're together again, with your dad—and he is your dad!—we're back with one another and that means that Pablo won't win the bet. So he's decided to brag to his best friend's son that it isn't a draw after all, saying to you, 'We'll never know which of the two of us, Cris or me, was born earlier, who is the eldest, but you're not really his son. I'm the real father. He's fucked all those women, but I'm the one who's going to have all the children. It'll be my genes that will keep on, generation after generation.' And even if you don't believe it, he'll feel good. Men are so delusional. It's all a mirage, like the ones we saw in Antarctica, but that's what Pablo needs, that's what he believes: that he beat McKenzie because he fathered McKenzie's only child."

"And he didn't?"

"Forget what he told you. I'm the mother and I'd know."

I couldn't forget it. Amanda Camila might really be my sister. And the Nana had known. She had known, I was sure, and had let it happen anyway.

So she had been, after all, devious and deceptive and devilish. One piece of information she had deliberately not passed on to my mother: that I wanted to fuck the daughter of the man who she thought was my father. What better revenge on the Baróns and the Wendells who had decimated her tribe, paid a pound sterling for every genital. Or if she was a Mapuche, what better way to screw the Spaniards who had cut off Galvarino's hands, subjected her kinsmen to servitude. Or if there was no tribal urgency in her plans but merely the need to rebel against her humiliation at the swimming pool when her feet had gathered dust and been forced away without the blessing of water, retaliation for Alvaro's expulsion from the community he had grown up in, what better way to express her superiority, bringing together the two children of Barón in an incestuous embrace the night she died, dying with glee because the joke was on them, the joke was on us, the descendants of the men who had come to despoil this valley and perpetuate themselves. Amanda and me, the dead ends of a supposedly superior civilization, the brother and the sister who would have a deformed offspring in a deformed land.

Unless my mother was right and I wasn't Barón's son. But could I believe her, a mother who had spent the last four sneaky months writing letters to try and undo the damage she had imposed upon her exiled son with her toilet seats and Che Guevara posters and

Inti-Illimani songs and breathless stories about McKenzie-induced multiple orgasms? Could I believe her when she had trained the Nanny to trick me, when she had lied to protect me, when there was no doubt she would lie to keep Barón from hurting her man, keep the *Ministro* from proclaiming victory? She wouldn't let him take her child from Cris now that I had finally gained my father McKenzie's comradeship, now that she was enjoying something more than his comradeship and would do anything to stop Barón from coming between them.

No, she wasn't telling me the truth. I made that decision right then and there, Janice, made it because it fit into the pattern of my incredible bad luck. With the way things had been going, with the curse of Che and now the curse of the Nana on top of that, her ghost careening into my life like a drunken army, I was pretty sure that the chances that my lover was my sister and that my child was my nephew or niece were better than fifty-fifty: if the gods had been playing with me and organized this whole intricate plot so that I could bask for one week in the illusion that I had finally found happiness before they let me really get it up the ass, what more perverse downfall than this one? It was so demented and twisted that it had to be true.

I told Amanda Camila.

She believed me. She was almost too quick to believe me, as if she had been looking for an excuse to break with me, to return me to my condition as brother instead of lover. As if this proved to her how right she had been when she had first greeted me, during those long months when we had been like siblings in her mind, even as I dreamed of sucking every last suckable thing inside and outside her body, of swimming up into her green eyes to see myself from inside her, even as I was engaged in those lecherous luxurious visions, she had nursed the intuition that we should stay apart, she had kept me from her body. And had enjoyed of me what I had truly enjoyed of her: the intimacy of our verbal intercourse, the companionship we could accomplish anyway, she thought, without sex.

An abrupt about-face like so many I had witnessed, her wild mood changes: with the same tenacity she had shown in her defense of the baby, she now wanted to erase it from her body, return us to where we had been forty days ago. She understood that only our child's death could restore us to the innocence she now longed for.

She asked me to make arrangements.

The sooner the better.

I turned to my Tío Pancho. I couldn't bring myself to ask the great McKenzie; I tried in fact to avoid crossing his path. My father—that's what I felt him to be, that's what I kept on calling him, that's what I still call him now—my father Cristóbal might have guessed something was wrong. He had that perception, that compassion for people in trouble, and I needed time to make myself a mask. He had taught me how to hide who I was from women, show only what they needed to see so they could fall for me. And now I had to perfect those very instruments to fool him, to keep him from ever guessing that Barón had penetrated Milagros before he could get to her. Me, Gabrielito, finally protecting him, paying through my silence for his lessons in love.

So it was Tío Pancho or nobody. Easy, because I didn't have to tell him the name of the girl. Not that he asked about her, either. Just the dates.

"How far gone is she?"

"A month or so."

"Will be born when, then?"

"I haven't calculated but—end of August. August 24, I think she said. Give or take a few days."

"The day Che Guevara was baptized," my Tío Pancho said. "Your kid would have been born the day Che's parents introduced him to God. What do you think of that?"

I thought it was one more sign of how snarled everything was in my *puto* existence, one more sign of my inability to escape the pestilence that Guevara was visiting upon me. Maybe he was organizing all this from *el más allá*, with help from the perverse God he had been introduced to.

"I don't think anything of it, Tío," I answered. "We just need to get rid of that baby. Will you help me?"

He would have helped me, he said, even if Che's soul had migrated into that child. Women had the right to decide what to do with their bodies—not that this right was recognized in Chile. Here the very people who had fought the dictatorship were—

"Tío, I need an abortionist, not a lecture. Will you help me?"

My Tío Pancho came up with the address of a doctor who had

once performed brilliantly for him many years ago. "I suppose he's still operating."

The doctor was providing full service. The only problem: he couldn't possibly accommodate anybody until next month.

"When did you want this done?" he asked, wiping his hands on a rag. He was his own secretary, his own nurse, his own receptionist. Ran a tight ship in that hidden clinic on Calle Arturo Prats.

"Tomorrow," I said.

"Tomorrow? If she's only a month or so gone, we can do it end of January, beginning of February."

"It has to be tomorrow."

"Listen, my man. Tomorrow's December 31. Last day of the year, in case you didn't know. Morning's booked. In the afternoon, I want to get ready for New Year's, make some *pisco sour*, steal a little siesta. With the wife we're going to Viña and see the fireworks."

"Skip the siesta," my uncle said.

"Now you're really asking too much."

"Not if we're paying double."

"You're paying double? Why didn't you say so? How about three o'clock in the afternoon?"

"She'll be coming by herself," I said. "She doesn't want anybody to accompany her."

"Which of you's the father?" the doctor asked.

"I am," I said, trembling, suddenly trembling.

He held his hand out. I looked at my uncle. He nodded. It was all right. This doctor with his thick lips and sleepy eyes wouldn't pocket the money and then not perform the operation. I counted out the cash on that table, all new bills. I had exchanged dollars that very morning.

"Next time," he said, "use a condom."

Advice he should have given Pablo Barón twenty-five years before. Or maybe it was Cristóbal McKenzie who needed to hear and heed his words. Both of them and I wouldn't be here, if both my possible fathers had put something between their sperm and my mother, I would be a happier person, Janice; I would have been so much happier if I had never existed.

I called Amanda, gave her the address, couldn't bring myself to see her face, touch her tummy, listen for life inside. I hung up before I would find myself convincing her to have the child and live forever in defiant and incestuous sin. I hung up and stepped out of the phone booth and immediately decided to book my ticket back to the States, to get the fuck out of Chile and return to New York and never visit this dump ever again. Without saying goodbye, not to any of them, especially not to Amanda Camila, just pack my bags quietly, leave a note saying, So long, I'm going home, see you in the next world. Not be here while they were extracting my seed from her womb.

All the seats for that night were taken, all the seats for January as well. It was summer vacation and Chileans were flocking in droves to Disney World; hardly anybody thought nearby Patagonia might be more fascinating. Full, every plane. But there did happen to be a seat available for the next night, December 31. "The last night of the year hardly anybody travels," the big-nosed girl at the American Airlines reservation desk explained. "People don't like to spend New Year's on a plane."

"I can't think of a better place to ring in the New Year," I said, "suspended in the air, between countries. I'll take it. I can celebrate over and over as the time zones change."

She smiled at me. It would have taken no effort to turn on the charm, seduce her with all the skill my father McKenzie had taught me, seduce her like my father Barón had seduced Carola and my mother and who knows who else. It would have been effortless, and I thought to myself, Why not? I'll just wait for her outside the ticket office and go from there. What better way to spend my last night in Santiago? The girl smiled at me from under her large nose and reminded me to make sure I arrived at the airport an hour earlier than usual to give myself time to exchange my current ticket.

"I've got plenty of time," I said. "How about you?"

"That depends," she said, "on what you had in mind."

"If you want to find out over drinks . . ."

But I wasn't there when she got off from work, she wasn't the female flesh I tasted that night.

No sooner had I left the American Airlines office than I saw a woman across the street, walking her cute ass through the milling crowds of Calle Agustinas, the late sun slapping her splendid bare shoulders. It was Cristina Ferrer, the woman I had told my father I was trying to hunt down, the woman my father, lying as usual, had told me he had never nailed, the woman I should have screwed and sent off to the abortion doctor instead of Amanda Camila.

She waved at me and I waved back.

I fucked her that night, Janice. No, I'm not making this up: I fucked her in a hotel near the Alameda, three, maybe four times. I hoped it was the hotel where my parents had conceived me—or maybe they hadn't, maybe it had been Barón and my mother the night before in the Casa Milagros. There was no answer in Cristina's *chucha*, no real pleasure in it, for that matter, no conversation after each savage session, no relief or resolution to be duplicating my father's story, the story in fact of either of my fathers. I guess I was looking for Amanda in Cristina's twat, looking for the woman I could never again make mine, looking for the woman who, at that very moment, was spending a sleepless, lonely night preparing to abort our child, I was looking for my sister and did not find her.

"You haven't called, you naughty boy," Cristina had said when I crossed the street to her. "It's the end of the year and you haven't called."

And I took her wrist and looked at her watch and said, "Doesn't look to me like the year's ended yet," as if I were in some sort of bad movie, but it worked. The worst thing about these phrases is that they often do the job. "A lot can happen in one night. And by the way, I'm not like my father."

"Oh?" Wondering, Cristina, if this meant that I wouldn't go to bed with her after all.

"I come back for seconds," I said.

And for thirds—with her and with others. In the days and nights to come, in Chile and Sevilla and ports in between, establishing a *catálogo* of my own, seducing them just for the hell of it, using the great McKenzie's technique and strategy and advice, but nothing else. No falling in and out of love. No remembering the name of each one, just the general blur of beds. Oh, I listened to each of them, listened for hours, had no deadline like my dad, my supposed dad, feigned interest in whatever they had to say, but was really tuning out, flying on autopilot, letting them gab away as if, fascinated with their brains, I couldn't wait to hear their next thought, when the only thing that I really wanted from them was that moment when I could smuggle myself inside their lower bodies and forget who I was for six, seven, eight instants, maybe more, the moment when I could throw up inside them from deep down below, trying to make believe it was my one true love down there, in there, underneath, who was clutching my buttocks so I would not slip out, while I prayed that I would open my eyes and we could talk each other into sleep, tell each other the deepest secrets, chat ourselves into a world that only we shared. But I would open my eyes and Amanda Camila was not there.

Instead: replicas and routines implemented and revealed that night with Cristina, my one true happiness dawning not each time I proved my mastery at holding back so she could achieve her shuddering orgasm, doing it not so she would be joyful but so I could feel good about myself, avenge myself on that fool Cara de Guagua I had been for so many years, beating my past self into the ground—my one true happiness coming when I finally fell asleep and erased this brain that remembers.

Did I dream at some point early in the morning that she woke me to say goodbye, that I muttered, I have something to confess. Did I tell her, I'm not a reporter, never was. She answered, I've got a little confession of my own—I never fucked your dad, just adored him from afar. Did I make this up? Invent that conversation with Cristina to make myself feel even more depressed? Because if I had met her before Amanda Camila that first evening I arrived in Chile, if I had known my father hadn't preceded me, wouldn't she have been the one I'd have made love to? Wasn't she one more opportunity gone wrong? I could hardly distinguish anymore what was real and what false: to sleep, that was real, to sleep and hope I would never wake up.

It must have been around eleven when the phone rang and I was roused and the creepy voice of the clerk at the front desk warned me that other guests needed the room or did I intend to pay for another day?

Cristina had paid for the night. Left me a note: "Next time, your turn. You're the best McKenzie of them all." I crumpled it, reached for the phone myself, dialed Amanda Camila's house. The maid answered that the young miss had gone out.

"Did she leave any message for me?"

"Tell him goodbye."

"That's all?"

"*Adiós*. Goodbye. I noted it down. She asked me to be sure to write it down so you knew."

A few hours left to kill before meeting my Tío Pancho. I called him up on that ugly hotel phone. There was one place I needed to visit before I left the country: the restaurant where he had made the bet with Cristóbal McKenzie and Pablo Barón.

"The bet I lost," he said, melancholy. I could hear the din of his co-workers in the background. His brother had found him a job—selling pension plans, selling security, Pancho said, to people who needed something else, needed insecurity so they could be adventuresome. But work was work, and always the doctrinaire materialist, he believed in work, labor, and was grateful to Cristóbal for pressuring one of the parents whose child he had returned safe and sound to try Francisco McKenzie out, was melancholy perhaps because he had promised to stay out of trouble, to not organize the other agents in a trade union, to not convince the pensioners to investigate who was investing their squalid savings in a market that might topple at any moment and leave them destitute in old age, to not point out to them the fine print that would screw them over when they complained. Melancholy because he had lost more than the bet.

"That one," I said.

"If you insist," he said. "Meet me there at two o'clock. That's as good a place as any to spend the time, you know, while it's happening."

As I left the hotel, I felt—I guess dirty is the best word, Janice, however clichéd, however obvious. With a grime inside the skin that I knew no water, no liquid on this planet, would ever wash clean. Never again would I be that little boy who climbed inside the shower with his dad, that young man who watched with his dad the water being loaded onto a ship bound for the iceberg. Condemned to be this failure as a brother and lover and father who had let his child be snuffed out of existence instead of helping it grow.

Brimming with these buoyant thoughts, I allowed my feet to stumble me unawares to the Alameda and the Cerro Santa Lucía. Five months after my first hopeful visit I arrived once more at that Cerro where Valdivia's letter promised those who settled that they would perpetuate themselves, where he had fornicated without remorse with Inés de Suárez under these mountains. I had visited it when I had been a virgin and my sister had been a virgin, the Cerro Santa Lucía.

Where you can pick girls up, where you can get raped, where you can get mugged.

Which is what happened to me.

I suddenly felt a tug at the back of my pants. I turned and caught a fleeting glimpse of a small urchin racing up the Cerro. He had stolen my money! Without thinking, I took off after him, running up past a terrace filled with statues, seeing the blur of the kid speeding away, up and up, past pseudo-colonnades and fake Roman aqueducts, until I reached a wide plaza at the end of which, on top of a giant boulder, was the statue of an Indian. I collared the boy just underneath that statue and was about to wrest my money from him when a group of other street kids surrounded me.

They were smaller than Choclo and his band, but there were enough of them to give me a second helping of what had been served up to me in that *población* five months earlier. This was going to be my farewell from Santiago. They were ready to leave me naked on this hill. While the sister I had made love to was being undressed under the glaring lights of that doctor a few blocks away. It was all lapsing into another nightmare.

"Leave him alone."

Not the voice of Ignacio. The voice of Carlitos. There he was, a bit taller than I remembered him, with a confident air I would never have suspected, this boy who had cried himself to sleep, who had held my hand on our way to the bathroom.

"It's Gabriel," he said. "Cristóbal McKenzie's son. The one who took care of me."

The other boys all stepped away.

"Oh, my God," I said. "Where have you been? My father and I have been looking for you."

He took the money from the urchin who had stolen it. "Here," he said, handing it to me. "We don't steal from friends."

"No," I said. "You need it. I don't want it."

I meant it. I thought here was a chance, one last chance before I left, to do something in this country, leave a microscopic mark of glory on somebody's life, bring him back home to my father.

"Come back with me," I said. "To the Casa Milagros."

Maybe that was why all this had happened: so I could salvage one small boy.

"No, Gabriel," he said. "Back there, I was scared. Look at me— here, I'm the king."

He showed me his small friends.

"Let me buy you something to eat," I said, almost pleading, needing to be rescued by my own goodness. "All of you."

He shoved the money at me, retreated a few steps to make sure I wouldn't try and force the bills on him.

"I don't think so," he said. "I don't want to go back there. I don't want you to convince me to go back."

Who knows if I would have been able to insist, who knows if over a hot meal we would have reached some sort of agreement that would have allowed me to return triumphantly to the Casa Milagros. Because at that moment a *paco* happened to saunter like a sick summer shadow into that *plazuela*. And the kids all scattered, each in a different direction.

Carlos raced up some steps and I followed him. But he had disappeared. Who was there, on a lovely esplanade at the very top of the Cerro, was Pedro de Valdivia himself, trapped in a cold slab of marble that might at some point have originally been white but that now was smudged dark, just like the city that he had founded and over whose thick horrible haze he uneasily presided, he who had said in his letter to the emperor that it was like paradise, full of greenery and mild breezes. On closer scrutiny, there were some white specks on his statue, tiny smears of shit provided by the birds who had been there before the conquistador of this valley arrived and would probably be there once I was as dead as Valdivia himself.

And then, from behind me, came music.

It was the lone sound of an Indian *quena* flute playing the very Inti-Illimani song I had heard below the loft that night in SoHo when I had broken off relations with this country. I wondered for an insane second whether the Compiler of My Life, whoever was typing my misfortunes on some screen, had not recorded that melody on some CD-ROM in the Sky for the express purpose of spiting me. That paranoid idea disappeared quickly because I whirled around and there, to one side of the open space, near a small chapel, sat a dream of a young woman, a native woman, by the looks of her, those dark slanted eyes, black hair, skin a deep bronze, the lovely shape of her skull, her delicate fingers plaintively playing her instrument. She noticed my interest and acknowledged it with a nod and continued playing, unaware that every note was reviling me for the wrong turn I had taken on that SoHo street when I was eleven years old. I wondered if my mother had not planned it all, the final spiral in her revenge. *Someday you'll come running, begging for me to tell you about Chile.* Maybe she had paid this Indian beauty to come and haunt me, maybe it was her diseased way of reminding me that I still owed Che Guevara, that I still had not paid my debt to Che Guevara, maybe Che himself had sent this musician my way.

I abruptly felt as sick as I had the afternoon I confessed my past to Nana. The smell of the anaesthesia and the blood from that doctor's butcher shop I had inhaled the previous day caught up with me, the smell Amanda would be breathing within a few hours, mixing with the summer smog, though what was really tainting and taunting me was the valley itself, millions of lungs mocking mine, breathing corruption into every poisonous pore. They were the contaminants and not the air. They were the ones who were punishing me. It had all started and ended there. Something had gone drastically wrong that night in Manhattan when the shout of "Che Guevara! *Presente!*" had moved me to deny the continent of my birth. All I needed was to have mounted those stairs to the loft, given the money back to my mother, and joined in the song they were all fervently intoning, that was all. And my fate would have twisted like a nickel in the wind. The next day the great McKenzie's insistent invitation to visit home would have arrived as it usually did and that time I would have said yes, I would have come here, to this city founded by Valdivia, and my dad would have offered me a couple of pointers, would have set me straight. Every other summer I would have come back and that would have been enough, he would have told me about his stupid bet before Mom had, I would have lain down below these mountains and timidly entered a Chilean girl, as it was always meant to be. Maybe it would have been this very princess I was listening to now, why not, why not her? And then I would have gone back and given you, my faithful Janice Worth, what both you and I wanted. And Amanda Camila would have been just another semi-relative at the edge of my consciousness, and the iceberg something I'd have read about in a newspaper item in New York as one more quaint and "chilly" thing these people from Chile were doing, and I'd never have killed my own daughter, because she would never have existed. That's how it should have been in an alternative existence, on the planet of possibilities that I had thrown away with my gift to those kids break-dancing on the Manhattan pavement. That would have lifted the curse of Che Guevara before it had a chance to bar my way home. That's how it should have worked out.

And then something even more bizarre happened. That Indian girl suddenly stopped blowing that Inti-Illimani melody into her *quena*, stopped in the very middle of the song, as if she could hear my silent prayers that she cease tormenting me. A heavenly respite that only lasted a few seconds. She started to play another tune, and guess what she plucked, amazingly, out of thin air? The one piece of music in the universe that could be guaranteed to disturb me more than the Inti-Illimani song, deride me with even greater cruelty: it was Mozart, the catalogue of Don Giovanni's conquests that Leporello delivers and that my mother had kept on playing in New York whenever I asked about my father. That native woman was tootling that aria and forcing me yet again to remember how the don doesn't care if they're fat or thin, blond or brunet, old or young—he knows what to do with them, envious Leporello belting it out, Leporello and now this Indian maiden here on the top of this Chilean hill. An Indian playing Mozart? Was I imagining this? Could it be true? Both of them ending with the remark that, of all the countries, Spain was the most prolific, the Spain from which Pedro de Valdivia had emigrated at about the time Don Juan was alive and pumping away; in Spain he's already fucked one thousand and three, *mille e tre*—and I couldn't stand it anymore, this dark-skinned angel had first reminded me of my father Che and how I had betrayed him and my mother, and now her second tune was gashing me with the knife of another betrayal. It had taken me less than a day to bed Cristina and chuck my damaged Amanda. I had to shut off the spigot of that Mozart song before I bled to death.

I rushed to the young woman's side as she began to improvise a combination, jazzlike, of the first song with the second one, intertwining them as my mother and my father had been intertwined not far from here to create me, in and out of each other, the melodies, the bodies, and I thrust my hand into my pocket and came out with the fistful of bills that Carlos had not wanted to receive because, like everybody else I had met on this trip, he did not want to be redeemed by me. I took that money and threw it down in front of the native musician, as if I were returning to the remote descendants of the Nana a small part of what Valdivia and his boys had stolen from her, as if this would rid me of the memories that woman was inducing in me, probing out of me like an incestuous scalpel. I threw it at her bare feet and whispered to her lovely indigenous mouth, "Stop, please stop." And she stopped. Stopped in utter astonishment and looked at the money as if she had never seen anything like it before, as if we had both been transported back to the foundation of Santiago when the Spanish had come with baubles and coins and the Mapuches had examined these objects with uncomprehending amazement. "No, wait," she said, her eyes flashing in liquid alarm, but I turned and left her, hurried down the steps to the next *plazuela* and, short of breath, staggered to the statue of the Indian I had passed on my way up.

And saw its name: Caupolicán.

Where had I heard that name before? The *teatro* where my father met Polo the night I was conceived! A beam of ashen Santiago sunlight hit the face of Caupolicán, and from behind me a voice I knew only too well crept up, made a comment.

"*Huelén,*" the familiar voice said, and I almost desired it to be Polo himself, who, through some pact with the demon deities of this valley, had managed to track me down in order to remind me that when I left tonight he would stay behind as my father's only son, the usurper of my heritage. But I knew with a sinking heart that it was someone worse: Max Behrends.

"*Huelén,*" Max reiterated. "The Mapuche word for pain. That's what the Mapuches had been calling his hill for centuries. Before any-body thought to name it after some Italian saint. Pain. You think they guessed hundreds of years before the Spanish came that they'd get shafted, that all they'd get from history would be a stake up their ass? A stake up his ass in particular. That's how he died, Caupolicán. They were going to burn him, but he converted, became a Christian—so they were compassionate, stuck a lance up his ass till he bled to death. Slowly."

I turned to go, but Max grabbed my arm in his Aryan grip. "Not so fast," Max said. "There's somebody I want you to meet. She could tell you something about this statue. For instance, why doesn't it have a stake up its ass?"

Had he gone crazy? Was this his revenge for my having separated him from Amanda Camila, to hold me hostage while he re-enacted his old role as tourist guide on this Cerro? To drag us back to our first meeting at the bottom of the hill, when he had pointed out to an eager camera that this had once been a cemetery for the *expatriados* from heaven and earth?

As usual, he had asked a question in order to answer it himself, show off how Chilean he was in spite of having been born in faraway Salzburg. "This statue doesn't have a stake up its ass," Max Behrends said, with the voice he used when being filmed. "It's a fake, not an Araucanian at all. Originally modeled by a Chilean sculptor for some gringos at the American embassy, inspired by an engraving of a noble Indian from a gringo novel, *The Last of the Mohicans*. Have you read it?"

"Listen, Max," I said, "I have a luncheon—"

"The gringos," Max went on, as if I hadn't spoken, "hated that statue. Of course. They didn't want one of their own stupid, fictitious cigar-store American Indians, they wanted an authentic, typical, and nonexistent Chilean Indian. So what did the sculptor do when they returned the statue to him?"

I didn't want to know, I didn't give a fuck. But I wasn't prepared to get into a fistfight. Max was bigger, in better shape, and had reasons to hate and hurt this audience of one he had captured and was boring to death.

"The sculptor turned right around and sold his masterpiece to the Cerro Santa Lucía, falsely claiming it was Caupolicán. And the Chileans loved it. They didn't care that it was copied from a book up north. That's the way it goes. First the Spanish stick a hot rod up Caupolicán's ass and then their Chilean descendants erect a statue without the pain, a worse crime, I think, than the original murder. One of the most famous statues in Chile—teaching schoolkids a debased version of their own history. Which is worse: to torture somebody or to forget it ever happened? Huh, Gabriel?" The pressure on my arm grew. "But why ask you when we can ask someone who hasn't forgotten, a real expert on the subject, someone who is coming our way right this moment. It's Victoria Huepimul in person."

I broke away from Max and she was there, the breathtaking native woman who had played the music. She had followed me down the steps and was now resolutely heading in my direction as if a stake were up her resplendent ass or, more alarmingly, as if she wanted to shove one up mine. She didn't do anything that drastic, fortunately: she thrust toward me, silently, reproachfully, the money I had thrown at her feet. I didn't take it. I sensed a connection to her and this money was my chance to stay in contact with that woman and her passion. And that's all my fickle heart could think of at that moment. Maybe a miracle would happen and she was the reason I had come to Chile, maybe everything wasn't lost after all. Like a little boy, I clenched my fists and put my hands behind my back.

"Have you two met?" Max asked, his blue eyes flitting between us both. "Victoria, have you—?"

"He thought I was a beggar, Max," Victoria said. "Your friend thought I was a fucking *conchuda* Indian beggar."

Max gently took her arm with the hand that had just been holding mine. "He's not really my friend, are you, Gabriel? Though he did me a service, Victoria. If it hadn't been for him, we wouldn't be together. This is Gabriel McKenzie, remember—"

"The guy who kept you away from that girl you fell in love with down in Punta Arenas?"

"The same son of a bitch. Never had a chance to thank him. Thanks to your maneuvers, Gabriel, I gave up on Amanda. And was freed to discover Victoria."

"I don't know what you're talking about," I said. "I've got to go."

But I didn't move. Victoria's eyes fixed me to that ground, anchored me to her pleasure. Suddenly, I understood the source of my fascination: she reminded me of the Nana in that photo, that Ona girl back in Punta Arenas who had called to me from across time and space and straits and desires. There was a touch of the Nana's wisdom in her eyes, her lips, the slope of her shoulders.

"I thought you'd enjoy meeting Victoria," Max said. "One of our great concert musicians, a wonderful composer. She plays the clarinet with the symphonic orchestra. Not bad, at twenty-six, to be heading the winds, huh? I understand why you might have been confused. I was confused the first time I saw her five months ago, on my birthday, to be exact, a present I did not at the time appreciate."

"Max Behrends," Victoria said, "you talk too much. Why don't you use your mouth to persuade your friend or your enemy or whoever the fuck he is to take his money back, so we can get out of here, okay? My rehearsal's been ruined."

"I've got an equitable, negotiated solution, *mi amor*," Max said. "You don't want to keep the money and he doesn't want it back, so the solution is . . . I keep it"—he plucked the money out of her hand—"in order to donate it to your Lautaro project. Right, Gabriel? A donation? From an expert on the Internet? I even toyed with the idea—one day when he came to see me with his father for reasons I still can't fathom—anyway, I thought he might even lend you a helping hand."

"You're an expert on the Internet?"

Was Victoria looking at me in a less aggressive way?

"My girl here has come up with an idea," Max went on. "She wants to wire up the Mapuche communities."

"Get them the best hardware and the latest software," Victoria said, surmising my mistrust, knowing nevertheless that I would understand better than Max would, this woman who had instinctively chosen the two songs that evoked in me the strongest memories. What a dream it would have been to make love to her, to chat with her after making love. Or was I using her to erase Cristina, erase Amanda? "Plug my nation in—Web sites, the works. A computer in every community center would make them competitive. Job offers to begin with, but our basic problem today is fragmentation, so networking among people who can't gather together anymore would re-create ties, coordinate efforts to get our land back."

"What Lautaro," I said, nursing the conversation, nursing the hope that someday it might be more than just that, "would have done if he were alive."

"Now you're getting it. At first, like you, Max didn't approve, didn't understand. He thought that I wanted to destroy my own culture. Max knew so much about the country but still thought of Indians in the way you did, some sad somebody on a hillside that you can toss money at paternalistically and go on your way. I taught him that a community that doesn't open to the outer world is going to die."

"Sure," I said. "Use the money for that project."

"Agreed," Max said, pocketing the bills. "Go and get your things, *m'hija*."

"So you'll help me?" Victoria asked.

"Of course. I'd love to."

We both watched her go back up the steps, disappear from view.

"Isn't she great?" Max asked enthusiastically. "She's going to do the music for my film. I heard her that day—"

"Your birthday," I said.

"Yes," he said.

"Your birthday," I repeated, thinking about dates. That meant he had met her on July 11, the day after I had been here myself and seen him exploring this same space. That meant that if I had gone up the Cerro Huelén or Santa Lucía or whatever this shit-pile park was called, I would have heard her before he had. I would have sat down on that same bench under the statue of the dead conquistador. I would have listened to those two songs. I would have spoken to her, she would have told me about the Lautaro project, I'd have offered my services to her instead of to Oscar and Nano. I'd have fallen in love with her then as I was in danger of falling in love with her now that all my bridges to Amanda Camila had been more than burned, more than despoiled. It meant that I had missed by a few feet, by a few minutes, what should have been my fate in Chile, to have met that woman who could have saved me and who now belonged to Max Behrends. He was flaunting her, that's why he had captured my arm, in order to tell me that she was expecting his child, to thank me for having hindered his access to Amanda Camila. When he had returned to Santiago and found the road to my Amanda blocked, the melody from that *quena* had come back to him one night when he couldn't sleep, he had rushed up the Cerro Huelén early the next morning and waited for Victoria hours on end. And when, in the afternoon, she had finally materialized as if from the future, he had sat silently listening to her whole concert, he had proposed that she write the score for the film, they had gone off to have a meal together.

Max had stolen my life twice, and if the first time I was unaware as we crossed each other in the Santiago airport when he arrived and I departed at six years of age, the second time, now that we were both twenty-three, I was the one who had paved his way. You must think I'm crazy, Janice, and I am, of course I'm crazy. Read the newspapers tomorrow: Terrorist Act in Sevilla, Explosion Greets Columbus Day, Mad Chilean Strikes Blow in the Name of Che Guevara. Tune into the news tomorrow and you'll see how crazy. But it's the truth: we were meant for each other, Victoria and the son of Pablo Barón. I could have given her all my Internet skills, I could have spent the rest of my life on the Lautaro project and we would have had children with the eyes of my Nana and I would not have ever known who my father was. I would never have needed to build my many traps, betray the woman who nursed me into life.

"Did you fuck her?" Max Behrends asked.

I looked at him as if he were mad and not me.

"Amanda Camila," Max said. "Did you fuck her?"

He must have seen the *huelén* in my eyes, the pain welling out of my eyes, he must have seen the answer in my eyes. Maybe for the first time since he glimpsed me at the bottom of this hill and then wove between those tables one week later in the Hotel Cabo de Hornos in Patagonia and then advised me to kill my father when I had visited his office here in Santiago, for the first time it dawned on him how deeply entangled we were. Something made him understand that he could have been *me*, that my pain could have been his, that a destiny that neither he nor I controlled had switched us, given him joy, given me the misery of being called Gabriel McKenzie. That's how it was, and Max would make sure that that was how it would remain.

"Stay away from her," he said. Like Pablo Barón so many months before, speaking of another girl. The same tone. "Go. Before she comes back."

I had nowhere to go, nowhere I wanted to go. I looked at Max, but there was not an ounce of pity in him.

"I said, Get the fuck out of here!"

I got the fuck out of there. I went to the restaurant where Cristóbal McKenzie had gone the day after he lost his virginity. Where else could I end up but where it had all begun?

It was still there, on Providencia. It was the same menu, maybe even the same waiter, my Tío Pancho wasn't sure but he seemed to be the same guy: still waiting tables, still eyeing each customer to calculate how much the tip might be, still offering clients the choice of seafood or steak, white Santa Rita or San Emiliano *tinto*. Just as he had plied his trade when I was not yet entirely alive, was creeping toward birth, could have been aborted if Pablo Barón had not defied Cristóbal McKenzie to state how he expected to spend the next twenty-five years, if Pablo Barón had not induced his best friend and rival to marry the woman he had discharged his seed into the night before. That's all it would have taken. Had Tío Pancho not come that day and started that conversation, I would not have existed, just as in one hour's time, at 3:00 p.m., to be precise, the child I had conceived inside my sister, Amanda Camila, would no longer exist. The waiter would have been here, perhaps even reciting the specials of the day to this very uncle of mine—but somebody else with who knows what troubles and what slowly maturing face would have been by his side. Anybody but me.

"That bet," he said now, "I don't regret having made it. I just regret having lost it. Not for me. For all the people who would be better off if there'd been socialism in Latin America, if we controlled our own destiny. Street kids whom your dad shouldn't be taking care of, whom we should all be taking care of. Who shouldn't even exist. No street kids in Cuba. No street kids in the Soviet Union. Now, of course, they'll start again. Corporations, street kids, prostitutes, you'll see what capitalism does to—you'll tell me that socialism hasn't exactly been a success story, that millions have died, innocent people. All right. But birth is painful. We make mistakes, and then we learn and then we rectify. But it won't go away, the dream, Gabriel, it won't, because capitalism can't solve the problems of the poor, can't make anybody really happy. It will end up self-destructing and destroying the planet as well."

I really did not feel like getting into a political argument with him, hearing him bet that in twenty-five years' time things would be different, that the Choclos of this world would have heroically manned the barricades and the Onas would be resurrected and the Larreas and their factories would be run by their workers, his prophecy that Carlitos would be Chile's president. Nothing would ever change. My dad McKenzie had been right. Or maybe my dad Barón had been right that if they did change, it would be oh so gradually, within the system. Or maybe Tío Pancho was right after all and people would get tired of being screwed and would tear it all down in disgust. But the point for me was that I didn't care who was right, because they couldn't change me. Nothing could change things for me, I was leaving tonight. This was my goodbye to Chile.

And even as I thought that, there was one last chance for a major alteration in my fortune, hovering in the air, one last chance ready to materialize right then and there, to land on that table. Too late, too late.

"Did you ever think the other two would win?" I asked, little suspecting the revelation my uncle was about to pull out of the past. "Not that you'd lose but that they'd win, both of them."

"Both of them," Francisco McKenzie repeated. "Can you keep a secret?"

"I'm great at keeping secrets," I lied to him.

"Barón's already lost," he said, attacking his steak with gusto, jabbing at it as if it were the abominable Dow-Jones average, the new Chilean pension plan that was being touted as a miracle all over the world, chewing it with those teeth that had only guzzled prison gruel for almost five years.

"What do you mean, he's already lost? Is Barón going to be sacked?" Did my uncle know something I didn't? Or was this one more delusion, a consolation, to imagine the traitor who had been in the resistance with him humiliated and forced to resign.

"Oh, no. He'll keep his job. He's doing just what he was supposed to: Pinochet's economic program without Pinochet. A few crumbs for the workers, big profits for the big companies. Did you know that Chile is more dependent than ever on foreign markets?"

"Tío, I know all the theory. Could you just tell me what you mean by his losing?"

Our *garzón* poured us some wine. Francisco McKenzie watched him, patiently waited till he had finished and withdrawn, before continuing. "My brother made sure," he said, "that even if they both made it to their fiftieth birthday having fulfilled their pledges, that even in that case, he would have an advantage over Barón."

"What do you mean, an advantage?"

"I was never in the running, Gabriel. It was all about them. First it's who was born first, then who's got the longest prick. They used to try to compare size as early as kindergarten, who can piss farther, that macho bullshit."

"So . . ."

"So my brother Cris decided early on, just in case, to stack the cards in his favor."

"How?"

"Think of it. Think of their relative strengths. Barón had all this political power and he used it, tried to use it—at least that's what Cris says and I believe him. So what did Cris have that could screw Barón? What is Cris good at? What could Cris do to a woman that would beat Barón, make a McKenzie the secret victor? Secret, that is, except for one witness—me. He told me. He needed me, the third one at this same table when we made that bet. He wanted me to know that, even if there was a draw at the end, he had won. Finally, in the real game, in the real world, he had beaten Pablo Barón."

"Amanda Camila?" I said, my heart sinking. It couldn't be—that my father had fucked her after all, that his oath to Barón had all been a sham, that she had lied to me.

"Amanda Camila," my Tío Pancho confirmed.

"He fucked Amanda Camila?"

"Fucked her? Hell, no. He's Amanda's father. He fucked her mother, fucked Marta. He did it to make sure he'd win no matter what. Did it on the day he calculated she'd be dropping an egg."

"Marta hated him, Pablo Barón said she—"

"What did you expect her to say? I love him, I'd screw him every day of my life if I could? Of course she allayed Barón's suspicions by telling him that Cristóbal McKenzie was a bad influence on him. But Marta had from my brother the one thing he'd never given any other woman except your mother—a baby. So Amanda Camila's your sister, Gabriel. How about that?"

Except she wasn't. If what my uncle was saying turned out to be true, she wasn't my sister. We had swapped fathers: she was the daughter of Cristóbal McKenzie and I was the son of Pablo Barón and—

"This can't be true," I said to my Tío Pancho. "Who else knows it, who can confirm what you're—"

"*Hombre*, take it easy." Francisco McKenzie was enjoying my distraught questions. "There's nobody else. Marta's dead, of course. And the other person who knew, she's also dead."

"Who?" I asked, even though I already knew the answer. Suddenly it was all clear to me, suddenly I understood it all.

"Your Nana, who else? She ended up knowing everything, that woman. She cornered your dad one day and asked him point-blank. In fact, that was the real reason she left his household. That rigmarole about waiting seven years for Milagros—*pura mierda*. You can believe me that she would have waited seven hundred years for Milagros to come home. No, it was to take care of McKenzie's other child, your half sister, that's why she agreed to serve that bastard Barón. She asked me what sort of man he was; we were still friends with Pablo back then but I was beginning to mistrust him. I could already see that he was heading for a compromise with Pinochet."

"Tío, please stick to the point."

"I told her he was a good man. Maybe I should have warned her off, but I think Nana would have gone off with him if he'd been Hitler, as long as she could make sure that Amandita had a woman to look after her as she grew. She was the daughter of the man Nana had chosen for her darling Milagros, that she had counseled Milagros to keep on loving in spite of all his playing around. So now she wanted to make sure that his daughter, that member of the family, would be protected by someone like her. Where are you going?"

I was going to save my baby.

It was ten to three and if I hurried I could make it. Again, it stood to reason: that condom Cristóbal McKenzie had given to Pablo Barón with the promise that he would never use it on the newborn Amanda Camila. It had been the very condom he hadn't used with Marta, the one woman he had fucked without protection, no latex between his sperm and her womb. The one time he broke his promise to my mother—because he wanted to win that bet more than he wanted to be true to her, he wanted to beat Pablo Barón enough to betray her trust that he'd never give another woman what he'd given her. Barón might be the most powerful man in the nation, but he had not been powerful enough to stop the McKenzie *pija* from entering the sacred space that Barón had reserved for himself and his heritage. No wonder Cris had avowed to his best friend that he would never fuck that little girl: it was his own daughter he was shielding from his ever-roving pecker. He was vouching that he would never commit with her the act of incest that I thought I had committed. The act I had not committed. Barón had been wrong. I was not Amanda's brother.

And the Nana had known. For me, that was the clincher, the one piece in the puzzle that was missing. I had kept asking myself how it could be that the Nana who seemed to love me and Amanda so fiercely would allow the two children of Barón to mate. My answer that she was a demon had been unfair. She was an angel. From the very start she had brought us together, was cheering us on, the son of the woman she adored coupling with the daughter of the man who had married that woman with vows of eternal love. She had urged Cristóbal's daughter on and urged the son of Milagros on, and when that son had confessed his tribulations to her she had given the information to Milagros so the letters could solve my problem. She had never expected either of us to discover who our true fathers might be. She had died in the night as we made love, she had transferred her soul to that child beginning to form inside Amanda Camila, she had blessed our union.

And it was still time to make it all right, to save that baby, to bring the Nanny's plans to fruition.

I knocked on the doctor's door.

Nobody answered.

I knocked again and saw a woman next door, on the threshold of her house, smoking a sullen cigarette, looking at me suspiciously as if memorizing my features would help her identify me when she informed the police, He's the one, he's the one who paid for the abortion. I turned the knob on the door and it opened and I went in.

He was cleaning up. There was blood on the operating table and he was swabbing it with a rag, the smell of formaldehyde sickening the air.

"What are you doing here? Who let you in?"

"Where is she?"

"She left. Who let you in?"

"She was supposed to be here at three."

He stopped what he was doing, went to the sink, and began to wash his hands. The water ran red. "Yeah, but she called to ask if I could make it a bit earlier and I thought, What the hell, I'll miss lunch, get it over with, maybe I can even take my siesta. But you haven't answered my question."

I sat myself down in a chair next to the operating table, sat down hard, vacantly. "She can't have left. It's somebody else. You must be mistaken."

He came over to me, wiping his hands. He wiped them in a special way, finger by finger, as if he were taking off a glove, meticulously, first the right hand, then the left, finger by finger. "It was *Ministro*

Barón's daughter, wasn't it?" He stood over me. He had one of these caps on, a sort of white fez, a dirty white cap. A fly was poised on it, ready to dart away at the first sign of danger. The fly stayed put, looking at me with the fracture of its million eyes. "It was Pablo Barón's daughter, wasn't it?"

"Yes," I said.

"I thought so. I couldn't quite place her, didn't mention it to her. It's always nice when you can identify patients. They always come with false names and once in a while you find out who it is. No, it's not blackmail, I'm not into that, you don't have to worry. In fact, this is for you."

He handed me the wad of bills that I had given him the day before, that my uncle had offered as an enticement to operate on the last day of the year.

I took it from him mechanically. My only thought was that I had lost her, I had come late, the baby was dead, the Nana's little breath of love was dead.

"I can't take your money, not for Barón's daughter," the doctor said. "He's a great man, that Pablo Barón. Because of him we have peace in this country, we finally have a chance. A brave man—to negotiate with the military, get them to give up power, get his own people to agree to those conditions—the sort of man we need in this country, reasonable, determined, forthright. I tell you, if his daughter's committed a silly sin, that's all right with me. Anybody who comes from that family deserves my respect. I'm not taking any money from a Barón."

If he'd only known that he had operated on a McKenzie and that the Barón child was the one in front of him.

I looked at the money in my hand.

"Keep it," the doctor insisted. "My contribution, my insignificant homage to a great man. And next time, use a condom, man. Even if it makes me poor."

"Where is it?" I asked.

"Where is what?" And when I didn't answer, he said, "You don't want to see it. There's nothing to see. I've already thrown it away."

Why did I want to punish myself? Why did I want to see more blood, the blood of menstruation delayed, the blood of Barón and McKenzie's first grandchild, both of them joined in that death that should have been a life, the blood that lost its way in Nana's arteries and burst into her heart and drowned it, all the blood that had flowed in this valley since Santiago had been founded—why did I want to see any more of it?

"What would it have been?"

The doctor turned off the lights, indicated the door. "You don't want to know."

"I want to know."

"A girl," he said. "Probably a girl, though that early on . . . "

We went into the street, he said Happy New Year to the sultry woman who was still smoking her cigarette—maybe he had performed a quick operation on her, given her a freebie just to keep her quiet and curdled. Who knows what secrets he knew, what wombs he had cleansed, what memories and hopes he had buried, what lives he had allowed to start all over again as if nothing had happened.

For one final instant I let myself believe—I say final because it was the last time; truly after that I did not, have never since believed—there was a chance for me, but then, at that moment, it flashed into me from some deep lullaby voice of the Nana inside that I could blot out the past like Chileans all around me seemed to be doing, I clung to the belief that people like me get one more try than they deserve, that I could, like my two fathers, lie and cheat and never really pay the consequences, do some good as well perhaps. A hallucination of the future visited me and told me that all I had to do now was talk to Amanda, take her entirely into my confidence, ask her forgiveness and forgive her, and start where we should have, start where I might have. That illusion.

It lasted what life lasts on this planet, nothing, what it took a bullet to rip into Che's body, what it took for the blood to split Nana's heart, what it took for that doctor to puncture that fertilized egg, that's how long I kept up my hopes that everything would be all right.

It was that slashed gleam of hope that did it, that sent me over the edge, brought me here to Sevilla to die. Waking from it on that street, knowing that nothing would ever change, I also knew that I never again wanted to trust in the benevolence of the universe, I never again wanted to fool myself into believing I could ever be happy. More than that, I knew that this was how whoever or whatever was playing with me had me trapped, that thing or person or destiny or whatever the hell you want to call it, that somebody who was amusing himself or herself or themselves at my expense, this was what they used, the blink of faith I had just experienced was what fueled me to keep going, keep trying, that was how I was being controlled.

Well, fuck you. I don't mean you, Janice, pitiful you on your pitiful couch yesterday, in front of your pitiful screen today. I mean the whoever it is that's been conducting his muddled experiment on me: Let's take this kid and mess him up real good, over and over, and each time things go wrong, let's offer him another shimmer of desire, another goal, another woman, another hole in another body, another father figure to model and guide his existence, a tiny glint of hope to keep him going when things turn sour. So we can amuse ourselves every time he picks himself up and heads for the blind future.

Well, fuck you, wherever you are, in heaven or hell or somewhere in between.

And inside the Fuck you to the planners of my life was the idea—not a grand revelation, not an orgasm of light streaming into my brain—that's when I understood that only by killing myself could I be free. Even if that is what the gods wanted me to do, even if they organized all this to drive me insane and end my life and have one last snigger at my expense, well, it didn't matter, because that would be the final act. They would have to go out and find somebody else to trifle and tinker and gamble with. This was in my hands, the thought crossed my mind as I leaned against the wall of the clinic where that doctor had operated on my hopes, put his hands and steel into the space where only I had been before with my aching love. This was the one thing I could do that would terminate this farce.

I knew who I was, there, on that desolate street of summer, I remembered the cemetery of the Cerro Huelén that Max first mentioned to me, those words of his that recalled the fate of the *expatriados*, those without a *patria*, without a land. That is where I belonged. Max had known it as he looked at me back then, at the bottom of the hill where Santiago had been founded and all our stories had started. I belonged with the heretics and the outcasts and the disbelievers. With the suicides—above all, that's where I belonged. With the murderers. I know it now here in Sevilla and fully realized it back then as we approached the last hour of the year when my Nana died. Needing her body to rock my body, take me in her arms, and tell me to keep on living, wipe away the rage. But I had finished her off, the last Ona, the stupid old beautiful bitch had died for me. Or maybe she wasn't the last Ona, as if that matters anymore. Mapuche or Fueguina or Aztec, I killed her as if I had pulled the trigger. We all killed her with our lies, her own lies of love for me killed her. Her love for Amanda Camila and for Milagros killed her, *mi novia*, my true bride, Nana should have been. Yes, we all did it, but I had left her alone to die in the dark, I had not taken her hand as she would have taken mine if I were facing death, I had not sat by her as she left this earth.

That was the one thing I could not forgive myself for. Lying, scheming, all that—I'd done nothing more than everybody else around me in Chile did for a living, starting with both my fathers. But letting her die while I washed the sex from my body, leaving her there alone when I could have cleared the hair away from her eyes even if she did not know I was nearby—for that there was no forgiveness. That I had not registered her last words or her last silence. There would be no sacred ground for me, no place on this earth I would ever be able to call my own. No bones would be left, no country to claim me, no children to remember my passing. Like Antarctica, except with no land underneath, no mountains cracking upwards, no hidden volcanoes, no islands with penguins, no cormorants, not even an albatross. No warmth. Only me. Ice to ice.

But I'll go out in style.

Payback time, Gabriel.

And that thought of suicide stayed with me. It stayed inside and grew when I went to Barón's house and spoke to Amanda Camila and did not tell her the truth, consoled her for our loss and let her assume that we were still brother and sister. It stayed inside me as I put her softly to sobbing sleep, kissed her hair on the pillow, switched off the light. It stayed inside me when I went to my room and, instead of packing my bags and leaving the country, decided to remain in Chile, because if I was to die, I did not want it to be alone, I wanted witnesses, and that is when a second thought intertwined with the first one: maybe I should not die by myself, maybe I should take somebody with me, Polo maybe, Max maybe, show them that they hadn't won, that I still held a card or two. I fell asleep with that new thought curled in my arms like a child and was awoken by my mother. "Gabriel, you're going to miss the New Year, hurry up," my mother who had written those letters out of love for me but whose love hadn't stopped her from ignoring that pain all the years in New York, my mother who had fucked two men in two nights without thinking of where that would leave me, split and adrift, so many years later. I smiled at her angelically, maliciously. "Sure, Mom. I'll be right down." She was excited. "They're planning their fiftieth birthday, Cris and Pablo," she said. "Pablo has to close the Expo '92 exhibition on October 12, so he's invited us all, you and me as well, to Sevilla. And Cris wants to go, he's ready to leave the country for the first time! As long as we're together." And I smiled some more. "That's great, Mom. We'll have the best time. I'll be right down." And Sevilla seemed as good a place as any other to rid the world of the vermin of myself. Don Juan's city, the city of Columbus, seemed the perfect place, in fact, and as to whom I would take with me on this voyage, not Polo, not Max—who cared about them? They were auxiliaries, bit players in this drama. The men who should die if I died were—

I saw them both together, hugging at midnight, ringing in the year of their fiftieth birthday, the year of America's five hundredth. I saw them holding each other as tightly as I had held onto my Nana the day I had arrived in this country, the way I would have liked to have embraced them, either one of them, just once like that. I saw them look into each other's eyes and hope the other had the best New Year ever, both of them hiding what each had done to the other and to me. Then they turned in unison, my two fathers noticed me, they emerged as if they were crabs coming out of that crippled ocean of people, all those kids celebrating 1992 in the Casa Milagros, all those friends of theirs dancing and kissing and sweating champagne, they came to me and folded their four arms around me simultaneously, all three of us squeezed together as if we were having an orgy. I felt their warm drunken breath on my neck, from one side and the other, their fingers clutching my shoulders and my ribs and my elbows. God, we love you, Gabrielito—both of them slobbering it into my ears—and I smiled back at them as if I believed them. I began to understand what I needed to do.

It was then, being held by them, that it all started to come together for me. I hated them so intensely that I did not even have to dissemble it: that's how natural it was, as much a part of me as my own breath or my own blood, a hatred so deep that it would never go away. Barón and McKenzie, who had had their pleasure with each other's women. Barón and McKenzie, who had denied me. Barón and McKenzie, who, each in his own way, used me to destroy the other. My father McKenzie pressing me to him, his whole body trembling next to mine. That's how close he'd been to my mom when he didn't make me, how close he'd been to Pablo Barón's wife when he made Amanda Camila. He had got to her first after all, the girl I loved. He'd been inside her years before I had, carried the seed of her body and her sex in his testicles. And the other body, my father Barón's body that had shuddered inside my mother to make me twenty-four hours before his best friend entered her, my father Barón who had lied to him about that, had kept that secret from him all these years and from me as well, my father Barón who had taught me to lie, to deceive those you love and screw them over if you can—that is the lesson he taught me with his buddy McKenzie, the lesson I had followed as if they had been dictating it to me, the fathers I had come to Chile to find.

I broke away from their embrace, afraid that they would smother me with the false words of their false love. Even then, with all that hatred spilling and swirling inside me like dark semen, I still didn't have a plan. Kill myself, yes. Kill them, probably. Sevilla, certainly. But how? To make what point?

As usual, I was adrift. I waited for some sign to come to me, some voice to rescue me, one other person, living or dead, to accompany me in my conspiracy, walk with me into the ice of death. And as if answering my prayer, my mother provided me with the name I was looking for. She had been yammering it at me and hammering it into the wall of my life for as long as I could remember. It was so simple and so obvious.

Toasts were being proposed and hers was the third.

First came Larrea: he wanted to drink to Cristóbal Colón and refrigeration, the two marvels of the last five hundred years, the man who had discovered us and brought us here like Moses over the desert of the Atlantic, and the technology that would bring the iceberg back to the *madre patria* to prove that we weren't all Indians.

Everybody drank to that.

Then came Polo: he wanted us to drink to the other Cristóbal, the McKenzie one, and his best buddy *Ministro* Barón, who in this coming year would be celebrating their half century on this planet together with the biggest party in Sevilla—we were all invited to attend.

Everybody drank to that as well.

At last, it was my mother's turn: another anniversary next year, she said, was the execution and burial of Che Guevara, twenty-five years since he had left America orphaned, since his hands like Galvarino's had been cut off. But he wasn't as dead as many people would like to think. He was coming back, and when he did, all hell would break loose. Here's to Che: may he return and live forever.

To that toast, people most emphatically did not drink. "Not to that maniac with his suicidal mission," one prim lady whispered to her husband. A few drained their champagne for Guevara, maybe one or two who thought it was chic to be left-wing and revolutionary, maybe a couple of the kids who had a vague idea of Che as somebody with long hair and glowing eyes. But most guests only put their lips to their glasses or pretended they hadn't heard.

McKenzie and Barón had heard, however, and cast sideways glances at each other, and in those glances I could see what they were both symmetrically and perversely thinking. Each of them was remembering how Che had led them to the body of Milagros Gallardo and to the bet at that table when they celebrated their twenty-fifth birthday, each of them planning to spring his little surprise on the other one on October 11 at precisely 11:59 p.m. in Sevilla, each of them savoring the moment when he would proclaim himself the victor—I fucked your wife, no, I fucked yours—both of them getting ready to tell their best friend that he had lost.

Only they wouldn't, I wouldn't give them the chance. I would be the one to tell them. In front of everybody, all those who had voyaged to Sevilla to honor the triple birthday, theirs and America's. Tell them they were both losers and that I was the one who had beaten them both because I was going to kill them and kill myself—in the name of Che, my real father.

Well, wasn't he? The man whose death had prodded me into life, prodded both Barón and McKenzie into the *rajadura*, the wound between my mother's legs. What would he have done if he were still alive? What would he have told his son Gabriel to do?

My Uncle Pancho had given me the answer that first time we'd talked in prison. Che would have blown the iceberg sky-high. Symbolic, it is true, but what other rebellion was possible today, when Che was being marketed by the Oscars and Nanos of the world, and the Indians he vowed to defend were putting their confidence in the Internet rather than the revolution, and the workers he was supposed to lead to victory were calculating in what corporate stocks to invest their pension funds—what better way to make a statement? I'm doing this to commemorate Che Guevara, the note I'd leave behind would say. I'd leave it for Cristina Ferrer to find at her hotel in Sevilla after Expo '92 ended: to protest the contamination of his memory. Not saying that I was also blowing up something more personal, for my own private reasons. Blowing up what joined me to my father McKenzie when I arrived in Chile, blowing it up, the ice that lured him down to Antarctica and made him accept me as his child. Blowing up what my father Barón had staked his future and his reputation on, the ice he used to bring me closer to him so he could play all the better with yours untruly. I'm the son of Che—Mom kept on saying it to me, you owe him, if not for him . . . Wasn't it Che who said that only violence can set the world right, put things back on course? I'd fuck the iceberg, just as the letters said.

And do it not only in the name of Che but in the name of the Nanny as well. Because she would have approved. She must have realized what I was doing, collaborated with my plot willingly, let herself be used. What better fate, she said one day, when I found her sighing over the death of a mother on one of her radio soaps. Why ask for more than to be eaten by those you love? She was eaten by me, had been secretly telling me all this time to eat her up. My secret secretary, writing out the letters I was dictating to her. Though she was really dictating them to me, so I could ultimately carry out those threats: there's something satisfying and almost smacking of true justice, yes, in my decision to explode the iceberg. I hadn't fully understood it back then, thought I was ghosting those letters, using Nana's laborious block capitals to manipulate my father and seek help. But in retrospect I see that I was writing my deepest intentions, my obituary, the many fragments of the iceberg I had anticipated the night I saw Antarctica on the many screens in New York, whispering to her how the iceberg would be sacrificed in Sevilla—everything in fact would be sacrificed, for my needs, anticipating the day, fifty years after my father's birth and twenty-five years after Che Guevara's burial, when I would end up destroying what I love.

Paying back to her, when you think of it, what my great-great-grandfather Wendell did, what my blood did to her blood, settling the debt. Completing the work she should have set herself instead of idiotically defending me, feeding me, singing me to sleep, taking the blame on behalf of her women, Milagros and Amanda Camila, taking the blame to free her men, Cristóbal and Gabriel, to roam and fuck some more—just a few more cunts before we die and disappear. She deserved something better than that final submissive message to the world. My Nana deserved to be there just like Che; my real mother and my real father would guide my hand, will be with me tonight, Janice, when I say goodbye to this world.

"Hey, everybody," I shouted to the rowdy crowd in the Casa Milagros, but not one of those people listened to me, not even Amanda Camila, who had managed to put on enough makeup to stagger forth into the New Year, determined to put bad times and dead babies behind her with the corrupt memories of 1991. Not even she heard my voice in the hullabaloo over what they all thought would be the best year in all their lives and in the life of the universe, not even she knew I existed. Polo did. He thrust a glass into my hand and, shouting *Feliz Año Nuevo* at the top of his lungs, he sprayed champagne into it and—"Oops"—he spouted it like a whale all over me, drenching me. On purpose. I answered by pretending I was slipping and grabbed hold of him, letting the glass fly. It bounced off him, soaking his shirt, and fell to the floor with a crash. Then they all looked up: people love to see something shatter, the glass there at my feet back then like the iceberg will be broken into a thousand particles in a few hours. That made them listen to me. Violence, Janice. Che knew what he was talking about. Nothing like a dash of violence for people to realize you matter.

"Oops," I said. "Sorry about that. But every accident has its benefits. And"—at this point addressing the expectant celebrants—"now that I have your attention, ladies, and if there are any gentlemen, yours as well, I want to announce my birthday present, what I'm going to give Cristóbal McKenzie and Pablo Barón."

"It's supposed to be a surprise," Jorge Larrea said. "Don't tell us."

"There'll be a surprise along with it," I said. "But I have to tell you now, because I don't want anybody else doing this. I want to be sure."

They all quieted down, waited for my announcement. I saw Polo, dripping and tense, I saw him get all nervous, anxious that I might offer his mentor something that would diminish his own gift. He shouldn't have worried.

"*Cazuela*," I said.

The folks at the party laughed.

"*Cazuela*," I repeated. "Nana's *cazuela*. That's what I'll cook for them and for whoever else is there that night. October 11, 1992. In Sevilla. All fresh ingredients. A Chilean dish in Sevilla. Cook it myself. From her secret recipe. That she confided only to me."

"That's a sweet idea," my mother said, kissing me.

"Beautiful," Amanda Camila agreed. Pale and shaky but full of hope, my Amanda, caught and bamboozled by the gods, believing like everybody else in the room that she could save herself, make things better. "Beautiful, Gaby. Nana would have been so happy."

"The best gift a son could give me," the great McKenzie said.

"You took the words right out of my mouth," Barón said, smirking to himself, his spectacles glinting like mine.

"I just want Nana to be there," I said to them. "I want her to smile on us, wherever she may be."

The rest was easy, has been easy.

Do I need to give you all the details?

How I convinced Pablo Barón and Jorge Larrea to put me on that boat, the *Aconcagua*, that was docking with the iceberg a few days later in Valparaiso on its way to Sevilla, how I wanted to make sure nobody would try to sabotage it before I did? How I accompanied my iceberg to the tropics, past the equator, following Drake's itinerary, listening to it growl and moan and call to me at night under the warm moon of the Pacific? How I came to Panama and crossed into the other ocean and left behind what Balboa saw and Magellan and Sarmiento de Gamboa navigated, entering the sea that Columbus crossed eight times in his four voyages, guiding the iceberg back the way the admiral came, that piece of Antarctica upon which it had been snowing for more than fifty thousand years when he first stepped on this land, on the land that the forefathers and foremothers of the Onas and my Nanny had touched? How I traversed the Sargasso Sea in reverse, murmuring the sights to the iceberg, blind in its container, telling it of the seagulls and the hot waves and the warm stormy clouds so different from the land of eternal ice of its birth, how I kept it company as if I were its Nana, escorting it toward the eyes of the world and toward death? How I suggested to the captain that we divert the ship to a different port to avoid the ecologists who might have injured it—Cadiz, I said—and how they listened to me, the defender of the iceberg, its lover—do you want to hear this, Janice? How our trucks sped along the cold steppes of Spain where Columbus returned when his journeys were over and the palm trees and the isle of the Caribs and the mythical mermaids were fading from his memory and he was heading for the other island of La Cartuja, where the World's Fair would commemorate what the courtiers of his time had denied him? How I rented this apartment in the street named after my extinct cousin Rodrigo de Triana, exiled forever from the sun of the New World his eyes had deflowered to no avail? How I surveyed day by day the installation of the Antarctic ice, heard its pain as Armando Jorquera worked with his saw on its blue fragments, how I watched carefully to make sure that nobody could harm it, that only I could harm it, that we would die together, both of us, the iceberg and me, how I became invisible like a postman, like the man who checks the water gauge, like the gardener who plants the flowers under the orange trees of the Alcázar, allowed to come in and come out by Don Jacinto's son Freddy as if I were the owner of the exhibition? How I became familiar with each stall in Sevilla's feria, each surrounding farm, began scouting the ingredients for that last meal? How I was there in April when the president of the Republic (but not Barón, not yet Barón, who was back in Chile running the country) inaugurated the pavilion, how I was there to watch the millions drink in the sights of that iceberg I had first recognized in Bahía Paraíso and convinced my father McKenzie to track down under the blanket of snow the next day? How they were astonished indeed by the new Chile, by *El Túnel de los Sonidos*, by the modern country we had become—does that really matter anymore? How I filled the days between April and October by picking up girls, picking them up in English and fucking them in Spanish, collecting nationalities the way children buy different Coca-Cola bottles of the countries they visit, German cunts and Pakistani cunts and a Russian hooker and one, I think, even from Senegal, though I couldn't tell you for sure because they form a blizzard, as if they were the same hole that I was trying to fill and that kept on reopening one or two nights later, an eclipse of skins and guttural throats in languages I did not care to learn a word of, not one memory of them tormenting my mind now, except maybe Cristina Ferrer, who reappeared from time to time to report on the World's Fair and the iceberg and to screw me, the best McKenzie of them all, how she dressed up like Carmen just for me and rolled cigarettes on her naked thighs as if she were in some sort of porno film—does any of this matter to you if it did not matter to me? How I celebrated my birthday, twenty-four years on this earth, July 9, 1992, the first anniversary of the day I desired to plunge into the inside of those green eyes of Amanda's, how I bought a ticket to see *Don Juan Tenorio* at the Teatro Lope de Vega, Zorrilla's play where the don is saved by the love of Inés, a nun, at the end—a false romantic ending instead of Tirso's scoundrel who was dragged to hell by the statue of the Comendador—how I left in disgust at the end of the performance and swore no woman would save me, save the iceberg, save my two fathers, who sent enthusiastic letters announcing their arrival soon, soon? How one day in early October I set out for Prague to meet Milagros and Cristóbal, who were taking the honeymoon they had never had time for, how they went to see *Don Giovanni* at the opera house where the first performance had been staged by Mozart himself, and how I went the same night to watch a puppet version of it, a buffoonish, slapstick, sprawling condensation in which everybody was a fool and everybody was saved? How all three of us arrived in Sevilla—Sevilla, Janice, which a thirteenth-century Moor described as a city whose inhabitants were the most frivolous and the most given to playing the fool—and there was my Amanda Camila, still thinking she was my sister while I still played the fool? Does it matter that I almost yielded to the temptation, seeing her resplendent, forgiving figure there, of wanting to start over, and how that very day we all went to *la corrida de toros* and I watched the bull be taunted into death, weakened and bled into death, and refused, unlike the forty thousand other spectators at *la real maestranza*, to take out my white handkerchief and give him a second chance, a lease on life? How I screamed with ritual glee as the sword went into the hump of his trembling back, enjoyed Amanda Camila's horror and compassion? Do you need to know how one day I accompanied her to the Archivo del Consejo de Indias to look up what Tomé Hernández, the sole survivor of Puerto Hambre, had dictated to a scribe about the Onas, how we strolled in the streets of El Arenal and tried every tapa in every bar as if we had forever in front of us, how I fooled her into thinking we had forever, and we sat in a café in front of *La Catedral* and refused to let the gypsies read our palms? Like a brother and sister, like two lovers who are too old to make love anymore, apparently at peace, she was ready, at least, to bury the past and face another day.

Details, Janice, so many days and details: how I said goodbye to the world, the whole world, there in Sevilla, a different pavilion each day, until I had exhausted every corner of the globe and was ready to leave this earth, had planned it all so I could have three days left in which to write and send this letter, the last task I required myself to complete before my mission ends: to have someone read this after I'm done, have you awaken in your own America, Janice, some day in mid-October of 1992, and find the last traces of my existence there, the explanation of why I left, why I never sent even a message, why you'll never hear from me again.

And that's all I need to tell you.

The day is drawing to a close on the Guadalquivir and the city of Don Juan is beckoning.

Am I really going to do it? Am I really going to kill myself and the two faces that spawned me twenty-five years ago while my mother's face, the third female face, watches, while Amanda Camila pleads with me not to do it? Am I really going to blow up the iceberg that I helped carve into birth?

That's for me to know and you to find out.

EPILOGUE

OCTOBER 9–12, 1992

•

"Io non morii, e non rimasi vivo"

(I did not die and I did not remain alive)

—ARIOSTO, *ORLANDO FURIOSO*, AS QUOTED BY

GIACOMO CASANOVA IN HIS AUTOBIOGRAPHY

You're not doing this right, *niño* Gabriel.

No, I don't mean your life. That's *más que claro*—even an idiot would realize the trouble you're in, the mess you've made of things since I haven't been around to help you. No, I mean the *cazuela*.

I've been trying to contact you since I died, *mi niño*, and now that I can finally do it, what's this, what am I seeing? That water's about to boil. Didn't I tell you that the water's supposed to be hot but not boiling, just hot enough to make sure that it'll be easier a few minutes later to pluck the feathers from the hen? Good. You've lowered the flame, extinguished it. Good. As if you could hear me. My friend who's right by my side, he's sure you can't, you won't, that it's useless to try and contact you. But look, I say to him, Gabriel's listening to me, Che, he's putting the hens in the water just like I told him.

"You told him while you were alive and he's remembering your instructions," Che says. My friend Che doesn't believe in this, any of it. He's cooperating with me because he has no other choice, really. He knows we'll be shut in here together for a long, long time and he wants to stay on my good side. It took me three days—counting time, that is, the way the living do on earth, Gabriel—three whole days to convince this Guevara fellow to help me help you. *Sí, tú*, I'm speaking to you, Gabriel McKenzie, there in the *Pabellón Chileno en Sevilla*, the son of my Milagros there furiously plucking the feathers off the dead hens, you see how smoothly they come off? Then, *mi niño*, you have to hang each bird over a slow fire—burn away those quills that are still left bristling in the skin, just like you burn the chafe after the harvest—and now this Guevara fellow speaks out. "Like the stubble of a beard on a man's face," he says, rubbing his own beard, and I welcome the fact that he's even decided to contribute that comment, though you won't be surprised to find out that he knows nothing about cooking, nothing about anything domestic. Maybe I should tell you right away that I don't see eye to eye with Che on everything, in fact, we agree on very little else, the two of us here, but that you're a fool, Gabriel McKenzie, it's God's truth, we both agree on that. And one other thing: that you shouldn't kill yourself or the others, we agree about that, if nothing else. If it's up to me I won't let this end tragically, and as for him, well, he's ready to act as my assistant, even if he is reluctant and *descreído*, still doesn't believe, even here, that God exists.

You hesitate, you look around as if I were in the room as you prepare the *cazuela*. But you can't see me. Can barely hear me. The echo of my echo. I could be confused with a breeze, but yes, it's me, your Nana.

You stop now for a second, you've already washed and rubbed the skin under the stream of water from the faucet, but now your fingers leave their task of cleaning out the *tripas* and the blood—don't forget to throw away the *interiores*, the heart and liver are no good for *cazuela*—you stand there as if transfixed and listen to my faint voice inside your head. You remember the voices that howled silently underneath the wind in Patagonia, the sad sound of ice on groaning ice in Bahía Paraíso, you wonder why now of all times you're recalling me, you wonder if I've forgiven you.

What if I were to tell you that I have nothing to forgive? You're not ready to accept that possibility, Gabrielito, not yet at least, not even ready to admit that you can hear me: guilt is eating you up alive. Look at how you're cutting the *gallina* with that kitchen knife, breaking the bones of the *espinazo* as if it were your own backbone you were gashing. Don't do that. When you put it in the broth it'll dissolve, and all those fractured tiny bones can stick in the throat. I told you that the first time I made *cazuela*, told you that the *espinazo* gives the soup a special flavor, you have to let it simmer in the pot along with the *cogote*, the neck of each hen you've just wrung, violently twisting it across your knee as if it were a human being, and you did it much too forcefully, not even asking the hen permission for taking its life, not even thanking it for giving up the sun and energy it has stored inside its juices, but you were lucky in this case that you did it with such hatred, because that's what convinced Che. When he saw your hands strangling the hens, one after the other, he said to me, "This kid's going to do it," Che said, "*este tonto*'s really going to kill himself and the others."

That's when he agreed to participate in this attempt to reach you. Because I needed him to say yes, this fellow Guevara, this Che fellow had to say yes.

How come we're together? Well, I'd have to explain certain things about how this place works. I'm calling it a place, a space, because I don't have another word, in fact I have no words at all here, just thoughts and they're translated into words for the benefit of mortals like you, Gabriel, but I can't say more about where we happen to be. My lips are sealed. No, I mean really sealed. Not sealed like I promised when you told me about your problems. I had to tell my shadow Milagros. I said I'd only tell my shadow, so I didn't really lie. Here I can't lie anyway, it's forbidden. I mean, there's no need to forbid anything because you can't lie: everybody and anybody can read your thoughts right on your forehead, glowing like wings, so why try to hide them? Though we're allowed to keep some secrets; some things we don't need to show or tell anybody. Che won't show me his pain, the pain in the hands that they—and me, well, the less said the better.

We're together, Che and your Nana, to get back to the question that you haven't asked but that you would ask if you'd heard even a hint of what I've been murmuring to you—and you mustn't let me distract you from the main task, getting that *cazuela* into shape. You put all those *presas de ave* in the pot, that's it. You've thrown out the almost boiling water and cleaned the pot and filled it with cold water now, placed the pieces in there with the pepper, the cumin, a small bouquet of parsley tied together with a thin string, oregano. Don't forget the salt. Don't light that fire until everything's in there, then let things boil for forty-five minutes. You'll need the time to get everything else ready. Anyway, we're together, Che and your Nana, because of you. That's what we've figured out, what I suggested to him when he asked who the hell I was as soon as I walked in the door, his first visitor in twenty-five years, this *vieja*.

I'm Mercedes, I say to him. He's shocked, hasn't seen a soul since he died, and it's me. I feel like reaching out, taking his hand, but that's frowned on here, it's not done over here, to touch one another. And certainly not to touch him.

"Mercedes what?" he asks.

Just Mercedes, I answer. I never use my last name. I'm a Nana.

"Used to be a Nana," Che says.

No, I answered him quite firmly. I'm still a Nana. Once a Nana . . . And my boy's in trouble.

I told him that for the last eleven months, earth time, that is, almost a year, ever since I passed away, I'd been pestering the people in charge, the people who run this *casa*, to pair me with someone who could help *mi niño*, nagging them so persistently, they said, that they finally sent me to him. This man Guevara, he's about ready to receive a visitor, they said and thrust me into the room where he'd been alone since his death, waiting, watching the world go mad, he says, twenty-five years to the day since he was killed.

You are what joins us, *niño* Gabriel. That's what I explained to Che. The fact that you're about to do this stupid murderous act in our name, my name and his name. The fact that I can't save you by myself. You're such a fool, *hijo*, that you need two guardian angels: one won't do.

Che said, "That boy of yours is in sad shape." He said it as soon as I told him your problems, and I answered, He's your boy more than he's mine. By the time Gabriel came to me you had failed, made a mess of things, Che, left him all confused with your sainthood that he could never live up to, your heroic poster on his wall, all that macho talk about how you hadn't died, and for a while after that we didn't speak to each other. But then I cooked Che something nice, *pastel de choclo* it was, and over our meal he told me some beautiful stories, he told me how he'd crossed the whole continent on his motorbike and about the wasted lives he'd seen and how he'd sworn that he would not let them waste, that this was the worst sin; he told me about the peasants up in the Sierra Maestra when he'd been a guerrilla. I liked the idea of a Sierra being a Maestra, a Schoolteacher, and he laughed at that, said Maestra meant the Most Important Sierra, and I said,

There's nothing more important than a woman who can teach the young, and he liked that, so we became friends again. And that's when I invited him to eavesdrop on you and your plans. We listened in on the letter you've been typing on that machine to that Janice woman whom you've never made love to, and I couldn't help myself. What a fool, *mi Gabriel*, I exclaimed, and Che nodded his head and sighed, and that's when I popped the question, did he think there was anything that could be done?

There's a rule here that you can whisper messages to the other side, try at least, as long as two sponsors approve the attempt to cross the border, and of the two, one must have personally known the subject who's still alive back on earth, and the other can under no circumstance have ever met that subject, cannot even have shared a moment on the planet with him. And Che qualifies by a thread as my collaborator in this stab at a breakthrough because he died the day before you were conceived. It's a rule to make sure none of us spirits, if that is what you wish to call us, decide to interfere in worldly matters on our own: you have to be supported by someone else. And let me tell you, it's pretty hard to convince the old-timers. I've gone to everybody under and out of the sun, Gabrielito, oh, you can believe me that I've been busy. Soon as I saw that you were headed in the wrong direction, the first one I approached was some *tipo* called Ramses the Second, a difficult old coot—rumor had it that he'd never helped anybody in all the time he'd been here—never so much as sent a dream somebody's way—and I was no different. He didn't even acknowledge my presence. I kept on trying, manifested myself to any number of others while you were destroying your existence and meeting that Max on the Cerro and planning death and heading for Sevilla, and each time all I got was a rejection: your Gabriel's a fool, not worth the effort. So I guess I'm lucky. Or you are. Or it's been planned that way. Because yours are not the only plans in the universe, Gaby.

Yes. Those are the rules, *mi niño*. As long as I don't *do* anything. Just voices, just these words inside you, Gabriel, which you'll attribute, according to Che, to your own psychosis. I think that's what he called it, I'm getting a real education up here like I never got down there, all these fancy words. At any rate, Che is sure you'll explain away what you're hearing as a delusion, won't accept that you're receiving a message from this island of afterdeath. I mean, what sort of spirit from beyond the grave tells one of the living to slice the carrots into small sticks after he's peeled them, what sort of unearthly voice, Che asks me, reminds the recipient to cut the onion in four—that's right, in four, and if you cry a bit it'll do you good, *mi niño*—and to make sure when he slips each piece into the water that it's floating and doesn't come apart and also to be careful not to overdo the onions, because they'll stink the whole *cazuela* up? Who would believe that a ghost would come all the way from beyond the beyond to give cooking instructions, Che wonders, when you could be shaping big issues, inspiring the world to change its ways, end poverty and injustice, haunting some capitalist's night?

You scratch my back, I say to Che, I'll scratch yours. First you save my boy, then you can concentrate on the world. And besides, I add, I know what I'm doing. If my Gabriel's not interested, he can switch me off right this minute as if I were an old radio station transmitting a nice tearjerker like the ones I used to like to listen to in the afternoons. Maybe that's how I want your story to end, *mi niño*, full of tears of joy. But it's really up to you. If your heart is not open, these words will slip by like the dirt on the *calabaza* that you're scrubbing clean, good boy, that's the way to do it. "That petit-bourgeois moron's switched you off before you even said the word *cazuela*," Che says. "Of all the people I'm given the opportunity to save, it's this immoral, apolitical, horny, weak McKenzie of yours. A gringo! A kid who preferred the United States to Latin America!"

He gets like that, angry at times, self-righteous. He insists whenever he can that I'm to blame for what happened to you. "It's symbolic," Che says. "If you had rebelled, if everybody like you had rebelled, none of this would have happened. The kid would have had an alternative instead of being screwed by everyone and trying to screw them back. People like you who don't do anything to change society are the ones who put the young in an impossible situation."

As for me, Gabriel, I think Che's to blame, though I won't tell him that. No need to get him upset and start another argument. I need him to help me out, but this Guevara man is in fact at fault. He is the one who proclaimed that by killing others you could solve the hurt of the world. He is the one—a man who abandoned his own family—in whose name you are doing this, killing your own father. And no, I won't tell you which of the two, Barón or McKenzie, is the real one; I wouldn't tell you even if the rules allowed it. Just like I won't tell you other things either, *mi niño*, things about myself, my secrets. What you didn't find out about me during my life I won't tell you from my death. *Ya te dije*: I won't tell anybody, not even Che. As if it mattered that much if I was an Ona or a Mapuche, if I'm a virgin or if I made love.

What's more urgent is to remind you, Gabriel, that you've left out the garlic. So, quick, plop it in. It's good for your memory, helps whoever eats it to have an alert mind. And now put the head of garlic in, the whole head, like you should.

See, I say to Che. You see how he can hear me?

Che shrugs his shoulders. We both watch you throw the slices of green peppers in there; the water is already boiling. You can cook them forever and they won't lose their flavor or their crispness. Isn't that a perfect pungent sharp smell that green peppers offer to the air? They're also pretty—they decorate and give *sabor* as well. But Che isn't cheered up. Sad, my Che is. So I feel like giving him a good hug, rocking him in my arms like I did you, Gabriel. He turns *melancólico* when he thinks of that other place, Bolivia, where his dreams did not come true, where people with my color skin and my dark eyes and their clothes in tatters and without shoes saw him go by in the jungle and did not join him, even betrayed him, the Indians did, to the authorities. He gave up his life for them and they didn't care.

"I'd do it again," he says. "What was I to do?" he asks. "Let them die? They were starving, their children were looking more like skeletons every year, they were losing their teeth and their language. And they're not much better off now than they were twenty-five years ago, and twenty-five years from now it'll be worse. So I was supposed to close my eyes and not give a damn. Like your *niño* Gabriel? Is that what I was supposed to do? Live my life as a doctor in Buenos Aires and cure a couple of patients and drink a thousand cocktails and fuck some women and then step off the face of the earth without changing any of the pain? Or cook like you did for the people who never even found out who you were? Who never asked you the right questions, any questions? Who kept living after you died as if nothing had happened?"

You never had a Nana? I ask him, keeping an eye on you, Gabrielito, making sure that you've cut the stems off the green beans.

"I did," Che says. "She came from Galicia, she raised me. My mother was always somewhere else, swimming, off by herself. I also had a Tía—Beatriz. I really loved her."

Ask your Nana, I say to him, ask her what it means to have a child held to your body, to bring him into the world not once, at birth, but over and over again in the many minutes and fruits of the day, to cook for that child. If you gave children milk, if you gave them the bottle like I did with Milagros and Gabriel, if you woke them up in the morning with a kiss like I did little Amandita, ask your Nana how you are woven together by the hand of God. Ask her if you would have ever cared about the poor if she had not kept the fire going, put a bandage on your wound, helped you to breathe when your lungs began to heave and die. Ask her what the world would be like if we were all like that with one another, all of us Nanas to one another. Ask her if she could ever abandon that child no matter what that child did, no matter what harm, ask her. Ask her if you would not do anything for one minute with that child, to tell him not to kill himself, not to kill others. Ask her.

"If they ever let me out of here," Che answered, "and I can find her, I'll ask her. But only if you ask your mother why she wasn't there for you, who killed her, who came and killed your people, who made you a servant and somebody else the master."

Maybe we have been put here together in order to learn. He'd been waiting for twenty-five years for somebody, anybody, to show up. When I came in three days ago, just as you started typing your letter, well, my Ernesto wasn't pleased. He wanted someone called Fidel, that fellow in Cuba. He wanted someone he could gab and discuss and conspire with for all eternity. "Instead," he complains, "after a quarter of a century with no company at all, just watching the world turn greedier and insane and slick and not a thing I can do to alter it from here, condemned to watching my image become a teacup or a T-shirt, who do they send me but you, old woman, *vieja*. Why you of all the possible dead in the universe?"

Maybe this is how we prepare for the next stage, we meet here and have it out, like two prisoners in a cell, like man and wife, like two best friends. Maybe he's my bridegroom for all eternity until I learn something from him or he learns something from me. Both of us died alone after all, more alone than when we were born. Who's to know?

Lovers brought together by their long-lost son, by you, Gabriel. To tell you we are not happy with these plans to destroy yourself and the iceberg.

And Che, by the way, wants you to know that there is no iceberg to unplug, to destroy. Yes, I know, I know, you've seen it, it's the same blue glare of ice that you saw torn from the legs of Antarctica, but he insists that it isn't. He's got good intelligence, he says. That's the most important thing, to have the right information, he says. "If I'd known they were heading me off at La Higuera . . ." Anyway, he claims that four nights before the inauguration of the expo back in April, the refrigeration system broke down. They brought in experts, they were desperate. The thing was melting in front of their eyes. By the time they fixed it, the iceberg had half melted, a good part of it was just a puddle, streaming into the sewer. So they got local ice, they mixed it in with the frozen core and ice flown in from Norway, they made a *menjunje*, a brew, like a *cazuela* in fact, *niño* Gabriel, and they cast the lights so it would look a transparent blue. I sense that he's saying this because he wants you to think that you'd only be blowing up an illusion, a mirage, he says, as false as the tomb of Columbus in the cathedral of Sevilla. You'd only be exploding Spanish water mixed in with a few shards from Chile and some crushed ice from the North Pole, Santa Claus ice, Che calls it, laughing, the North and the South finally meeting with no one to take a photo of the occasion. The truth is, I don't know what he's talking about. But if it helps you to refrain from using those sticks of dynamite, well, bless my companion Ernesto, good for him. He's beginning to believe that we can turn this around. He's starting to view this as a real challenge, almost like a guerrilla campaign: infiltrate the world and snipe at it, establish a *foco* and rescue a lost soul. But even if I welcome his increasing enthusiasm—which may come from the smell of that *cazuela* that is wafting through the *aire* so deliciously that it even reaches this beyond where we watch you—I prefer to trust something else to convince you. Let's say you don't blow up the iceberg. We still haven't solved the real problem: what's in your heart, how you hate yourself, how you've ended up hating all of them and wanting them dead, how blind you've been all through your life to the roads you could have taken, the people who could have really helped you. If we don't solve that emptiness inside you, that strangling of hope as if it were the

347

delicate twisted neck of a bird, it's all the same how real or how false that piece of ice is. It's no more than that. A piece of ice. And it means only what you want it to mean. No more. No less.

And for that, what we need is a change of heart. With less than an hour and a half to midnight. And I have nothing else at hand but the *cazuela*. It's the only one that can whisper to you. It's human and vegetable and animal and liquid, food that you chose yourself, that I taught you to cook when I was alive. The only way for you to start seeing what you should have seen all this time and . . . Though this is not why I'm speaking to you. I haven't contacted you from so far away just to scold you. What you don't understand by yourself, *mi niño*, it's useless to say anyway.

"Why are you wasting our time, then?" Che asks, suddenly skeptical again.

To open a space for him, for Gabriel McKenzie. That's all we can do. Keep the fools in this world company and let them figure it out for themselves. Just open that little space where you can breathe. A space where God can show herself. God! Che scoffs. But you don't need to listen to him, that nonbeliever. Things could be worse here, I say to him. "Yes," he says. "They could have forced me to put on a Mickey Mouse mask and show visitors around, greet newcomers, cheer up children who have just died of cancer or whose teenage parents have thrown them in the garbage, or tell an old man who was evicted from his hellhole of a room after his hands built that city, tell that man who died of starvation on the streets he paved, tell him that it's all right, he got what he deserved, the universe is fair when some get nothing and others get all. They could have punished me with that sort of madness. Worse still, they could have reincarnated me as a millionaire. Instead, I'm here with you. And you're not a bad sort," Che says. "A bit of an ass licker, a bit of a traitor to your class, but you can learn."

"Thanks," I say. "You're not that bad a sort yourself. I appreciate that you've offered to help save one. Just one, I say. The one who deserves it least. The one who is beyond redemption."

"The Christian delusion," Che says.

"I don't care what you call it," I say. "Just one. If you can find it in your heart . . ."

Che sighs. He thinks of all the years ahead of us. "So how do you intend to convince your *niño* Gabriel?" Che asks. "Your child seems to be rather determined to carry out his plans."

I don't answer Che. Because . . . the cooking needs my attention. Gaby, keep your eyes on that *olla*, the hens are about to be done. While they're still *blandos*, that's when you put the green beans in—in they go, thinly sliced, almond-shaped so the seeds look like eyes peeping at us, and I am looking at you, all the dead are looking at you from the eyes of the green beans. Now this would be when you should pour the rice in as well, though I like your decision not to use any rice tonight. It adds to the substance, that's true, but you're not poor, you don't need to fill ten bellies with food that should be eaten by two or three. When I was a girl we used to put a lot of rice in the *cazuela* but I've always thought the perfect world would be one where you use rice for other things, not to fool a hungry stomach.

"Hey," Che says, "you're learning, old girl. You'll turn into a revolutionary yet. Though you haven't answered my question. How are you—"

I shush him up. This man's got to learn to keep quiet when important things are happening, and that pot's been on the fire for forty-five minutes, right, *mi niño*, and now's when you put in what can't be overcooked. What you've been preparing in a separate smaller pot, just as I told you, boiling it apart for thirty minutes in just a bit of water with salt, whole potatoes, and big pieces of yellow pumpkin. Lord, how I loved *calabaza* when I was alive, and I see you've also managed to find corn, clean, beautiful ears stripped of their long beards.

"All of them from the New World," Che says. "You realize that now he's cooking what the Indians discovered and gave to humanity. Your brat could put a tomato in there and then it'd be perfect," Che says. I tell him to please mind his own business, *cazuela* doesn't have tomatoes, even if they are American plants.

"*Cazuela*," Che says, "I get it. The meeting of the hens and carrots and onions from the Old World with the vegetables and tubers from the New one, that's what you're teaching him. How it all comes together, the two worlds can come together instead of tearing him apart."

That's not what I'm teaching him at all, I say. Just the joy of cooking for somebody else. If Gabriel could only understand, if you could, Ernesto Guevara, then we'd be in better shape. And you've almost diverted Gabriel's attention with your intellectual musings, he almost made a mistake. Right, *mi amor*, you add the water in which the potato and pumpkin and corn have been cooking, slowly, using the *tapa* of the pot to strain it, that's the way, into the main pot, the larger one where the hens are ready. And be sure to keep the vegetables apart till the last moment, especially the potatoes—they are so greedy, they love to absorb the taste, dissolve, they are really badly behaved. But we love them anyway, don't we?

"Potatoes," Che says. "Let me tell you how the discovery of potatoes changed the history of Europe, like sugar did later. If there hadn't been that sort of cheap, substantial food around, there'd never have been an industrial revolution, though when the famine came to Ireland—"

Later, Doctorcito Guevara, we'll speak about this later. What we want to make sure of now is that the *cazuela* not only tastes like heaven but looks *una maravilla* as well. Because Gabriel's scraped the carrots and then fried the gratings in oil until they're ready. Look at that dark orange color that you're supposed to add to the soup at the very last moment so it doesn't look sickly. Many years ago people used to think a yellow greasy look was a sign of health. But it's much nicer if you have a deeper, rich color. I feel like coming back to life only to savor a bit of it with a spoon. Not all illusions are bad, Gabrielito. Once in a while it's all right to fool others, hide from others, pretend things are prettier than they really are.

So now you're almost ready and you can hear the guests in the next room. You can hear the champagne bottles being uncorked as the birthday approaches—and now's when I can answer Che's question, how do we convince him to end the five hundred years with a feast and not with an explosion, how do we convince him that it's better to be alive than dead?

"Hold it," Che says. "I want it clear that I'm not against violence. In the case of the iceberg, it's silly, counterproductive. But violence against those who have used institutional violence to keep illegitimate power . . ." Che wants that clear. He wants it on the record. What record, I ask, what are you talking about? "I'm still in favor of violence," he says, "haven't changed my ideas this much, not this little bit."

Well, I answer him, if you haven't changed your ideas one little bit, then you're probably somewhat of a fool yourself. A good fellow, great heart, my boy Che, but I don't see that you've made the world much better by what you did. But you'll have plenty of eternities ahead to make me see the light. Now we have an immediate problem. An urgent problem. In a bit under an hour it will be time for Gabriel to take out that gun he has smuggled inside one of those empty pots, and he's going to point it at Cristóbal McKenzie and at Pablo Barón and will have his eager Tío Pancho tie them up to one of the columns of the iceberg and then he'll make a speech in which he'll invoke your name and maybe even mine and then he'll tell Amanda and Milagros and all the other guests to leave and then he'll light the fuse and then they'll be dead—and you can discuss politics and injustice and revolution when you meet him here in this room, you'll have all the time out of this world to convince him what he should have done. But if we don't save him now, right now, he'll never even have the chance to do it. Right? So stop asking him to desist in the name of the great ideals and the future of mankind, because that won't work with him. It may have worked with you, but not with him. That's why he is who he is. Like most of the people alive, he's not listening to what you have to say. They didn't listen back then, they're listening even less now. So—are you ready to help me?

"You're the boss," Che says, "like the father of Milagros used to say, like McKenzie used to say, like Barón used to say."

For once, they're right. I am the boss.

Look, I say to Che, my boy's already softened. He doesn't even realize that it's happening, the food has been talking to him, each potato has been telling him what it meant to sleep in the earth, each ear of corn has been murmuring that under the ice there is land, under his ice is land, the smell wafting out of the pot has been talking to him.

Now is the crucial moment. Now Gabriel has to allow the *cazuela reposo*, let it settle, rest, doze before being served. If he remembers my instructions, he'll warm up the plates. But never ever make people eat things boiling hot. Now's when he has nothing to do with his hands but wait five, ten minutes. Amanda Camila comes in and he asks her, oh so gently, as if he loves the way her name sounds, loves to have her name in his mouth, asks her if she'd mind telling everybody to take their seats at the table in front of the iceberg, that he'll start serving the plates with the Nana's *cazuela* very soon.

Yes, *mi niño* Gabriel, you like things hot. Even as a child you were always demanding I warm the milk more, more, but there's also patience, *mi niño*. I've told Che this because he doesn't seem to know much about patience either. He's also too much in love with heat and fire, but he nodded his head and said something about objective conditions. I don't know what that means, but I do know that you shouldn't eat your food before it's ready, you shouldn't push things too hard or they'll push back. And besides, you need to give all those wonderful cooked things time to get to know one another quietly, not in the agitated boil but the way you say goodbye when the family's journey together has been good and the journey coming up promises to be even better, time for them to say to one another, See you inside a plate, inside a mouth, down a throat, through a stomach, turned into energy, that man and that woman will use me tonight to make love. I will be there with you, brother potato, sister carrot, as they make love.

Only five or ten minutes, this settling-in process.

Just enough time to take a last breather before you serve, trying to portion it all out equally, like a mother with her chicks, the way I taught you before you even knew how to walk.

Listen to the food, Gabriel. It's telling you that this is not going to end the way you planned. You look in that soup and you see me, how I brought you into this world, how I allowed your mother to give birth to you, how I steered her into Cristóbal's arms. I am responsible, finally, for your existence. You belong to me, you belong to others. You're not going to die without having given the others something of yourself.

I won't let you. *No te dejaré.*

Can you hear me?

You want guarantees that everything is going to turn out all right, that if you allow yourself this reprieve, if you go back on your vow to blow everything up, you won't find yourself full of grief.

I can't give you that guarantee. The guarantee that hope is rewarded.

Will you get together again with Amanda Camila, will she want to, do you feel you can risk it? I don't know, I can't tell. Will your mother stay on with Cristóbal McKenzie, who may or may not be your father, will he love you if he thinks you are not his son? Will Pablo Barón guide the country into the twenty-first century, will he be able to love Amanda if he finds out she may not be his daughter? Will you emerge from the pavilion tomorrow as October 12 breaks open the night and will a tall woman walking as if on air approach you and say, I'm Janice, I tracked you down and I don't need any letter from you to know that we should start all over again, come back to the States with me, the world is born all over again every second, some come and some go? Is that what the future holds? Or will she not be there and will there instead be a message from Oscar and Nano that they've found the money for your magazine and are ready to go into business with you—a solution that Che definitely disapproves of but that millions would jump at? Or will you send Oscar and Nano a courteous refusal and return to Chile and find Victoria and offer her your help, even if you have to fight Max, get beaten up by Max, offer Victoria your services, your skills, that brain of yours, those hands you hate so much, in the hope—you are male, after all—that one night when she's peering over your shoulder at what you are tap-tap-tapping on your computer, you'll both fall into bed? Or is it Patagonia you want to return to, want to start seeing, and Antarctica, really, really seeing it instead of passing over its surface in search of your own image? Take the iceberg, true or false as it may be, back to its mother, back to Paradise Bay? Is that what you want? I don't know. Che doesn't know or won't say. How are we to guess where your human heart will take you? If you won't wander forever?

So now you ladle it out into the dishes, all in a row, the dish for Milagros and the dish for Amanda Camila and the dish for Cristóbal McKenzie and the dish for Pablo Barón and the dish for Polo and the dish for each and every one of the guests, Armando and Larrea and Tío Pancho, all of them here at the end that is a beginning, and finally a bowl of *cazuela* for yourself, Gabriel. The fact that you are going to serve yourself food and eat what I helped you cook—no, it won't erase the past, the past is always there even when we don't remember it. You won't get rid of it that easily, no, that's not what I'm promising you. I'm promising you that if you put one piece of hen on each plate, one potato, one slice of pumpkin, one third of an ear of corn, if you sift through the bottom of the soup and make sure each and every one of them—including you, include yourself among them!—has some vegetables, some green beans, some onions, if then, only then, you ladle out the broth itself, where all the best of every last thing in that *cazuela* has deposited its hope, as has been happening since the world was made, since the earth has been loving us enough to keep us alive, I'm promising you that this will taste like heaven. That's all I can promise, and no guarantees about what might happen after that. You could slip on a banana peel outside the pavilion and break your neck and die in a hospital in Spain like Columbus did or you could see the light and understand how humanity can be saved and go on to be one of the great men of the next century, but I can tell you this: if you add the final touch of coriander, if you finish this *cazuela* by sprinkling on the cilantro as you should, this I can promise you: your *cazuela* will be as good as anything I ever cooked.

So now you're ready.

They are calling you from the other room.

Amanda Camila and Cristóbal and Polo and Milagros and Pablo and Francisco.

Your family.

You hesitate. I see you hesitate. You look at the match in your hand. The last time you used a match, from the same box, it was to light the flame with which you cooked the soup that you must now serve for the fiftieth birthday of the two men who made you who you are.

Now the moment of truth, the moment of fire, has finally come. The moment when you will decide whether what you have just cooked is the last supper of America's first five hundred years or if it's our first breakfast, whether the next five hundred years are going to be any better.

Che and I look at your eyes, try to guess from your eyes what you will do.

This is the moment I choose to reach across the infinite space that separates us and take one of Che's hands in my hand. Yes. One of his hands.

It is the first time somebody has touched him since he died, the first time I have touched somebody. It is forbidden. It is not what we do over here.

Háblale, Che, I say. Speak to him. Let him hear your voice as well as mine.

Che looks at you, Gabriel, he looks at you in front of all those plates, the steam from the food rising up to your eyes, and then he begins to sing, he sings something in a low voice. It is a language I have never heard. "*Nonantzin,*" he sings, "*ihcuac nimiquiz mitlecuilpan xinechtoca.*" And then he translates: "My little mother, when I die, bury me next to your home and when you make tortillas by the door, then start to cry for me. *Ihcuacu tiaz tetlazcalchihuac ompa nopampa xichoca.* It's in *Nahautl,*" Che whispers. "The language of your cousins, the Aztecs. I learned it in Mexico from a woman who died of asthma, she died because she had no medicine, no medical attention. She died like all the mothers of the world die. This is what she left me, this song, a contemporary song." Che hums the melody a bit more and then goes on in that deep, sad voice of his: "And if someone comes to ask you, little mother, Nonantzin, why do you cry? *Ihuan tla acah mit-zlatlaniz: Nonantzin, tleca tichoca? Xiquilhuiz ca xocohui in cahuil ihuan in nechochoctia ica cecenca popoca.* Little mother, if someone comes to ask you, why do you cry? Tell them that the wood is green and that it is the smoke that makes you cry. It is the smoke that makes you cry."

Now Che puts his head on my lap and I let him do it. I rock him gently. *Mi niño*, I say to him, I'll take care of you. Until the end of time.

And then together we wait, the two of us, his broken hand in my hand, his head in my lap, we wait from so near and so far for your decision, Gabriel McKenzie, we wait like two lovers about to give birth, we wait as if the fate of the world depended on it.

I wish to thank history for providing me with the incredible central event of this novel: the fact that in 1992 the Chilean government did indeed exhibit an iceberg from Antarctica in its pavilion in Sevilla as part of the World's Fair. It was this bizarre way of celebrating the five hundred years since Columbus's voyage across the Atlantic that allowed me to first conceive the idea behind *The Nanny and the Iceberg*. As I imagined the rest of the story, I did my best to investigate and follow carefully the true historical trajectory of that real-life iceberg. I documented, for instance, the date when the project was announced, the date when the expedition to Antarctica was organized and who was on board the ship, and the dates when it arrived in Spain and when it was dismantled. But these factually correct incidents are the only ones in the novel that have not been fabricated. All the characters, situations, dialogue, threats, and escapades are entirely my invention.

I wish to stress this circumstance. Many of the people involved with the project of the iceberg—those who were enthralled by it and those who were its detractors—are friends or acquaintances of mine. One of my next-door neighbors in Santiago, for example, was the artistic adviser to the project. The entrepreneur whose company organized the installation of the iceberg and of the pavilion itself is the brother of one of my good friends: that same young boy whom I used to watch playing soccer in his parents' garden was extremely helpful many years later when I came to question him about the motives behind this attempt to sell a different image of Chile. Not to mention that my good friend and former brother-in-law, the very talented filmmaker Ignacio Agüero, was on that expedition and filmed it, producing a weird hallucinated movie documenting the whole voyage. I would not want it thought that I had him in mind when I made up an absolutely different filmmaker. Having already endured a bothersome experience with my play *Death and the Maiden*, which people (not only Chileans) treated as a tragedy à clef, pestering me at great length about the "true" identities of the characters, particularly determined to identify the invented lawyer, Gerardo Escobar, with a friend of mine who was serving on the Chilean Truth Commission, I hope my protestations will guarantee that it is useless to seek historical models for the men and women in *The Nanny and the Iceberg*. I am sure that some stubborn readers will nevertheless try to figure out who Minister Pablo Barón really is and will probably see in him a not-so-veiled reference to Enrique Correa, who served in Patricio Aylwin's democratic government as a sort of minister for information and was, I believe, greatly enthusiastic about the iceberg's being transported to Sevilla. No such parallel or connection crossed my mind.

If it is history that is to blame or to praise for the iceberg's existence and certainly for the fact that Chile's transition to democracy after the Pinochet dictatorship was indeed accompanied by a process of euphoric and accelerated modernization as well as by bouts of collective and selective amnesia, it gave me a very different sort of helping hand by supplying me with a group of real people who nourished me as I navigated the many waters of this story.

As always, my first thanks go to my wife and first reader, Angélica, without whose presence, patience, and critical judgment I would have been unable to write this or any other book. And there was always the cheerful camaraderie and advice of my sons, Rodrigo and Joaquín, and my daughter-in-law, Melissa. My assistant, Margaret Lawless, efficiently kept the world away while I created this other world, and Debbie Jakubs, my friend and favorite librarian (at Duke University), found all the texts I needed, the whole gamut, from South Pole expeditions to Ona Indians. Other essential clippings were provided by Justo Alarcón of the Biblioteca Nacional de Chile, by my sister-in-law Nathalie Malinarich, and by my dear *suegra* Elbita, whose packages arrived every week with their Southern Hemisphere messages. Mariano Fernández, the undersecretary for foreign affairs of Chile, was the first to offer a free trip to Antarctica, for which I will ever be grateful. Jin Auh, my agent at the Wylie Agency, was always enthusiastic and extremely supportive. Nor can I forget the encouragement of Antonio Skármeta and Eugenio Ahumada, who, from Chile, kept feeding me information and much-needed gossip. And one morning, walking on a beach in California when the book was already finished, Deena Metzger revealed to me the story of the orphaned elephants of Africa that I employed as one of the novel's opening epigraphs.

My editor at Farrar, Straus and Giroux, John Glusman, worked overtime to beat a difficult schedule and ended up supplying me, as he has in the past, with exceptionally intelligent and sensitive comments, urging me to find ways of giving this unwieldy saga the shape its protagonists, father and son, deserved. I deeply appreciate his commitment and loyalty to my vision. Other useful ideas about characters and plot development were generously furnished to me by my faithful and perceptive British editor at Hodder, Carole Welch. Copy-editor Roslyn Schloss provided valuable and painstaking suggestions that made the text better. Thanks also to Professor Gabriella Nouzeilles of Duke University, born and bred in Patagonia, with whom I had several entrancing conversations about the wind, shipwrecks, and madmen in Tierra del Fuego.

Other friends gave me other gifts when I most needed them, on two successive December nights in Paris in 1997 when I was trying to figure out far from my home in Durham how Gabriel's journey ends. The first evening I had dinner with Toni Morrison, whose remarks about black nannies and white children triggered an idea that was already percolating somewhere in my brain. And the next night I went to visit John Berger, who has nursed me with friendship and wisdom for over twenty years and who helped me, with one visionary suggestion, to find the key to Gabriel's possible redemption. As that same magic evening was drawing to a close, I was bequeathed yet one more revelation: Birgitta Leander (an anthropologist friend and the wonderful wife of my pal Raúl Silva Cáceres), who had been listening to my conversation with John, started all of a sudden reciting in Nahautl and then translating first into English and then into Spanish the Aztec poem that I later decided to incorporate at the end of the book. It was as if she knew I needed those exact verses—needed them not only for *The Nanny and the Iceberg* but for myself, for my life, for questions I had been praying for an answer to.

This false story that shadows real historical events was born, therefore, under the benevolent eye of many powerful godfathers and godmothers, all of them more substantial than my characters. Perhaps, given such auspicious allies, Gabriel's journey may find its way to the right port of call. It's what I hope as author of this story. And I am, after all, both its father and its mother.

October 11, 1998